She scanned the court,
searching for him.

Now that she could see all ten basketball players close up, she came to a startling realization. Apparently, vampire men were extremely handsome.

Then *he* broke from the pack, and she forgot all about the other handsome guys. Good God, he was magnificent. Stealthy, graceful, and wild. Exotic. She covered her mouth when a strangled whimper escaped.

And his head turned. His steps slowed to a stop.

Her hand fluttered down to press against her chest. Oh God, he was looking right at her. Her heart pounded, thundering in her ears. His loose black hair was wild about his shoulders. His black T-shirt was stretched tight across a muscular chest. His golden brown eyes narrowed on her, and his gaze sizzled through her, hot and electric.

"Carlos!" a teammate yelled just as he hurled a pass.

Bam! The ball slammed against Carlos's head, and he stumbled to the side.

By Kerrelyn Sparks

EAT PREY LOVE
THE VAMPIRE AND THE VIRGIN
FORBIDDEN NIGHTS WITH A VAMPIRE
SECRET LIFE OF A VAMPIRE
ALL I WANT FOR CHRISTMAS IS A VAMPIRE
THE UNDEAD NEXT DOOR
BE STILL MY VAMPIRE HEART
VAMPS AND THE CITY
HOW TO MARRY A MILLIONAIRE VAMPIRE

KERRELYN SPARKS

EAT PREY LOVE

AVON

An Imprint of HarperCollins*Publishers*

AVON BOOKS
An Imprint of HarperCollins*Publishers*
10 East 53rd Street
New York, New York 10022-5299

*In memory of all the beloved pets
who filled our lives with joy
for too short of a time —
Liesl, Precious, Megan,
and Lestat, the original Mr. Foofikins.*

Acknowledgments

*H*ow could I possibly write humor without those people who bring joy into my life? For all the hours of laughter and sushi, I must thank my dear friends and critique partners: MJ, Sandy, and Vicky. My thanks to my husband, who still makes me laugh like he did on our first date many years ago. My thanks to my children, who fill me with pride and joy. My thanks to my editor, Erika Tsang, and all the professionals at HarperCollins. I love working with you all! My thanks to Michelle Grajkowski of Three Seas Literary Agency, who miraculously manages to be a fortress of strength and sweetness at the same time. And many, many thanks to all those who read my books and keep coming back for more. Your notes and e-mails are greatly appreciated!

Chapter One

*C*aitlyn had been warned never to come near this place. Gutsy or foolish, she didn't know which category she fell into, but it was too late to worry about that now. She had arrived.

Her rental car's headlights illuminated a smooth, black-topped driveway. Tall trees arched over the road, their skeletal branches grasping like gnarled fingers at the starlit sky. She suppressed a shudder and focused instead on the patches of bright yellow daffodils scattered over the grounds.

Looking for the positive, she would call it. Foolhardy, some might say. But when facing the unknown, she'd learned in her twenty-six years that keeping a good attitude was critical. The fact that the grounds appeared well-maintained was a good sign. And the security guard at the entrance had seemed friendly, checking her ID and welcoming her with a smile.

Think of this as an adventure. You love adventure.

Even so, her grip tightened on the steering wheel as she watched the heavy wrought-iron gate swing shut in her rearview mirror. The metallic clang echoed around the barren trees and vibrated through her bones.

She was locked in.

Dad had to be wrong. This place couldn't be dangerous. She'd looked it up on the Internet before coming. Romatech Industries manufactured synthetic blood, then shipped it to hospitals and clinics around the world. The CEO and inventor, Roman Draganesti, was credited with saving thousands of lives every year. Who could object to that?

She proceeded down the long driveway that snaked through extensive grounds. Maybe Dad was referring to the bombing she'd read about. That had happened three years ago, though, and nothing dangerous had occurred since then. She was perfectly safe, she assured herself, as a dimly lit, sprawling building came into view.

Neatly clipped hedges lined the wings that spread from the building's center. Overhead lamps shone down on the dozen or so cars in the parking lot, while insects buzzed in each lamp's halo of light. She parked her rented Camry and glanced warily at the entrance.

Dad was being overly dramatic, that was all. But why would he want to keep her away from her sister? Was he concerned that a reunion would cause her emotional distress? Caitlyn had to admit she didn't know what to expect from a sister she hadn't heard from in six years.

She'd been shocked when two days ago she'd received a card from her older sister. Shanna had acquired a new last name: Draganesti. Was she married to the CEO of Romatech? When had that happened? Shanna had included a photo of her son and daughter, and she'd invited Caitlyn to a birthday party for Constantine, who was turning four in late March.

Caitlyn had stared, dumbstruck, at the photo for five minutes. She hadn't known she had a nephew and niece. Mom and Dad had never mentioned it. How could they fail to brag about their grandchildren? The invitation had arrived at the extended-stay hotel where Caitlyn had found a room after returning to the States a week earlier. How had Shanna known where she was?

The last communication she'd had from Shanna was a birthday card in July 2004. Shortly after that, Shanna disappeared without a trace. Almost a year later, Dad had announced that he'd located her. She'd been given a new identity through the Witness Protection program.

Dad had been vague on the details, only saying that she was lost to them forever. They must all stay away from a place called Romatech Industries. Shanna had changed. She could no longer be trusted. She was to be avoided at all cost.

She's still my sister. Caitlyn had to know the truth. She climbed out of the car with her handbag and gift for Constantine. Dad would go ballistic if he knew she was here. He was already pissed by her recent fiasco. The fact that she'd made a mistake for good reasons didn't matter. She was still screwed. Her career ruined. Blacklisted from the

State Department. No job, no home, and a quickly dwindling amount in her savings account.

Coming here to see Shanna could be another mistake, but dammit, she wanted her sister back. And she'd never been one to shy away from a challenging situation. She slammed the car door to accentuate her rebellious determination, then marched toward the entrance.

She was about twenty minutes late, having made some wrong turns. She knew her way around Minsk, St. Petersburg, Bangkok, and Jakarta, but White Plains, New York, was a foreign land to her. She could hear shouts and laughter in the distance, so hopefully that meant the party was still in full swing.

Her stride slowed as a nagging question returned, one that had bothered her since she'd first opened the invitation. Who would throw a birthday party for a four-year-old at nine o'clock at night? Granted, she didn't have any experience with raising children, but still, didn't kids usually go to bed about that time?

She paused mid-step when the front door swung open. A column of light spilled out, framing the dark silhouette of a huge man.

"Miss Whelan?" His voice was deep and gravelly. He moved to the edge of the light and became more visible.

"Yes." Another security guard, Caitlyn assumed, since he was well over six feet tall and looked as indestructible as an army tank. He was dressed in the same khaki pants and navy polo shirt as the man at the front gate.

"How do you do? I'm Howard Barr." He motioned to the open door. "Come in."

"I hope I'm not too late." Caitlyn stepped into a wide foyer and glanced around. Potted plants, nice artwork on the walls, a gleaming marble floor . . . and no Shanna. No one there at all.

She swallowed hard as the huge security guard shut the door and locked it. "Shanna's here, isn't she?"

"Sure. The party's in the cafeteria. I'll take you there in just a minute." Howard gave her an apologetic look as he stepped behind a table. "I have to check your bags first. Standard procedure, nothing personal."

"I understand." Caitlyn placed her bags on the table. "Is there still a problem with people bombing Romatech?"

Howard shook his head as he rummaged through the silk handbag she'd bought in Singapore. "It's been calm lately."

"It seems like an odd place for a child's birthday party."

He shrugged. "Shanna set up a nursery next to her office, so the little ones spend a lot of time here."

"Oh." Shanna had an office in a scientific research facility? "I thought my sister was a dentist."

"She is. She has a dental office here." Howard slid her red silk handbag to her with a puzzled look. "You didn't know that?"

"No. I've been out of the country and . . . out of touch. I didn't know she had children or that she was even married until I received the invitation to this party. Her husband is Roman Draganesti?"

"Yes." Howard frowned as he plunged his large beefy hands into the gift bag. "I can't believe you didn't know."

Caitlyn winced. The blue and red crepe paper she'd carefully arranged was being crushed. "For some reason, my dad never told me."

Howard's fists tightened, smushing the crepe paper even more. "That . . . sorry. I guess I might as well tell you. Your dad's not very popular around here."

"He doesn't seem very fond of you guys either."

Howard grunted and pulled out the fire engine she'd bought for Constantine. "This is cool. I had one of these when I was a kid."

He was changing the subject, as if she wouldn't notice. "Do you think Constantine will like it? I didn't know what to buy for him." She'd bought all sorts of stuff—a book, a DVD, a dinosaur, and the fire engine—hoping that if she hit all the bases, one would result in a home run.

"Yeah, he'll love this stuff." Howard jammed the fire engine back into the gift bag, then frowned at the mangled crepe paper. He attempted to fluff it up but only succeeded in ripping the paper. "Damn. I'm just making it worse. Mom always said I was a bear in a china shop."

"I thought that was a bull."

He grunted and slid the present back to her. "Sorry."

Her beautifully packed gift bag looked like it had been mauled by a grizzly. Howard seemed genuinely embarrassed, so she gave him a friendly smile. "Don't worry about it. I doubt a four-year-old boy cares about aesthetics. It's what's inside that really counts."

He nodded, clearly relieved. "I'm glad you feel that way. You . . . may need to remind yourself of that before the night's over."

Was that some kind of warning? Caitlyn slipped the long strap of her handbag over her head and shoulder, grabbed the gift bag, and followed the security guard to the end of the long foyer. They passed through a set of double doors, then entered a long hallway, lined on one side with windows. A courtyard and garden was visible through the glass.

On the other side of the courtyard, she could see the cafeteria through another wall of glass. It was well-lit, with colorful balloons gathered in bunches and obstructing her view of the people inside.

Howard led her to the right, then turned left into an intersecting passageway that linked the first wing to the second. The hallway continued, lined on both sides with glass. Not soundproof, for she could hear shouts and laughter from outside. She slowed, glancing out the windows on the left.

Off in the distance, past the cafeteria, she spotted a basketball court. It was brightly lit and currently filled with players.

"They've got quite a game going on." Howard paused beside her to watch. "Roman had that court put in last summer, but it's usually just him, Tino, and Phineas playing. Tino was excited about having enough guys at the party for two full teams."

"You mean Constantine is playing?" Caitlyn

stepped closer to the glass. As far as she could tell, all the players were grown men and teenage boys.

"That's Phineas there, doing a slam dunk." Howard motioned to the left end of the court.

Caitlyn smiled as the young man celebrated with an exuberant rendition of a chicken dance. The guys were obviously having a great time, but as big and athletic as they all looked, she was worried they would run over her young nephew. She searched the court for a little boy, then halted, her gaze fixated on the most glorious representative of manhood she'd ever seen.

Smooth and stealthy, she thought, as the man ran down the court. He glided with such effortless grace it was like he was standing still and the earth was doing the moving. His shoulder-length black hair blew back, revealing a classic profile— straight nose, sharp cheekbones, strong jaw.

Time seemed to slow as her vision sharpened, taking in every detail. She detected some sort of tattoo along his neck. His jaw was shaded with a hint of dark whiskers. A glint of gold gleamed on his earlobe. An earring. Exotic. Dangerous. So very masculine.

A big redheaded man moved into his path to block him, but he dipped around his opponent with ease and kept going. So graceful, and yet so strong. He reached the free throw line and leaped into the air, twisting to catch the basketball hurled in his direction, then rotating in the air to neatly deposit the ball through the hoop.

Howard snorted. "Show-off."

The man landed lightly on his feet as his team shouted in celebration. He grinned.

And Caitlyn was lost.

She slowly became aware that Howard was nudging her. "There's Tino. Do you see him?"

What? Who? She pressed a palm against the glass, surprised to find herself light-headed. She inhaled sharply. *Sheesh*. The man had smiled, and she'd forgotten to breathe. Forgotten to think. She'd slipped into some sort of trance.

Temporary insanity. That had to be it, 'cause the man was definitely not her type. She'd always dated the clean-cut, shirt and tie, neatly combed hair, corner office type of guy. Intellectual and predictable. Easily managed and easily forgotten when the lure of adventure called. And it always did.

Caitlyn had never been able to resist the exotic. Exotic languages, foreign locales. It was the reason she'd joined the State Department. She'd worked all over the world, and she thrived on the excitement. But even though she'd put her physical self in stressful situations, she'd never done that with her heart. When it came to relationships, she'd always played it safe.

This man was dangerous. She could feel it in her bones. He could slide right under a woman's skin and take hold of her heart. If she had any sense, she'd stay away from him. Unfortunately, her sense was in question. She'd been warned to stay away from Romatech, yet here she was.

She took another deep breath and eased her grip on the gift bag. She'd been clutching it so tightly, the handles had dug into her palm.

"There's Tino. By the other goal." Howard pointed.

She spotted her nephew for the first time and smiled. He was even more adorable than he'd looked in the photo. Blond curls and an angelic sweet face. Her earlier concern rushed back. "He's too little to play with adults. They'll run him over."

Howard chuckled. "Tino can hold his own. He has . . . special skills."

Skills? What kind of skills could a boy have to help him compete with guys over twice his size? And who was the mystery man who'd made her forget space and time?

"Come on. I'll take you to Shanna." Howard headed down the hall to a set of double doors.

Caitlyn followed slowly, peering out the window to make sure her nephew wasn't being trampled. The gorgeous mystery man was playing defense now, guarding the big redheaded guy who had possession of the ball.

Constantine was still stationed underneath the goal. The redheaded guy tossed the ball to him, and he caught it. The other players ran toward him, and Caitlyn slowed to a stop, worried for his safety.

He jumped.

Howard grabbed her arm. "Come on, let's go."

Her jaw dropped as Constantine's jump went higher and higher. "What the . . . ?"

"Come on." Howard tugged, managing to make her stumble a few steps. "Shanna wants to see you."

Caitlyn's heart raced. Her nephew was now as high as the goal, and he easily dropped the ball through the hoop. His team cheered as he landed on the cement.

She gave Howard an incredulous look. "Did you see that? He just jumped ten feet in the air!"

"Well, yeah. I told you he has some special skills."

"Like what? Flying?" She glanced out the window again. The guys were playing in a normal manner now, as if nothing strange had just happened.

A chill tickled the back of her neck. This was too weird. "Is this related to the reason my dad told me never to come here?"

Howard winced. "Please don't tell your father what you saw. He might reject Tino, and it would break the little guy's heart. Tino's a great kid—"

"Who can fly?"

Howard frowned as he opened the door. "It's not my place to say. Shanna will explain it to you."

Caitlyn glanced inside at the cheerful balloons and happy people. The chill on her neck skittered down her spine. *It's just a birthday party for a little boy. No big deal.* Then why did it feel like she was about to tumble down the rabbit hole?

It's an adventure. You love adventure. She squared her shoulders and strode into the cafeteria. It was a large room with glass walls on two sides, overlooking the courtyard, the basketball court, and landscaped gardens in the distance.

Howard motioned to the first table, which was laden with gifts, and she set her crumpled gift bag there. The next table boasted a punch bowl and trays of finger food. Across from it, a table held a large chocolate sheet cake with *Happy Birthday, Constantine* written in bright red icing. Another table was topped with tubs of ice containing bottles. Beer, she assumed, for the adults.

Finally, she reached the tables where people were sitting. All female, she noted as she searched for her sister. Her eyes widened at the sight of one woman with purple spiky hair. She estimated about ten women her age, all happily chatting with each other. A handful of younger girls sat with them.

But no Shanna.

"You must be Shanna's sister!" A beautiful brunette stood and hurried toward her.

"Yes. I'm Caitlyn." She smiled briefly as everyone at the tables hushed and looked at her.

"Where's Shanna?" Howard grumbled.

"She'll be right back," the brunette continued in a crisp British accent. "She's in the washroom, helping Heather. Both the twins needed their nappies changed." She grinned and extended a hand to Caitlyn. "It's so lovely to meet you. I'm Emma MacKay, Tino's godmother."

Did you know he can fly? Caitlyn refrained from asking the question out loud and shook the woman's hand.

"I'll head back to the security office," Howard grumbled.

"Thank you," Emma told him. "Be sure to come back later for a bit of cake."

"Will do." Howard smiled a farewell at Caitlyn, then lumbered from the room.

"Let me introduce you to everyone." Emma began calling their names, but there were too many for Caitlyn to keep up with at once. She smiled and waved as they all greeted her.

"And this is your niece." Emma moved behind

a chair where a little girl was sitting. "Sofia, this is your Aunt Caitlyn."

"I'm happy to meet you, Sofia." Caitlyn's heart squeezed in her chest as the little girl gazed at her with wide blue eyes. She was beautiful. Her eyes were like Shanna's, but she must have inherited her black, wavy hair from her father.

"Hi," Sofia said softly, then glanced over her shoulder at Emma. "I thought you were my aunt."

Emma smiled and brushed the girl's hair over her shoulder. "I'm a pretend aunt. Caitlyn is your real aunt."

"I don't have any aunts," one of the other little girls muttered. "They were all killed."

Caitlyn's breath caught. She tried to recall the girl's name. She was one of Tino's classmates.

Emma moved over to the little girl and touched her shoulder. "Coco, I would love to be your aunt."

"Me, too." The woman seated next to Coco gave her a hug.

All the women echoed a desire to be Coco's aunt.

"Me, too!" Sofia cried. "I want to be an aunt."

Caitlyn smiled. Shanna was fortunate to have such caring friends. From the loving way they interacted with each other, it was obvious they were a close-knit group.

With a small jolt, Caitlyn realized these people were Shanna's family. They knew Shanna better than she did.

A twinge of annoyance needled her. She'd only been nine years old when Shanna had turned fifteen and taken off to a boarding school across the world. Caitlyn had sorely missed her only sister. She'd written letters, but never received a response. Shanna had simply left her family behind. And she'd acquired a new one.

Caitlyn knew she should be happy for her sister, but damn. Why hadn't she been good enough for Shanna? She'd spent most of her teenage years feeling lonesome and abandoned. It was clear her father didn't approve of Shanna or her new family. And he didn't even know the full story—that her son could *fly*.

"Here's Shanna now." Emma motioned to the double doors.

Caitlyn spun around, her heartbeat shooting to a fast pace. Tears threatened at the sight of her sister. Shanna was accompanying another woman, and each carried a baby.

Shanna still looked much the same, with her strawberry blond hair and blue eyes. She'd matured some, naturally, since Caitlyn had last seen her, but the years had only added a warm and beautiful glow.

Shanna's face lit up. "Caitlyn!" She rushed forward and passed the baby she was holding to Emma.

Caitlyn wasn't sure how to greet the sister she hadn't seen in years, but her awkward hesitation quickly passed when Shanna threw her arms around her in a big hug.

A few tears escaped as Caitlyn held her sister tight. It had been so long, but finally, she had her sister back.

"Look at you." Shanna leaned back and tears glistened on her cheeks. "You're all grown up. And so beautiful."

Caitlyn wiped the tears from her face. "I always thought you were the beautiful one. I missed you."

Shanna hugged her again. "Did you meet everyone?"

"Emma introduced me. Your daughter's precious."

"I totally agree." Shanna grinned. "You need to meet the birthday boy, too. He's outside playing basketball."

And flying up to the hoop. Caitlyn needed to get her sister alone so she could ask a few pertinent questions.

"Oh, you haven't met Heather." Shanna motioned to the pretty redhead who was holding a squirming baby in her arms. "I was helping her with the twins, Jean-Pierre and Jillian."

"This is Jillian." Emma strapped the little girl into a high chair and handed her a cracker.

"They're adorable." Caitlyn admired the two dark-headed babies. "How old are they?"

"Eight months." Heather placed the little boy on the floor, and he shot off in a fast crawl. She sighed. "He'll be halfway back to Texas before the party's over."

The women laughed.

"I'll watch him." A young redheaded girl jumped to her feet and ran after the baby.

"Thank you, sweetie." Heather smiled at Caitlyn. "That's my daughter, Bethany, otherwise known as Assistant Mommy and Lifesaver."

"Older sisters are good to have." Caitlyn glanced at her sister. *And really painful to lose.*

Shanna blinked and gave her a curious look. "We don't have to be separated ever again."

Caitlyn gulped. Had Shanna read her mind? They'd been so close when young, always in tune with each other's thoughts and feelings that she'd often wondered if they shared some sort of odd connection. It was a few years after Shanna's departure that Caitlyn had realized the full extent of her own unique abilities. She'd written about it to Shanna, knowing her sister would understand, but there'd never been a response.

"Shanna was telling me about your family while we were in the restroom," Heather said. "You lived in a lot of foreign countries."

Caitlyn nodded. "Yes, we lived in Poland, Belarus, Latvia—all over that area."

"And Mom home-schooled us," Shanna added. "I swear, every time Caitlyn went out to play, a stray dog or cat would come up to her. Drove our mom crazy 'cause there were too many to keep, and she'd have to find homes for them."

Caitlyn smiled, remembering her favorite kitty, a solid black cat she'd named Mr. Foofikins. Now she understood why animals came to her, but at the time, in her youthful ignorance, she had assumed everyone could understand the noises made by their pets.

"And every time we moved to a new place," Shanna continued, "Caitlyn was the first to pick up the new language. She was incredible. I swear she could learn a language in a month."

Caitlyn's face grew warm as all the women expressed amazement.

Emma watched her closely. "Is it true you know over a dozen languages?"

Caitlyn nodded. She had an odd suspicion that Emma's interest in her was more than casual.

"How long does it take for you to learn a language now?" Emma asked.

Caitlyn hesitated before answering. "A few hours." Her face burned hotter when the ladies gasped. It wasn't like she'd mastered some fantastic skill. It was simply a weird gift she'd been born with. Once she'd figured out she was a psychic linguist, she'd honed the talent to her present level of expertise. It wasn't something she usually talked about, since most people refused to believe she could understand any language she heard. They either thought she was lying or loony.

"That must have been extremely useful for your job with the State Department," Emma observed. "They were wrong to let you go."

Caitlyn stiffened and glanced at her sister, who stepped closer and lowered her voice. "I told Emma you were looking for employment."

"How did you know?" The State Department had done a good job of hushing up her big mistake.

"I called Mom to invite her to the birthday party," Shanna continued quietly. "After she gave me an excuse for not coming, she told me what had happened to you and that you were here in New York, looking for a job. She said Dad wanted to hire you for his team. I wanted to give you an alternative, so I asked Emma to find you."

Emma smiled. "I'm one of the owners of MacKay Security and Investigation."

So that was how they'd tracked her down at her hotel. Even so, Caitlyn was stunned that her mom hadn't wanted to come to her grandson's birthday party. "I don't understand why Mom and Dad aren't here. Or why Dad told me never to come here."

Shanna winced. "I was afraid of that." She leaned closer. "I just want you to know that you're not alone. You don't need to stay at a hotel. We have a townhouse in Manhattan that's mostly empty, and you can live there as long as you need to."

Caitlyn swallowed hard. "That would really help."

"Emma and I thought you might like a job with MacKay Security and Investigation," Shanna continued.

A job offer? This was the last thing she'd expected at her nephew's birthday party. She turned to Emma. "That's very kind of you, but I have no experience in the security business."

Emma dismissed that with a wave of her hand. "We conduct investigations all over the world. Your linguistic abilities make you ideally suited for that kind of work."

"Thank you. I'll be glad to consider it." Caitlyn looked over the faces of Shanna's friends and realized her sister was attempting to draw her into her family, a family her father didn't approve of.

"Before you consider anything," Shanna said with a worried look, "you need to know all the facts. About us."

The chill returned to tickle the back of Caitlyn's

neck. Her instincts flared. The entrance to the rabbit hole loomed before her, gaping ever wider and enticing her to fall in. As much as she loved adventure, she wasn't sure this was a place she wanted to go. Her dad certainly didn't want her involved with these people.

But her sister was here. She didn't want to lose Shanna again. She didn't want to lose her niece and nephew. *I saw Constantine fly.* How could Shanna possibly explain that?

Shanna winced. "I'll do my best."

Caitlyn stiffened. "You're reading my mind."

Chapter Two

*C*aitlyn took a deep breath to calm her racing heart. Maybe she shouldn't be so shocked. She was a psychic linguist, so it was entirely possible that her sister had psychic abilities, too.

Shanna motioned for her to accompany her to the refreshment table. "I'm not making a conscious effort to read your mind. I want to respect your privacy, but some of your thoughts are so intense, I'm catching them."

Caitlyn glanced back at the other women across the cafeteria. They were busily chatting, so thankfully, she could now speak privately with her sister. "You have telepathic powers."

"I'm usually better at blocking messages than sending or receiving," Shanna confessed. "But with you, I've always had a strong connection. Remember when we were young, and we'd always—"

"Finish each other's sentences," Caitlyn said

with a sad smile. If their connection was so strong, why did her sister leave her?

"Are you telepathic, too?" Shanna asked.

"I don't think so. Most of my psychic ability is centered on language."

"You have a rare gift." Shanna ladled some punch into two red plastic cups. "When I was at boarding school, I would think of you often and dream about you at night. You were surrounded by snow, and you wore a bright red woolen coat and mittens."

Caitlyn's breath caught. From the ages of ten to twelve, she'd worn a bright red coat.

Shanna passed her a cup of punch. "Later on, I saw you in Washington, D.C., then you were back in the snow. A few years ago the dreams changed. I saw white sandy beaches and palm trees. Elephants and tigers."

Caitlyn gulped down some punch. "I graduated from Georgetown University before joining the State Department. I was stationed at Minsk, then Bangkok and Jakarta."

Shanna's eyes glimmered with tears. "I always hoped I was seeing images from your real life. I missed you so much."

Then why did you leave me? Caitlyn blinked back tears and grabbed a paper plate featuring a red cartoon car. "I don't know anything about your life. I didn't even know you had a husband and children."

"Dad didn't tell you?"

"No." Caitlyn put some crackers and sliced cheese on her plate. "He just warned me never to come here."

Shanna sighed. "Well, I'm glad you did. Thank you."

Caitlyn took another sip of punch. "Why didn't our parents come?"

"Mom does whatever Dad tells her to do. And Dad . . . well, he doesn't approve of me." Shanna motioned to some chairs next to the table heaped with gifts. "Did you know Dad works for the CIA?"

"Yes." Caitlyn set her cup and plate on the table, then took a seat. "I used to think he worked for the State Department, but when he helped me get a job there, he confessed it was only a cover, and that he'd always worked for the CIA."

Shanna nodded. "For the last six years or so he's been in charge of a secret group called the Stake-Out team. Emma MacKay used to work for him."

"Really?" Caitlyn glanced over at Emma, who was helping the baby Jillian eat.

"And another employee at MacKay S and I, Austin Erickson, worked for Dad."

"Can I ask why they left?" Caitlyn figured it had something to do with her father's overbearing personality. The thought of having him for a boss was definitely making her think twice about accepting his job offer. She topped a cracker with a slice of cheese and bit into it.

"They couldn't agree with the mission of the Stake-Out team," Shanna explained. "Dad's investigating a group of . . . people with the ultimate objective of hunting them all down and destroying them."

Caitlyn swallowed hard as the cracker stuck in her throat. "Terrorists?"

"Some of them are. I know all about it 'cause Dad tried to hire me, too. Our psychic power is inherited from Dad, you know. Our brother didn't seem to get any."

"I know, but what does that—"

"Everyone on the Stake-Out team needs enough psychic power to resist mind control," Shanna continued. "Dad's enemy has the ability to control minds and erase memories. He considers them a dangerous threat to mankind."

"They sound dangerous."

Shanna sighed. "Some of them are, but not all of them. The ones I know are perfectly nice."

Nice mind controllers? Caitlyn had to wonder if Shanna's mind was being controlled if she thought some of them were nice. This had to be the source of the friction between her dad and her sister. "Who exactly are we talking about?"

Shanna hesitated, then whispered, "Vampires."

Caitlyn blinked. "What?"

"Dad is hunting vampires."

Caitlyn sat back. She couldn't be hearing this right. "You mean he's gone off his rocker?"

"No, he's perfectly sane. That's why he calls it the Stake-Out team. You know, staking vampires."

Goose bumps prickled Caitlyn's arms. Her dad and sister were crazy. She rose to her feet. "Is this some kind of joke? Some kind of . . . party game? I don't find it amusing."

"It's not a joke." Shanna regarded her seriously. "Vampires are real."

"They're make-believe."

"They're real." Shanna lifted a hand to stop further objections. "I know it comes as a shock. If you don't want to believe me, you can ask anyone else here. Or ask Dad. He wants to hire you, so he must be planning to tell you."

A chill skittered down Caitlyn's spine. It couldn't be true. How could her sister lie to her? Then again, what could Shanna possibly gain by making this up? But wouldn't it be foolish for her to trust Shanna? She hadn't seen her sister in years.

She would have to talk to Dad about this. But what if he claimed it was true and he was hunting vampires?

Her thoughts swung back and forth, truth or lie, the pendulum increasing in speed, faster and faster till she felt dizzy. She slumped in the chair. "Are you seriously telling me vampires are real?"

"Yes, I am." Shanna nodded. "And I should know."

A frisson of alarm shot through Caitlyn, and she sprang to her feet. This was why Dad had warned her never to come here. *Shanna has changed. She can no longer be trusted. Stay away from her at all cost.* "You're a vampire?"

Shanna's eyes widened. "No. I'm the same as I ever was."

"Oh, thank God." Caitlyn pressed a hand to her chest and collapsed onto the chair. "You scared me to death."

Shanna smiled. "Relax, sweetie. I'm not a vampire." She patted her arm. "My husband is."

"Ack!" Caitlyn jumped back to her feet. "You—You're married to a dead man?"

"He's not dead. He's outside playing basketball."

"But—" Caitlyn frowned, trying to make sense of this. "Isn't he . . . sorta dead?"

"He's Undead."

The dizziness returned and Caitlyn sat down once more. "I don't really see the difference."

"Dead is dead all of the time, but Roman's only dead when the sun is up."

Caitlyn rubbed her brow. She was still tumbling down the rabbit hole and couldn't tell which end was up. "So he's fifty percent dead?"

Shanna chuckled. "I guess you could say that. But boy, when he's alive—" She sighed with a dreamy look on her face. "He's totally alive. All night long."

With trembling fingers, Caitlyn grabbed her cup and gulped down the rest of her punch. Apparently, vampires were good in the sack. Who would have guessed? Her thoughts returned to the gorgeous mystery man on the basketball court. Was he one of the Undead? Was he available? Could he give her the same sort of dreamy, well-satisfied look that Shanna had?

Caitlyn slapped herself mentally. What was she thinking? Within seconds of learning about the existence of vampires, she was imagining having sex with one? It was the damned lure of the exotic. It always tempted her. "Does he bite you?"

Shanna's mouth twitched. "Not for food. Roman and all the good Vamps drink synthetic blood."

"And you're happy, married to a vampire?"

"Oh, yes. And I'm not alone." With a grin, Shanna motioned toward the other women. "A lot of my friends here are married to Vamp men."

Caitlyn had to admit they all looked happy.

They were also very pretty. Apparently, vampires were drawn to beautiful women. Would the mystery man find her attractive? Would he even notice her? She groaned inwardly. She needed to stop thinking about him. But it was so much easier to think about a gorgeous man than to deal with this strange new reality that had broadsided her out of nowhere.

Vampires. Her brother-in-law was a vampire. And what were her nephew and niece? "I saw Constantine fly up to the hoop. Is he some kind of mini-vampire?"

Shanna laughed. "He's a normal little boy. He eats and sleeps and goes to school."

"And flies?"

"He doesn't fly. He levitates."

Of course. That was so much better. "Shanna, sweetie, that's not normal."

She waved a dismissive hand. "What is normal? We were never normal, not with our psychic abilities. Tino comes by his abilities in the normal way. He inherited them from his parents."

"I didn't think vampires could have children." Caitlyn gritted her teeth. "But then I never bothered to learn much about vampires, 'cause I never thought they existed."

Shanna gave her a wry look. "You'll get used to it. My husband is a scientific genius, so he figured out a way for Vamp men to father children."

"Great." Hybrid children? Caitlyn wondered just how deep this rabbit hole went.

Shanna glanced sadly across the room. "Unfortunately, it's impossible for a Vamp woman to carry a child."

Caitlyn looked warily at the women. "Are you telling me there are vampires in this room?"

Shanna nodded. "You see the two women getting bottles from the tub of ice? They're Marta and Vanda, both Vamps."

So the purple-haired woman was a vampire. Caitlyn eyed the bottles suspiciously. "That's not beer, is it?"

"It could be Bleer. Part beer, part synthetic blood. Or it might be Chocolood, blood and chocolate. Roman manufactures a whole menu of Vampire Fusion Cuisine."

Caitlyn took a deep breath. Vampire Fusion Cuisine? Vampire men fathering babies and playing basketball with their levitating sons? It was all too much.

"And you met Emma," Shanna continued. "She's a Vamp."

Caitlyn sucked in another breath. She was getting light-headed. "I shook hands with a vampire? You handed a baby over to a vampire?"

Shanna frowned. "Emma's wonderful with the children. It breaks my heart that she can't have any of her own."

Caitlyn glanced at Emma, who was still taking care of the baby, Jillian. "I don't understand. Didn't you say she worked for Dad?"

"She was mortal then and a vampire slayer, but some Malcontents captured her and nearly killed her. The only way Angus could save her life was to transform her. It devastated him to do it, but they're happily married now."

"Great." Caitlyn rubbed her brow. "And who are the Malcontents?"

"Evil men who became evil vampires. They refuse to drink synthetic blood. They feed from mortals and enjoy terrorizing and murdering them."

Caitlyn grimaced. "So there's a bunch of blood-sucking killers out there?"

Shanna nodded. "We're at war with them."

"Are they the ones who bombed Romatech?"

"Yes. They'd like to destroy us. And the synthetic blood that's manufactured here. It took Dad a few years to admit that there are two factions in the vampire world: the good Vamps like you see here, who risk their lives to protect mortals, and the Malcontents."

"And where does Dad fit in?"

"Right now, we have an alliance with him so we can help each other defeat the Malcontents." Shanna sighed. "But once we succeed, I'm afraid Dad will focus his attention on getting rid of all Vamps." Her eyes glistened with tears. "Once the witch hunt begins, where will it all end? My children are half vampire."

Caitlyn gulped. "No." She touched her sister's arm. "I can't believe Dad would ever harm his own grandchildren."

Shanna grabbed Caitlyn's hand and squeezed. "He thinks Tino is completely mortal. Please don't tell him—"

"I would never," Caitlyn assured her. "I could never allow an innocent to suffer." That was exactly what had caused her fiasco at the State Department.

"Thank you." Shanna hugged her. "So now you need to know what the job offer is about. MacKay

S and I provides security for good Vamps like Roman. And they investigate and hunt down Malcontents. You would get to travel all over the world, using your language skills to help them with their investigations. And you'll be making the world a safer place for mortals. Would you like more information from Emma?"

"Not really. To be honest with you, I need some time to assimilate all of this. Part of me is still thinking this is a weird dream and I'll wake up."

"I understand, but there's actually more stuff I need to tell you."

Caitlyn lifted a hand to stop her. "Not now, please. I'm feeling a little . . . dizzy with information overload."

"All right. We'll stop for now. I'm sorry to shock you so much, but when I heard Dad was planning to hire you, I wanted to show you our side of the story before you made up your mind. At least now you have a choice."

"I'll think about it." Caitlyn stood. And she would definitely talk to Dad to see if his story matched up. "Maybe I should go."

"Oh no!" Shanna jumped to her feet. "You just got here. And you haven't met Roman and Tino. Please stay a little longer."

One look at Shanna's beseeching blue eyes and Caitlyn knew she couldn't go. She was finally reunited with her only sister. How could she let something like a little vampire problem come between them?

She winced. Okay, the vampire problem wasn't little. It was colossal. It was freaking bizarre. But even so, she wasn't prepared to reject her sister over it. Or her innocent young nephew and niece. "I'll stay, but I'd like to be alone for a little while." So she could pinch herself to make sure she was awake.

"There's my office. You could use that." Shanna's eyes lit up. "Or you could take a walk in the garden. It's beautiful right now. The bulbs are blooming."

"That sounds good."

"Perfect. Come on." Shanna led her past the women, who smiled and waved.

Caitlyn waved back, forcing a smile. No wonder she'd sensed how close-knit these women were. They were all keepers of the Big Secret, the hidden world of vampires.

Shanna exited a glass door into the courtyard. Caitlyn steeled her nerves as she joined her sister. *Great.* Now she was outside with a bunch of bloodsuckers playing basketball. The shiver that skittered down her spine wasn't caused entirely by the chilly night air.

She reached beneath the strap of her handbag to fasten the top button of her bright yellow cardigan sweater. Her gaze wandered over the basketball players as she looked for the gorgeous mystery man. She didn't want to admit it to herself, but chances were he was a vampire.

A shocking image speared her thoughts. Shanna's daughter had black hair. "What does your husband look like?"

"He's gorgeous." Shanna led her closer to the brightly lit basketball court. "Golden brown eyes, shoulder-length black hair."

Caitlyn gulped. *Oh, God, please don't let me be attracted to my sister's husband.*

"Hey, Teddy," Shanna greeted a young man with a white stripe bleached down the middle of his dark hair and a referee whistle looped around his neck. "This is my sister, Caitlyn."

Teddy glanced up from his stopwatch and clipboard. "Nice to meet you." His attention returned to the game.

Caitlyn leaned close to her sister. "Is he . . . ?"

"He's mortal like us," Shanna reassured her. "So how's the game going, Teddy?"

He checked his stopwatch. "Two minutes to go in the last quarter. Claws ahead by two. Oh, another slam dunk by Phineas." He marked his clipboard. "Fangs are tied."

"Go, Fangs!" Shanna pumped the air with her fist, then grinned at Caitlyn. "Tino's on the Fangs team."

Caitlyn's eyes widened as her nephew floated up in the air to give Phineas a high five. "He's flying again."

"Levitating," Shanna yelled over the shouting players. "See the guy next to Tino? That's my husband Roman."

Caitlyn let out a whoosh of air in relief. Roman was good-looking, all right, but he wasn't her gorgeous mystery man. She scanned the court, searching for him. Now that she could see all ten players close up, she came to a startling realization. Apparently, vampire men were extremely handsome.

Then *he* broke from the pack, and she forgot

all about the other handsome guys. Good God, he was magnificent. Stealthy, graceful, and wild. Exotic. She covered her mouth when a strangled whimper escaped.

And his head turned. His steps slowed to a stop.

Her hand fluttered down to press against her chest. Oh God, he was looking right at her. Her heart pounded, thundering in her ears. His loose black hair was wild about his shoulders. His black T-shirt was stretched tight across a muscular chest. His golden brown eyes narrowed on her and his gaze sizzled through her, hot and electric.

"Carlos!" a teammate yelled just as he hurled a pass.

Bam! The ball slammed against Carlos's head and he stumbled to the side.

"Carlos!" his teammates shouted in dismay.

He rubbed his head, then glanced again at Caitlyn. He didn't attempt to stop his redheaded opponent, who took the ball. As far as Caitlyn could tell, he wasn't paying any attention to the game. He was completely focused on her.

"Uncle Angus!" Tino yelled from beneath the goal.

The redheaded man tossed him the ball. Constantine levitated up to make a basket.

Teddy blew a whistle. "Game over. Fangs win!"

Constantine's team whooped in victory and took turns tossing the birthday boy into the air. The other team soon joined in the celebration.

Caitlyn noticed Carlos talking to the redheaded man, the one her nephew called Uncle Angus. The two men strode through a glass door leading to the first wing and disappeared down a hallway. A jab of disappointment pricked her. He hadn't bothered to meet her.

"Mommy!" Constantine ran to Shanna and flung his arms around her. "Did you see me? I made the winning basket!"

"You were fantastic!" Shanna lifted him in her arms. "I'm so proud of you."

"He scored more points than I did." Roman wrapped an arm around Shanna's shoulders and kissed her cheek.

"That's because Uncle Angus always passes the ball to me," Constantine boasted. He looked at Caitlyn curiously. "Hello."

"This is my sister, Caitlyn," Shanna told him. "Your aunt."

"Then you know Grandpa?" Constantine asked, his blue eyes wide with hope. "Did he come with you?"

"I'm afraid he couldn't make it." Caitlyn ached for the little boy. "But I'm delighted to finally meet you."

"Me, too." He grinned and reached out to her.

Caitlyn's heart squeezed in her chest as she took him from her sister and felt his little arms wrap around her neck. In that instant she knew she could never let anyone hurt this little boy, no matter what kind of blood flowed through his veins.

"Thank you for coming." Roman extended a hand to her.

She swallowed hard.

Tino pulled back to look at her. "You're afraid?"

"No, I'm fine." She quickly shook hands with Roman.

"Caitlyn just found out about vampires," Shanna explained, "so she's still in shock."

Roman nodded. "You have my word, Caitlyn, that no harm will come to you here."

"Let's have cake and ice cream!" Constantine wiggled out of Caitlyn's arms. "Come on."

"I'll join you in a little while." Caitlyn tousled his blond curls. "Save a piece of cake for me."

"Okay." He ran inside when his dad opened the door.

"See you soon." Shanna smiled, then entered the cafeteria with her husband.

Caitlyn retreated across the basketball court as all the players and spectators hurried into the cafeteria. She spotted a gazebo in the distance and strode toward it. The strains of "Happy Birthday" wafted toward her, and she glanced back at the cafeteria. The song ended with applause and laughter. Apparently, vampires liked to party.

She wrapped her bright yellow cardigan around herself to ward off the chilly night air and resumed her stroll toward the gazebo. The farther she walked, the darker it became. Her red silk embroidered handbag bounced gently against her hip.

The stone-flagged path led her up a gentle incline. Clumps of yellow daffodils sprung from the grass. Hyacinths in shades of purple, pink, and white added their sweet fragrance to the air.

As she neared the gazebo, the unmistakable sounds of passion drifted from the interior. She halted as a woman let out of long, soft moan.

"Oh, Robby, we need to stop. We're missing the party."

"I canna wait another minute," he grumbled in a low voice. "I need you now, Olivia."

The woman let out another long moan that Caitlyn could only interpret as surrender. She tiptoed across the grass, headed in another direction. A feminine squeal emanated from the gazebo, followed by a masculine growl.

Sheesh. Caitlyn hurried away. Apparently, vampires were very seductive. Images of Carlos flitted through her mind but she shoved them away. He wasn't interested in her. He'd looked her over, then walked away.

She spotted a cement bench underneath an oak tree and strode toward it. She couldn't put off reality any longer. She needed to deal with it. *Vampires.*

She skimmed her fingertips along the rough bark of the oak tree. According to her sister, vampires were as real as this tree. Now she understood Howard's cryptic warning that it was what was inside that really mattered. The Vamps appeared to be generous and kind. And they wanted to protect mortals from the bad vampires.

Caitlyn sat on the bench. What was she going to do? First, she needed to talk to Dad and make sure this was all real. She had a terrible feeling deep in her gut that it was. After all, Shanna's husband manufactured synthetic blood—a perfect job for a vampire who didn't want to bite people. And her dad had warned her never to come here. It explained why he refused to let her mom visit her grandchildren. He considered this enemy territory.

As far as Caitlyn could tell, she had three choices.

First option: she could pretend none of this had ever happened. She could find employment that had nothing to do with vampires. She could lead a normal life.

Boring. She never did boring. She loved adventure. And she was not the type to hide from reality.

Option two was accept her sister's world and family and take the job with Emma MacKay's company. She could work all over the world and meet a lot of interesting . . . people, alive and Undead. Major drawback: danger from the bad vampires.

Option three was also accepting the world of vampires, but taking the job with her dad. As a member of the CIA Stake-Out team, she'd have an exciting life, fighting bad vampires. Unfortunately, she'd never been the sort to engage in physical conflict. And what if Dad decided Roman, or worse, Constantine, was bad?

She sighed. At least now she understood the animosity between her dad and her sister.

"Damn," she whispered. She was going to have to choose which side of the family feud she was on.

Chapter Three

I'd like to go as soon as possible," Carlos told his employer as they strolled down the hallway to the MacKay security office.

Angus MacKay frowned. "I'd feel better about this if ye had some real evidence."

Carlos understood his boss's hesitation. Angus had financed his last two expeditions, one to Belize and one to Nicaragua. Both trips had yielded zero results. "Actually, it's the best lead I've had in years. According to Pat, the informant saw a wild jungle cat change into a human after it was killed."

Angus halted mid-step. "That is promising. But what if he's making it up?"

"Pat believes him."

"And who is Pat?" Angus resumed his walk to the office.

"Professor Supat Satapatpattana from the Chulalongkorn University in Bangkok. I call him Pat for short."

"I wonder why," Angus muttered as he pressed his hand against the security pad by the office door.

"Chula is a prestigious university, and Pat is a well-known anthropologist. He wouldn't have passed the report on to me if he didn't believe it was true."

Angus nodded. "Then ye'll have to check it out. Go ahead with yer plans." He opened the door. "Howard, how's it going?"

Carlos exhaled with relief. Maybe this time he would succeed. It had been five years since the Summer of Death, five years since he'd witnessed his family and friends being slaughtered. As far as he knew, he and five orphans were all that were left. He had to find more of his kind. He had to find a mate.

Howard's and Angus's conversation faded into background noise as memories bombarded Carlos's mind. So much death. The stench of burning bodies. The choking smoke of burning villages. His parents gone. His brother gone. Everyone murdered. Everything destroyed.

At first the memories had hounded him constantly, dragging him into an ugly pit of despair. Now they only haunted him once a day. Time hadn't erased the pain. It only made it easier for him to project the image that he was all right.

He'd become a master of pretense and illusion. He'd learned as a young child how to hide in the Amazon jungle, camouflaging himself so he couldn't be seen. Now he was able to hide in plain sight. No one knew the real him. No one . . . except Fernando.

Since the Summer of Death, Carlos had gone on a total of five expeditions. All had failed. He took a deep breath to steel his resolve. It didn't matter if this last glimpse of hope teetered on a vague rumor. He would keep hunting until he succeeded.

He wandered over to the wall of surveillance monitors. The daily deluge of pain had faded away for the time being. Angus was bragging about how well his godson, Tino, could play basketball.

Carlos was glad the birthday boy's team had won, but the shape shifter team had come mighty close to victory. If he had caught that last pass, the Claws would have won. He didn't want to dwell on the cause of his stupid mistake. *Her.*

He'd never felt such an immediate attraction before. A potent mix of desire and passion had slammed into him like a charging bull, leaving him dazed and breathless. Proof positive that he'd gone too long without a woman. For a few glorious seconds he thought he'd found the perfect woman.

But one sniff had crushed his hopes. Reality had crashed down on him so hard, he'd hardly felt the ball smacking him upside the head. She wasn't a shifter. She wasn't the one for him. The sooner he found his true mate, the better.

He studied the monitors. No one in the parking lot or the foyer. The hallways were empty. Everyone seemed to be in the cafeteria partying. He should be there with his adopted children. But he'd needed to talk to Angus about the new expedition.

And he needed to avoid *her*.

His chest tightened when he spotted her on a monitor. She was approaching the edge of the garden where it melded into the woods. Her bright yellow sweater and blond hair made her look like sunshine in the midst of darkness. What was she doing here? If she'd come for Tino's party, why was she missing it?

"Who is she?" He pointed to the monitor, attempting to keep his manner nonchalant.

Howard glanced up. "That's Caitlyn Whelan, Shanna's sister."

Carlos's hand curled into a fist. *Merda.* Sean Whelan was her father? The man was a bigoted fool. Still, he was not someone the Vamps wanted to anger. They needed their alliance with him in order to defeat the Malcontents and keep themselves safe.

That meant Carlos needed to stay away from his daughter. A dalliance would upset Sean and the Vamps.

But to be honest, Carlos had already known she was forbidden. She was a disaster disguised as paradise, the kind of woman a man could never forget and never leave. He couldn't allow himself anywhere near her. His fate was written in stone. To ensure the survival of his species, he had to find a mate just like him.

Angus sauntered toward the wall of monitors. "She looks a lot like her sister."

Not at all, Carlos thought. Her eyes were more

turquoise in color. Her face was more oval-shaped. Her nose was sprinkled with a few freckles. Her hair was longer and a more golden shade than Shanna's strawberry blond hair. He shook his head ruefully. Was there nothing he hadn't noticed about her and already committed to memory?

Howard leaned back in his chair behind the desk. "Did you know Sean didn't tell her that Shanna was married or had children?"

"Och, what an arse," Angus muttered.

When it came to Sean Whelan, Carlos was tempted to use more colorful language. "She's missing the party."

"She's probably in shock." Howard propped his feet up on the desk. "Shanna was going to tell her about vampires."

Angus nodded. "That was Emma's idea. She thought it would be better for Caitlyn to hear the news from her sister." He glanced at her on the monitor. "She seems to be taking it well."

Howard snorted. "Because she's not running for her car, screaming her head off?"

Carlos gave Angus a curious look. "Why did Emma want her to know the truth?"

"We're hoping to hire her."

"What?" Carlos stepped back.

"We'd rather have her working for us than for her father and his bloody Stake-Out team."

Carlos gulped. He couldn't work alongside *her*. If they stationed her here at Romatech, he'd have to put in for a transfer. Better yet, he'd just depart immediately for Bangkok. "I need to leave on my trip right away."

"What trip?" Howard asked.

Carlos quickly explained. "I'll take the first available flight."

Angus's brow creased with a frown. "Why the big hurry?"

"Why not?" Carlos countered. "Things are slow right now, with Casimir and the Malcontents in hiding. You don't really need me here. And you know I have to find a mate. I've been looking for five years. I'm not getting any younger."

"I understand, lad." Angus rested a hand on his shoulder. "I'm just concerned about yer children. I hear they're having some trouble adjusting to the new school and new country. I'm no' sure ye should be leaving them right now."

Carlos groaned inwardly. He knew the orphans were having a rough time. All the more reason for him to find a mate. Coco was only six years old. Raquel was nine, and Teresa twelve. They needed a mother. They needed a woman who could guide them through the shape shifting process when they reached puberty. The change could happen any time now for Teresa. Carlos could feel the clock ticking.

Angus's cell phone rang, and he retrieved it from his pocket. "Aye, I'll be there soon."

The big Scotsman's normally gruff voice had softened, a sure sign he was talking to his wife, Emma. His eyes widened. "They're missing? Doona worry, sweetheart. We'll find them." He hung up.

"Who's missing?" Carlos asked.

"Coco and Raquel." Angus studied the monitors. "Emma was fetching cake and ice cream for the children, and when she came back to the table, the two lassies were gone."

Howard dropped his feet to the floor with a thud and stood. "They couldn't have gone far."

Carlos felt the usual heaviness in his chest whenever a problem arose with the children. They were suffering, and he didn't have a clue how to make it better. His pretense that everything was fine wasn't working. He knew how to save people physically, but emotionally? Whenever the children looked at him with all that pain glimmering in their teary eyes, he cringed inside.

He spotted movement on a monitor that showed the garden. Someone was hiding behind a big rhododendron. His heart twinged. The poor girls didn't want to be found.

He motioned to the quivering bush. "They're hiding there. I'll get them." He could return them to the party, but God help him, he didn't know what to tell them. For the last few years, he'd entertained them with jokes, amateur magic tricks, and trips to the ice cream parlor to make the tears go away. It wasn't enough, but how could he open his heart when all he had to offer was pain and despair?

He left the security office and trudged down the hallway to the side exit. The heaviness in his chest bore down on him, making it hard to breathe. The orphans thought he was their hero, the bravest man in the world, the one who had rescued them from a horrible death.

He couldn't let them know the truth. He was brave enough to face the physical pain of death, but when it came to emotional pain, he was a clueless pretender. Worse than that, he thought with a snort. He was a damned coward.

Caitlyn was deep in thought as she sat on the bench beneath the oak tree. If vampires were real, what other strange creatures could exist? Elves? The tooth fairy? Big Foot?

A sound close by made her jump. She turned and spotted someone behind the oak tree. Definitely not Big Foot. Not big at all.

She rose to her feet. "Hello?"

The little girl peered around the tree. Tears glistened in her big brown eyes and her bottom lip trembled.

"Coco, no," another girl whispered from behind a nearby bush. Her voice carried a slight accent and sounded tense with pain. "Leave the lady alone."

"It's all right," Caitlyn assured them. Were these hybrid children like Constantine? Whatever they were, they were certainly upset.

Coco rounded the tree and approached Caitlyn quietly. She had a lost, frightened look in her eyes that Caitlyn had seen many times in her life, every time a stray kitten or puppy came to her for help.

She sat on the bench and patted the space beside her. "Tell me what's wrong, Coco."

The little girl climbed onto the bench and wiggled up close.

The second girl, who appeared a few years older, ventured closer. "I forgot your name."

"I'm Caitlyn. And you are?"

"Raquel. Raquel Gatina." She lifted her chin proudly. "We're from Brazil."

Coco's thin shoulders shook as she burst into tears. "I want to go home. I . . . I'm so tired of this English. It's hard."

"Sweetie." Caitlyn patted her on the back. "You speak whatever you like. I'll understand." Her comprehension would be immediate, but it would take a while before she could start responding in the girls' native language.

Raquel stepped closer. "Are you serious?"

"Try me."

Coco gazed up at her. "I feel bad," she said in Portuguese.

"Why do you feel bad?" Caitlyn asked in English.

The girls exchanged surprised looks.

"Coco's mad at Constantine," Raquel explained in Portuguese. "She says she hates him."

"I don't want to hate him," Coco wailed. "I like Tino. But it's not fair!"

Raquel sniffed. "Tino has family and friends. We don't."

Caitlyn's heart squeezed. "You have each other. And from what I could tell, every woman at the party loves you and wants to be your aunt."

Raquel frowned and kicked at the ground. "They just feel sorry for us because we're orphans."

"Tino has a mommy and daddy and a sister," Coco whispered. "My mommy and daddy and sister are dead."

Caitlyn gulped. "How did that—I'm sorry. I'm sure you don't want to talk about it."

Raquel perched on the bench next to Coco. "Some bad men came to our village and killed our families. They hate us because we're different."

Caitlyn sucked in a deep breath. Good God. Were the girls' families killed because they were vampires? That was unconscionable. It reminded her of racial purging. It could not be allowed to continue.

She was struck suddenly with a moment of crystal clarity. If she took the job offered by Emma MacKay, she could work to protect innocent children like Coco and Raquel. And her niece and nephew.

Coco tugged on the sleeve of her cardigan sweater. "Am I bad 'cause I'm mad at Tino?"

"No, sweetie. It's normal to be envious when someone else has what you want for yourself."

"I really do like him." Coco sniffled. "I want to be happy for him, but it's not fair."

"I know." Caitlyn stroked the girl's long black hair. "But in a strange way, you can be happy that the world isn't fair."

Raquel stiffened. "But it should be fair."

"Think about it," Caitlyn said softly. "In a world that was totally fair, everything that happened to you would be because somehow you absolutely deserved it."

Raquel's mouth dropped open. "We—We didn't deserve it."

Coco sat up, her eyes wide with horror. "The bad men came because I'm bad?"

"No!" Caitlyn grabbed the girl by the shoulders. "You are good. You are a sweet, innocent child, and there is no way you could ever deserve what happened."

Raquel jumped to her feet. "Then why did it happen?"

Tears filled Caitlyn's eyes. "Oh, honey, I don't know why there's evil in the world. I think it has something to do with free will, so people can decide to be good or bad."

"I want to be good," Coco whispered.

Caitlyn blinked back her tears. "Sweetie, you are good."

"If we're good, why did that bad thing happen to us?" Raquel cried.

Caitlyn winced. She was in seriously over her head. "I don't know. It shouldn't have happened to you. I'm so sorry that it did."

Coco burst into tears and threw her arms around Caitlyn's neck. Raquel sidled closer, looking hesitant to ask for comfort.

"Come here." Caitlyn pulled the older girl onto her right knee. Her own tears spilled over as she listened to the girls' soft cries and felt their small bodies tremble.

Great job, she chided herself. Instead of making them happy, she'd brought them to tears.

She thought back to when she'd been stationed in Thailand and she'd visited the Tiger Temple. She'd asked a Buddhist monk the same question Raquel had asked her. He'd simply smiled and said it was better to consider all that was good in the world that brought love and joy. She pointed out that he'd avoided giving her a real answer.

"Sometimes there are no words to answer. Only love," he replied. "And love is always the best answer."

So she sat silently, hugging the girls and hoping it was enough to give them some comfort.

Slowly, a sense of purpose and completion

seeped into her. She'd been fired from the State Department because she'd interfered with local customs in order to help an innocent woman. She didn't regret her actions. She'd do it again in a second.

Maybe that was her true mission in life. Protect the innocent. She was here at this moment because these girls needed her. Her whole life had been a maze of turns and decisions, all leading to this.

"I'm going to be here for you," she whispered to the girls in Portuguese. She wouldn't let anyone harm them because they were different.

"You know our language?" a deep masculine voice asked in Portuguese.

With a gasp, she turned her head. Good God, it was him. The gorgeous mystery man. The vampire.

Carlos.

Chapter Four

*C*aitlyn dragged in a shaky breath. What was it about this man that made her feel so raw and ragged? It was as if every nerve cell was exposed and vulnerable. And instead of frightening her, it excited her.

He stepped out of the shadows, moving so stealthily and quietly she wondered how long he'd been there. How much of their conversation did he hear? Since he obviously spoke Portuguese, he would have understood the girls.

"Uncle!" Coco scrambled off the bench, ran to him and flung her arms around his waist.

Uncle? Caitlyn watched as he patted the girl on her back. Was the uncle an honorary title? Coco had said her family members were dead.

Raquel approached him slowly, as if afraid her need for affection would be rejected.

Caitlyn exhaled with relief when he drew the

girl closer. Somehow, he didn't display the same gracefulness he had while playing basketball. His movements seemed hesitant and awkward.

"Are you all right?" he asked quietly in English.

"Yes." Raquel motioned toward Caitlyn. "We made a new friend."

His gaze shifted to Caitlyn and his eyes narrowed. "Yes, I know."

She had a strange suspicion that he was annoyed with her, but that didn't make any sense. "How do you do? I'm Caitlyn Whelan."

"Yes, I know."

She waited for him to introduce himself, but he simply watched her, his amber eyes gleaming and intense, as if he were sizing up his prey. Maybe to a vampire, she *was* prey. She suppressed a shiver. "You're Coco's uncle?"

His mouth thinned. "I'm her guardian. We need to get back to the party. Thank you for your assistance."

He *was* annoyed. Why would he object to her helping the girls? Caitlyn looked at Coco and Raquel. "If you ever need to talk again, I'll be happy to listen."

Coco grinned and ran to her. Raquel followed, and Caitlyn wrapped her arms around them, pulling them close. When she noticed Carlos scowling at her, she couldn't resist needling him.

She smiled a sweet invitation. "Group hug?"

His gaze drifted down to her feet, then inched slowly back up. "I don't do groups."

Her skin tingled with sensual awareness, but she refused to let him know how much he unnerved her. "I don't do strangers."

His wide mouth curled up on one side. "I don't consider you a stranger. I know your name."

"You didn't tell me yours."

His eyes glimmered with heat. "Yes, I know."

She suspected he was playing cat and mouse with her. She lifted her chin. She was not the sort to accept the role of mouse.

Coco tugged on her sweater. "Will you come to the party with us?"

"You go on with your . . . uncle," Caitlyn replied. "I'll see you in a little while."

" 'Bye!" The girls ran back to Carlos.

He inclined his head at Caitlyn. "Good evening." He turned to escort the girls back to the cafeteria.

"So long." Caitlyn couldn't resist one last jab. *"Carlos."*

He stopped and looked back at her. A flash of heat flared in his amber eyes, and her skin prickled with excitement.

"Catalina," he whispered. Then he turned and walked away.

Catalina. The name sizzled through her. Maybe he was just translating her name into Portuguese, but she could have sworn he'd made it sound like an endearment.

With shaky knees she sat on the bench. She fumbled through her silk handbag for a tissue, then wiped her damp cheeks. The two girls had touched her heart. And Carlos—what was he doing to her? If he came back and asked for a pint, she'd actually be tempted to bare her neck. Did all vampires exude that sexy seductive charm?

But she'd seen other vampires on the basketball court. It was only Carlos who was affecting her like this. She looked in his direction, but he and the girls had moved out of view, blocked by a huge rhododendron bush.

"Carlos!" a female voice yelled. "We need to talk."

Caitlyn eased to the other side of the oak tree. There in the shadow she had a good view. A young man and woman approached Carlos and the girls.

In a low voice Carlos urged the girls to go on to the cafeteria. "I'll be there soon." He walked a few steps with them, then watched them continue past the gazebo.

"Is it true?" the young woman asked. "You're leaving on another trip?"

Carlos turned to face the young man and woman. "Yes. Angus approved it."

"Howard mentioned it at the party," the young woman continued impatiently. "And he said you wanted to leave right away?"

"That's true." Carlos's gaze shifted toward the oak tree and his eyes narrowed.

Could he see her? Caitlyn moved farther back into the shadows and slipped her white tissue back into her handbag. Maybe vampires had superior night vision.

"How long do you intend to be gone?" the young woman demanded.

Carlos sighed. "However long it takes. A month, maybe more."

"You can't leave for a month," the woman insisted. "Your children need you. You're their hero, Carlos. They know they would be dead if you hadn't rescued them."

"They'll be fine, Toni," Carlos gritted out between clenched teeth. "They'll be at school with you."

"Aye, and 'tis at school where they're having problems," the young man said with a Scottish accent. "Emiliano is picking fights with Phil's boys."

"I'll talk to him before I go," Carlos grumbled.

"And what about the girls?" Toni asked. "They need you, Carlos."

"They need a mother!" Carlos yelled. "And I need a mate."

Caitlyn gasped. He was looking for a mate? What kind of mate? His gaze shifted toward her, and his eyes glittered with a hard, angry look.

"You—what?" Toni stepped back, apparently stunned.

"You heard me," Carlos growled.

"Ye want to get married?" the Scotsman asked.

"Don't look so shocked, Ian. Didn't *you* want to get married?"

"Aye, but—"

"You can't get married," Toni declared. "You're gay."

Caitlyn snorted. Were they crazy?

Carlos glared at her in the shadows, then shifted his gaze to Toni. "I never said I was gay."

"Of course you're gay," she insisted. "I saw you dance the samba in a hot pink sequined thong."

Carlos shrugged. "So? You said I was very sexy. You were practically drooling."

Ian stiffened. "When was this?"

"Before I met you," Toni muttered, then turned back to Carlos. "And what about Fernando? Whenever he came to visit, the two of you would hug and kiss."

"We kiss on the cheeks." Carlos waved a hand in dismissal. "That's not strange in our culture. If you choose to misinterpret it—"

"But Fernando's gay," Toni interrupted. "He said he was."

"Yes, he is," Carlos said impatiently. "But I am not."

"Bloody hell." Ian walked away a few steps. "I knew it."

Toni gestured wildly with her hands. "You let me think you were gay!"

"I had my reasons," Carlos grumbled.

"To purposely mislead me?" Toni planted fists on her hips. "You used to watch me get dressed. How could you?"

Carlos shrugged. "You never told me I had to leave."

"Because I thought you were gay!" Toni shouted. "You—You pervert!"

Carlos frowned. "There's nothing perverse in enjoying the sight of a woman's body."

"Oh really? Well, enjoy this!" Toni slapped him so hard the sound echoed across the garden.

Carlos stumbled back. Caitlyn winced.

He rubbed his cheek. "*Menina*—"

"Don't *menina* me! I trusted you!" Toni drew back her hand to slap him again.

"Stop!" Ian pulled his wife back. "That's no' the way to handle this."

"Thank you for understanding," Carlos murmured.

"Och, I understand it verra well," Ian said. "Ye

ogled my wife under false pretenses, ye bloody bastard." He punched Carlos in the face, knocking him flat. "Now, that's the way to handle it."

Caitlyn's mouth dropped open. Apparently, Carlos was getting his comeuppance for being naughty, but really, how could those people ever think he was gay? He could make her breathless with just a look.

"Come on, Toni." Ian grabbed his wife's hand and led her back to the cafeteria.

Carlos sat up with a groan.

Caitlyn winced at the sight of blood trickling from his nose and lip. She retrieved her small pack of tissues from her handbag and hurried toward him. "Are you okay?"

"I'll live." He pressed the back of his hand against his nose.

Did the scent of blood make him hungry? "Here." She passed him a tissue.

He tilted his head back and held the tissue against his nose. "Well, *menina*. Did you enjoy the show?"

She crouched on the flagstone path beside him. "It was . . . interesting."

"What a relief. I would hate to be boring." He frowned at the blood-soaked tissue.

"I doubt you're ever boring." She handed him another tissue. "Do you really dance the samba in a hot pink sequined thong?"

He pressed the fresh tissue against his nose with his head still tilted back. "Not on the first date."

She smiled. "It seems like every time I see you, your head is getting pummeled."

"It must be your lucky night."

She took another tissue and dabbed it against the blood that had oozed from the corner of his mouth. His bottom lip looked swollen and puffy. She touched it lightly with her fingertip, wishing she could kiss it.

She glanced at his eyes. They were closed, so she took advantage of the opportunity to look him over close up. His eyelashes were thick and black. His hair was shoulder length and very silky. His skin was surprisingly tanned for a vampire. The short sleeves of his black T-shirt were tight around his biceps. His shoulders were broad, his chest muscular. A tattoo in red and black circled around his neck to his collarbone, but too much of it was hidden beneath his T-shirt for her to make out the design.

She tried to wipe up the blood on his chin, but the tissue tore against his dark whiskers. "I don't know how that woman could ever believe you're gay."

He opened his eyes. "I let her believe it."

"I would never believe it." She met his gaze. "I saw the way you looked at me."

The golden tint in his brown eyes glimmered like amber. "I never looked at her that way."

Caitlyn's face grew warm. She brushed the bits of shredded tissue from his chin. "Why did you want people to think you're gay?"

He shrugged. "It was easier that way. I didn't have to worry about women pursuing me."

She sat back. "Because there are mobs of drooling women stalking you?"

"In Brazil, yes. There were many beautiful

women who would come on to me. It was very tiring."

She snorted. "Poor baby."

He arched a brow. "The illusion worked in Rio, so I tried it in America. It helps keep women at a distance—"

"Because their natural tendency is to throw themselves at you? Of all the . . ." Caitlyn scrambled to her feet.

He stood. "You're angry?"

"More like disappointed. And annoyed. The size of your ego makes the Amazon River look like a—a drainage ditch."

"It's not a matter of ego, *menina*. It is simply fact. My kind tends to attract women, and I didn't want to take advantage of that."

She hesitated. He could be right. Women might be naturally attracted to vampires. She'd certainly felt an immediate attraction. It was to his credit if he was trying not to capitalize on it.

He stuffed his bloody tissues in a pocket of his jeans. "I pretended to prefer men, so I could keep myself free from temptation."

"And it worked?"

"Yes." He gave her an intense look. "Until now."

She gulped. Was he thinking about biting her? He had lost a little blood. "If you're hungry, there are some bottles in the cafeteria."

He tilted his head. "I like real food."

Did he mean fresh blood? "I thought you were resisting temptation."

He stepped toward her. "You're making it very hard for me."

She eased back. "Look, I know you're really gorgeous and all that, but I'm not going to let you bite me."

He halted with a jerk. Anger flashed in his eyes. "I would never bite you. There is nothing on earth that could make me bite you."

"What?" Suddenly, she felt strangely insulted. "Are you saying my blood isn't good enough for you?"

He blinked. "What?"

Dammit, it was her childhood all over again. She'd always feared her sister had abandoned her 'cause she wasn't good enough. Now she was being judged less than worthy by a hungry vampire.

She tossed the bloody tissue at him. "Suck on your own blood, Carlos!" She stormed past him.

"Wait." He grabbed her arm, but she wrenched herself free.

"Why are you so angry?" he demanded.

Tears crowded her vision. How could she tell him how much her heart had filled with hope and desire? "You don't think I'm good enough for you."

His eyes glistened with pain. "I never said that."

She lifted her chin. "You don't have to. I know when I'm being rejected." She turned on her heel to march off.

"*Merda,*" he growled behind her.

She was suddenly whipped around and pulled hard against his body.

"Oof." She planted her palms against his solid

chest. "What are—" She stopped when he seized her jaw with one hand.

He leaned forward, his amber eyes blazing into hers. "You have no idea how much I want you."

Her lips opened with a small gasp, and his mouth was instantly there. She stiffened, taken aback by the taste of blood and how quickly he'd pounced.

Then she realized his fingers were gently stroking her neck. His lips were softly moving against hers. He planned to lure her in with tenderness. And it was working.

His swollen bottom lip pressed gingerly against her. She suspected he was feeling more pain than pleasure, but it wasn't stopping him. She leaned into him, and with a low growl he deepened the kiss. The sound was so low and exotic, it reverberated through her bones, making her want to melt at his feet. Her heart pounded. Her hands smoothed up to his shoulders, then around his neck. Silky strands of his hair brushed against her forearms, sparking an electric spurt of tingles across her skin.

"*Menina*, Catalina," he whispered as he dusted her face with kisses.

She moaned and pressed herself against him. The hard ridge in his jeans was unmistakable. Heat sizzled through her and a desperate desire seized her. "Carlos."

He growled low in his throat once again, then planted his mouth on hers. The gentleness was gone, replaced by a hunger that made her squirm. She gasped against his mouth when he cupped her breast and squeezed.

He broke the kiss and leaned back. A stunned look crossed his face when he glanced down at his hand on her breast. He pulled his hand away and stepped back. "What am I doing?"

"I don't know," she gasped for air, "but you're doing it awfully well."

"I—I had no right to kiss you."

"I didn't object. I was actually participating. I thought you might have noticed."

"But we can't . . . we can't ever . . ." He dragged a hand through his hair. "I'm sorry."

Why was he apologizing? Granted, it was the hottest kiss she'd ever experienced, and he was practically a stranger, but it wasn't a disaster. "Don't worry about it. This sort of thing happens." *Once every million years.*

He shook his head, frowning. "I shouldn't have done it. Forgive me."

A frisson of alarm shot through her. Did he actually regret the kiss? Did he never intend to kiss her again? It didn't make sense. He'd clearly wanted her. He'd said so. The hard lump in his jeans said so.

He turned away, scowling at the ground. "I think you should return to the party. I'll follow in a few minutes."

She considered arguing with him but didn't think it would work at the moment. He was too upset with himself, too determined to push her away.

This wasn't going to be the end of this, she decided. She would visit Romatech regularly to see Shanna and her children. And she would try to see Coco and Raquel again, too. There was no way

Carlos could avoid her. If the attraction between them was real, it would grow. He couldn't stop it.

"I'll see you later, then." She strode toward the cafeteria.

The noise inside was deafening. Children were chasing each other around tables. Balloons were popping. Adults were in small groups, talking. Every time Constantine opened a new present, a cheer erupted. Caitlyn eased through the crowd till she reached her sister.

Shanna grinned at her, then her smile faded as her eyes narrowed. "Are you all right?"

"I need to talk."

Shanna took her arm and led her into the kitchen. She poured a glass of water. "You look hot and flushed, which is odd since it's chilly outside."

Caitlyn sipped some water and set the glass on the stainless steel counter. "I'm seriously leaning toward accepting the job with Emma's security company."

Shanna's face lit up. "That would be wonderful! We would see each other all the time."

"Yes."

Shanna studied her sister's face close up. "You look like you've been kissing someone."

"Maybe because . . . I have been kissing someone."

Shanna gasped and stepped back. "My God, Caitlyn. You just got here. You're already—isn't that kind of quick?"

Caitlyn gave her an annoyed look. "Believe me, I don't usually throw myself at men the first time I see them. But these vampire guys . . . well, they're really attractive."

"Who was it?"

"Carlos."

Shanna's mouth dropped open.

Caitlyn reached for the glass to drink more water.

"Give me that." Shanna grabbed it and gulped down a few swallows. "You kissed Carlos?"

"Yes."

Shanna drank some more water. "Are you sure?"

Caitlyn snorted. "Yes. I did manage to learn his name before I jumped him. I have some scruples, you know."

Shanna set the empty glass on the counter. "I want you to stay away from him."

"What?"

Her sister gave her a stern look. "Don't get involved with him."

"How can you say that?" Caitlyn's temper flared. "Do you think I'm not good enough for a vampire? You've got a vampire. Why can't I have one?"

"Cait!" Shanna reached out to her. "Sweetie, he's not a vampire."

"What?"

"Carlos is not a vampire."

Caitlyn slumped against the counter. Her attraction to him wasn't caused by a supernatural allure? She could have sworn he was . . . special somehow. "He's a regular guy?"

"Not exactly." Shanna winced. "Some of the guys who work the day shift for MacKay Security and Investigation are . . . different. They're shape shifters."

Caitlyn stared at her sister. The rabbit hole had just reopened. She collapsed onto a stool. "Carlos is a . . . ?"

"Shape shifter. They can change into animals."

Caitlyn gulped. "Like a werewolf?"

"Phil and some of the boys are werewolves," Shanna explained. "And of course, Howard Barr is a bear."

"A *bear*?" Caitlyn motioned toward the dining room. "There's a bear over there? Where?"

"There." Shanna pointed at Howard. "A were-bear."

Caitlyn touched her brow. "I'm losing my mind."

"I should have warned you." Shanna shook her head. "It just never occurred to me that you would . . ."

"Lock lips with the first man to cross my path?" Caitlyn asked dryly.

"You have to understand. We shouldn't anger Dad more than necessary. He's going to be pissed if you take the job with Emma. He's already furious that I'm married to a vampire. If he finds out that you're involved with a shape shifter—"

"I know," Caitlyn muttered. "He'll have kittens."

Shanna snorted. "No, Cait. *You* would have kittens. Carlos is a were-panther."

Chapter Five

*H*ere." Shanna set a plate of birthday cake and a cup of punch on the kitchen counter, then perched on a stool next to Caitlyn. "The all-natural remedy for coping with stress: chocolate."

Caitlyn slipped a small bite of chocolate cake into her mouth.

"Better?" Shanna asked with a strained smile.

Caitlyn nodded. No doubt her sister was worried about her. She'd sat on a stool for five minutes frozen in shock, not uttering a sound. She ate another bite of cake. The rich, gooey texture melted in her mouth, erasing the lingering taste of blood. His blood. From his kiss.

A were-panther. She'd kissed a were-panther. A Brazilian were-panther.

She sipped some punch. The last thing she probably needed was a sugar rush. Her heart was already racing. "I'm falling for a giant Mr. Foofi-kins," she whispered.

"Excuse me?" Shanna gave her a wary look.

She thinks I've gone over the edge. "When I was young and you left home, I was . . . really lone-some. Dylan was always off somewhere playing soccer, and he didn't have time for a little sister. Mom was always kind, but detached, like she wasn't quite there."

Shanna nodded. "I know. I'm sorry."

Then why did you leave me? Caitlyn had wanted the answer to that since she was nine years old, but she didn't ask it now. She was afraid she would hear what she'd always suspected. *You're not good enough.*

"About a month after you left," she continued, "a little black kitten came to our back door. I loved it at first sight, but as usual, Dad insisted we take it to a shelter. It turned out that the kitten had feline leukemia, and the shelter wanted to put it down."

"How terrible," Shanna murmured.

Caitlyn's eyes blurred with tears. "I begged Dad to let me keep it. I told him I had no one to love. So he relented. I adored Mr. Foofikins. I gave him all the love I could, but he died about a year later."

Shanna touched her shoulder. "I'm so sorry."

Caitlyn wiped a few tears from her cheek. "Why don't you know about him? Didn't you read my letters? I wrote all about him for months. I even sent pictures."

Shanna sat back. "You wrote to me?"

"Yes. Every week for months. I . . . I stopped when you never replied."

"Oh my God." Shanna pressed a hand to her chest. Tears shimmered in her eyes. "I never received any letters from home."

Caitlyn blinked. "You didn't get my letters?"

"No." She shook her head, her face deathly pale. "I . . . I thought you'd all abandoned me."

"I thought *you* abandoned me."

Shanna shut her eyes briefly with a pained look. "How could he . . ."

"What? Who?"

Shanna grabbed Caitlyn's hand. "What's important is we're back together now. No one can separate us."

Caitlyn squeezed her sister's hand. "Agreed."

"Good." Shanna helped herself to a sip from the cup of punch. "I think you've been through enough for now, so if you want more information about the job, can you come back tomorrow night to talk to Emma?"

"Sure."

"I'll get you a key to the townhouse so you can move in tomorrow."

"That would be great. Thank you." Caitlyn ate another piece of cake.

"We have a few friends staying there while they're in town. Jack and Lara and Robby and Olivia. They work for MacKay S and I." Shanna gave her a curious look. "I suppose you know that Carlos works for MacKay, too."

"I sorta figured that."

"I hope he's not the reason you're considering the job."

Caitlyn shook her head. "No."

"Good." Shanna looked relieved. "I know you loved your little black kitty, but Carlos is not a giant Mr. Foofikins. My husband has fought in a few battles with the Malcontents, and he's seen the were-creatures in action. They're not cute and cuddly. They're deadly and savage."

And sexy as hell. Caitlyn sighed. Who would have thought a jungle cat could kiss that well? "Do you think they can be trusted?"

"I trust them completely," Shanna admitted. "But only when they're in human form. Once they transform, I'm never quite sure how much control they have over the beast."

Caitlyn shivered. She knew her sister was trying to scare her away from Carlos. But the lure of the exotic always pulled at her. God help her, she knew the truth about Carlos, and it only made him more exciting.

"Toni, pick up. I know you're there." This was Carlos's third attempt to call Toni MacPhie.

She'd returned to Dragon Nest Academy after the party had ended last night. A group of Vamps had teleported the mortals and shape shifters who lived at the school back to the dormitories. His adopted children had gone back.

Carlos had remained at Romatech, spending the night in one of the bedrooms in the basement. He hadn't slept well because of *her*. One minute he was chastising himself for kissing her, and the next he was replaying the kiss in his mind and wanting more. When he finally fell asleep, he dreamed about her. And him. Rolling around naked in the jungle. Then he woke with an erection and started the whole process all over again, beginning with the chastising.

During the day, he was on guard duty at Romatech, protecting the Vamps who were death-sleeping in the basement. Howard, the other day guard, was usually at the Draganesti home in White Plains, so he could guard Roman and his Vamp bodyguard, Connor. This left Carlos alone all day, bored and yawning with sleepiness because of *her.*

He couldn't allow himself to get involved with her. He had to get away. He'd spent the last few hours planning his trip so he could leave tomorrow. But before he left, he needed to make arrangements for his adopted children. And he needed to patch things up with his friend Toni.

"*Menina,*" Carlos continued to talk to Toni's answering machine. "How long are you going to stay mad? Do you need to slap me again?"

There was a click as someone picked up the phone.

"I ought to clobber you," Toni said. "You deserve it."

"Oh come on, you always knew I was naughty." He lowered his voice. "Would you prefer to spank me?"

She snorted. "Bad kitty. I still haven't forgiven you."

"What if I told you that out of all the girls I've ever helped dress, you were the prettiest?"

"Gee, thanks," she muttered. "And what about the ones you helped undress?"

"I made them purr."

She scoffed. "Do you realize how pissed Sabrina's going to be when I tell her?"

"Sabrina's always pissed."

Toni laughed. "Yeah, but at least now she'll be pissed at you and not me."

He shrugged. Toni's former roommate was still struggling with the fact that her best friend had married a vampire and become the headmistress of a school for shape shifter and hybrid children. "How is her orphanage coming along?"

"She's doing great," Toni replied, "but she's still mad that I'm working here and not with her. So why did you mislead us, Carlos?"

"I was worried about the two of you living alone, especially with Sabrina being a rich heiress. I was afraid someone would try to take advantage, so I wanted to keep an eye on you. At the same time, I didn't want you to interpret my concern as something romantic. I have to keep myself unattached until I can find a were-panther mate."

There was a moment of silence while Toni considered his words. "You did a good job of convincing us you were gay."

"I'm good at pretending." For five years he'd been pretending everything was fine and life was one big carnival. The daily deluge of pain threatened to break loose. *Merda.* Couldn't he go one day without having to relive the Summer of Death? "My . . . twin brother was gay."

Toni gasped. "You have a twin? You never told me that."

"*Had.*" Carlos rubbed his brow. "It's normal for us to be born in litters of two or three."

"You . . . lost him?" Toni asked gently.

The pain spilled over and flooded his senses. His brother. His parents. His village. All gone. Everyone dead.

"Carlos?"

He shoved the pain back, but the effort made his head throb. "Yes?"

"I'm sorry. I don't really know what you or your children went through, but I know it must have been traumatic. Those kids are hurting."

"I know. If I can just find more of our kind, then they won't have to feel so alone. And if I can find a mate, then they'll have a mother. Someone who can give them . . . comfort."

"I think they need *you*, Carlos."

He frowned as the throbbing in his temples increased. How could he help them get over something that he couldn't get over? "I called Fernando. He's much better with them than I am. He agreed to visit them at school while I go on this trip. I was hoping you'd let him live in the dorm."

"He's the one who was taking care of the kids while you were at NYU?"

"Yes. In Rio."

"Hmm. I'm wondering if there's anything he can teach, so we can hire him," Toni murmured. "Is he a were-panther?"

"No. He's a geek. Knows everything about computers and modern technology. He taught me everything I know."

"That sounds promising," Toni said. "We could use a computer specialist. And if he can help the kids feel better, then I'm all for it."

"Great. Thank you." Carlos checked off one of the major concerns on his to-do list. With the children taken care of, he was free to leave on his trip.

"When are you leaving?" Toni asked.

"Tomorrow, I hope." He just needed to get Angus to okay it. "I'll call Fernando again, and he'll catch the next available flight."

"All right. Good luck, Carlos. I hope you find your mate."

"So do I." Carlos hung up. He rubbed his temples, trying to relieve the pain. *Think positive.* He'd soon be trekking through the mountains of northern Thailand, hunting for were-panthers. And this time he'd find them. He'd find his mate, and she would be all he'd ever hoped for. Everything he'd ever imagined.

The vision that filled his mind was Caitlyn Whelan.

"No!" He jumped to his feet and paced across the office. *No, no, no.* She wasn't the one.

The alarm sounded on the desk. He always set it to go off at sunset. Down in the basement, Angus and Emma would be wakening. Phineas, too. Other Vamps, like Jack and Robby, had opted to stay at the townhouse on the Upper East Side. Their mortal wives were with them, guarding them during the day.

Carlos strode to the desk to turn off the alarm. He straightened the papers that described his travel plans. He paced back to the wall of surveillance monitors. Soon, he would see the Vamps exiting their rooms in the basement.

His attention was snagged by a monitor that showed the front gate and driveway. A car was arriving. That was unusual. It was too early for the Vamp employees at Romatech to show up for the night shift.

The phone rang, the sound grating against his headache. He rushed to the desk to answer it.

"Front gate," the guard identified himself. "Caitlyn Whelan has arrived."

Carlos's heart lurched in his chest. "All right. Thanks." He hung up.

He strode back to the monitors and spotted her pulling into the parking lot. The front door at Romatech was locked. The last of the mortal employees had left an hour ago. He'd have to let Caitlyn in. He'd have to see her.

He noted Angus and Emma on another monitor. They were entering the elevator. Phineas ran to join them.

Meanwhile, Caitlyn had parked her car. The front door opened and a pair of long bare legs stretched out. He sucked in a deep breath. Holy Mary, Mother of God. How short was her skirt? He leaned closer and his breath fogged up the monitor.

"Damn." He pulled the hem of his polo shirt up to his chest to wipe the monitor.

On another monitor, Angus, Emma, and Phineas exited the elevator. Carlos dashed over to the desk phone and called Phineas on his cell.

"Yo, Catman, what's up?" Phineas asked.

"Caitlyn Whelan is approaching the front door," Carlos reported.

"Shanna's sister? Man, I missed meeting her last night." There was a pause, then Phineas continued, "Emma says she'll let her in."

"Good." Carlos exhaled in relief as he hung up

the phone. He would avoid seeing her tonight, then he would leave for Thailand tomorrow. The throbbing in his head eased.

He opened the door to let Angus and Phineas inside.

"Anything happen during the day?" Angus asked.

"No." Carlos grabbed his report off the desk. "I was able to complete an itinerary for the trip. As you can see, there's a flight tomorrow night."

Angus shook his head, frowning. "I'm sorry, lad, but we canna let ye leave just yet."

Carlos swallowed hard. "I thought we agreed that I could go as soon as possible."

"Aye, we did. But there are a few matters we have to take care of first. We need to find a replacement for you, and we—"

"Man, that chick is hot!" Phineas stood in front of the monitors, watching Caitlyn and Emma in the foyer.

Carlos's hands fisted around his papers.

Angus glanced at the young vampire from the Bronx. "I hope ye're no' referring to my wife."

Phineas snorted. "I don't have a death wish. No, I'm talking about the blonde. She's bootie-licious. Grade A smoking hot female."

Carlos felt a strange compulsion to rip Phineas's throat out. Which was odd, 'cause he really liked Phineas.

Angus chuckled. "Och, I'm sure Shanna will be pleased to hear yer description of her sister." He turned to Carlos. "Back to business."

Carlos glanced down at his papers. *Merda!* They were scored with slashes, half shredded. He thought he'd only clenched his fists, but somehow his claws were extended. Normally, they only did that if he was in danger. Or if someone he loved was in danger.

Dammit, no. He didn't want to think about that. He mentally forced his claws back in and slipped the mangled papers into a folder.

"We may have an assignment for you to complete before you go," Angus continued, watching him curiously. "A new employee who will require training in self-defense. You're the best we have in martial arts, so we'd like you to teach her."

Her? Carlos's headache returned full force. He glanced at the monitor that showed Emma and Caitlyn walking toward the security office. "You want me to teach her?"

"Aye." Angus nodded. "If we can convince Caitlyn Whelan to work for us, ye'll be her trainer."

Chapter Six

*I*n the parking lot at Romatech Industries, Caitlyn climbed out of her rental car and winced when she saw how far her skirt had ridden up during the drive from Manhattan. She tugged the hem down to its proper length just above the knees, then buttoned her jacket. She checked the interior of her leather portfolio again to make sure her résumé and referrals were inside.

She'd decided a few hours ago to take the job at MacKay Security & Investigation. An interview with her father had helped her make up her mind. Sean had asked her to meet him at the Federal Building, and there in his office, he'd revealed the shocking news. Vampires were real, and by joining his Stake-Out team, she could help him wipe the hideous bloodsuckers off the planet.

At first she pretended to be shocked, but there'd been no need to feign a reaction. Her dad seemed to forget she was in the room. He paced about, waving his arms wildly, shouting and cursing. In the end her shock had been real. Sean was so consumed with hatred for vampires, she feared he was no longer rational. He clearly wanted them dead. All of them.

Her chest had tightened with a terrible fear that somehow he would convince himself that Shanna's beautiful children were spawned by the devil and therefore needed to be destroyed. After ten minutes of listening to her father's virulent rant, she stood up and announced her regret that she couldn't accept his job offer.

"What?" he shouted. "You can't refuse. You have a moral obligation to help me fight these monsters."

"I—I can't. I'm sorry."

He muttered another curse as he paced across the room. "I don't blame you if you're scared. Those damned parasites are scary."

So are you. "I'm sorry, Dad." She'd left in a hurry and taken a taxi to Central Park. She'd walked down the paths, barely noticing the bright patches of daffodils as she wrestled with all the recent twists and turns in her life. She'd grown up trusting her father and believing Shanna had abandoned her. Now everything was upside down. Vampires. Shape shifters. Malcontents. A father obsessed with killing them all.

And in the midst of all the confusion, the innocent faces of Constantine and Sofia invaded her mind and filled her heart with warmth. She remembered the tearful joy of being reunited with her sister. She recalled the feel of Carlos's arms around her, the touch of his lips against hers. And she remembered the way Coco and Raquel had needed her. She had felt such a strong sense of purpose and completion, as if she'd been given a sacred mission to protect them.

Her dad promised a life motivated by hate, while her sister's world offered a life filled with love. In the end the decision was easy.

Caitlyn had driven to Romatech, ready to accept the job with MacKay Security & Investigation. She wore her most expensive suit and high heels. She'd twisted her long hair into a neat bun at the nape of her neck. Instead of her red silk embroidered bag from Singapore, she brought a black leather handbag.

As much as she wanted this job, she was still wary about entering the world of vampires. Just in case it was dangerous to display a bare neck in their presence, she'd knotted a silk scarf around her throat.

As she strode toward the entrance, her heart began to pound. Was Carlos inside? Had he thought about her at all?

The door opened and Emma MacKay greeted her. "Come in."

"Thank you." Caitlyn stepped into the foyer, her stiletto heels clicking on the marble floor. Maybe she'd overdressed. Her new boss was dressed simply in jeans and a green sweater. Hard to believe she was a vampire. Emma looked and acted so normal.

Emma locked the door and pressed some buttons on a security panel. "We have to be careful at night because that's when the Malcontents might attack."

"Shanna told me a little about them," Caitlyn said. "They hate the synthetic blood that's manufactured here."

"Yes. They adhere to an archaic belief that vampires are superior and have the right to use and abuse mortals however they like. The truth is they were a bunch of thugs when they were alive and becoming Undead has only made them worse. They're a bunch of vicious killers, and we're doing our best to defeat them."

Caitlyn suppressed a shudder. Shanna had made the job sound like an exciting adventure— traveling around the world, making it a safer place for mortals—but now she wondered just how dangerous this job could be. "What kind of powers do the Malcontents have?"

"Levitation, teleportation, mind control, super-speed, and enhanced senses," Emma explained as she led Caitlyn down a hallway on the left. "But don't worry. We have some excellent Vamp warriors on our side with the same powers. And we have employees with all kinds of talents and abilities. Shape shifters, mortals—in fact, we recently hired a mortal who can detect lies. Robby's wife, Olivia MacKay. You may have met her."

"I did. When I moved into the townhouse this morning, I met Olivia and Lara."

Emma smiled. "Aren't they lovely?"

"Yes." Caitlyn had taken an instant liking to them both. She realized that Olivia had been the woman in the gazebo the night before. Of course she didn't meet the man who had made Olivia squeal. He was dead during the day.

"I'm a bit concerned that I don't have the right credentials for this job," Caitlyn admitted. "Lara told me she used to be a police officer. And Olivia worked for the FBI."

Emma stopped her with a touch on the shoulder. "They have their own talents, but yours is truly unique. You can learn a new language in a few hours, right?"

Caitlyn nodded. "And I can understand any language that's spoken."

Emma's eyes widened. "That's amazing. Good heavens, we could have used you a month ago. We were hunting for Casimir in Bulgaria, and none of us knew the language."

"Who is Casimir?"

"The leader of the Malcontents." Emma gestured to the right. "This is the nursery for Shanna's children, and next door is her dental office. They should be arriving soon."

The top half of the nursery door was open. Caitlyn peered inside and saw shelves full of toys, books, and stuffed animals. A rocking chair sat in the corner. The carpet was printed to look like a town with streets and buildings.

She smiled to herself. Her sister might have given birth to half-vampire children, but she was managing to give them a fairly normal childhood.

Emma sighed. "I have to be honest with you. We have no plans to ever put you in a dangerous situation, but we're dealing with a dangerous enemy so it could still happen. Every MacKay employee undergoes some self-defense training just to be safe. Are you all right with that?"

Caitlyn swallowed hard. There was no avoiding the potential danger. Even if she had joined her father's Stake-Out team, she would have needed to be prepared for a possible confrontation with a Malcontent. At least by working for MacKay S & I, she'd be surrounded by Vamps who possessed the same powers as the Malcontents. And she'd be able to see her sister, niece, and nephew. "I understand the danger."

Emma nodded. "We'll do our best to keep you safe." She snorted. "Shanna would probably stake me in my sleep if I let anything happen to you."

A door opened down the hall, and a big man in a kilt stepped out. Caitlyn recognized him as the redheaded man who'd played basketball the night before.

"Angus." Emma strode toward him, smiling. "This is Caitlyn Whelan."

He extended a hand. "Pleased to meet you, lass."

Caitlyn shook hands with him. "Thank you."

Angus wrapped an arm around Emma. "Have ye convinced Miss Whelan to work for us yet?"

When Emma hesitated, Caitlyn spoke up. "Yes, she has. I would be delighted to work for you."

Emma's face lit up with a big grin. "That's super!" She hugged Caitlyn. "Thank you, dear."

Angus chuckled. "Excellent."

"Yo, dudette." A tall male filled the doorway, grinning at Caitlyn. He was dressed in khaki pants and a navy polo shirt. "Welcome to the hood. I'm Phineas McKinney, aka Dr. Phang."

Caitlyn remembered him from the basketball game, too. "You're a vampire doctor?"

"I'm the Love Doctor." He winked. "Available every night for consultation regarding your romantic queries."

"Thank you. I'll keep that in mind."

"I'm sure you've noticed all the happily married couples around here." Phineas flipped up the collar on his polo shirt. "Is it a coincidence that all this conjugal bliss abounds while the Love Doctor's in the house? I think not."

Angus snorted. "Doona let his jesting fool you, Miss Whelan. Phineas is a fierce warrior on the battlefield, and the enemy has learned to fear him."

"Oh yeah, I'm bad." Phineas moonwalked back. "Bad to the bone, baby." He spun in a circle, then went up on his toes. "Ow!"

"And if he can behave in a professional manner"—Angus gave him a pointed look—"I'll be promoting him to head of security here at Romatech."

Phineas halted in the middle of his dance routine, his eyes widening with shock. "No shit? I mean, really, sir?"

Angus's mouth twitched. "Really. Ye'll be in charge here. Connor will still be around, but his main focus is keeping Roman and his family safe."

"Aye, aye, Captain." Phineas saluted.

Angus turned to Caitlyn. "Ye'll have to undergo some self-defense training. Carlos has been assigned as yer trainer until he leaves on his trip."

Caitlyn took a deep breath. Where was Carlos

going? Was it the trip he had argued about last night before getting slapped and punched? He'd mentioned something about needing a mate, but she didn't want to dwell on that. The important thing now was that he was going to train her. That meant time alone together.

"Let me get the forms for you to fill out." Emma slipped into the office, and Angus followed her.

Caitlyn stepped inside and was instantly intrigued by the wall of surveillance monitors. She spotted the main foyer and hallways in Romatech and recognized the cafeteria. She saw the front parking lot and the basketball court. The gazebo and gardens.

She gulped with a sudden thought. If anyone had been in this office last night, they would have seen her and Carlos kissing. She struggled to remember. When she'd returned to the cafeteria, Howard had been there, eating cake. Maybe the kiss was still secret. The hottest, most glorious kiss of her life.

She turned away from the monitors and noticed that the back of the office was caged off. What a huge arsenal of guns, rifles, and swords! Her skin prickled with alarm.

The most violent act she'd ever perpetrated in her twenty-six years was the smashing of cockroaches with her rain boots. And that had been a traumatic experience, considering the gargantuan size of roaches in Southeast Asia. She might be a complete wimp when it came to a big, vicious vampire with fangs.

Think of this as an adventure, she reminded herself. She'd always hated violence, but she loved adventure. And she wasn't one to give up easily. She'd been brave enough to live in strange, exotic places. Strong enough to survive even though she'd always felt alone.

She wasn't alone now. She would have Shanna and these new friends. As she mentally calmed herself, she became aware of a prickling sensation on the back of her neck, as if she was being watched. She turned slowly. Phineas was lounging in a chair in front of the desk. He gave her a friendly smile.

She smiled back. It wasn't him. This was something hot and . . . dangerous, like she was being targeted as prey. Angus and Emma were standing in front of the desk, their backs to her as they rummaged through papers.

She stiffened. Seated behind the desk, barely visible in a narrow gap between Angus and Emma, was Carlos. He was staring at her with those intense eyes that glowed like amber. Every nerve fiber inside her sizzled.

She lifted her eyebrows. Was he just going to sit there and refuse to talk to her? "How do you do?"

His jaw ticked.

Angus turned toward her. "Miss Whelan, I believe ye met Carlos last night."

She opened her mouth to say yes, but was taken aback by the twinkling amusement in Angus's eyes. Did he know about the kiss?

"We met." Carlos stood slowly. "Briefly."

"I saw him playing basketball," Caitlyn murmured.

"Oh yeah, man." Phineas leaned back in his

chair. "Carlos was the star player on the Claws team. He leaves those wolfie boys in the shade."

"Aye." Angus gave Carlos a pointed look. "I believe ye scored big last night." He glanced at Caitlyn, then back at Carlos. " 'Twill no' interfere with yer duties, will it?"

Carlos's tanned face took on a reddish hue. "No, sir."

Caitlyn felt her own cheeks warm with a blush. *Angus knows.*

"We've added more security measures at the townhouse," Angus continued. "Phineas and Carlos, I'd like for ye to move back there. We doona need one of our guards here if all the Vamps do their death-sleeping at the townhouse. Since Miss Whelan is living there, 'twill make it more convenient for you, Carlos. Ye can train her during the day while ye're guarding the Vamps."

Carlos nodded. "I'll pack my things." He skirted the desk and strode from the office.

Emma gathered up a stack of papers. "Come with me, Caitlyn. You can fill these out in the conference room."

Caitlyn followed her into the hallway. As Emma entered a room across the hall, Caitlyn paused to watch Carlos. He had almost reached the foyer. He was dressed like Phineas, with a navy polo shirt and khaki pants, but the ordinary clothes couldn't hide the extraordinary way he moved. Stealthy and controlled, masculine yet graceful. She could imagine him as a cat stalking prey in the jungle.

He turned into the foyer, glanced back, and stopped. For a sizzling moment their eyes met. Then his heated gaze meandered down her body and lingered on her bare legs, before heading back to her face. Her knees grew weak. How much beast lurked beneath his handsome human exterior? Would he purr if she tickled him behind the ears?

"Caitlyn?" Emma called to her.

"Yes." Reluctantly, she turned away from Carlos's hot amber gaze. She entered the conference room, then took a seat in the chair that Emma indicated. With great effort, she attempted to shove all thoughts of Carlos away so she could concentrate on business.

"We have some forms for you to fill out." Emma placed the papers on the table in front of her. "And you can choose which kind of insurance plan you want."

"Thank you." Caitlyn retrieved a pen from her portfolio, along with her résumé and referrals.

"I'll issue a sidearm to you while you work. Be right back." Emma strode from the room.

A sidearm? Caitlyn swallowed hard. Her father had always owned guns, and he'd taught her and her brother about gun safety. Over the years, he'd taken Dylan often to a shooting range. He'd only taken her once. No doubt the humiliation had been too much to bear.

She groaned inwardly. Should she admit to Emma how much guns scared her? Or how she couldn't hit the side of a barn?

She shook the doubts away. Her disastrous trip to the shooting range had been ten years ago. She would do better now. She had to. Her life might depend on it.

Her dad's stash of weapons made more sense

now that she knew he'd always been employed by the CIA. As a young girl, she'd grown up believing he worked for the State Department in a peaceful office setting. He'd lied about that. Now she was left wondering what other lies he'd told. Why hadn't Shanna received any of her letters?

She pushed aside her suspicions and started filling out the forms. After a few minutes, Emma entered the room and set a small box on the table.

"This is plastic short-range training ammunition." She opened the box so Caitlyn could see the contents. "I've issued you a nine millimeter automatic. Carlos is busy packing, so I asked Phineas to take you to our indoor firing range down in the basement."

"Okay." Caitlyn cast a wary look at the ammunition. Even though the bullets were plastic, they still looked pointed and deadly.

Emma perched on the end of the table. "Carlos is in a hurry to go on his trip, so if you don't mind, he'll start your self-defense training tomorrow."

Caitlyn's heart pounded in anticipation. "Okay."

Emma watched her closely. "Remember how I said vampires have enhanced senses? I can actually hear your heartbeat. It just sped up."

Caitlyn's face grew warm. "I'm . . . excited about this new job."

"Angus told me what he saw on a monitor last night."

Caitlyn winced. "It was nothing. Really." Just the hottest kiss she'd ever experienced.

"Well, perhaps Angus exaggerated." Emma

smiled. "He can be such a hopeless romantic. He said you and Carlos shared a kiss that was so hot, he feared you would set the garden on fire."

It was that obvious? Caitlyn's cheeks blazed with heat. "I . . . it just happened. I don't usually kiss strangers."

"I'm not judging you." Emma touched her arm. "I'm just concerned for you."

Caitlyn let loose a deep sigh, and her shoulders drooped. "Shanna told me not to get involved with him."

Emma's gaze was full of sympathy. "That may be for the best. He's leaving soon on an expedition to hunt for more of his own kind."

"Were-panthers?"

"Yes. They're an endangered species," Emma explained. "As far as we know, he and his five adopted children are the only were-panthers left."

Caitlyn's heart sank. Now she knew why Carlos was rejecting her. He needed a were-panther mate.

Emma gave her a curious look. "But it does seem odd that he would kiss you when he's planning to leave."

Caitlyn shrugged. "It was . . . just one of those things. I won't have any trouble working with him."

"You don't want to kiss him again?"

Caitlyn opened her mouth to agree, but her throat constricted and she couldn't force the words out. Good God, she was dying to kiss him again.

"Oh, dear." Emma sat back. "Perhaps we should have Lara or Olivia train you."

"I want Carlos," she blurted out, then winced.

"I mean in a professional type of relationship. Strictly business."

Emma snorted. "I know a Freudian slip when I hear one." She tapped her fingers on the table. "Interesting."

"He is."

"I meant the situation." Emma gave her a worried look. "You need to think about this."

Caitlyn sighed. She knew that, but whenever Carlos was around, her thinking process went haywire.

Emma stood and gathered up the papers. "We're done here. Phineas will take you down to the firing range."

Chapter Seven

*C*arlos strode down the hall toward the MacKay security office, his duffel bag in hand, his head throbbing, and his angry frustration barely in check. Caitlyn Whelan was screwing up everything.

He'd wanted to catch a plane to Thailand tomorrow, but no. He had to stay in New York so he could train *her*. He couldn't refuse when Angus was the one funding his trip.

He'd wanted to hunt for his mate, full of anticipation for discovering the perfect were-panther woman, but no. Caitlyn Whelan kept invading his thoughts and dreams. He had a doomed feeling that no woman of any species would excite him like she did.

How could fate be so cruel? He snorted. Why did he even question it? He'd already lost all his family and most of his species. No one knew better than he did how cruel life could be.

He'd paced angrily in his bedroom in the basement for twenty minutes before packing his few belongings and heading back to the office. Hopefully, she would have finished filling out forms by now. Hopefully, she would be on her way back to the townhouse.

But he would still have to live there with her. And train her. *Merda.* Maybe she would be like Toni and learn martial arts quickly. Or maybe she'd be like Lara and Olivia and already know how to fight and wield a weapon. That would be even better. A few days of training and he'd be able to leave.

But would he be able to forget her?

He heard a squeal from the nursery that sounded like Constantine. The Draganestis must have arrived while he was downstairs.

He jogged up to the half door to peer inside. Tino was all right. He was opening a birthday present from his grandfather.

"This is cool, Grandpa!" Tino admired a boxed remote-controlled police car. "Thank you!"

"You're welcome." Sean Whelan's usual harsh expression melted into a loving smile as he tousled the little boy's blond curls. "I'm sorry I had to miss the party."

"That's okay." Tino hugged him, then went to work ripping open the box.

Sean glanced at Carlos and frowned. "I've seen you around here before. Who are you?"

"This is Carlos Panterra, one of our day guards," Shanna quickly explained before he could answer.

She was sitting in the rocking chair, holding Sofia in her lap.

Sean continued to regard Carlos suspiciously. "Are you a mortal, then?"

Carlos gave him a bland look. "At the moment."

Sean's blue eyes narrowed. "Explain."

Carlos shrugged. "Why should I?"

Sean stepped toward him. "I could haul you in for questioning. What kind of accent is that? Where are you from?"

Carlos's jaw clenched. One more reason Caitlyn was all wrong for him. Her father was an asshole. He smiled slowly, envisioning Sean's reaction if he found out about the kiss Carlos had shared with his daughter.

A sudden hot blast crashed against his brow, wiping the smile off his face. He immediately blocked Sean's attempt to invade his mind, but it took all of his concentration. For a mortal, Sean's psychic power was incredibly strong.

"You're not getting in, Whelan," Carlos gritted out.

"Dad, leave him alone," Shanna muttered.

Sean dropped the mind probe but continued to glare at Carlos. "You're not a normal mortal."

"He's a shifter," Shanna explained. "I told you Angus had a few in his employ."

Sean gave his daughter a horrified look. "He's one of those damned werewolves? And you let him around the children?"

"Carlos is nice," Tino mumbled. "I like him."

"Me, too," Sofia said.

Sean frowned at the children. "You'd better stay away from him when there's a full moon."

"The children are perfectly safe," Shanna insisted.

"Yes." Carlos leaned against the door frame, crossing his arms. "It's been ages since I gobbled up a small child for breakfast."

Tino giggled.

Carlos winked at him. "You might be good with ketchup."

"It's not funny," Sean growled. "Werewolves are too dangerous to be around children."

"I disagree, since I know some children who are werewolves," Carlos said. "Besides, I'm not a wolf."

Sofia stretched her arms out, grinning. "He's a big kitty cat!"

"A what?" Sean asked.

"I'm a were-panther," Carlos said.

Sean grimaced. "Shit, that's even worse. Jungle cats are notorious man-eaters."

Carlos glowered at him. "I spend most of my time in human form. Even as a panther I retain my human thoughts and feelings, so I don't appreciate being called a cannibal."

Sean grunted, glaring at him.

Carlos smiled. "Nice to meet you." He winked at Tino. "Enjoy your new presents." He strode down the hall to the MacKay security office. What he needed was some aspirin and a big steak dinner. Then he could settle into his old bedroom at the townhouse and try not to think about *her*.

He was swiping his card when Emma opened the door to let him in. He spotted Angus sitting behind the desk.

Carlos dropped his duffel bag on the floor. "I'm ready to go to the townhouse if one of you can teleport me there."

Emma perched on the corner of the desk. "Do you mind staying a little late tonight? We're expecting some MacKay employees here in about ten minutes for a strategy meeting."

"All right." So his steak dinner would be delayed a few minutes. He could handle that as long as he didn't have to deal with *her*.

"Could you go down to the firing range?" Emma asked. "Caitlyn's there with Phineas, and she needs to be warned that her father's on the premises. She might not want to see him right now."

Damn. "Why don't we just call Phineas?" He reached in his pants' pocket for his cell phone.

"We tried," Angus explained. "But he dinna answer. He must be . . . verra busy with her."

Carlos's hand flinched around his cell phone. *Merda.* He was reacting like a jealous lover. He took a deep breath to calm the raging beast, then made sure his claws hadn't emerged before removing his hand from his pocket.

He realized Angus and Emma were watching him curiously. *They know about the kiss.* A shot of pain speared his temple. "I'll be right back."

A few minutes later Carlos swiped his ID card through the security pad next to the indoor firing range and slipped inside. Both Phineas and Caitlyn were wearing headphones and didn't hear him enter. He leaned against the wall, crossing his arms over his chest as his gaze meandered over her body.

Her feet were spread wide to maintain balance. Her legs were long and tanned, beautifully shaped. Her wide stance stretched her gray skirt taut around her thighs. If he was one of the wolf shifters, he'd be drooling by now.

She'd removed her jacket, and her sleeveless silk blouse clung to her torso, clearly showing the elegant line of her back and how it narrowed into her waist. He wondered if the rose-colored silk was the same color as her nipples.

Bam! She stumbled backward from the recoil but managed not to fall over. At the far end of the room the large paper outline of a man remained perfectly still.

Carlos sighed. So much for his hopes that she would already know how to shoot. She was woefully inexperienced.

Next to her, Phineas slid his headphones off to rest around his neck. "Damn! You missed again."

She ripped off her headphones and dumped them on the counter in front of them. "This is so frustrating. I'm doing everything you said."

"I know what's wrong," Carlos said.

With a gasp, she spun toward him.

He winced and held up his hands.

"Whoa!" Phineas shoved her hand down. "Remember the first rule I told you? Don't point your gun at anyone unless you want to kill him."

"But who knows what a lady wants?" Carlos murmured.

She glared at him with a look that could kill.

"Right now I'd like to hit the damned target. I'm halfway through my box of bullets and I haven't come close."

"You're too tense." Carlos pushed off the wall and strode toward her. "Kick off your shoes."

"What do my shoes have to do with anything?"

"You're teetering on those high heels," Carlos explained. "It's distracting you."

"Yeah." Phineas nodded. "She has been stumbling a lot."

"Fine." She kicked off her shoes. "What now?"

He smiled slowly. "Your skirt's too tight. It's restricting your movement."

Her eyes narrowed. "I'm not taking off my skirt."

"Damn." Phineas slapped his leg. "That was a good try, Carlos."

She snorted. "Do you have any useful suggestions?"

"Yes." Carlos's gaze lingered on her sweet mouth. He could think of a lot of suggestions. "Will you do as I ask?"

She licked her lips. "Maybe."

He motioned with his hand. "Turn around. Face the target."

She turned her back to him and rested her hands on the counter, the gun still gripped in one hand.

Carlos waved at Phineas to leave, but he just grinned. He wandered over to a chair and plopped down, obviously determined to enjoy the show.

Carlos moved behind Caitlyn, placed his fingertips on her shoulders, and she flinched.

"Shh, *menina*." He pressed her shoulders down. "You're hunched up to your ears. You need to relax."

"How can I relax when I'm holding a freaking gun? I'm not a violent person."

"Any person can be violent." He leaned toward her and breathed in the sweet scent of her hair and skin. "Close your eyes."

"Why?" She turned her head slightly, and her temple brushed against his mouth. She looked away, her muscles constricting under his hands.

"Relax." He gently massaged her shoulders. "Close your eyes, *menina*."

"What are you going to do?" she asked with a breathy voice.

"I'm going to tell you a story." He stroked his fingers along the tender skin of her neck and paused when she shivered. *Merda.* She was so susceptible to his touch. And she smelled so good, it took all his control not to pull her into his arms and kiss her senseless. "Close your eyes."

"I don't trust you."

"Catalina," he whispered. "You have the gun. You have the power. Close your eyes."

She lowered her head and her eyes flickered shut.

He leaned close, his lips next to her ear. "You have a lover."

"I don't think so." Her shoulders rose, tensing again.

"Play along with me."

"You wish."

He dug his fingers into her shoulders, pressing

them down, and she moaned. "You were madly in love with him. You gave him your heart, your soul. But then he did you wrong."

"He kissed me, then acted like it was a mistake?" she muttered.

Carlos winced. "Yes, that is exactly what the bastard did. Now open your eyes and shoot him in his black heart."

She lifted her head, clasped the gun with both hands, and took aim. *Bam!* She swayed back from the recoil, bumping against Carlos's chest. He steadied her, holding her against him. The paper man shuddered with a hit.

"You did it!" Phineas ran up to the counter and pushed the button to activate the pulley that would slide the paper target close to them.

"Damn, woman." Phineas gave her a horrified look. "Remind me never to make you angry."

Caitlyn gasped as the paper came close enough for her to spot the bullet hole with her mortal vision. "Oh dear."

Carlos winced. She'd blasted the man right through his balls. "Well, I think we should be positive about this."

She looked over her shoulder at him with a grateful smile. "That's what I always say. We should look at the bright side."

Carlos returned her smile. With a small mental jolt he realized his headache was much better. The scent and feel of her was so damned sweet.

"There ain't no bright side," Phineas objected. "The man's got no gonads."

"But she hit the target," Carlos said.

"The man has got no gonads," Phineas repeated forcefully.

"It was an accident." Caitlyn set her gun on the counter. "I was aiming for his chest."

"You blew his pecker into Connecticut," Phineas muttered.

She grinned. "I think you have issues, Phineas. It was only a paper pecker."

"The worst kind," Carlos added.

She laughed, and his heart stopped. She sounded like music and tinkling wind chimes and the trill of birdsong all in one. Making her laugh made him feel like he could conquer mountains.

"Would you like to practice some more?" he asked.

"I think I should stop while I'm ahead." She ejected the cartridge from her automatic. "My ears are ringing."

Carlos removed his cell phone from his pants' pocket. Maybe enough time had passed and her father was gone. "I'll see if it's okay for you to go upstairs."

"Why wouldn't it be okay?" she asked.

He hesitated. "Your sister and the children are in the nursery."

"Oh, I'd love to see them." Caitlyn slipped her shoes back on and reached for her suit jacket.

"And your father's there," Carlos added.

She paused with her jacket half on. "Oh."

"He brought a present to Tino," Carlos continued. "Angus and Emma sent me down here to warn you. They figured you wouldn't want to see him right now."

"Oh, man." Phineas shook his head. "Your dad's

gonna be pissed when he finds out you're working for MacKay."

"He has to find out sooner or later." Caitlyn finished putting on her jacket. "I might as well get this over with."

"Are you sure?" Carlos asked.

She took a deep breath. "Yes. I made my decision, and I'll stand behind it." Her eyes hardened with a glint of anger. "Besides, I have a few questions for my father."

Chapter Eight

Caitlyn exited the elevator and strode across the foyer. Just as she entered the hallway, she spotted her father leaving the nursery. His head turned at the sound of her heels on the marble floor. His eyes widened.

She steeled her nerves for his reaction.

"Caitlyn," he demanded, "what are you doing here?"

She continued to walk calmly toward him. "I work here."

He flinched, then his face turned red. "The hell you do. Is this some kind of sick joke?"

Shanna peered out the open top half of the nursery door and gave Caitlyn a worried look. "There's no reason for anyone to get upset. I'm sure we can discuss this in a rational manner."

"It's really quite simple," Caitlyn added. "I've

accepted a job with MacKay Security and Investigation."

"No!" Sean's face grew a darker red and his hands fisted. "I've lost one daughter to this foul place. I refuse to lose another!"

"There's nothing wrong with this place." Caitlyn stopped across the hall from the nursery.

"It's infested with vermin," Sean hissed. "Foul creatures of the—"

"Enough!" Shanna stepped into the hall, closing the nursery door behind her. She lowered her voice. "Don't talk like that in front of my children."

Sean ground his teeth as he visibly fought for control. "This is a nightmare." His head snapped to the side and he glared. "Get lost. This is a private conversation."

Caitlyn whirled around and found Carlos walking toward them. Damn. He didn't follow instructions well. She'd told him and Phineas that she wanted to handle this alone.

"Don't mind me," Carlos muttered as he strolled by. "Just passing through. I have a meeting to attend."

Sean waited till Carlos swiped his ID card by the MacKay security office, then he stepped closer to Caitlyn. "I can't believe you did this to me. Do you know how hard it was to get the CIA to accept you? They were not impressed by the fiasco you created at your last job."

Caitlyn glanced at Carlos. He'd paused outside the door, his head cocked in a way that made it obvious he was listening. Damn him. Though she probably deserved it for eavesdropping on him last night. "I wouldn't call it a fiasco."

"It got you fired," Sean argued.

"It saved a woman's life." She noticed Carlos had stopped pretending not to listen. He was now leaning against the door, studying her with his gleaming amber eyes.

"It caused a scandal," Sean said. "I had to call in some major markers to get you a job working for me."

"I appreciate your efforts, but I decided to work here."

"That's ridiculous." Sean gave Shanna an angry look. "This is your fault, isn't it?"

Shanna frowned. "I invited her to Tino's party last night and explained the situation to her."

"You mean you brainwashed her," Sean growled. "You were always the one to cause problems."

"She did nothing wrong." Caitlyn jumped to her sister's defense. She had a terrible feeling there were secrets she still didn't know about. "I could see with my own eyes that the vampires, mortals, and shape shifters here have combined to make one loving, supportive family. And I'm happy to be a part of it."

"I will not allow it," Sean growled. "You will not live with these monsters!"

"I'm not a monster!" Tino yelled.

Caitlyn gasped when she saw the little boy had levitated so he could see over the closed bottom half of the door. "Dad!" she shouted, drawing his attention to her before he could turn. "My mind is made up." She noted with relief that Shanna was hurrying into the nursery to grab Tino.

"Cait, you're not thinking clearly," Sean said, facing her. "Who would you trust the most— vampires or the government?"

She tilted her head. "That's a tough one."

Carlos chuckled.

Sean spun toward him. "What the hell are you doing, listening in on us?"

Carlos smiled. "Good night, sir." He glanced at Caitlyn and switched to Portuguese. "Brava, *menina.* You're a brave and fearless fighter."

Her heart swelled at the compliment. "Thank you."

"What did he say?" Sean demanded as Carlos slipped inside the MacKay office.

"Nothing," she mumbled. She noted with relief that Shanna was now holding Constantine. The little boy's secret was safe.

"I'm not letting this go," Sean warned her. "I'll talk to MacKay myself and get him to release you."

"You will let it go." Caitlyn lifted her chin. "Or I'll ask Mom why Shanna never received any of the letters I wrote to her."

Sean's face paled. "I . . . don't know what you're talking about."

"After Shanna left home, I wrote letters to her, lots of letters, and Mom gave them to you so you could mail them from your office."

Sean shrugged. "They must have gotten lost. Or maybe we had the wrong address."

"Or maybe you never mailed them," Caitlyn said quietly.

Shanna shook her head sadly. "Cait, let it go."

"Right," Sean agreed. "It was a long time ago. Water under the bridge."

"It was a bridge I never got to cross," Caitlyn snapped. "I needed my sister. I felt all alone and abandoned. And Shanna felt abandoned, too."

Sean crossed his arms, scowling at her. "You have no reason to complain. You were well provided for, both of you. You always had everything you needed."

"Except each other," Caitlyn muttered.

Sean's mouth thinned. "I thought it was for the best."

Caitlyn planted her hands on her hips. "And I'm doing what I think is best. I'm working for MacKay. It's my decision, and I expect you to respect it."

With a groan, Sean shook his head. "It's a big mistake, but I guess you'll have to learn the hard way. Whatever you do, please don't get involved with a vampire. I know they're somehow attractive to females, but—"

"It's all right, Dad. I won't fall for a vampire. I promise." Because for better or for worse, her interests were focused on a shape shifter.

When Carlos stepped inside the security office, he discovered the meeting had already commenced. Angus sat behind the desk, talking, while Emma perched on a corner. The two chairs in front of the desk were occupied by Lara and Olivia. Their Vamp husbands, Jack and Robby, stood behind them.

The Draganestis' daytime bodyguard, Howard Barr, eased behind the desk to select a bear claw from the doughnut box on the console. As a were-bear, Howard constantly ate as if he were preparing for a winter's hibernation. Roman's nighttime bodyguard, Connor Buchanan, leaned against a wall, his arms folded across his chest. Next to him was J.L. Wang, a fairly new Vamp who had worked with Olivia at the FBI. Ian MacPhie had teleported in from Dragon Nest Academy and brought Phil Jones, the werewolf, with him.

Phineas was missing. Since Caitlyn had asked him and Phineas to let her deal with her father alone, Phineas had gone outside to do his rounds. Carlos spotted him on a surveillance monitor, zipping over the grounds at vampire speed.

Carlos had been too curious to stay away from Caitlyn's conversation with her father. He preferred to think of it as curiosity. Not protectiveness. Even though he had been prepared to punch Sean if necessary.

Caitlyn had handled the situation remarkably well. Carlos doubted she was very strong physically, but mentally and emotionally, she was tough. He'd heard her the night before, talking to Raquel and Coco. She'd helped them more in just a few minutes than he had in the last five years. It had sorely aggravated him at first, but now he realized he was grateful for the compassion she'd shown to his girls and the comfort she'd given them. She was brave in a way that he was lacking.

And she was monopolizing his thoughts, dammit. He pushed her to the back of his mind and concentrated on the discussion at hand. Robby MacKay was voicing his frustration over their inability to locate Casimir.

"Aye," Angus agreed. "The bloody coward is too good at hiding."

"Could be worse," J.L. observed. "At least when he's hiding, he's not killing people."

"Aye," Connor muttered. "When he stops leaving a trail of dead bodies, he's impossible to find. He could be anywhere. And if we get close, he only has to teleport away."

"We need to keep watch on his entry points into America," Jack warned. For safety reasons, a vampire either used a sensory beacon to teleport somewhere or he would go to places he'd teleported to before. Those locations would be embedded in his psychic memory.

"We know of several places he's teleported to," Robby said. "Apollo's compound in Maine, the coven house in New Orleans, the campground south of Mount Rushmore, and the federal prison in Leavenworth."

"And those farmhouses in Nebraska," Olivia added. "My old boss at the FBI will let us know if anything happens in Nebraska or Leavenworth."

"I've asked the werewolves in Maine to keep an eye on the compound," Phil said. "And I've contacted some Lakota Indians who can shift into wolves. They've promised to watch over the area around Mount Rushmore. The Black Hills are sacred to them. They want no more spilled blood there."

"Excellent." Angus nodded. "Now let's move on to some new assignments. Zoltan Czakvar is hunting for Casimir in Eastern Europe, and he'd appreciate some help."

"We can go," Robby offered. He looked at his newly wedded bride. "If ye doona mind being stationed in Budapest for a while."

"I'd love it." Olivia leaned close to her husband. "We'll be close to my grandmother on Patmos."

"Aye." Robby nodded. "I can teleport you there on the weekends."

Angus fumbled through the papers on the desk. "We have a request here from Rafferty McCall, the West Coast coven master. Two of his members have disappeared in San Francisco and he'd like some help investigating it."

J.L. Wang raised his hand. "I'll go." Although he'd only been a vampire for a short while, he'd previously served as a special agent for the FBI, and so completed his training at MacKay S & I in record time.

"Verra good." Angus passed J.L. a sheet of paper. "This has all the information ye need to get started. Ye can teleport there tonight."

Olivia touched him on the arm. "We'll miss you. Be careful."

"And we have a request from Jean-Luc," Angus continued. "His coven in Paris has reported a resurgence of Malcontents."

"They probably figured it was safe to move in since Jean-Luc is still hiding in Texas," Robby said.

"We can go to Paris," Jack offered, then glanced at his wife Lara. "Is that all right with you?"

She snorted. "Are you kidding? Let's go pack."

Jack chuckled and kissed her cheek.

Carlos stifled a groan. It was so damned easy for the Vamps to find a mate. Any woman, mortal or Vamp, would do. They didn't have the survival of an entire species hanging on their selection.

Phineas entered the office. "Hey, dudes. What's up?"

"We're about to congratulate you for becoming the head of security here at Romatech," Angus announced.

Everyone in the room applauded as Phineas gave them high fives and knuckle pounds. "Oh yeah, baby, who's bad?"

"I'm sure ye'll do an excellent job." Angus stood to shake his hand. "Continue to monitor our spy, Stanislav."

"Will do," Phineas assured him. "Stan's my man."

"And we have a new employee living at the townhouse in Manhattan," Angus continued. "Shanna's younger sister, Caitlyn Whelan."

"She's a hot babe." Phineas grinned at Carlos, who scowled back.

"We hope to get her trained as soon as possible," Emma added. "Her unique ability to understand any language could prove invaluable for discovering information on Casimir."

Murmurs spread across the room as everyone marveled over Caitlyn's special talent.

"How fast do ye think ye can train her, Carlos?" Angus asked.

All eyes in the room shifted to him. Carlos's jaw ticked. "A few days. A week at the most."

Phineas snorted. "Are you kidding? She's a complete rookie. And you guys do not want to know where that girl aims her bullets."

"She hit the target," Carlos defended her.

"One hit out of twenty attempts," Phineas muttered.

Carlos groaned inwardly. He was so screwed. "My trip can't wait for weeks or months. Maybe Phineas or Toni can train her."

"Give it a week, Carlos, and then we'll reassess the situation," Angus told him. "Emma and I will be leaving in a few days for Moscow to assist Mikhail with his search for Casimir. Everyone has their assignments, so off ye go."

After a round of good-byes and hugs, people began to teleport away.

Ian approached Carlos with a sheepish look. "Sorry about the punch last night."

Carlos shrugged. "I deserved it."

"Aye." Ian grinned. "That ye did. Toni told me about yer trip. I wanted to wish you good luck finding yer mate."

"Thank you. Fernando should be arriving in New York in two days. He'll help you take care of the children."

Ian nodded. "I expect you to come see them before ye go." He stepped back, grabbed Phil by the arm, then teleported to the school, taking the werewolf with him.

Carlos grabbed his duffel bag. The room was clearing out fast. "I need to hitch a ride to the townhouse."

Emma approached him. "Caitlyn will be driving there soon, and I hate for her to be alone after the confrontation she had with her father. Do you mind accompanying her?"

Carlos gritted his teeth. How could he say he wanted to avoid her when it was his job to train her? But he needed to avoid her. Every time he came near her, he ended up touching her. And liking it too damned much.

Emma regarded him curiously. "Are you all right? You seem a little tense."

"I'm fine," Carlos growled. "I'll go with her."

Chapter Nine

I'm not a monster," Constantine mumbled, his face buried in his mother's sweater.

"Of course not." Shanna held him tight and nuzzled her cheek against his mop of blond curls. "You're my brave little boy."

Tears sprang to Caitlyn's eyes as she let herself into the nursery. How could Dad say such hurtful things in front of his grandchildren? But it was just as much her fault for confronting him in front of them.

Sofia sniffled, all alone in the rocking chair. "Why doesn't Grandpa like us?"

"He doesn't know you." Caitlyn rushed over to gather the little girl in her arms.

"He's known me since I was a baby," Constantine grumbled.

"I'm afraid he's blind in some ways," Shanna told him. "But it's Grandpa's problem. Not yours."

Sofia wrapped her little arms around Caitlyn's neck and gazed into her eyes. "You're not like Grandpa."

"No." Caitlyn smiled, her heart swelling with love. "I've been all over the world and seen thousands of children, so I know a little angel when I see one."

"Like me?" Sofia asked, her eyes wide.

"Yes, like you." Caitlyn kissed her niece's brow, then hugged her tight.

Shanna smiled at her over her son's head and mouthed the words *Thank you*.

Caitlyn nodded. "I still have some questions."

"I'm sure you do." Shanna glanced at her watch, then set her son on the floor. "Tino, you only have about ten minutes to play with your new toys before it's time to go to school."

"Oh." Constantine grabbed his new fire truck off a shelf. "Sofia, you want to see how the ladders work?"

"Okay." The little girl squirmed in Caitlyn's arms, so she set her down.

Shanna opened a side door. "My office is in here. We can keep an eye on them until Radinka comes."

"Radinka?" Caitlyn followed her into a waiting room.

"My assistant. She was at the party last night. You probably met her."

Caitlyn lifted her shoulders in confusion. "I've met a ton of people lately. I can't keep them all straight." Except for Carlos. He definitely stood out.

"Radinka is my lifesaver. She watches the kids

when I have a patient." Shanna left the door open, then motioned to some chairs in the waiting room. "Have a seat."

Caitlyn sat in a chair where she could see into the nursery. "I'm sorry I talked to Dad in front of the children," she whispered. "I should have realized—"

"Don't blame yourself." Shanna sat beside her. "Dad is always one inch away from blowing his top whenever he comes here. It was actually a relief when he didn't show up for the party. Tino was free to be himself."

"It worries me how hateful Dad is toward your friends and your husband."

Shanna squeezed her hand. "I'm glad you're able to accept them."

Caitlyn took a deep breath to steady her nerves so she could pose the question she'd wanted to ask since she was nine years old. "Why did you leave all those years ago?"

Shanna gazed into the nursery with a faraway look in her eyes. "I didn't want to go. Dad said I needed some real school records in order to get into college, but I found out later that it wasn't exactly true."

"He told me it was your idea, that you wanted to leave."

Shanna shifted in her chair to face her. "I didn't want to go. I was miserable without you, and I couldn't understand why you never responded to my letters."

Caitlyn's throat constricted. "You wrote to me?"

"Yes. You never got my letters, did you?"

"No." Caitlyn shook her head. "And you never got mine." Tears threatened to escape. All those years of pain and loneliness and now she knew who had caused it—her own father. "Why did he make you leave?"

"I wondered that for years." Tears glimmered in Shanna's eyes. "I thought I must have done something wrong. I felt like I'd been kicked out of the family."

"I'm so sorry." A tear ran down Caitlyn's cheek. She felt a twinge of guilt that she'd doubted her sister. She'd been selfish, too, only considering her own pain, and never imagining what it had been like for Shanna.

"A few years back when Dad found me, he admitted the truth." Shanna snorted. "I guess I did do something wrong when I was a teenager. After years of blocking psychic power from Dad, I developed a lot of strength. Whenever he tried to control me, I would erect a psychic barrier that he couldn't penetrate."

"Dad was trying to control you?"

Shanna hesitated, frowning at the carpet. "Did you ever wonder how Mom always remained so calm? Even when Dylan broke a leg skiing, she was steady as a rock. No emotion, no fears."

Caitlyn shrugged. "That's just the way she is."

"Like she's muffled in a cocoon of blankets? Cait, maybe you were too young to remember, but she wasn't always like that. When I was little, she was full of laughter and always had a hug for everyone."

"Mom?"

"Yes. But she'd also freak out over things. She

hated living abroad and was always begging Dad to bring us back to the States."

Caitlyn frowned. "I don't remember that."

"You were just a baby. And then, all of a sudden she changed. She became calm and controlled." Shanna grimaced. "Dad's control."

Caitlyn's heart lurched. "What exactly are you saying?"

"Dad has been using his psychic power to control Mom. Or as he puts it, he's been helping her for her own good."

"No," Caitlyn whispered.

"I'm afraid so. And when he discovered he couldn't control me, he was worried that I'd mess up his plans."

"That's why he sent you away?"

Shanna nodded. "I know it sounds terrible. Well, it *is* terrible, but it's the truth. He admitted it to me."

Caitlyn shuddered. "Poor Mom."

Shanna sighed. "I think there may be more to the story. I've asked Mom, and she doesn't have any memory of the summer before I left."

"You think Dad wiped it?"

"Yes. I don't know why."

Caitlyn rubbed her brow. This was worse than she'd ever imagined. But when she thought back to all the times her mom had reacted—or rather, *not* reacted—to the normal stress of their daily lives, she knew it was true.

Anger boiled up in her. It was bad enough that Dad had separated her from her sister, but how dare he turn their mother into a robot!

She jumped to her feet and paced across the

floor. More tears welled up in her eyes. It wasn't every day that you found out your dad was an utter asshole. Part of her didn't want to believe it. But she'd always known he was a control freak. And deep inside, she'd also known that something was wrong with Mom. It had been impossible to connect with her on an emotional level.

That was why Shanna's departure had devastated Caitlyn so much. She'd depended on her sister for love and companionship.

And Dad had purposely sent Shanna away. Tears streamed down Caitlyn's face, and she angrily brushed them aside. "I can't believe you still talk to Dad. Or even allow him on the premises."

"I understand your anger. I felt it, too. But I've had a few years to adjust. I understand now that I have to involve Dad with our lives so he can see how good the Vamps are."

"So he won't target them for . . . termination." Caitlyn paused in her pacing to look at her nephew and niece. They were so beautiful and innocent. "You have to protect them, too."

"Yes. It's better for Dad to feel attached to them."

Caitlyn turned to face her sister. "Do you know if he was controlling me or Dylan?"

"I don't think so. Dylan was always busy with his sports, so he was hardly ever home. You were young and eager to please. I don't think Dad ever needed to use mind control on you. I was the one who gave him trouble."

Caitlyn winced. "I'm so sorry."

Shanna waved a dismissive hand as she stood. "It's not your fault. Let's put it all behind us, okay?"

"How can I? I suffered for years, feeling lonesome and abandoned. And you were suffering, too! Dad had no right to separate us."

"He couldn't control me. He probably thought I'd be a bad influence on you." Shanna snorted. "He still thinks I'm a bad influence on you. But it's all over. We're together now. That's what really counts."

Caitlyn rushed to her sister and hugged her. "I'm so glad you're all right, that you found new friends, and you have such beautiful children."

Shanna smiled and wiped her sister's cheeks. "No more tears, okay? Everything will be all right."

Caitlyn nodded, although she still felt shaky inside. The last two nights had completely turned her world topsy-turvy. Creatures who should be monsters were now her friends. And her dad was looking like the real monster.

She needed to get away from it all. "I think I'll go back to the townhouse now." She needed a long hot bath and a good night's sleep.

"Okay," Shanna said. "Maybe we can come see you tomorrow. Late afternoon?"

"Hello, my darlings," a woman with an Eastern European accent said from the nursery.

"Radinka!" Tino shouted. "Look at my new fire truck."

Shanna strode into the nursery, bringing Caitlyn with her. "Hi, Radinka. Remember my sister?"

"Yes, of course." Radinka extended a hand. "We're so happy to have you join us."

"Thank you." Caitlyn shook hands with the older woman, then realized she wasn't letting go.

"Ah." Radinka squeezed her hand and studied her carefully. "Yes. I see love in your future. A very passionate love."

Caitlyn's face grew warm. "Okay." She tried to withdraw her hand, but the older woman held tight.

"Hmm. It is a forbidden love," Radinka murmured.

Shanna leaned close to Caitlyn and whispered, "She's a bit psychic."

"A *bit?*" Radinka released Caitlyn's hand and gave Shanna an incredulous look. "Wasn't I right about you and Roman? And Emma and Angus? And Darcy and—"

"All right." Shanna laughed. "You're extremely psychic."

"Thank you." Radinka set her handbag on the table and began unbuttoning her coat. "Now if I could just find a match for my son."

"Gregori is the vice president of marketing here at Romatech," Shanna explained.

"I like Gregori!" Sofia whirled around in a circle.

Radinka snorted. "I've never met a female who didn't. I don't know how I'll ever get him to settle down." She removed her coat. "By the way, Shanna, he's your first appointment tonight. He should be here in fifteen minutes."

"Good evening," a masculine voice came from the hallway.

Caitlyn stiffened. She'd recognize that voice anywhere.

"Hi, Carlos!" Tino skipped over to the door.

Caitlyn turned and found his golden brown

eyes focused entirely on her. Her heart pounded. Her throat constricted, making her breathless. Oh God, she couldn't handle an encounter with him now. She'd had enough drama for one evening.

"Ah, interesting," Radinka whispered.

Shanna shook her head at Radinka, then gave the shape shifter a bland look. "Can we help you, Carlos?"

"Emma sent me. May I have a word with you, Caitlyn?"

She swallowed hard. "My training doesn't start till tomorrow, so I'm going back to the townhouse now."

His eyes gleamed amber. "We didn't think you should drive back all alone. Emma thought you might be upset after the confrontation with your father."

"I'm fine, really." Caitlyn turned toward the others in the nursery. "It was nice to meet you, Radinka. Shanna, I'll see you and the kids tomorrow. 'Bye."

Tino and Sofia hugged her, then Caitlyn opened the nursery door to leave.

Carlos stepped back to let her pass. "You've been crying," he whispered.

A shiver skittered down her back. "It's nothing." She headed to the conference room to collect her handbag and portfolio.

He hovered in the doorway with a duffel bag in his hand. "You've been through a lot this evening. Why don't you let me drive?"

Just what she needed, another controlling man in her life. "No thanks. I'm fine." She swung her handbag onto her shoulder and marched out the door.

Carlos strode alongside her. "Let me put this another way. I . . ."

She glanced at him. He was clearly struggling to get something out. "What's wrong? Cat got your tongue?"

He gave her an annoyed look. "This cat is fine. I . . . I actually need a ride back."

She snorted. "Can you say pretty please?"

He halted, glowering at her. "No, I can't. I could easily hitch a ride with one of the Vamps."

"Fine." Tears blurred her vision and her voice cracked. " 'Cause I really want to be alone right now." Shanna might think everything was settled, but Caitlyn was still reeling from everything she'd just learned. Her dad had purposely separated her from her sister and he'd turned her mother into an emotionless shell.

His expression softened. "Catalina, you shouldn't be driving when you're this upset."

She couldn't bear for him to be nice. Sympathy would make her crumble faster than anything. "Don't tell me what to do. I hate controlling men. I hate—" Tears threatened to fall, so she whirled away before he could see them and strode down the hallway to the foyer.

Dammit! She wiped a tear off her cheek. She *was* upset. All those years when she feared she wasn't good enough, she had suffered needlessly. It hadn't been her fault. Or Shanna's fault. They'd been cursed with an asshole for a father.

She barged through the front doors into the parking lot. Cool air stung her wet cheeks. She hurried to her car, set her portfolio on the trunk, then fumbled in her handbag for the keys.

"It's a rental car, right?" Carlos asked. "Why don't you let me drive?"

She spun around to face him. "You're still here?"

"I never left. You're too upset to know when someone's two steps behind you. You shouldn't be driving."

"Don't tell me what to do!"

"I'm a friend, Catalina," he growled. "I am not your father."

With a cry of exasperation, she tried to shove him away.

He grabbed her arms and pulled her back, slamming her against his chest. His eyes gleamed with anger . . . and something else.

Desire. Her breath caught. Her handbag and keys tumbled from her grasp to land on the asphalt pavement. "Do it," she whispered, sliding her hands around his neck. "Kiss me."

The muscles in his neck strained. His grip on her arms tightened. "No."

She pushed him away, and he released her. They stood a foot apart, staring at each other, breathing heavily.

"The cameras are on," he said softly. "I'm not giving Emma and Angus another show to watch."

Caitlyn lifted her eyebrows. "Then you'll kiss me in private?"

His amber eyes burned into her. "No." He leaned over, scooped her keys off the ground, then unlocked the passenger side door. He opened it and gave her a fierce look. "Get in."

She snatched her handbag off the pavement and grabbed her portfolio off the trunk. Rejected again. Just as well. The last thing she needed in her life right now was another domineering male. She tossed her belongings onto the floor, then climbed into the car and settled on the seat. Her tight skirt hitched up quite a bit, but she didn't tug it down. She glanced up at Carlos to see if he'd noticed.

His jaw ticked, and he slammed the door shut.

With a snort, she fastened her seat belt. This was going to be a fun ride.

Chapter Ten

*T*his was going to be a ride from hell, Carlos thought as he drove through White Plains. It was damned hard to concentrate with her tight little skirt halfway up her thighs. He glanced over. More than halfway.

The little minx was doing it just to torture him. As a shifter, his senses were sharper than a normal human's. He could see quite well in the dark, well enough to spot the little black mole on the outside of her left thigh. He could also smell the scent of her hair and skin. He could hear her breathing faster than normal. She was still upset.

Or turned on. Desire had sizzled in her blue eyes when she'd wrapped her hands around his neck and pressed her sweet body against him.

Merda. A week with this woman was going to drive him loco. By the time he went on his expedition in the jungle, he would have a crazed mind . . . and blue balls. Even now his trousers felt uncomfortably tight.

He turned right onto a busy avenue. "Are you hungry? I'm starving."

She regarded him nonchalantly. "What do you eat? Field mice?"

He shot her an annoyed look. "No. I'm a big cat. I could take down a horse."

She grimaced. "You eat raw meat?"

Lift that skirt a little higher and find out. He flexed his hands on the steering wheel. "I was thinking about stopping at a restaurant. Would you care to join me?"

She shifted in the car seat to face him, causing him to glance at her legs once again. "Are you asking me out?"

"No."

"Will you purr if I tickle you behind the ears?"

"No."

"Will you dance the samba for me in your hot pink sequined thong?"

"No."

"Do you always say no?"

His mouth twitched. "No."

She sighed and tugged her skirt down a bit. "I'm afraid I was a bit rude."

He shrugged. "No more than usual."

She swatted his shoulder. "I'm not rude! Well, not normally." She adjusted the collar of his polo shirt.

Holy Mother of God, would she stop touching him? "Are you hungry? 'Cause I'm still starving here."

"All you think about is food."

"Not really." He glanced at her legs.

"I think I just want to take a hot bath and go to bed. I've had a lot thrown at me the last two nights. I'm mentally and emotionally exhausted."

"I could order the food, and they'll deliver it after we get home."

"That sounds good, actually. Really good."

He pulled into a parking lot. "That's one of the important rules about being a day guard. I can't leave the sleeping Vamps unprotected, so I learned how to get things delivered."

"I see."

He pulled his cell phone out to call his favorite restaurant. "I'm having a sirloin steak. Rare."

She made a face.

"Does that lovely expression mean you would prefer something else?"

She smiled. "Do they have seafood?"

"I'll check." He placed his order, then inquired about the menu. "Pecan-crusted salmon?" he asked her.

Her blue eyes widened. "That sounds heavenly."

He placed the order, set his phone on the console, then drove back onto the avenue.

"You mentioned last night that you're going on a trip," she murmured.

He shrugged.

"Emma told me you're going on an expedition to find more of your kind. She said you and your children are an endangered species."

"I'd rather not talk about it." He turned onto the Bronx River Parkway.

"You told your friends last night you were hunting for a mate."

"Don't want to talk about it." If he confided in her, it would generate a sense of closeness, and that would only increase the torture.

With a sigh, she scrunched down in her car seat. Unfortunately, that made her skirt slide higher up her thighs. About an inch to be exact.

"You were crying earlier." The second the words left his mouth, he slapped himself mentally. He couldn't afford to have her confiding in him either.

"I was upset. Furious, actually. At my father. Not you."

He glanced at her. She was staring out the side window. The line of her jaw and slender neck was beautiful. *Merda*. He had to stop thinking like that. "Do you want to talk about it?"

"No."

"Your dad mentioned some sort of fiasco that got you fired."

She gave him a pointed look. "Don't want to talk about it."

He gritted his teeth. "I guess we'll just be quiet then."

"Fine." She crossed her arms over her chest. "Actually, I think I am a little mad at you. You keep sending out mixed signals."

His jaw ticked. "How's that?"

"You kissed me with a ton of hot, desperate passion, then acted like it was a mistake."

"It was a mistake."

"If the hot, desperate passion was real—and it

certainly felt real—then how could it be a mistake?"

She had him there. He could claim the passion wasn't real, but she'd know it was a lie. "I have to find a were-panther mate. The survival of my species depends on it."

She was quiet for about two blessed minutes, then she finally spoke. "You have no choice in the matter?"

"No."

"What if you can't find any were-panthers?"

He swallowed hard. "I will. I have to."

"And if you find a mate, you'll marry her?"

His throat constricted.

"Even if you don't love her?"

"I have no choice." *Merda*, she made it sound like a prison sentence.

"How long have you been looking?" she asked.

"Five years." Five years since the Summer of Death. "I've been on five expeditions."

"Where?"

He sighed. "You ask a lot of questions."

"I'm . . . curious."

"Curiosity killed the cat."

She smiled. "Then I should be safe. Where are you going this time?"

"Thailand. A small town in the northern Highlands."

"Chiang Mai?"

He glanced at her, surprised. "You've heard of it?"

She laughed. "I've been there. I was stationed at the embassy in Bangkok for a year, and they sent me to Chiang Mai for a few weeks."

"Are you familiar with Chulalongkorn University?"

"Chula? Sure." She shifted to face him. "You think there are were-panthers in Thailand?"

"There's a rumor that some poachers killed a wildcat in the mountainous area to the north, and when the cat died, it turned into a human."

"Is that what happens when were-panthers die?"

"It's common for most were-creatures."

She nodded. "Do you speak Thai? Or any of the dialects you might come across in the Highlands?"

Carlos's grip tightened on the steering wheel. He could tell where she was headed. "My professor friend at Chula will find me a guide and translator."

"A complete stranger? How can you trust someone like that?"

She had a valid point. When the guide he'd used in Nicaragua had realized Carlos was a were-panther, he'd tried to capture him and sell him to a billionaire animal collector. "I'll be fine."

"I think you need me."

"No!" His heart lurched. "I can hire a translator."

"And how will you know if he's telling you the truth? I have contacts in Bangkok and Chiang Mai. I know the language, the culture, and the landscape."

His heart thundered in his chest. "You're not going."

"I know the markets, the local food."

"This is not a shopping trip! It's an expedition."

She lifted her chin. "I can do that. I've ridden elephants. I've petted tigers."

"*What?*"

"At the Tiger Temple. The Buddhists monks raise them. They're adorable. So cute and furry."

"*Menina*, I'm going into the jungle. The tigers will not be *cute*."

"All the more reason why I should go. Dogs and cats are naturally drawn to me because I can understand them, so if there are any were-panthers, they'll come—" She gasped. "Oh my gosh, that's why Coco and Raquel came to me. They're little kitten were-panthers, aren't they?"

Carlos groaned. "You're not going."

"I can think of a hundred reasons why I should."

"I can think of a hundred why you shouldn't! Jungle, Caitlyn. No cute little kittens. Scorpions, deadly spiders, spitting cobras, pit vipers, poisonous centipedes as long as your forearm."

She flinched.

"Will they be drawn to you, too?" he continued. "Do you understand the hissing language of a cobra before it strikes?"

"No. I only understand mammals." She shuddered. "Reptiles and bugs are . . . different. They don't want to communicate with us. All I feel is indifference and . . . disdain."

"You can't go into the jungle, Catalina. You can't shoot worth a damn. You can't protect yourself."

She frowned at him. "I'll learn."

"You'll be a burden."

"I'll be invaluable as a translator. I want to help."

"Why? I'll be looking for a *mate*, Caitlyn."

"You said it yourself. Raquel and Coco need a mother. I can help find them one."

He gave her an incredulous look. "You would risk your life to help them?"

"Didn't you?"

He turned his head front. Yes, he'd risked his life to rescue the children. And he'd died. Twice. He was now on his third life out of the nine allotted to his species. But Caitlyn only had one life. He couldn't allow her to risk it. "My decision is final. You're not going."

He could feel the angry glare directed at his face.

"Umph." She settled back in her seat, scrunching down and causing her skirt to hitch up another inch.

He groaned inwardly. That was the main reason she couldn't go. Her presence, her scent, her beautiful body, her heroic spirit and compassionate nature—it would be a constant, relentless torture.

With a twist in his gut he realized she was the perfect woman for him in every way but the only way that really mattered. She'd even be perfect for his adopted children.

He couldn't do it to her. Not if he truly cared about her. And he did care.

He glanced at her and noted one of her fingers tapping against her hand. Her eyes were narrowed. She chewed on her bottom lip. *Merda*. She was strategizing.

She wasn't giving up.

Chapter Eleven

*C*aitlyn groaned at the insistent knocking on her bedroom door. She opened one eye to glance at the window. Dim city lights filtered through the sheer curtains, but it was still dark. "Go away," she mumbled and dragged a pillow over her head.

"Caitlyn, wake up!"

She recognized Carlos's voice. Now he wanted to talk? Last night, while they'd eaten their gourmet delivered meals in the kitchen, he'd barely said a word. Two words, to be exact. *Good night.* Then he'd gone to his bedroom.

The knocking continued. "Come on, Caitlyn. It's almost dawn." The doorknob rattled.

He was trying to come in? Of all the nerve. "I'm up, already!" She fumbled along the top of the bedside table. No lamp. Great. She slid out of bed and squinted her eyes to see. She could barely make out the door frame across the room.

She shuffled around the edge of her bed, then rammed her toes into a box. "Ouch!" She jumped to the side and slammed her shin into the footboard. "Ouch! Damn!" That was going to leave a bruise. She hadn't finished moving in, and her room was a maze of boxes and suitcases she could hardly see.

"What's wrong?" Carlos demanded from the hallway.

"You," she muttered.

"I heard that. I have super hearing and vision."

"Well, isn't that just *super.*" She swiped her hands along the foot of the bed. Hadn't she left a robe there? "So do you have X-ray vision like Superman? Can you see through the door?"

"No."

She enjoyed taunting him. He deserved it. "What a shame. Since I'm standing here stark naked." She gasped when the door crashed open. Light spilled in from the hallway, surrounding his tall frame. "You pervert!"

He scoffed. "You lied."

"You broke my door!"

"Only the lock. The door still works." He flipped on the light switch close to the door frame.

"Ack!" She covered her eyes from the sudden bright light. "What are you doing here?"

"It's called a job, *menina*. I believe you've had one of those before?"

"Very funny." She lowered her hand and noticed he was focused on her nightie. More than focused. His eyes were glued to her clingy, silk leopard print nightgown. Since she was a bit on the tall side, the baby-doll top barely skimmed the top of her thighs. No doubt, a hint of her matching leopard print panties was showing. And if the hot gleam in his eyes was any indication, he'd noticed.

Instead of making her angry, it made her feel tingly and seductive. If he was going to choose an unknown were-panther lady over her, he might as well know what he was missing. She flipped her hair over her shoulders. His laserlike gaze didn't budge. "Hello? My face is up here."

His gaze lifted slowly, but hit a snag at her chest. She glanced down to see if she'd fallen out. It happened sometimes when she slept on her side. No, no such luck.

She sighed. What was her problem? She was acting like a cat in heat, and she never did that. She would normally be appalled for a strange man to see her like this.

She scanned the floor for her missing robe. "I thought we were going to start my training in the morning."

"We are."

"Then why did you wake me up? It's still night." And she hadn't slept worth a darn.

She'd replayed the recent revelations about her father a dozen times in her mind. The only way she'd managed to forget her anger with her dad was to think about her plans to accompany Carlos on his trip. Ah, there was the robe. It had fallen off the other side of the bed.

"Sunrise is in fifteen minutes," Carlos explained. "Phineas, Emma, and Angus will be tele—" He stopped with a strangled sound.

She froze, wondering what was wrong. She'd

leaned over to pick her robe off the floor. Glancing back, she noted his eyes were wide-open, blazing with heat, and that he was gazing directly at her— *Oops.* She straightened with a jerk. She'd forgotten how much her French-cut panties exposed. Just the act of leaning over had given her a blasted wedgie. And given him an eyeful.

She slipped on the silk kimono-style robe she'd bought in Hong Kong. It was bright red, just a shade darker than her cheeks, no doubt. "You were saying?"

Amber flecks glittered in his eyes. "They'll be here any minute now, and I'm sure they'd appreciate seeing how eager you are to start your new job."

"Okay. I'll get dressed, then."

He nodded. "I'll meet you in the kitchen. Wear some gym clothes."

Gym clothes? She noticed for the first time that he wasn't wearing the usual khaki pants and polo shirt. He was dressed in a white T-shirt and judo pants, and his hair was pulled back into a ponytail. "I thought we were going to practice shooting."

"We'll be doing a lot of things. Fencing, karate, kick-boxing, wrestling. What do you usually do for cardio?"

"I . . . shop?"

He stared at her with an incredulous look.

"I moved here yesterday. Had to carry all these boxes upstairs. It was quite a workout." She didn't mention that Lara and Olivia had helped her.

His gaze wandered over all the boxes and suitcases. "All this stuff belongs to you?"

"They're my treasures. I always visit local markets whenever I'm in a new country. Or city. Or . . . village. That's a lot of walking, you know. Very healthy."

He cocked an eyebrow. "Put on some gym clothes. I'll meet you downstairs in five minutes." He turned on his heel and strode away.

She glared at him and shut the door. Men never understood how important her treasures were to her. Not that they were expensive treasures. Some of them had been incredibly cheap. But each one meant something to her, and she took them everywhere with her.

She opened the nearest box and smiled. "Hello, my darlings." Her Russian nesting dolls were cradled in a thick woolen sweater she'd bought in Poland. She'd started collecting matryoshkas as a young girl, so she had over a dozen now. She grabbed two of the wooden dolls and set them on an empty bookshelf. Out of all the bedrooms on the first floor, she'd picked this one because of the two empty bookcases that could hold all her treasures.

Five minutes? She winced, remembering Carlos's demand. That was hardly reasonable. She rushed into the bathroom. No time for a shower. At least she'd taken a bath the night before.

Four minutes later she stood in a lacy bra and panties in front of her open closet, chewing on her bottom lip. *Gym clothes*? She pushed two evening gowns and three cocktail dresses aside. She'd learned early on at the State Department that she was expected to attend some glamorous functions at the embassies.

Business suits, no. She pushed them to the side. Jeans and T-shirts? She put on a turquoise T-shirt, then moved to the dresser. In her pajama drawer she found a pair of gray boxer shorts. They looked sorta like gym shorts, so she pulled them on and tightened the drawstring around her hips. Carlos had been barefoot, so she'd do that, too.

She ran into the bathroom to brush her hair one more time and add some gloss to her lips. Strawberry flavored, as Carlos would discover if she could manage to get him to kiss her again.

"Hmmph." She fluffed up her hair. Even if he found a were-panther woman, the old cat might be mangy and decrepit, with a crooked tail and snaggly teeth.

She couldn't blame him for wanting to discover more of his kind, but *marry* one of them? That was crazy. Just because a woman was a were-panther didn't mean she would be automatically compatible with him.

But it wasn't crazy for him to try to save his species. She sighed. She knew she shouldn't flirt with him, but it was damned hard to pretend she wasn't attracted to him, especially when she knew he was attracted to her.

Part of her understood she should respect his wishes to find a were-panther mate, but another part wanted to scream at him that he'd never find anyone as well-suited for him as her. Their kiss had sparked more than a physical response. It had touched her heart with a feeling of completion, much like the strong connection she'd felt toward the girls, Coco and Raquel. How could her feelings for him be wrong when it felt so right?

There was a naughty desire deep inside her to see how far she could push him. It wasn't something she was proud of, but it was there. A wildly romantic fantasy that he would ache for her so much he'd be willing to toss aside all his concerns just to be with her.

Don't be selfish, she chided herself. This wasn't a fantasy where he could fall madly in love with her and everything would magically work out.

Frustration seeped inside her, and along with it came an unfortunate impulse to tease and torment him. *It's not his fault he has to reject you.* She would try to make sure their time together was fun. No ill feelings. Maybe a little friendly flirtation would be harmless.

She padded down the carpeted stairs to the kitchen on the ground floor. He was alone at the table, spooning cereal into his mouth.

"You're late," he grumbled. "They've already gone to their bedrooms."

She glanced out the kitchen window. "But it's still dark."

"As soon as the sun rises, they keel over dead, so they need to be prepared ahead of time." Carlos sipped some coffee. "Phineas went downstairs to the guardroom. Angus and Emma are in their usual place on the fourth floor."

Caitlyn poured herself a cup of coffee. "Do they stay here often?"

"Either here or the basement in Romatech, depending on the current level of violence. Things are calm right now, so we're safe to stay here." Carlos pointed at an empty bowl on the table across from him. "Have some breakfast."

She wandered to the table, wrinkling her nose at the cereal he was eating. "What is that? Meow Mix?"

He shot her an annoyed look. "It's the only cereal in the house. We'll have to buy some supplies today." He pointed to a legal pad next to him on the table. "I'm making a list. If there's anything you want, tell me."

She set her coffee mug down and poured some cereal into her bowl. "I'll go the store, if you like. Shopping is my specialty, you know."

He merely grunted and drank more coffee.

Sourpuss. She stifled a laugh when she realized he really was a puss.

He arched a brow. "Something funny?"

"No." She hurried to the fridge to fetch some milk. "You're kidding." She pulled out the carton. "Full fat?"

"So?" He spooned more cereal into his mouth.

"I'm used to skim." She splashed a tiny bit into her bowl. "This will taste like cream." She stifled another laugh. *Of course the kitty likes his cream.*

He frowned at her. "What's so amusing?"

"Nothing." She beamed. "I'm a naturally positive, happy person." She returned the milk to the fridge. She spun back toward the table and he quickly focused on his cereal bowl, shoveling the last of it into his mouth in a few quick bites.

Her mouth twitched. She'd caught him ogling her rump. "So where's Lara and Olivia? Are they too busy with their Vamp hubbies to eat breakfast with us?"

Carlos sipped some coffee and avoided looking at her. "They're gone. They were in town for

Tino's birthday party and now they're off on new assignments."

"Oh." She approached the table and sat across from Carlos. "So we're the only live ones in the house today?"

"Yes." He jumped up and took his empty cereal bowl to the sink. "I'll see you in the basement in five minutes." He nearly ran out the door.

Caitlyn smiled as she wrapped her hands around her warm coffee mug. This was going to be fun.

It was living hell.

She had hoped to have a little flirtatious fun, but Carlos was all business.

After going downstairs to the basement, she discovered him in a large game room standing next to a billiards table. With a slow smile she sashayed up to him. "Do you want to shoot pool?"

"No." He motioned to the table where he'd laid out a variety of knives, wooden stakes, and swords. There was also a burlap mannequin stuffed with straw resting on top of the table. "This is our pretend vampire—a vicious Malcontent who wants to kill you."

Caitlyn made a face at the straw-filled dummy. "Igor."

"Excuse me?"

"I named him Igor."

"Fine." Carlos handed her a wooden stake. "You've discovered Igor in his death-sleep. Take this stake and drive it through his heart."

She fingered the stake. "What if he's not a Malcontent? What if he's a double agent pretending to be a Malcontent? I would need to thoroughly investigate him first."

"Your investigation is over. This vampire's not a double agent. He has to die."

"Isn't he, by definition, already dead?"

Carlos's jaw shifted as he ground his teeth. "He'll wake from his death-sleep and rip your head off. The only way you can survive is to kill him now."

"Okay, okay." She pointed the tip of the stake where she estimated his heart would be and gave him a little poke. "There. That'll teach him."

Carlos gave her an incredulous look. "You didn't even break the skin. I've seen mosquitoes do more damage than that."

"I'm not a violent person, okay? With my special language skills, I've always relied on communication to—"

"Stab him!"

"All right!" She grimaced and raised the stake above the dummy's chest. Still, she hesitated. The thought of actually plunging a sharp object into a body was so grotesque.

"He thinks you look fat in those shorts."

"Aagh!" She stabbed him, then gasped and jerked her hand away. "Oh my gosh." She stepped back, staring at the embedded stake.

"Not violent, huh?" Carlos smirked.

She glared at him. "Don't push me."

With a chuckle, he yanked the stake out of the dummy. "Now you can learn how to fight a Malcontent who's awake."

She crossed her arms, frowning. "Emma said I would be helping with investigations. They don't expect me to jump into a fight with the Malcontents. They have warriors for that."

He scoffed. "If a group of Malcontents attack, do you think they'll leave you alone because you're mortal and didn't sign up for the fight? You'll be our weakest link. They'll attack you first."

She gulped. "But the Vamps would be there to protect me, right?"

"They would try, but if they're fighting for their own survival, you could be on your own." He fitted a hangman's noose around the mannequin's neck, then climbed onto a chair to attach the end of the noose to a pulley attached to the ceiling.

He jumped to the floor, then set the chair against the wall. "Now Igor is awake and moving." Carlos pulled on a rope, and the mannequin rose in the air. "Take the stake and kill him."

She picked up the wooden stake and slowly approached Igor.

"You'd better be quick," Carlos warned her as he jerked repeatedly on the rope, making Igor dance. "If he gets his hands on your neck, he'll rip your head off."

Again with the head ripping. Caitlyn grimaced and held up the stake. She bent her knees in time with the bouncing Igor. It was a bit like jumping rope, Double Dutch style. She'd been good at that as a young girl. It was all about timing.

She waited as he descended to the bottom of his bounce, then pounced, ramming the stake into his straw body.

"Got him!" She jumped back, grinning.

Igor grew still. Carlos winced.

Her smile faded. "I—I think you must have

pulled him up a little quicker than I anticipated."
Poor Igor had a massive stake embedded in his
groin.

"Please tell me you were aiming at his chest."

"Of course I was." She shrugged. "At least now
he can't father any evil Malcontent babies."

"He never could. Vampires are infertile. All
you've done is piss Igor off. He'll make a grab for
you and—"

"Rip my head off, I know."

Carlos arched a brow at her, then retrieved the
chair and released Igor from the pulley. "The best
way to survive a vampire attack is to never let
them get too close."

" 'Cause they'll rip my head off," she muttered.

"Exactly." He hung Igor up against the far wall.
"If you can throw a knife and hit him in the heart,
you can avoid hand-to-hand combat. I'll show you
how it's done."

She stepped back as Carlos selected a vicious
looking knife off the billiard table. He took aim
and threw. The knife spun through the air, and
thwack! It pierced Igor right through his straw
heart.

"That would turn him to dust." Carlos jogged
up to the mannequin and ripped the knife out.

"Is stabbing them in the heart the only way to
stop them? It seems so violent." She gave him a
playful smile. "Have you tried economic sanc-
tions?"

He snorted, then walked back toward her. "You
can set them on fire, burn them with sunlight, or
cut their heads off."

"Sounds like fun," she muttered.

He handed her the knife. "Your turn."

She gripped the handle and reared her hand back. It had to be like throwing a softball. Unfortunately, she'd never been good at that.

"Wait." He grabbed her wrist. "You're holding it too tight. Relax." He loosened her fingers.

Tingles spread from her fingers and up her arm. She drew in a sharp breath as her heart began to pound.

His eyes met hers briefly, then he let go and stepped back. "Throw. Throw it hard. Turn Igor into dust."

"Okay." She reared back, then threw the knife hard. It arched in the air, then plummeted to the floor with a clatter halfway to Igor. She winced. "I . . . missed."

Carlos was silent a moment. "Is that as hard as you can throw?"

"I don't really know. I stopped throwing things at people when I was two."

He retrieved another knife from the table. "Try again."

She gave it all she had, but the knife clattered onto the floor a few inches from the first.

"You don't have any upper body strength," he muttered. "Do you ever do push-ups?"

She gave him a flirtatious smile. "Of course. There's nothing sexier than a Wonder Bra."

His gaze dipped briefly to her breasts and his jaw ticked. "Come on." He motioned for her to follow as he strode toward the fallen knives. He picked them up and handed her one.

"Try again." He stepped back.

She flung the knife. It spun nicely toward Igor

but hit his chest with the handle and clanged to the floor.

"Not bad." He handed her the second knife. "Put more power into it."

"Agh!" She threw the knife with every bit of strength she could muster. It flew toward Igor, and *thwack!* "I did it!" She turned to Carlos, grinning.

The stunned look on his face made her glance back at Igor. She winced.

Carlos gave her a wary look. "I'm detecting a certain pattern here." He walked over to Igor and yanked the knife out of his groin.

"I really was aiming at his chest."

Carlos snorted, then picked the second knife off the floor. "I was going to do fencing next, but I can guess how that would end."

She frowned. "It's not a big deal. It's not like Igor needs his equipment."

"You would be fencing against me." Carlos walked toward her, his eyes gleaming. "And I definitely need my equipment."

Her heartbeat raced as he came closer and closer. He stopped just an inch away from her.

"Down on the floor," he whispered.

Chapter Twelve

*H*e was playing with fire but couldn't resist. She looked so damned hot with her hair loose about her shoulders, her long bare legs, and her tight little T-shirt that moved with every breath she took. Her face was flushed with exertion. And something else—desire.

It hung heavy in the narrow space between them, seeking to pull them together like a magnet. He'd made the mistake once of kissing her. It had taken all his strength to step back and resist taking more.

And now she was slowly lowering herself to her knees in front of him. His groin tightened as she reached eye level with his white karate pants. *Merda*, why was he torturing himself? He wanted her. She wanted him. She'd practically begged him to kiss her last night. If the damned cameras hadn't been on, he might have succumbed.

From the minute he first laid eyes on Caitlyn, he'd been gripped with a desperate desire, and it was only getting worse with each day. *Take her. On the floor. Now.*

He clutched his hands into fists. It was wrong. He couldn't take pleasure from her when he had no intention of staying with her. His future had been decided long ago during the Summer of Death.

He gritted his teeth. "Give me twenty."

Her eyes widened. "Twenty?" She glanced warily at his pants. "You must have awfully good stamina."

Hot blood rushed to his groin, causing him to swell. He stepped back. "Twenty push-ups."

"Oh." She made a face. "There's no way I can do twenty of those."

"Then you need to do them every day until you can." He motioned with his hand. "Come on. Get started."

"Okay." She balanced herself on her hands and toes with her arms locked straight. She bent her elbows and descended toward the floor. Halfway there her arms shook and she collapsed onto the floor. "Okay, that's one."

"One-half," he muttered. "Try doing it on your knees."

She snorted. "I bet you say that to all the girls." With a groan, she lifted herself up.

"Your body should make a flat line. You're sticking your rump in the air." He leaned over and gave her rear end a light slap.

"Hey!" She glared at him over her shoulder. Before she turned away, a mischievous look gleamed in her eyes. She collapsed onto the floor. "That's two."

"One and a half. And you're supposed to control your descent."

She lifted herself up again, pushing back to stick her rump out even more. She glanced at him with an expectant look.

Naughty little minx. "You want to be spanked?"

Her mouth twitched. "Do you?"

He groaned. "You can finish on your own later."

"My life story," she muttered as she rose to a standing position.

He clenched his fists to keep from grabbing her. *Stop playing with fire.* He needed to stick to business.

"I'd better check on the Vamps." He strode toward the basement dormitory where Phineas was sleeping. "I have to check on them every few hours to make sure they're okay."

"What could go wrong?" She followed him into the dark dormitory. "Aren't they dead during the day?"

"Yes." He flipped on the lights. "This is just a precaution."

"In case of what? Can they grow more dead?"

"In case someone manages to sneak into the house undetected to do them harm." He scanned the large room. It was mostly empty now, just a few twin-sized beds. "When I first started working here, there were a few Highlander guards, and they slept in coffins down here."

"You're kidding."

"No." He walked toward Phineas's bed. "Angus

had the coffins removed. If anyone in law enforcement was to present us with a search warrant, the coffins would have been hard to explain."

"So would the dead bodies." She glanced curiously at Phineas. "He looks like he's sleeping."

The young Vamp had sprawled on the bed on his tummy with an arm dangling over the edge.

Caitlyn giggled as she drew closer. "Look at his boxer shorts. They're perfect for a Love Doctor."

Carlos frowned at the white satin shorts with red hearts. His frown deepened when he realized Caitlyn was openly studying the half-naked Vamp. He grabbed the sheet at the bottom of the bed and covered Phineas up.

Her mouth twitched. "Right. He might catch his death of cold. Does he have a girlfriend?"

Carlos's chest tightened painfully. "Why do you want to know?"

She smiled. "I was just wondering if the Love Doctor had his own lady love."

"He does," Carlos said quickly, then reconsidered. "Well, he hopes he does. He's been pursuing a mortal woman named LaToya, but I believe she told him to take a hike."

"Oh, how sad." Caitlyn picked a photo frame off Phineas's bedside table. "Is this his family?"

"Yes, his aunt, and his younger brother and sister. Phineas supports them all."

"He's their hero." She set the photo down. "If they're still alive, then he must be a fairly young vampire?"

"Yes, just a few years." Carlos shifted his weight. "Why are you so interested?"

She shrugged. "I've been plunged into a whole

new world that I need to learn about. It's all fascinating, really."

"You find vampires fascinating?"

"Yes." Her mouth curled up as she gave him a flirtatious look. "Shifters, too."

His chest tightened. And then his groin. "You're not turned off by claws and teeth—"

"And fur balls?" She grinned. "As far as I'm concerned, the more exotic, the more I like it."

A low growl rumbled in his throat, and her smile faded. Her eyes widened with a big turquoise take-me look.

Merda. He hadn't meant to growl. He was losing control. With a mental shake, he strode toward the door. "I need to check on Angus and Emma."

She followed him up the back stairs to the foyer. "I think I'll take a break and grab something to drink in the kitchen."

"You should come with me."

She gave him a dubious look. "To the fourth floor?"

"It'll be good cardio for you." Carlos jogged up the stairs. "Come on."

She groaned, then ran up the stairs after him. On the third floor landing she stopped to catch her breath.

"Come on." He continued to climb.

"What's the hurry?" She trudged up the stairs. "It's not like they're going anywhere."

"Keep moving. It'll help you get in shape." He sprinted up the last few steps to the fourth floor. "This is the room Angus and Emma use." He opened the door and flipped on the lights.

Caitlyn winced as she joined him. "I would be

so angry if somebody turned on the lights while I was sleeping."

"They're not sleeping." He spotted them in bed, then crossed the room to make sure the aluminum blinds on the windows were shut tight.

"Oh my gosh, look." Caitlyn slowly approached the bed.

Carlos glanced over and noted the Vamp couple appeared to be naked. A bedsheet covered the bottom half of their bodies, and Angus's broad back and arm hid Emma's breasts.

Caitlyn quickly dragged the comforter up to their shoulders. "I think they were making love," she whispered.

"None of our business." Carlos headed back to the door.

"They were gazing into each other's eyes." Caitlyn clasped her hands together and her eyes gleamed with moisture. "They died in each others' arms. It's so beautiful."

Carlos paused at the door with his hand on the light switch. "Death is never beautiful, *menina*."

She turned to look at him with her misty blue eyes. "You saw most of your kind die, didn't you?"

He glanced away so she wouldn't see his face twist with pain.

"Did you lose your family?" she asked softly.

He pushed away the images of his dead parents and brother. He couldn't afford to confide in Caitlyn. She was such a compassionate soul, she would try to comfort him, and that would be a disaster. He'd suffered for so long, he would be powerless to resist her.

He switched off the light. "Let's get back to work."

He headed down the stairs, reminding himself not to touch her. He was too close to the breaking point.

Would this day of torture never end?

Would this day never end? Caitlyn asked herself after an hour of lifting weights and jumping rope. The man was trying to kill her. She felt sweaty and grimy, and he still looked gorgeous, like it was all a walk in the park.

They moved on to the punching bag. The first time she jabbed the damned thing, it rebounded and smacked her in the face. After thirty minutes of learning how to execute jabs, hooks, and upper-cuts, her arms were sore and aching.

She stumbled when Carlos had her perform a combination.

"Don't lose your balance," he warned her. "Keep your knees bent. Stay light on your feet. Shift your weight."

She shot him an annoyed look. He'd been barking out orders like a drill sergeant. "My arms are falling off."

He scowled at her. "Fine." He strode toward an exercise mat. "We'll do some tae kwan do. I'll show you some of the basic kicks."

Caitlyn hated to admit it, since he was torturing her, but she loved watching him move. He was so strong and graceful at the same time.

He moved off the mat. "Now you try."

She bowed to him, repeated every kick he'd performed, then bowed again.

His eyes widened. "You've studied martial arts."

She shrugged with a smug smile. "A little. I wanted to be able to shop without getting mugged. I take my shopping very seriously."

He snorted. "Let's see how well you can defend yourself." He stepped onto the mat and bowed to her.

She bowed back, then took a defensive pose. When he advanced with a slow and basic set of punches, she blocked them all. "You're babying me."

"Just trying to see what you're capable of." He grinned. "This is great news. I'll be able to train you much faster than I had originally thought."

So he could leave sooner to find his perfect mate. A twinge of anger needled her. She wasn't good enough for him. She wasn't furry.

He stepped back. "Let's see what you can do. Attack me."

Oh, she felt like attacking him now. She moved toward him with a quick succession of jabs and kicks.

He smiled as he easily blocked her. "Not bad."

She jumped back, glaring at him. "Don't patronize me."

"*Menina*, I'm truly glad you've had some training. We need to work on your kicks, though. You need to aim for your opponent's chest to make him lose his balance. Now came at me and kick as high as you can."

"You got it." She swung her right leg up.

He grabbed her foot one inch away from his groin. "Not funny, Caitlyn. I'm not the straw dummy."

"I didn't aim—"

"Do you have something against a man's balls?"

"No! I'm just not very limber." She hopped around on one foot. "Can you let me go? I'm about to fall."

He dropped her foot. "Try it again. And aim for my chest this time."

She winced. She'd aimed for his chest the first time. She leaned back to kick as high as she could but put so much power into the swing of her leg that both feet flew up and she fell, landing with a smack on her back.

"Ow." She lay there dazed.

"Sorry about that." He leaned over, offering her a hand to help her up. "Are you okay?"

The amused look on his face made her snap. He'd tortured her for the last few hours. And he was eager to leave her so he could find a mangy were-panther.

She grabbed his hand, rolled halfway up, then jerked hard, making him fall on top of her. His weight knocked her breathless for a second, but the victory was worth it.

"Sorry about that," she said sweetly. "Are you okay?"

He lifted himself onto his elbows and frowned at her. "Not a good strategy, *menina*. You don't want your opponent on top of you."

"Really?" She rubbed a bare foot against his leg and wrapped her hands around his neck. "I kinda like it."

The golden flecks in his eyes glittered like amber. His jaw shifted as if he was grinding his teeth.

She slipped her fingers under the neckline of

his white T-shirt and tugged it down. "I've been wanting to see your tattoo for days." It looked like a black panther leaping through flames.

He grabbed her wrist. "Stop it. We can't—"

She shoved him. Since he'd been supporting himself on only one arm, he lost his balance and landed on his back. She straddled him, sitting up on her knees. "Don't tell me what I can't do."

He attempted to sit up, but she pushed him back down, pinning him down at the shoulders.

His eyes gleamed. "I could get up if I wanted to."

"Then I guess you don't want to." She lowered her hips until she was sitting on his groin.

He hissed in a breath.

"Sorry," she murmured. "I was aiming for your chest."

His mouth twitched. "That's what you always say." His smile turned into a grimace. "You naughty minx. You're torturing me."

"I hope so. 'Cause you're torturing me, too." She moved her hips to rub herself against him. He was already swollen. And hard.

"Catalina." He placed his hands on her face. His breaths were quick and choppy. "You've got to stop me."

"No."

With a growl, he flipped her onto her back and claimed her mouth with his own.

Chapter Thirteen

To hell with it all. He wanted her. He wanted to taste every inch of her. He wanted to make her squirm in his arms and scream his name and beg for more.

A low growl rumbled in his throat as he kissed her. All the hunger he'd kept locked away broke free, and he ravaged her lips. His mind whirled with a frenzy of passion, yet somehow he managed to make an important observation. She wasn't afraid of him. She seemed every bit as frantic and determined as he was. That in itself filled him with awe.

"Catalina," he whispered as he nuzzled her neck. Her scent filled his nostrils, sending a cascade of pleasure through his mind before rushing to his groin.

"Yes." She skimmed her hands down his back and lifted a knee to rub against his hip.

He planted a hand on her thigh and squeezed. He nibbled her lips while his hand slid up her thigh and under the loose opening of her gray shorts. There it was. That beautiful round butt he'd seen that morning when the little minx had mooned him. He'd wanted to grab it for hours. He dug his fingers underneath her underwear so he could clasp her bare ass.

She moaned, her breath sweet against his mouth. He invaded her mouth with his tongue, and she met him with equal passion. She tugged at his T-shirt, gathering it underneath his armpits so she could rake her hands down his back.

He broke the kiss just long enough to pull his T-shirt over his head. He fell onto his back, rolling her on top of him. She traced his tattoo with her fingers, then bent down to tickle it with her tongue.

With a groan, he slipped his hands underneath her T-shirt. "Sit up."

"Mmm?" She lifted her head with a questioning look.

He unhooked her bra, then whisked her T-shirt and bra over her head. She gasped with surprise, then gasped again when he pushed her onto her back.

"Catalina." He'd never seen such lovely breasts. Full, with plump pink nipples that pebbled as he watched.

Her chest heaved with quick breaths. She reached for him, wrapping a hand around his neck. "Kiss me."

He touched his lips to hers and relished their softness and sweet strawberry taste. He kissed the base of her neck, then scraped his jaw against a breast.

She moaned, arching toward him. The hardened tip of her nipple nudged at his lips, and he couldn't resist. He clamped his mouth around the nipple and suckled hard.

"Carlos," she cried, raking her hands into his hair.

He released her nipple and blew on it. She shuddered. A surge of joy swept through him. Victory. Possession. With a grin, he glanced at her face.

He froze. She was looking at him with so much tenderness and trust.

And he couldn't be trusted. If he found a werepanther woman, he would marry her.

The truth hit him like a sledgehammer, and he reeled back from the pain. Caitlyn deserved more than a romp on the floor. She deserved loyalty and . . . love.

Her eyes clouded with concern. "Carlos?"

He scrambled to his feet. "Forgive me. I had no right."

She struggled to sit up. "You wanted this. I did, too."

"We can't!" He stepped back. "I'm sorry."

Her eyes glimmered with tears. "Don't apologize for how you feel. There's . . . something between us. You know it."

"I'd better go." He strode to the door, then halted. "I can't go. I'm on duty." He glanced back, wincing at the tears in her eyes. "We'll . . . take a break. Maybe after you've rested awhile, you can do the grocery shopping. I would do it, but I can't leave the Vamps unprotected."

"I left my heart unprotected," she muttered.

Her words hit like the jab of a knife. "I'm sorry. I . . . I'll see you later." He ran up the stairs as if he could run away from the pain he'd caused. Beautiful Catalina. How could he do this to her?

He sprinted up the stairs to the office on the fifth floor, then paced around the large room, breathing heavily. Coward, he chided himself. Running away from his crime. He ought to go back to the basement and let Caitlyn slap his face.

What was she doing to him? He couldn't let her get ahold of his heart. He had to stay away from her. For her own protection. If he kept succumbing to passion, he could end up doing the unthinkable.

Just bite her, an inner voice nagged him. *Then you can have her forever.*

"No!" he shouted, stopping to clench his fists.

He couldn't bite her. It was too dangerous. He'd seen mortal women die, writhing in agony, their bodies unable to sustain the massive genetic change that came with transforming into a different species. Caitlyn was strong mentally and emotionally, but physically she was soft.

So soft. Her legs, her breasts. He groaned. His erection strained against his karate pants.

He couldn't train her anymore. That was obvious. And yet, he still needed to get her trained, so he could leave for his trip.

"*Merda*," he growled. *Merda* was right. He was in deep shit.

* * *

"Surprise!" Tino bounced into the foyer, followed by his little sister.

"Oh my gosh!" Caitlyn feigned shock even though she wasn't surprised. Her sister had called earlier to let her know they would be arriving about six-thirty.

Shanna set two heavy tote bags on the floor so she could give Caitlyn a hug. "How are you?"

"Mommy!" Sofia covered her ears. "The noise is too loud!"

"What noise?" Shanna looked confused, then glanced at the security monitor by the door. "Oh. The alarm went off."

"It did?" Caitlyn shut and locked the front door. She hadn't heard anything.

"You have to turn it off before opening the door." Shanna punched some numbers on the keypad. "It's set at a high frequency that only Vamps and shifters can hear." Her gaze settled on her daughter. "Sofia, you could hear it?"

The little girl nodded.

Caitlyn felt her skin tingle with goose bumps. It wasn't just a reaction to Sofia, it was . . . him. She could actually feel his presence.

She glanced at the staircase, and sure enough, Carlos was there on the first landing. The alarm must have lured him out of hiding. He'd spent the rest of the day barricaded in the office on the fifth floor. She'd done the grocery shopping around noon, and when she returned she noticed the empty plate in the sink. He'd come downstairs to eat lunch while she was gone.

His eyes met hers for a sizzling moment before

he looked away. She turned her back to him so he wouldn't see how much she was hurting.

Shanna touched her son on the shoulder. "Did you hear the alarm?"

"No," he grumbled, then lifted his chin. "But I can teleport and Sofia can't."

"Tino." Shanna gave him a look of warning. "This isn't a competition. Sofia's gifts may be entirely different from yours."

Sofia nodded and gave her brother a prissy look. "I'm different."

"Yes, you are." Shanna leaned over to hug her daughter.

The phone on the nearby console rang.

"Oh, that'll be Howard." Shanna strode toward the phone. "He'll want to know why the alarm went off."

"He knows?" Caitlyn asked.

"Sure. He knows everything that goes on here." Shanna answered the phone.

Caitlyn winced. She glanced at the stairs and Carlos had disappeared.

Shanna listened on the phone for a moment. "Okay." She turned to Caitlyn. "Howard wants to know if you've learned how to operate the alarm system."

Caitlyn shook her head. "No." As long as Carlos was avoiding her, she'd have a hard time learning anything.

"I'll show her how it works," Shanna told Howard, then waved at a camera. "Don't worry about us. As you can see, we're perfectly safe." She hung up.

Caitlyn stared at the surveillance camera in shock. "Howard can see us?"

"Sure," Shanna answered. "He's able to monitor whatever goes on here. It's another safety precaution."

Caitlyn gulped. "How many cameras are there?"

Shanna shrugged. "A few. None in the bedrooms, of course."

"How about the basement?"

"I don't know. Maybe." Shanna gave her a curious look. "Are you all right? You seem awfully pale."

It was bad enough that Angus MacKay had watched her kiss Carlos in the garden at Romatech, but now she had to wonder. Had she performed in an R-rated sex video for Howard? She cast a wary look at the camera. "Does that red light mean it's turned on?"

"Yes." Shanna tilted her head, her eyes narrowed. "Is something wrong?"

"I'm hungry!" Tino announced as he attempted to lift one of the tote bags.

Shanna rushed over to grab the bags. "Let's go to the kitchen then." She smiled at Caitlyn. "I hope you like chicken."

In the kitchen, Caitlyn helped her sister set the table and divvy up the food. The whole time, she wondered if there was a camera in the basement, and if so, was it turned on?

She sat and stared at the grilled chicken thigh and coleslaw on her plate. She had to know. Now.

"Excuse me." She stood and eased toward the door. "I'll be right back."

The children paid her no mind, but Shanna gave her a worried look.

Caitlyn dashed downstairs to the exercise room in the basement. She halted, her heart lurching in her chest. There *was* a camera. And the exercise mat where she'd rolled around with Carlos appeared to be in its range of view.

She stepped closer, examining the camera. No red light. It wasn't turned on.

For now, but what about that morning? She swallowed hard, then wandered up the stairs to the kitchen.

"Are you okay?" Shanna asked.

"Sure." Caitlyn sat at the table and stared at her food. Maybe Carlos would know.

She jumped to her feet. "I think I'll take some food up to Carlos." She heaped chicken and mashed potatoes on a plate. "He's on the fifth floor. Apparently there's an office up there."

Shanna smiled. "That's Roman's and my old room. It's a long climb. Why don't we just call him to join us?"

Sofia nodded, her mouth full of potatoes. "I like Carlos."

"He's . . . busy." Caitlyn tossed a biscuit on the plate. "I'll be right back." She needed to talk to him in private.

She dashed up the stairs as fast as she could, then stopped outside the fifth floor office, gasping for air.

Carlos opened the door and looked her over. "Are you having a heart attack?"

She glared at him. Her heart was already breaking, thanks to him. She marched into the office and plopped the plate down on the desk. "I brought you supper."

"Thank you." He shut the door and approached her slowly. "How are you doing?"

She pressed a hand to her chest. "I'll catch my breath soon."

"I meant . . . about earlier."

"Oh?" She raised her eyebrows. "Are you referring, by any chance, to the most humiliating rejection of my life?"

He winced. "That would be it."

"Do you really care?"

"Yes, I do. I hate causing you pain."

"You have a strange way of showing it. You've been avoiding me for hours."

He raked a hand through his loose black hair. "I have good reason. But you don't need to worry about it ever happening again. I asked Toni to take over your training."

Ouch. She lifted the plate. "Chicken."

He arched an eyebrow. "Are you calling me—"

"If it looks like chicken and tastes like chicken—"

"Yes, I'm afraid." He stepped toward her, his eyes glittering with anger. "I'm afraid of endangering your life. I'm trying to protect you, Caitlyn."

She plunked the plate down on the desk again. "Protect me from what?"

He gritted his teeth. "There are things you don't know—"

"Then tell me!"

"I *am* telling you! I'm dangerous for you."

Frustration seethed in her. "Why should I believe you when it feels so right? Don't tell me you don't feel it!"

"What we feel doesn't matter—"

"It's *all* that matters!"

He closed his eyes briefly, his forehead furrowed. "Catalina, I cannot bear to hurt you anymore. Please go."

Tears stung her eyes. Rejected twice in one day. That had to be a new record. She walked to the door. She was halfway out when she remembered the reason why she'd come. "Was the camera on in the basement this morning? Did we give Howard a show?"

He looked back at her, his eyes glimmering with pain. "No, *menina*. No one knows what we did."

That was a relief, although it did little to soothe her aching heart. She trudged down the stairs as tears threatened to fall. Dammit. Why was she letting him get to her? She'd known him a total of three days.

But somehow the last three days seemed like half of her lifetime. Her world had turned upside down, and vampires and shape shifters had tumbled out. She'd found her sister, acquired a nephew and niece, and discovered her father was a mind-controlling monster. She had to be too confused and disoriented to know if she was genuinely attracted to someone.

She paused on a landing. Her attraction to Carlos had been immediate, the first time she saw him, and that had happened before she knew about vampires and shifters. Everything she'd found out since—that he'd rescued the were-panther children and adopted them, that he was trying to save his species, that he was helping the Vamps defeat the evil Malcontents—it all added up to a man who exuded strength and honor. *Face it. You're falling for him.*

A tear rolled down her cheek. He felt the attraction, too. She knew it. He'd kissed her and touched her with a sense of awe and reverence. She hadn't imagined it.

She wiped her cheeks and proceeded down the stairs. She wasn't giving up. Love was too rare and valuable. She hadn't given up on her sister. She wouldn't give up on Carlos.

Chapter Fourteen

What's going on?" Shanna whispered to Caitlyn as she finished loading the dishwasher.

"Nothing."

Shanna stashed the leftovers in the fridge. "You didn't eat, and you're as jumpy as a jackrabbit."

"I'm not hungry right now. I'll eat later." Caitlyn dried her hands and smiled at the children. "How would you like to see my treasures?"

Tino's eyes lit up. "Do you have pirate treasure?"

"Sure. Come on." She waved for the kids and Shanna to follow her upstairs to her bedroom. She'd spent most of the afternoon unpacking, so the bookcases were now full.

"Oh, how pretty!" Shanna smoothed her fingers along the yards of embroidered silk that Caitlyn had draped over the canopy frame of the queen-sized bed. "You brought this material back with you?"

"Yes." Caitlyn had turned her plain canopy into an exotic rainbow with a different color of silk cascading down each corner of the bed, tied to the bedposts with silk scarves.

Tino glanced at her bed, clearly unimpressed. "Where's the pirate treasure?"

"Here." Caitlyn removed a carved rosewood box from a bookshelf. "Inside, you'll find coins from countries all around the world."

"Cool." Tino set the box on her dresser and opened it.

Caitlyn separated one of her Russian nesting dolls so Sofia could see the hidden doll inside. "You keep opening them until you reach the baby."

Sofia's eyes widened. "Can I do it?"

"Yes." Caitlyn handed it to her, and a sudden thought occurred to her. For years she'd hoarded her treasures as if they were her family. She had a real family now, so she no longer needed empty substitutes. "I missed your last birthday, Sofia. Would you like to keep the doll?"

Sofia's face lit up with a grin. "Yes! Thank you!" She hugged Cait, then ran to the dresser next to Tino. "Look!" She lined up the first two dolls. "This is the daddy, and this is the mommy." She opened up the second doll. "This is the big brother, Tino."

Constantine frowned at the third doll. "That's not me. That's a girl."

Sofia ignored him and kept opening dolls. "And this one is me, and this one is my baby!"

"Thank you," Shanna whispered. She sat on the bed and motioned for Caitlyn to join her. "So are you going to tell me what's going on?"

Caitlyn climbed on the bed and winced. "I am so sore. Carlos nearly killed me this morning." In more ways than one.

Her sister gave her a sympathetic smile. "I know how it is. Roman insisted I learn some self-defense, too." She lowered her voice to a whisper. "Is Carlos behaving himself?"

"He's avoiding me." Caitlyn shrugged. "That probably comes as a relief to you."

"I want you to be happy. And safe."

Caitlyn wondered again why Carlos considered himself too dangerous for her. Was he referring to the emotional pain she would suffer if they grew attached to each other and then he dumped her for a were-panther woman? Or was there more to the story that he wasn't telling her?

With a sigh, she sat up and crossed her legs. "Enough about me. I want to hear about you and Roman. How on earth did you meet a vampire and fall in love?"

Shanna smiled. "It's a long story."

"I like this story." Sofia struggled to climb onto the bed with her Russian nesting dolls. "Tell it again, Mommy."

"Okay." Shanna pulled Sofia up into her lap. "Once upon a time, your mommy was working the night shift at a twenty-four-hour dental office called SoHo SoBright."

"I like this part." Tino scrambled onto the bed. "The bad guys were after you."

"Yes," Shanna agreed. "I was in the Federal Witness Protection program after testifying against the Russian Mafia in Boston."

"That's why you disappeared?" Caitlyn asked.

Shanna nodded. "I was given a new name and identity, but the bad guys found out where I was. They were coming after me when a strange and very handsome man appeared in the clinic—"

"Our daddy!" Sofia bounced on the bed.

"Yes. Roman had lost a tooth. A fang, actually. I thought it was a canine tooth from a dog or a wolf, so I refused to help him at first."

Caitlyn grinned. "He lost a fang?"

Shanna nodded, smiling. "He had one night to get it fixed, or he'd be a lopsided eater for all eternity."

Caitlyn laughed. "How does a vampire lose a fang?"

Shanna rolled her eyes. "He . . . bit something he shouldn't have."

"It was VANNA," Tino announced.

Shanna stiffened with a shocked look. "How do you know about that?"

"Gregori told me," Tino said. "He keeps her in the closet in his office."

Caitlyn gasped. "He keeps a woman in a closet?"

"She's not a real woman," Shanna muttered.

"She's a big rubber lady," Tino said. "Gregori has VANNA White in his closet. He let Phineas keep VANNA Black."

"What?" Caitlyn was still confused.

"VANNA stands for Vampire Artificial Nutritional Needs Appliance," Shanna explained. "They're life-sized female toys with synthetic blood pumping through them. It was Gregori's brilliant idea so Vamps could pretend they were still biting women. They asked Roman to test the doll, and he lost a fang."

Caitlyn snorted. "Is this for real?"

"I'm afraid so." Shanna gave her son a disapproving look. "Gregori shouldn't have told you about her."

"He put underwear on her before he let me see her," Tino said.

Shanna groaned. "I need to have a long talk with Gregori. He went over the line."

"That's what Connor said." Tino wrinkled his nose, trying to remember. "He told Gregori to shut the hell up. Then Gregori told him he was an old grouch because he never got any and Connor should borrow VANNA for the night. Then Connor said if he was ever desperate enough to tup a rubber woman, he'd—"

"Enough!" Shanna cried with a horrified look.

Caitlyn covered her mouth to keep from laughing.

Shanna shook her head. "I need to have a long talk with Connor, too. They've got to stop treating you like you're one of the guys."

Tino lifted his chin. "I *am* one of the guys." He tilted his head. "What's a tup?"

Shanna grimaced.

"Who is Connor?" Caitlyn jumped in to change the subject.

"He's Roman's bodyguard," Shanna grumbled. "He guards us at night. He's a medieval Scottish warrior."

"So he's a Vamp." Caitlyn searched her memory. She'd met so many new people in the last few days. "And Gregori is Radinka's son? How can he be a Vamp with a mortal mother?"

"He's a young Vamp," Shanna explained. "He was attacked in the Romatech parking lot by some Malcontents, and Roman had to transform him in order to save him." She bit her lip. "Speaking of Gregori, I sorta asked Radinka to have him take you around and introduce you to the vampire world."

"What?"

"It'll be fun," Shanna insisted. "Gregori's lots of fun."

"I like Gregori," Sofia said.

"Everybody does," Shanna agreed.

"What?" Caitlyn repeated. "I don't even know him."

Shanna checked her watch. "Roman will be waking up any minute now, so we should get back home. And you'll want to get ready for Gregori. He'll be here in about thirty minutes."

Caitlyn huffed. "You set me up on a blind date with a vampire?"

"It's not a date." Shanna scooted off the bed. "Believe me, you don't want to date Gregori. He's a bit of a playboy. Radinka's afraid he'll never settle down and give her grandchildren."

Caitlyn scrambled off the bed. "So you set me up with a vampire *playboy*? Oh yeah, now I feel really safe."

"Relax. He's just going to show you around the new and exciting world of vampires. Think of him as a tour guide."

Caitlyn stepped closer to her sister. "You're doing this to keep me away from Carlos, aren't you?"

Shanna winced. "Okay, I admit it. I'm worried about you and him being alone here at the townhouse all night."

"I can take care of myself, Shanna. I can't believe you did this to me."

"That's what sisters are for." Shanna shooed her children out the door. "Dress nice. Knowing Gregori, he'll probably take you dancing."

"Another guy who likes to samba?" Caitlyn muttered.

Shanna laughed. "No. With Gregori, it's all disco."

Thirty minutes later Caitlyn descended the stairs in a flirty black cocktail dress and red-hot high heels. She loved dressing up for a night on the town, so she decided to forgive her traitorous sister for interfering in her life. It had been months since she'd had an official date, so she wasn't in a position to complain that her date wasn't officially alive.

Beggars can't be choosers, she told herself as she reached the foyer. She'd practically thrown herself at Carlos, and that hadn't worked out well at all. He was still hiding in the fifth floor office.

She draped her red pashima shawl around her shoulders, then checked inside her red beaded evening bag. Cell phone, ID, red lipstick, some cash for emergencies. Maybe she should jam a bottle of synthetic blood in there in case her date got a little peckish.

The doorbell rang, and her nerves jangled. *Relax. It's just a date. With a vampire.* She strode toward the front door, her high heels clicking on the marble floor.

She peered through the peephole and spotted a tall man standing on the porch in a pool of light. He looked very dapper in his tuxedo, and she reluctantly acknowledged that he was handsome. But not nearly as handsome as Carlos.

She punched the intercom button on the security pad next to the door. "Just a minute. I have to turn off the alarm."

"Don't worry, Toots," a deep voice came through the speaker. "We've got all night."

Toots? This might be the shortest date on record. When Carlos called her *menina* and *Catalina*, her heart went pitter-pat and her body melted like warm chocolate. Toots was just plain annoying. She punched in the numbers her sister had showed her, then opened the door.

He smiled as he entered the foyer. "Wow! My mom said you were pretty, but what an understatement. Girl, you are smokin'!"

Definitely a player. "How do you do? I'm Caitlyn Whelan."

"Gregori Holstein." He shook hands with her.

She bit her lip to keep from giggling when she noticed his long black cape lined with red silk. "A vampire in a cape? Isn't that a bit clichéd?"

"Nothing clichéd about me, Toots." He adjusted his black onyx cuff links. "I just happen to be classy." His green eyes gleamed as he looked her over. "So are you. Nice dress. Nice legs. Nice shoes."

"Nice uppercut." She fisted her right hand.

He laughed. "Aren't you glad you were forced to go out with me?"

"I believe you were coerced, too."

He feigned a look of horror. "And it's sheer torture. How will we survive the night?"

She shook her head, smiling. "I'm afraid my sister is just using you to keep me away from someone else."

"Keep you away? That's odd. My mother's instructions were entirely different." He cocked his head toward the stairs, then whispered, "I can hear him. He's coming."

She glanced at the staircase but couldn't see Carlos. Or hear him. She gasped when Gregori suddenly pulled her into his arms. "What are you doing?"

"Following instructions," he whispered in her ear. "Carlos has reached the landing. I'm supposed to make him terribly jealous."

"What?" Caitlyn turned her head, accidentally brushing her forehead against Gregori's jaw. Radinka wanted Carlos to be jealous?

"It's working," Gregori murmured against her temple. "He's about to rip the banister in two." He grabbed her chin. "Don't look. He's glaring at us with laser-strength eyeballs. The heat alone would melt your skin off."

She laughed and gave Gregori a shove.

He stepped back, glancing toward the stairs. "Oh, Carlos. What a surprise. How's it going, bro?"

Caitlyn flipped her hair over her shoulder and shot a nonchalant look in Carlos's direction. Her heart stuttered at the intensity of his eyes and the barely contained tension in his body. Good Lord, if he just crooked a finger at her, she would run to him. Gregori was fun, but Carlos was fire and passion. A wildcat, dark and forbidding.

Her breath hitched when she saw his hand on the banister. Sharp, lethal claws had extended from his fingertips to dig into the wood. A shiver shimmered down her arms, prickling her skin.

He didn't scare her. God help her, he ought to, but he didn't. She wanted those claws to peel her clothes off. She wanted his mouth on her bare skin again.

She glanced at his face, and his jaw ticked.

"Well." Gregori watched them, his eyes twinkling with amusement. "It's been swell chatting with you. See you later, Carlos."

He inclined his head, his amber eyes gleaming.

Gregori opened the door and ushered Caitlyn out. "Sheesh, you two have got it bad." He shut the door.

"Is it that obvious?"

Gregori escorted her down the stairs to the sidewalk. "You took one look at him and your heartbeat shot off like a rocket. Vamps can hear heartbeats, you know."

"So I've been told."

"And Carlos looked like he wanted to perform open heart surgery on me with his claws."

Caitlyn grinned. "Your mother told you to make him jealous?"

"She thinks you two are meant to be together." Gregori pressed a hand to his chest. "I'm heartbroken, naturally, that I can't have you for myself."

"Right." He didn't appear to be suffering in the least. "There's no one special for you, Gregori?"

"Nope. And that's the way I like it." He strutted toward a black Lexus sedan. "I'm too sexy for my fangs, too sexy for my cape." He opened the car door for her. "Let's go dancing, Toots!"

Chapter Fifteen

*T*ime to get up, Caitlyn." Carlos knocked on her door early the next morning.

He heard a low moan. No doubt she didn't realize his sense of hearing was just as good as a Vamp's. Gregori must not be aware of that fact, either. Carlos had heard their conversation the night before as he'd descended the stairs, so he knew their date had been arranged. He also knew Gregori's alleged affection for her had been staged. But that didn't made it any easier to watch. Jealousy had surged inside him like an imprisoned wildcat snarling and slashing at the bars of his cage.

He'd had enough. He refused to play games with Gregori or anyone else who found his predicament entertaining. And he didn't want to endure any more from Caitlyn. Just being in her presence was painful. Her turquoise eyes, her luscious body, her intoxicating scent, her brave spirit, and her sassy attitude—it all added up to sheer torture. He'd never craved a woman like this before.

The only way to find relief and keep her safe was to leave. As soon as possible.

"Caitlyn, wake up." He knocked on her door again. This time he heard a muffled response. "Toni will be here soon."

"Okay!" she yelled.

He headed down the stairs, then paused on the landing to check the banister. Last night while Caitlyn was on her date, he'd gone to the nearest hardware store. Then he'd filled the gouges in the banister with wood putty. It had dried overnight, but needed to be sanded. With any luck, no one would ever know how much damage he'd caused.

"Something wrong?" Angus asked at the foot of the stairs.

Carlos straightened with a jerk. "No. You're back early." He noted the bottle of Bubbly Blood and two champagne flutes in Angus's hands. "Special occasion?"

"Aye. 'Tis the anniversary of Emma's first night as a vampire."

"Oh. Congratulations."

Angus snorted. "I wasna with her that night. I felt too guilty for what I had done to her."

Carlos swallowed hard. At least Emma had survived the transformation. He feared Caitlyn wouldn't. The guilt would be too much to bear.

As Angus climbed the stairs, his eyes glimmered with emotion. "I'll always be there for her now."

Carlos lowered his voice. "I need to talk to you about Caitlyn. I asked Toni to take over her training."

Angus paused on the landing, frowning. "We only asked for a week, and ye canna do it?"

"It's . . . complicated."

"Only if ye make it that way." Angus glanced up the stairwell. "I fought my attraction for Emma, but in the end I had to learn to trust the power of our love."

"The best thing I can do for Caitlyn is to stay far away from her."

Angus didn't look convinced. "Emma's waiting for me. Can we discuss this tonight?"

"All right. But first, I have to go to Dragon Nest Academy. Fernando will arrive this evening, and I need to take him there so he can be with the children."

Angus nodded. "That'll be fine. Emma and I need to go there, too, to check on security before we go to Russia. We'll talk tonight. Cheerio." He bounded up the stairs, his blue and green plaid kilt swishing around his knees.

Carlos sighed. If only he could find a werepanther mate that inspired the sort of devotion Angus felt for his wife. What if he never found a woman he wanted as much as Caitlyn?

He descended the stairs and found Phineas in the kitchen, sitting at the table.

"Yo, Catman." Phineas saluted him with a glass of synthetic blood. "What's up?"

"The usual." Carlos retrieved a new box of cereal from the pantry. "How was Romatech tonight?"

"Quiet. Emma and Angus took over for a few hours so I could visit my family."

"That's good." Carlos set a bowl and spoon on the table, then noticed Phineas was frowning at his glass of blood. "What's wrong?"

Phineas took a sip from his glass. "My little brother's graduating from high school this spring."

"That's great." Carlos fetched the milk from the fridge. "You must be very proud of him."

"I am. He's real smart. Smarter than I ever was. I want him to go to college, but he says I've been supporting them for too long and he needs to help out."

Carlos poured some cereal into his bowl. "Maybe he can work part-time while he goes to college."

"That's what I said. I gave him the speech about how important it is to get an education, but he says I'm making good money without a degree, so why should he bother to get one?" Phineas sighed. "I don't know what to do, man."

Carlos splashed milk on his cereal. "I finished my master's degree while I was working here."

Phineas's brown eyes lit up. "Maybe I could get my brother a job here, and he could go to night school like you did. And then I wouldn't have to keep the vampire stuff a secret from him anymore."

"Your family doesn't know you're a vampire?"

"No. I'm not supposed to tell them. My aunt's diabetic, and her eyes are so bad she hasn't realized that I'm not aging. But sooner or later my little brother and sister will notice."

Carlos nodded. "Eventually they'll start looking older than you."

"Yeah, I know." Phineas downed the last of his drink, then clunked the empty glass on the table. "Hell, maybe *I* should go to night school. You know, make a good example."

Carlos smiled. "Your family is fortunate to have you."

Phineas snorted. "I still haven't convinced LaToya that I'm a good guy." He took his glass to the sink. "I need to shower and get ready for bed."

Carlos ate some cereal. "You might consider wearing pajamas now that there's a female training in the basement."

"Snap!" Phineas whirled around. With a grin, he pointed a finger at Carlos. "You are busted, bro. You just failed the Love Doctor's test."

"What test?"

"I purposely wore those shorts to see if you would object to the lovely Caitlyn Whelan observing my abundantly sexy body. You are one jealous man, bro."

Carlos scoffed. "I don't care what you sleep in. If you want to offend Caitlyn, go ahead."

Phineas smirked. "Then you won't mind if I sleep on my back, stark naked."

"Then you won't mind if I let Caitlyn use your body for target practice. You know where her bullets and knives always end up."

Phineas grimaced. "Don't let that wild woman near me."

"Then wear some clothes," Carlos growled.

"Okay, I will. But you're still busted, bro. I know

you have the hots for her. The Love Doctor is finely attuned to all matters of the heart."

Carlos sighed. Everyone seemed to know he was attracted to her.

Phineas went downstairs to the basement. A few minutes later Ian and Toni arrived. Ian grabbed a bottle of synthetic blood from the fridge, then headed upstairs to the fifth floor bedroom for his death-sleep.

Toni fixed herself a bowl of cereal and sat at the kitchen table across from Carlos. "So what's going on? Why can't you train Caitlyn?"

"I need to go on my trip. You're a damned good fighter, so you'll make a good teacher."

"I can't do this every day." Toni ate some cereal. "I need to be at the school. It's a full-time job."

"I'll talk to Angus tonight. We'll figure something out." Carlos rubbed his brow. This whole situation was so damned frustrating. Attracted to a woman he couldn't have. Forced to scour the jungles of the world, searching for a were-panther mate to help his species survive. Cursed with the need to continuously reject Caitlyn.

How could he risk her life? He already lived with the ghosts of his twin brother and parents. He already struggled with the memories of seeing two tribes of were-panthers slaughtered. Their deaths haunted him, but if Caitlyn died, it would be even worse. It would be unbearable, because it would be entirely his fault.

He turned his head as Caitlyn shuffled into the kitchen, barefoot, wearing jeans and a T-shirt. She looked tired, sleepy, and as adorably sexy as ever.

Frustration ripped through him like a physical pain. "You're late. Again. All the Vamps have gone to bed." He immediately felt bad for snapping at her, but the damage was done.

Anger glinted in her eyes and she scowled at him. "Good morning to you, too."

Toni chuckled and extended a hand. "It's good to meet you, Caitlyn."

She shook hands. "You must be Toni. I'm sorry Carlos forced you to be my trainer when he chickened out."

Carlos stiffened. "I didn't chicken out."

Toni's eyes widened.

Caitlyn heaved a tired sigh. "I'm afraid I won't do very well today. Carlos left me so sore." She gave him a pointed look. "Even my lips are worn-out."

"Enough," he growled.

Toni's gaze switched back and forth between the two of them. "What is going on here?"

"Nothing," he said. When Caitlyn snorted, he added, "She's just tired and cranky. She stayed out too late last night."

"I was home by midnight," Caitlyn protested.

"It was 12:23," he muttered.

She arched a brow at him. "Were you watching the clock? Maybe you're jealous."

"Of what?" he snapped. "A fake date that was arranged for the sole purpose of tormenting me?"

"Good grief," Toni whispered. "I feel like I've stepped into a war zone."

"We're not at war," he grumbled.

Caitlyn lifted her chin. "He's in denial about us."

"I deny nothing." He stood, pushing his chair back with a screech. "Half the vampire world knows we're attracted to each other."

Toni sucked in a breath. "Oh my gosh."

Carlos gritted his teeth. "But nothing will happen between us. I'm going on my trip to find a were-panther mate, and you're not coming with me."

Caitlyn's eyes narrowed. "We'll see about that."

"Okay, truce." Toni took her cereal bowl to the sink. "Carlos, leave. Go make yourself useful. And Caitlyn, I think we'll start with pummeling the punching bag."

"Sounds good to me." Caitlyn grabbed a granola bar and bottle of water, then stalked out of the kitchen.

Toni headed for the door, then glanced back at Carlos with a sly grin. "That was quite a catfight. I think you've met your match."

"No." He glowered at her. Nothing on earth could make him endanger Caitlyn's life.

"Dammit," Caitlyn muttered. She'd tried three times to throw a knife at Igor, but each time the results remained the same.

"Well, at least you're consistent." Toni yanked the knife out of Igor's groin.

"I really was aiming for his chest."

Toni strolled toward her with an amused look. "Are you sure you're not still harboring some anger toward Carlos?"

"No. Okay, yes. But I don't have a secret desire to castrate him. It would sorta defeat the purpose of lusting for him, don't you think?"

Toni chuckled as she set the knives on the billiard table. "I am still in shock. I can't believe you two are . . . involved. Just two days ago, I thought he was gay."

Caitlyn's gaze wandered to the mat where she and Carlos had rolled around in passion. "Definitely not gay."

"I can see that. The sparks were flying off you two."

With a shrug, Caitlyn slumped against the billiard table. "You heard him. He's determined to reject me."

"Ian didn't think I was right for him either, at first, but I changed his mind."

"How?"

"Fight for him and don't give up." Toni yawned. "These men can be a little slow, but eventually they come to their senses."

"Well, that's reassuring." Caitlyn folded her arms across her chest. "How long have you known Carlos?"

"About five years. He was my next door neighbor when we were going to NYU. You couldn't ask for a better friend. He helped me rescue my roommate when she was in trouble. And he saved my life once."

He was a true hero, Caitlyn thought. She'd accused him of being a chicken, but she knew better. She knew he was brave and strong and everything she'd ever wanted in a man. "He rescued the were-panther children, too."

"Yes. I don't know much about that other than he and Fernando ended up as the kids' guardians."

"Is Fernando a were-panther, then?" Caitlyn asked.

"No, he's mortal. I don't know how he fits in exactly. Carlos has always been very close-mouthed about whatever happened in Brazil. But you should be able to meet Fernando this evening. He's flying in to stay with the kids while Carlos goes on his trip."

Caitlyn nodded. "I would like to meet him. And I'd like to see Raquel and Coco again."

"They told me about you. They really like you." Toni yawned again. "I'll make sure you get to visit the school this evening."

"Thank you. Where is the school?"

"The location is secret. A Vamp will teleport you there."

Teleport? Caitlyn smiled. That would be an adventure in itself. "Great. I'm looking forward to it."

Toni headed for the door. "Let's take a break. I'm used to taking a nap in the middle of the day, so I can stay up late at night with Ian."

Caitlyn followed her up the stairs. "A nap sounds wonderful. I didn't get much sleep last night."

They crossed the foyer to the main staircase and found Carlos on the landing. He appeared to be sanding a spot on the banister.

"What's wrong?" Toni asked.

He straightened with a jerk. "Nothing."

A surge of tenderness spread through Caitlyn. How adorable could he be? He was repairing the holes he'd made with his claws. She wanted to run up the stairs and smother him with kisses. She wanted— Her thoughts jolted with a sudden realization. She wanted to love him. She wanted to take him to her bed and never let him go. This was more than an attraction. More than lust. More than curiosity. She was falling in love.

He came slowly down the stairs. "I just checked on Angus and Emma. They're fine."

"We're taking a break for a few hours," Toni explained as she started up the stairs. "I'll be on the fifth floor."

"All right." Carlos reached the base of the stairs.

"I'm going to bed," Caitlyn whispered.

His gaze met hers, and she could swear the amber flecks in his eyes were smoldering like hot coals.

Why don't you join me? She wished she had the nerve to say it out loud. If the heat in his eyes was any indication, he was already thinking it.

"Sleep well, Catalina," he whispered, then strode to the kitchen.

Her heart sank as she watched the kitchen door swing shut in his wake.

"Hey," Toni said softly, halfway to the landing. "Don't give up."

Caitlyn nodded and headed up the stairs. She knew Carlos was attracted to her. He'd admitted to it himself. So why was he fighting it so hard? What was he protecting her from?

After a long nap, she took a hot shower and readied herself for a trip to the school where Raquel and Coco lived. She called Shanna to learn more about the Dragon Nest Academy. Her sister had founded the school so that hybrid, shape shifter, and a few mortal children who knew too much could all learn in an environment where they would be free to be themselves.

The current roster of students included Constantine, a group of ten outcast werewolf boys, five were-panther children, and two mortal students, Bethany and Lucy.

As the sun neared the horizon, Caitlyn left her room to go to the kitchen. Just as she started down the stairs, the doorbell rang. She quickened her steps so she could answer the door, then halted on the landing. Carlos was already at the security panel, punching in the number to turn off the alarm. He opened the door to reveal a tall, handsome man with dark hair and a wide grin.

"Carlos!" The man stepped into the foyer, rolling a large suitcase behind him.

"Fernando." Carlos grabbed him by the shoulders and quickly pecked each cheek. "Thank you for coming, my friend."

Caitlyn recognized the language as Portuguese. She hesitated on the landing, reluctant to interrupt their reunion, but not wanting to eavesdrop, either.

Fernando let a large tote bag slide off his shoulder to land on the floor. "You know I'd do anything for you." He wrapped his arms around Carlos in a tight embrace.

Carlos returned the hug, his eyes squeezed shut. As the two men continued to hold each other, Caitlyn's psychic senses tingled. There were no words spoken, no language for her to comprehend, but still, she could feel a communication passing between the two men.

Goose bumps skittered up her arms. This was

deeper than communication. There was a connection between them, something that tied the men together. It was both strong and tender, and it had her completely confused.

Her mind raced, searching for an explanation. They were both guardians of the children. Had they rescued them together? Did they witness the murders and face death together in order to save the children? Whatever had happened, she sensed it had been traumatic for both men.

Fernando leaned back and placed a hand on Carlos's cheek. "I missed your face."

Caitlyn's breath stuck in her throat. There was no mistaking the love in Fernando's eyes. And Carlos, his eyes were glimmering with tears. She pressed a hand to her chest. Was this why Carlos kept rejecting her? But he'd said he wasn't gay. It didn't make sense.

She stepped back. She had no right to witness this.

Carlos lay his hand on top of Fernando's and removed it from his cheek. "You miss *his* face."

His face? Caitlyn tumbled deeper into confusion.

Fernando stepped back, looking away from Carlos with a pained expression. Caitlyn eased back, but her movement caught his eye.

"We have company," Fernando murmured, still speaking in Portuguese.

Carlos glanced at her, and his jaw ticked.

"I'm so sorry," Caitlyn said in English as she hurried down the stairs. "I didn't mean to interrupt. I was just going to the kitchen to find some supper."

"I ordered some pizzas," Carlos grumbled. "They'll be here soon." He motioned to his friend. "This is Fernando Castelo."

"How do you do? I'm Caitlyn Whelan." She rushed forward to shake hands with him.

"Ah, you are Caitlyn." He smiled, speaking with a slight accent. "Coco and Raquel told me about you on the phone. They like you very much."

"The feeling is mutual," Caitlyn assured him. "I can't wait to see them tonight."

"What?" Carlos frowned at her.

"I'm going to the school with you," Caitlyn explained.

Carlos shook his head. "No, you're not."

"Yes, I am." Caitlyn lifted her chin. "Toni invited me."

Carlos's frown deepened into a scowl, and she glared back.

"Interesting," Fernando murmured. "Could I interrupt the staring contest, Carlos? I've been on a plane since yesterday, and I'd like to clean up a bit before we see the children."

"Of course." Carlos's face flushed a ruddy color. "You can use my room. I'll show you." He grabbed the handle of the big roller suitcase and hauled it up the stairs.

Fernando picked his tote bag off the floor. He leaned close to Caitlyn and whispered, "Don't worry. He's not gay."

"I heard that," Carlos growled from the stairs.

Fernando chuckled, then winked at Caitlyn and followed Carlos up the stairs.

She watched the two men disappear up the stairs. How did a mortal man like Fernando end up as a co-guardian for five were-panther children? There was a great deal she still didn't know. If she let Carlos go on the expedition without her, she might never get to know him better. He might find a were-panther mate and forget all about her.

If she wanted a chance with him, she needed to accompany him. Tonight, she would make her case to Emma.

Chapter Sixteen

Oh, I like it," Caitlyn said as she entered Coco's and Raquel's dorm room at the Dragon Nest Academy. "It's so colorful."

"This is my bed." Coco leaped onto a twin bed with a bright purple comforter with hot pink hearts.

"Mrs. MacPhie let us pick out our own stuff," Raquel said in Portuguese. She climbed onto her bed, covered with a hot pink comforter dotted with purple princess crowns.

Caitlyn perched on the end of Coco's bed as she looked around. The walls had been painted pink, and a purple shag rug rested on the floor between the two beds. Toni had tried hard to make the two girls feel welcome. Even so, the dresser and bedside table looked sadly bare of toys and girly things.

Caitlyn dug inside her silk tote bag and pulled

out two Russian nesting dolls. "I have too many of these, so I was hoping you would look after these two."

"Oh, they're pretty." Coco crawled up close.

The little girls gasped when Caitlyn pulled one of the dolls apart.

"There's another one inside," Raquel whispered.

Caitlyn handed each girl a matryoshka.

"Thank you!" They quickly opened each doll, laughing and chattering in Portuguese.

Caitlyn smiled. Her treasures were bringing her even more joy now that she was sharing them.

She'd been at the school for over an hour now. It had taken a few trips for the Vamps to teleport her, Toni, Carlos, and Fernando and his luggage. The were-panther children had been eagerly awaiting their arrival, and the foyer had filled with happy squeals and laughter as they hugged Fernando.

Caitlyn couldn't help but notice that he was much more at ease, hugging and talking to the children, than Carlos. She didn't doubt that Carlos loved them. She could see it in his eyes. And she knew he was fiercely protective of them. But for some reason he was reluctant to bond emotionally with them.

The oldest were-panther child was sixteen-year-old Emiliano. He was lanky and a bit awkward, but Caitlyn had no doubt that he would eventually be as handsome and graceful as Carlos.

The next two were-panther children were twelve-year-old twins, Teresa and Tiago. Teresa was wearing a ton of makeup, as if she desperately wanted to look about eight years older. Caitlyn made a mental note to herself to get to know her better, so she could convince the girl she was naturally beautiful and didn't need to try so hard.

When Raquel and Coco ran up to hug Caitlyn, her heart squeezed. The nine-year-old and six-year-old always looked so young and vulnerable to her. She suspected they touched her so much because she had been nine years old when Shanna had left. She'd felt abandoned and alone, even though she still had parents and a brother. Raquel and Coco were even more alone.

All of Caitlyn's life, lost cats and dogs had come to her for help. Instinctively, they had known she would understand them and open her heart to them. With Raquel and Coco, that phenomenon had risen to a new level, and her heart had responded.

They walked on each side of her, holding her hands as Toni took everyone on a tour of the school. Dragon Nest Academy was housed in a three-story H-shaped mansion. The center section was reserved for administrative offices and schoolrooms. The west wing held dorm rooms for single males on the second and third floors. A few married couples, like Ian and Toni and Phil and Vanda, had rooms on the first floor.

The east wing was for single females. Coco and Raquel shared a room on the second floor, and they had been eager to show it to Caitlyn. She'd gone with them while Carlos helped Fernando move into his new room in the west wing. Fernando had announced he was officially ready to crash after his long plane trip.

Caitlyn lounged back on Coco's bed. "Where is Teresa's room?"

"She's next door," Coco said as she spread the five nesting dolls out across her pillow.

"They lock the east wing off every night," Raquel said.

Caitlyn sat up. "You can get out, can't you? In case of a fire?"

"Oh yeah, we can get out," Raquel said. "But no one can get in."

Coco laughed. "Uncle Carlos is afraid one of the werewolf boys will like us. He said dogs and cats can't mix."

Caitlyn snorted. "I have news for you. All men are dogs." After the girls laughed, she continued, "You guys are too young to worry about boys."

Raquel stacked her dolls back together. "Uncle Carlos says we are the most precious girls on the planet. The future of our species depends on us."

Caitlyn winced. Carlos shouldn't be laying such a heavy burden on these children. She'd have a word with him.

"Teresa is supposed to marry Emiliano," Coco said.

"Teresa's only twelve," Caitlyn protested.

"Oh, it won't happen for a long, long time," Raquel assured her. "Like about five years."

Caitlyn grimaced. "Is Teresa okay with this?"

Raquel shrugged. "Emiliano's the only one she can marry."

"He likes her," Coco said. "He looks at her when we're eating lunch." She grinned at Raquel. "I saw Tiago looking at you."

Raquel snorted. "He has big ears. You can have him."

Coco chewed on her bottom lip. "Maybe we can share him."

"You can't share a husband!" Raquel crossed her arms and made a sound of disgust.

"Wait a minute!" Caitlyn stood. "You are way too young to be thinking about marriage."

Raquel scowled at her feet. "We have to save our species. Uncle Carlos said so."

Caitlyn groaned. "Uncle Carlos should be smacked upside the head."

Raquel and Coco giggled.

"I'd like to see that," Coco said.

"If anyone could smack him, it would be Caitlyn," Raquel added.

The two girls looked up at Caitlyn with admiration and hope in their eyes. Her heart expanded and her mind hardened with resolve. These girls deserved a childhood that was free of the heavy burden of saving their race. They'd already suffered enough. They needed to have choices in life. If she could help Carlos find more were-panthers, it would ease their burden. And it would enlarge the list of potential mates in their future.

"I need to talk to Emma." Caitlyn headed out the door. "I'll be back in a little while."

After ten minutes she located Emma and Angus in a security office on the ground floor. They were discussing something with Ian MacPhie.

"Are you ready to go back to the townhouse?" Emma asked.

"I'd like a word with you, if you don't mind."

Caitlyn waited for Ian to leave the room, then launched into her proposal.

Angus and Emma looked surprised. When they didn't respond right away, she pressed on. "I have contacts at the embassies in Bangkok and Chiang Mai. I know the Thai language. I'm also familiar with the dialects used by the hill tribes where Carlos will be going."

Angus held up a hand to stop her. "I believe Carlos has already arranged for an interpreter."

"But can he trust a stranger?" Caitlyn asked.

"She has a point there," Emma murmured. "Didn't Carlos have trouble with his translator in Nicaragua?"

"She'd be invaluable as a translator, I grant you that." Angus gave Caitlyn a worried look. "But can ye manage a trek into the jungle?"

"We may not have to go into the jungle," Caitlyn said. "I have always attracted dogs and cats. They seek me out the same way Raquel and Coco did in the garden at Romatech. I believe if I was with Carlos, the were-panthers would come to us."

"How interesting." Emma perched on the edge of the desk.

"I visited a hill tribe before when I worked for the State Department," Caitlyn explained. "I think we could simply stay with the tribe and the were-panthers would find us. It would keep Carlos from wandering aimlessly about the jungle."

Angus rubbed his chin, considering. "Ye make a good case for yerself. How does Carlos feel about yer idea?"

Caitlyn shifted her weight. "Well, he—"

"He's against it for sure," Emma said. "He probably thinks it's too dangerous for you."

Caitlyn made a face. "He sorta mentioned that."

"It *is* too dangerous for you," Angus grumbled.

Emma rolled her eyes. "The men always say that. But if you think you can handle it, Caitlyn, I see no reason why you shouldn't go."

Caitlyn grinned. "Thank you."

"I just want to know why," Emma continued. "Why are you willing to do this? I realize you're attracted to Carlos, but he's doing this to find a mate."

"I know." Caitlyn sighed. "I know I might lose him. But I still want to help him. And I want to help the children."

Emma nodded. "All right. I say we let her go." She gave her husband a questioning look.

Angus hesitated. "Are ye sure ye want to do this, lass? It could be dangerous. At the least, 'twill be verra uncomfortable."

"I'm sure."

Angus nodded. "Then ye have my blessing. I'll tell Carlos of our decision."

After Carlos finished helping Fernando move into his new room in the west wing, he headed for the security office to talk to Angus.

"Carlos?" Teresa approached him in the main hallway. She appeared nervous, her teeth stained red from chewing her bottom lip, which was covered with a thick coat of lipstick. "Can I talk to you? In private?"

"Yes." His immediate worry was that one of

the werewolf boys had developed a crush on her. The school had ten teenage werewolf boys living on campus, all training to become Alphas, and Teresa was the only girl close to their age. It didn't help matters that she was trying to look older. He wondered if he could manage to tell her to lay off the makeup without hurting her feelings.

He followed her into a room filled with tables and chairs and a television.

Teresa paced around the room. "This is the teachers' lounge, but it's empty now."

"I can see that." He watched her pace nervously for a while. Whatever was bothering her, she was having a hard time talking about it. "Have any of the boys been bothering you?"

"No." She clutched her hands together.

Another possibility occurred to Carlos. She might have started menstruating, which meant the time for her first transformation would be with the next full moon. "Are you close to the time for your first shifting?"

"I—I don't know. I don't think so." She took a deep breath. "I don't want you to go on your trip."

"Fernando will be here—"

"It's not that," she interrupted. "I don't want you to risk your life again just to find a mate."

Carlos sighed. "You know I need a mate. And you and the other girls need a were-panther woman who can guide you when the time comes for your first shifting."

Teresa lifted her chin. "I don't need anyone to help me. I can take care of myself. And I can take care of you. I want to be your mate."

Carlos stepped back in shock. The notion was so ludicrous, he nearly barked with laughter. Instead, he turned his back to her and cleared his throat. *Merda!* How could he tell her this was ridiculous without hurting her feelings?

He turned slowly, schooling his features. "It's kind of you to make such an offer, but I'm afraid you would leave Emiliano devastated."

"He'd get over it. He can have Raquel, and then Tiago can have Coco. You see, it works out perfectly."

Carlos edged toward the door and pushed it wide open. "Emiliano is perfect for you. He's sixteen—"

"He's a boy. He can't compare to you. He doesn't have the extra powers that you have."

"I wouldn't wish my extra powers on anyone. The cost was way too high."

Teresa stepped toward him. "I know how much it cost you. You suffered through all that in order to save us. This is the least I can do to pay you back."

"You don't owe me anything, Teresa."

"But I love you," she insisted.

He winced. "Hero worship is not love. You don't know about love yet. You're too young—"

"Don't tell me that!" she cried. "I saw my parents butchered and thrown on a fire to burn. I've been through more hell than other people twice my age."

Carlos's heart wrenched in his chest. He had a tough enough time dealing with the memories that haunted him daily. How on earth could these children handle it? "*Menina,* you're twelve years old. I'm twenty-eight. It can't happen."

Tears streamed down her face. "I only want to help. Don't hate me."

Merda. He'd completely bungled this. And now he was afraid to even hug the girl when she was crying. "I could never hate you. Do me a favor, okay? Take a seat and don't move."

She sat at one of the tables. "I'd do anything for you, Carlos."

He groaned inwardly and ran to the administrative office. Luckily, Toni and Ian were there. He explained things quickly, and Toni rushed off to comfort Teresa.

Carlos paced across the office. His expedition couldn't wait any longer. He needed to get away from Teresa. And Caitlyn. He turned to Ian. "Do you know where Angus is?"

"He's in the security office with his wife and Caitlyn Whelan."

Carlos stiffened. What was Caitlyn doing with them? A niggling suspicion tickled the back of his neck. She'd better not be doing what he thought. He rushed into the hall just as Angus exited the security office. "I need to talk to you."

"Good. I need to talk to you." Angus opened a door. "This conference room is empty. Come on in."

Chapter Seventeen

*N*o! She's not coming." Carlos paced around the conference table. Fear and rage stormed inside him, growing in intensity till his skin tingled with the desire to shift. But this wasn't a physical foe he could conquer. This was a deep anguish over the fear that he would cause Caitlyn's death.

Angus sat at the head of the table, calmly watching Carlos as he prowled about the room. "She has contacts. She knows the languages. Hell, she understands every language. Ye couldna ask for a better interpreter—"

"I know all the reasons," Carlos interrupted. "I've heard it before. She's still not going."

"Ye prefer to traipse about the jungle with no idea where the big cats are? She can draw the cats to you, lad."

She can draw me to her. "It's too dangerous for her."

"She says she can handle it."

"She can't! She may be mentally and emotionally strong, but physically, she's a powder puff."

"She's going," Angus said softly. "I'm paying for the expedition, so the decision is mine."

A flash of anger ripped free from Carlos's control. His arms shimmered a second, then his hands shifted into large black paws with sharp, lethal claws. He sucked in a deep breath and concentrated hard. Beads of sweat popped out on his brow, but he succeeded in changing his hands back to normal.

Angus sat forward, leaning on his elbows. "Ye can partially shift? I heard ye can shift without a full moon, too. Ye must be an Alpha?"

Carlos shook his head wearily. "That's a werewolf term. It's completely different for cats."

"How so?"

Carlos groaned. "It has nothing to do with my trip."

"I doona care. I want to know how it works for yer kind."

Carlos slumped into a chair. He really didn't want to talk about this, but he supposed his employer had the right to know. "Were-panthers start off at level one. They shift each month on the night of a full moon. That is the only time they shift."

Angus nodded. "Like Emiliano."

"Yes." Carlos rubbed his brow. "I'm at level three, so I have more power. I can shift whenever I like. I'm faster and stronger. And I can communicate telepathically while in feline form."

"Interesting. What did ye do to reach such a level?"

Carlos twisted his mouth into a wry smile. "It doesn't require a lot of training like the wolves do. It's quite simple, really. You only have to die."

Angus sat back. "Die?"

Carlos nodded. "I died twice saving the orphans. I'm on my third life. That tale about cats having nine lives is true for were-panthers."

Angus stared at him, dumbfounded. "Ye died? Twice?"

"I really don't like to think about it."

"But yer people were slaughtered. If ye can come back to life, why did they no'—"

"Their bodies were hacked into pieces and thrown into a fire." Carlos closed his eyes briefly, trying to chase away the memories. "There's no way to come back from that."

"I see. I'm sorry."

Carlos took a deep breath. "I have witnessed enough death. I cannot endanger Caitlyn."

"Lad, if ye stay with a hill tribe and let the cats come to you, then she should be reasonably safe."

"Danger from the jungle is one thing, but she's in danger from me. Don't you see what she's up to? She'll use this trip to . . . seduce me."

Angus's mouth twitched. "A fate worse than death."

"It would be."

"Why? Can ye no' restrain yerself?"

Carlos clenched his fists to keep his claws from springing out. "You don't understand how much I want her."

A glint of anger sparked in Angus's eyes. "Aye, I do. I understand verra well how a man can ache and long for a special woman. But if ye want Caitlyn so much, why are ye hunting elsewhere for a mate?"

"She's not a were-panther."

"So? Can ye no' bite her and make her one? That's how the werewolves do it."

Carlos jumped to his feet and paced around the table. "It's not that easy. Changing from one species to another causes a massive genetic shift. I've seen mortal men and women die, writhing in agony, unable to survive the transformation."

Angus grimaced. "That sounds awful, but there must have been some mortals who survived the change. Ye look a lot more European than native American. Yer tribe must have brought mortals in and made them into shifters."

"That's true," Carlos conceded, "but it happened gradually over five hundred years. When the Portuguese explorers first arrived, they mated with our women. The children from those unions were mortal, but we believe they retained some latent were-panther DNA. Over the years, with all the cross-mating that occurred, there are probably thousands of Brazilian mortals with some were-panther DNA."

"Has this been documented?" Angus asked.

"No. It's just a theory, but we believe the mortals who already possess some of our DNA are the only ones who survive the transformation. We have no way of knowing, really, since we don't want to be tested in a lab and have our existence exposed."

Angus nodded. "Understandable. Maybe Roman can test it in his lab."

"Even if the theory is correct, it's not going to help us. I don't see how Caitlyn could possibly have any latent were-panther DNA. If I bite her, it would probably kill her. I can't take that chance. I care too much about her."

Angus tapped his fingers on the table. "I understand yer fear. I felt responsible for Emma's death. 'Twas a terrible time for me."

Carlos sat back down. "I can't travel with her. I have to keep rejecting her, and it hurts her feelings."

"Then tell her the truth. She deserves to know why."

Carlos stiffened. "No. She might decide to take the chance."

" 'Tis her life. I believe it is her choice."

"No!" Carlos sprung back to his feet. "I'm not giving her a choice. If she dies, I couldn't live with it."

"If she lives, ye would both be verra happy."

"I'm not gambling with her life." Carlos dragged a hand through his hair. "That's what caused the massacre. My cousin married a woman from Sao Paulo, and she wanted to become a were-panther like him. She died one week after their wedding. Her father was a powerful businessman, and he went berserk with rage when he learned what had happened. He was the one who sent the thugs to murder us."

Angus went pale.

"Imagine how Sean Whelan would react if I kill

his daughter." Carlos collapsed in the chair. "He'd find a way to destroy us all."

"Then ye must be careful no' to bite her. If ye love her, ye will protect her." Angus rose to his feet. "But I want her on the trip with you. She can help you more than anyone. Ye should be able to leave in a week."

"Yes, sir." He'd keep his hands off Caitlyn. He had to.

Angus strode to the door, then paused. "Before ye leave, I want you both to give blood samples to Roman."

"Why?"

Angus smiled sadly. "I'm no' sure, but if anyone can figure out a way to help you two, 'twould be Roman."

Caitlyn was giddy with excitement as the day neared for their departure. She hoped her enthusiasm would be contagious, but Carlos remained angry and aloof. He insisted she continue her training with guns, knives, and martial arts, and he taught her himself. He worked her hard, continuously reminding her that if she didn't toughen up, the jungle could kill her. She suspected he was taking revenge by making her miserable. At any rate, she was too sore and exhausted to flirt with him.

She contacted her friends at the embassies in Bangkok and Chiang Mai and arranged for visas in case she and Carlos stayed in the country over thirty days. She made flight and hotel reservations. She did everything she could to prove her usefulness to Carlos, and he managed to grumble thanks a few times.

Shanna drove them to the airport to see them off. She hugged Caitlyn fiercely as Carlos unloaded their bags. "I just got you back in my life. I can't believe you're going."

"That makes two of us," Carlos muttered.

Shanna pinned him with a stern look. "Don't you dare let anything happen to my sister."

He stiffened with an indignant look. "I'll protect her with my life."

Caitlyn batted her eyelashes at him. "That's so romantic."

He scowled at her.

Shanna eyed the two backpacks in his hands. "Is that all you're taking?"

Caitlyn made a face. "He insists we travel light."

"You don't roll a twenty-nine-inch upright suitcase through the jungle," Carlos grumbled.

Shanna smiled as she adjusted her sister's khaki-colored fedora on her head. "You look like a female Indiana Jones."

Caitlyn glanced down at her khaki pants and hiking boots. "All I need is a bullwhip."

"We'll be buying our weapons after we arrive," Carlos announced. "I've already made arrangements."

Shanna turned to Caitlyn with beseeching eyes. "This sounds dangerous. Are you sure you should do this?"

"No, she shouldn't," Carlos growled.

"Yes, I should," Caitlyn insisted. "Don't pay any attention to him. He's an old sour puss."

He snorted.

Shanna hugged her once again. "I'm going to leave before I start crying." She drove away.

Forty-five minutes later Caitlyn settled in the window seat next to Carlos on the 747 that would take them to Bangkok.

She fastened her seat belt. "Wasn't it wonderful of Angus and Emma to spring for first class tickets?"

"Yes."

"It's an incredibly long flight, you know."

"Yes."

"They'll show us a movie or two."

"Yes."

She leaned close to him, smiling. "I love traveling with you. You're so agreeable."

He gave her an annoyed look. "Are you going to talk the whole time?"

She smiled sweetly. "Yes."

He groaned and closed his eyes.

After take-off, the first meal was served, then the lights were dimmed. Many passengers tilted their seats back to try to sleep.

Caitlyn turned her head to look at Carlos. His eyes were closed, his brow smooth and relaxed. She admired his thick black eyelashes and sharp nose. A gold stud gleamed in his ear. His jaw was shaded with dark whiskers. Overall, the most gorgeous man she'd ever known.

He'd mentioned once before that his kind tended to attract women. She'd seen proof of that just walking through the airport. Female heads turned in his direction when he passed by. Something about being a cat, she supposed. One young woman had literally walked into a wall while ogling him, and another tripped and fell over a suitcase.

"Do you grow whiskers?" she whispered.

He grunted, his eyes still shut. "Didn't shave this morning."

"No, I mean real whiskers. You know, when you . . ."

He opened his eyes to frown at her. "I'm not talking about it here. There's not enough privacy."

"But I want to know what it's like. I'd love to see you when you're—"

"No, you wouldn't. It would mean we're in danger." He angled his body in his seat to face her. "I've given this a lot of thought, and I want you to pretend to be my wife on this trip. It'll be the best way for me to protect you."

Her mouth dropped open. "You're proposing to me?"

"*Pretend* wife. Just to keep you safe."

"Ah." She smiled. "But will I be safe from you?"

His jaw ticked. "Yes."

"I already booked two rooms in Bangkok and Chiang Mai."

"We'll change it to one. I'll sleep on the floor."

"That doesn't sound very comfy."

"In a few days we'll be sleeping in the jungle. How comfy does that sound?"

She grimaced. "I was hoping we wouldn't have to leave the hill tribe. They have little houses on stilts."

"One more thing I want you to understand. I'll be in charge on this trip."

She arched a brow. "Really? I didn't vote for you."

"I have more experience. If things get dangerous, you need to do exactly what I tell you to do. It's the best way to keep you safe."

"Fine." She crossed her arms. "And since we're making demands like a dictator, I have one. Don't let your professor friend and your guide know that I can understand every word they say."

"Why would you want to deceive them?"

"So I can see how trustworthy they are." She smiled grimly and repeated his words. "It's the best way to keep you safe."

"Fine." He lounged back in his seat. "I guess we have each other's backs."

"I'll take whatever body part you can give me."

He snorted.

"I also want to know all about you."

He shrugged. "No point."

"I disagree. If I'm going to help you, I need to know as much as possible, especially if I'm going to pass as your wife. In fact, you'll have to act a lot more friendly and affectionate to me, or no one will believe we're married."

He smirked. "I didn't say we were happily married."

She swatted his shoulder. "There you go, ruining our marriage before we can even get started."

He chuckled.

She smiled. "Now that's more like it. After all, I have to assume you like me if you were willing to marry me."

"*Pretend* marriage. And I like you very much. That's why I'm so worried about your safety."

Her heart swelled at the compliment. "That's why you were such a slave driver this last week?"

"Yes. And I was angry that you wheedled your way into my plans."

"I just want to help you and the children. Now tell me everything you can."

"It's not private enough here."

"Tell me in Portuguese. I'll understand." She patted his hand. "Please."

Carlos heaved a sigh. "Fine. But first you have to tell me why you lost your job at the State Department."

She gave him an annoyed look. "That's old news."

"As your pretend husband I should know. Did you accidentally stab an ambassador in the groin?"

She laughed. "No. I helped a woman leave the country. She's with friends now in the States, and she's safe."

"She was in danger?"

"Her father had her marked for an honor killing. He wasn't happy with some of the Western ways she'd adopted."

Carlos grimaced. "That was a reason to kill her?"

"Yes. He raised a big stink about me helping her escape. I got in trouble for interfering, but I'd do it again."

Carlos nodded, his eyes glimmering in the dim light. "You are a brave woman, Catalina."

Her heart expanded and she gave him a sly smile. "You must be proud to be my husband."

"Pretend husband."

She touched his hand. "Now it's your turn to talk."

He settled back into his seat. "What do you want to know?"

Chapter Eighteen

*C*arlos glanced across the aisle. The elderly woman seated there had taken sleeping pills and was nodding off. Everyone had pulled the shutters down on their windows, and the first-class cabin was dark and quiet. The only sound he could hear was the hum of engines. Even though the plane was full, he felt oddly alone with Caitlyn. Even more odd, he felt at peace.

For the first time in five years there was someone willing to accompany him on an expedition, someone willing to brave the discomfort and danger. For so long, he'd struggled against his predicament all alone. He was truly grateful that Caitlyn was with him, although he wasn't about to tell her that. After years of being haunted with horrible memories, he looked forward to seeing her bright and happy face every day. Her optimistic, courageous attitude soothed his pain and gave him hope.

He figured she'd ask him about the Summer of Death. It was a topic he always tried to avoid, but in her case, he decided it would be good for her to understand the extent of devastation his people had suffered. If she knew how important it was for him to locate a suitable mate, she might find it easier to let him go.

"How was your life growing up?" she whispered in English.

He switched to Portuguese in case anyone seated nearby was still awake and listening. "It was always a dual life. We spent the summer months in the tribal village. Those were the easy days when we were free to roam the jungle and be ourselves. In the winter, we lived in the city but would return to the village for the night of the full moon."

"And that's when you would . . ."

"Shift, yes. Though it doesn't happen until a child reaches puberty."

"So Raquel and Coco haven't done it yet."

"No." He realized she was being careful not to say anything too provocative in English. "Teresa and Tiago haven't either. Only Emiliano."

She nodded. "Where did you live in the winter?"

"Rio. My dad was a newspaper editor."

"You're kidding."

"No. He loved the job, and it put him in a good position to make sure no rumors were ever printed about our people."

"Ah. Clever."

A wave of grief seeped into his heart. "Yes. He was a smart man. A wonderful father and the leader of our tribe."

She placed her hand on top of his. "You lost him."

"He was murdered when our tribe was attacked five years ago. I call it the Summer of Death."

"I'm so sorry. Coco and Raquel spoke briefly of it. It still causes them so much pain."

Carlos nodded. He was reluctant to admit how bad he was at comforting the children. He didn't know how to give them peace when he had none for himself.

"You call it a summer," Caitlyn whispered. "It lasted longer than one day?"

"Yes." Her hand still rested on top of his. It felt so good that he entwined his fingers with hers. "There were two tribes in the jungle about twenty miles apart from each other. My brother and I were in a Jeep, going to the other tribe."

"You have a brother?"

"Had."

She gasped. "Oh no."

"Erico and I were going to visit a cousin. We'd missed his wedding a week earlier 'cause we were in college taking final exams. We heard screams in the distance. Terrible screams. And there was smoke billowing in the air, with a horrendous smell. We pulled the Jeep over, took out our knives, and came up on the village from behind."

"The attack had already begun," she whispered.

He closed his eyes briefly as the memories shot

through his mind. "They had machine guns. Those who tried to run away into the jungle were mowed down. Others cowered in their huts, but the bastards went from home to home. You could hear the gunfire and screams."

Caitlyn squeezed his hand. "What did you do?"

"Erico and I sneaked into the back of the nearest hut. We found Teresa and Tiago and got them to the Jeep. We went back . . ." That was when he'd seen one of the thugs dragging a little boy out of his hiding place beneath a canoe. Carlos threw his knife and killed the thug, but when he tried to rescue the little boy, they were sprayed with bullets. The boy died. Somehow Carlos managed to make it back into the jungle before collapsing.

That had been his first death. Erico had carried him back to the Jeep and driven him and the children home. A few hours later he'd wakened to his second life.

"You went back?" Caitlyn asked. "What happened?"

He hesitated. Did he really want to tell her that he'd died? Twice? Doing so had given him extra power, but he'd never viewed that as a great achievement. It was more of a colossal failure. Would she even want to go into the jungle with him if she thought he couldn't protect her? Hell, he'd failed to protect himself. Twice.

He cleared his throat. "We went back. Everyone was dead. Their bodies were thrown into a fire, and the whole village was burned to the ground."

"Why would they do such a horrendous thing?"

Carlos shrugged. "Anger. Hatred. Greed. The man behind it all wanted revenge. Then he tried to buy up the land afterward."

"Has he been arrested?"

Carlos shook his head. "My brother and I pressed charges against him. I guess he figured the best way to avoid getting arrested was to kill the witnesses."

"So he attacked your father's tribe?"

Carlos tilted his head back, closing his eyes. He and Erico had worried there would be a retaliation, but their father had insisted they press charges. He'd also armed the men in the village and prepared them for a possible attack. Still, it clawed at him. "My people might still be alive if I hadn't pressed charges."

Caitlyn leaned close and spoke for the first time in Portuguese. "Don't you dare blame yourself. You did the right thing. I'm sure your father agreed."

"He did." Carlos opened his eyes and felt blessed to have Caitlyn so close, gazing at him with so much compassion in her lovely turquoise eyes.

"I have a strong feeling that the monster who murdered the first tribe was going to come after your tribe no matter what," she continued. "He was out to destroy your people."

Carlos nodded. "That's what Fernando says."

"How does he fit into the story?"

"Erico met him in college and they became very close. After the first massacre, Erico and I took Tiago and Teresa to Rio, and Fernando's parents took care of them. Fernando wanted to help our people, so he went with us when we returned to the tribe."

"And that's when the attack happened?"

"Yes." Carlos sighed. "The murderers attacked at night, killing the two men on guard duty before they could raise the alarm. And then the slaughter began."

Caitlyn shuddered.

"Erico convinced Fernando to take the Jeep down a path where he could hide it in the jungle. My people tried to fight, but they'd only get off a shot or two before they were mowed down by machine gun fire. I saw my parents die."

Caitlyn grimaced. "I'm so sorry."

"The bastards started a huge fire to burn the bodies. While they were busy with that, Erico and I sneaked from hut to hut, looking for children who were still alive. We found Coco, Raquel, and Emiliano, then ran, carrying them to the Jeep. Then we went back to look for more survivors. And we were both shot."

"Oh, no."

"Erico's wound was worse than mine. I managed to carry him a little ways into the woods before I passed out. I'm fuzzy on what happened after that. At some point Fernando found us. He carried me to the Jeep, then ran back to get Erico." Carlos squeezed Caitlyn's hand as tears blurred his vision. "Erico was gone. They'd found him and thrown him onto the fire."

Caitlyn pressed a hand against his chest. "I'm so sorry." A tear rolled down her cheek.

"Fernando took me and the children to his parents' home in Rio." Carlos didn't want to admit that he'd died a second time. "After I recovered, I tried to deal with things. I leased the tribal lands to an oil company that wanted to drill, then I used that money to buy a house in Rio so the children would have a home. When Fernando offered to share guardianship with me, I was grateful for his help."

"It was very kind and generous of him."

"He felt it was the best way to honor Erico's death. He loved Erico so much." Carlos blinked back tears. "We lived in the house with the children. People assumed Fernando and I were in a relationship. We were, I suppose, but not in a sexual way. I don't know how I would have made it through those first few months without him. He was a rock for me and the children."

"You were lucky to have him."

"Yes. But it took me about a year to realize what it was costing him. Erico was my twin."

Caitlyn gasped. "Identical?"

"Yes. And every day, Fernando would see my face. My presence was a torture for him. I would catch him looking at me with so much love and pain . . . I knew I had to leave."

"That's so sad." Another tear rolled down her cheek.

Carlos brushed it away. He was having a hard time keeping his own tears at bay. "I've always had this terrible fear that Fernando couldn't tell us apart when he rescued me. Then when I regained consciousness, he realized he'd saved the wrong twin."

"Oh, Carlos." Caitlyn placed her hands on his face. A tear escaped down his cheek, and she wiped it with her thumb.

"I've never told anyone this before," he whispered. "For five years I've been afraid that Fernando regrets saving me. Now he's stuck with the brother who can't love him."

"Don't say that. He went back for your brother, right? He intended all along to save you both. He never chose between the two of you. The choice was taken away."

Carlos squeezed his eyes shut. "I miss my brother so much. And I know the children are hurting, but I don't know what to say to them."

She lowered her hands. "You're doing fine."

He opened his eyes. "Do you understand why I have to find a mother for them?"

"Yes."

He touched her cheek. "I'm sorry it can't be you."

"So am I."

With a sigh, he dropped his hand. "Sometimes it hurts to do the right thing."

She nodded. "It hurt you to tell me everything, but I'm glad you did. Thank you."

He settled back in his seat. She'd misinterpreted his statement. What was hurting him the most was rejecting her. If only . . . but it did no good to avoid the truth. He couldn't have her.

"Let's get some rest." He closed his eyes and listened to the rustling sounds she made as she nestled underneath a flannel blanket. Eventually he heard her breathing become slow and even.

He opened his eyes to look at her while she

slept. Her soft cheeks glistened from the tears she'd shed for him and his family. His chest tightened. He was awed by her determination to help him and the children. Awed by how quickly and thoroughly she could open her heart to someone. She was beautiful, clever, loyal, and brave.

He nudged her head over till she was sleeping on his shoulder. Her scent filled him with a sense of comfort and peace. As he drifted off to sleep, he realized he felt much more than desire and passion for Caitlyn.

He loved her.

Caitlyn yawned again as they walked across the campus of Chulalongkorn University. Even though she'd managed to sleep a little on the long flight, she was still exhausted.

"You don't have to do this," Carlos said. "The professor speaks English, so I don't need an interpreter. You could go back to the hotel and sleep."

"I'm fine. I'm enjoying the walk." It felt good to stretch her legs. She took a sip from her water bottle. The weather was warm, but she was glad they'd come in early April. A few months later the rains would begin.

After arriving at the Suvarnabhumi airport in Bangkok and changing some dollars into baht, they'd taken a cab to their hotel near Embassy Row. The taxi driver had jabbered nonstop in broken English while he careened down busy streets, narrowly avoiding other cars and claiming that traffic lanes and signs were merely suggestions. Caitlyn figured his hyperactive behavior was linked to the five empty energy drink bottles in the front seat. Carlos had muttered something about the jungle being safer.

They'd checked into the hotel, a very posh place that Caitlyn had used for visiting dignitaries when she'd worked at the embassy. They'd cleaned up and eaten some Pad Thai at a local restaurant. Another cab ride dropped them off at the university on Phayathai Road, near the science buildings where Carlos's contact had his office.

"He's expecting us?" Caitlyn asked as they entered the faculty building.

"Yes. I called him while you were in the shower." Carlos punched the button on the elevator. "He's on the third floor."

A few minutes later, Carlos knocked on an office door. A short man with a round smiling face answered. He wore thick round glasses that made his eyes look huge. A few strands of black hair were combed across the bald spot on top of his head.

"Ah, you must be Carlos!" He pressed his hands together close to his chest and bowed slightly. He glanced curiously at Caitlyn. "You brought a pretty lady with you."

"My wife. Caitlyn . . . Panterra."

Caitlyn smiled in spite of the twinge of annoyance she felt. Carlos had nearly choked saying her name.

"Your wife?" The professor blinked his big owlish eyes. "I didn't know you were married."

"He never mentioned me?" Caitlyn heaved a tragic sigh. "I'm afraid he gets so wrapped up in his work that he forgets all about me."

Carlos shot her an annoyed look. "I could never forget you." He gritted his teeth. "Darling."

"Oh, you're so sweet." She squeezed his arm, inadvertently pressing her breasts against him.

He arched a brow at her. "Let me introduce you to Professor Supat Satapatpattana."

"Delighted to meet you, Professor Salapatty-patman." She pressed her palms together and inclined her head.

"It's Satapatpattana," Carlos murmured.

Caitlyn gave him a wide-eyed look. "Isn't that what I said?" She'd warned him ahead of time that she might act a little ditzy so no one would suspect she could understand other languages.

The professor chuckled. "Please, call me Pat. Come, sit down." He circled behind his desk and took a seat.

Caitlyn and Carlos sat in the two chairs facing him. She set her leather handbag and bottle of water on the floor by her feet.

"I have to say that I am very excited about your mission," Pat began. "If we can prove there are humans who have the ability to shift into cats—" His eyes lit up. "It would be the greatest scientific discovery of our time!"

"Indeed," Carlos murmured.

"And to be a part of this momentous discovery," Pat continued, his face beaming. "It would be a great honor for me. And the university."

Caitlyn almost felt sorry for Pat. If Carlos did find some were-panthers, he would never admit to it. The professor's hopes were doomed from the beginning.

Pat slid a map across his desk. "This is for you. I have circled in red the area where the cat shifter was killed."

"Alleged cat shifter," Carlos said as he took the map.

"Surely you must believe it is true," Pat protested. "You have come all this way. You must believe the shifters really exist."

There was a desperation in the professor's eyes that worried Caitlyn. Did he have a different motivation than his fifteen minutes of fame?

Carlos cleared his throat. "To be honest, Pat, there are rumors of strange creatures all over the world. Big Foot, Sasquatch, the Loch Ness monster. It's extremely hard to find definitive proof."

"We have proof, an eyewitness account." Pat's hands clenched into fists. "I am positive you can find these cat shifters. You must."

Definitely something fishy going on. Caitlyn kept her face blank and pretended to be engrossed in the map Carlos was holding. A red circle had been drawn around a hilly area northwest of Chiang Mai.

Pat took a deep breath and relaxed his hands. "I have arranged for a guide who will meet you in Chiang Mai. His name is Tanit, and his English is good."

"Great. Thank you." Carlos folded the map carefully. "Our plane is arriving there tomorrow at four-fifteen in the afternoon."

"I can't wait." Caitlyn grinned, feigning a bubbly excitement. "I read about it online when I booked the hotel." She avoided saying that she'd been to Chiang Mai before. "There's this old city that's surrounded by a moat. And then there's a nightly bazaar, so I can go shopping."

Carlos stiffened. "No, no shopping."

"We have to buy stuff for the children."

"Anything you buy would have to be dragged along for the entire trip. We don't have room in our backpacks."

"I'll buy little things."

The professor shook his head and muttered in Thai, "Definitely married." He switched to English. "I will call Tanit immediately to let him know when to meet you at the airport."

"Thank you." Carlos rose to his feet. "I appreciate your help."

"Here." Pat gave him a business card. "This has my office number and my cell phone number. Call me anytime, day or night."

"Thank you." Carlos slipped the card into his trouser pocket.

"And if you find out anything about the cat shifters, you must call me immediately," Pat insisted.

Caitlyn's instincts prickled with suspicion. She leaned over to retrieve her handbag, then decided to leave her water bottle there. She stood, hitching her handbag over her shoulder. "It was nice to meet you, Pat."

He nodded, smiling. "I am very excited and hopeful for your success."

As Carlos walked her to the door, she said just loud enough to be heard. "I'm so glad we're going to have an interpreter. Their language is so confusing. The words are a mile long."

Carlos nodded. "I know."

She stepped into the hall with him, and he closed the door. She pressed a finger to her lips and leaned against the door to listen.

His eyebrows lifted in an unspoken question.

She heard Pat's voice inside, waited a moment, then cracked open the door.

Pat looked up with alarm, his cell phone by his ear.

"I'm so sorry," she whispered as she tiptoed into the room. "Don't mind me. I just left my water bottle."

Pat nodded with a grim smile. "It's all right, Tanit," he murmured in Thai on the phone. "It's just his wife."

There was a pause, then Pat continued, "I don't know why she came, but I don't think she'll give you any trouble. Just remember your priorities here. Do whatever you can to help them find the cat shifters."

Caitlyn made a pretense of looking around the chair Carlos had sat in.

"Mrs. Panterra?" Pat spoke impatiently. "You weren't sitting in that chair. Your water's over there." He pointed to the other chair.

"Oh." Caitlyn looked surprised. "That's right." She shook her head sheepishly. "Jet lag. I can't think straight anymore." She leaned over to grasp the water bottle. When Pat had motioned with his hand, she'd spotted an odd tattoo on the inside of his wrist.

"Call me immediately if you find a cat shifter," Pat said in Thai on the phone. "We must find one for the Master."

The Master? Caitlyn strode to the door, then smiled at Pat as she exited. She motioned for Carlos to follow her to the elevator. Thank God she'd come along on this trip.

She had a terrible suspicion Carlos was walking into a trap.

Chapter Nineteen

*I*sn't it lovely?" Caitlyn asked, looking out the restaurant window.

"Yes." Carlos took another bite of Kaphrao gai. The green chilies set his mouth ablaze, and he reached for his glass of water.

They'd met their guide, Tanit, at the airport in Chiang Mai. He'd driven them to their hotel, then to this restaurant overlooking the Mae Ping River. In the distance Carlos could see the mountains of brilliant green vegetation beneath a fiery sky, ablaze with the setting sun. Caitlyn had taken the seat by the window, and he sat next to her. The air was filled with exotic, delicious smells: curry, chilies, garlic, and basil.

Tanit sat across the table, fidgeting with his chopsticks. "Chiang Mai is a very beautiful place." He was a young, slim man who seemed eager to please, but Carlos sensed that he was nervous.

"We have many national parks. Mountain biking is very popular and looking at the elephants. We also have many lovely temples. The Wat Chiang Man was built in 1296 and houses the Crystal Buddha."

"That sounds interesting, but this is a business trip," Carlos said. "I assume Pat told you what we were looking for."

Tanit nodded as he pushed the fried rice around his bowl. "It is . . . most unusual."

"I think it's exciting." Caitlyn grinned. "But let's not leave till tomorrow. I want to go to the bazaar tonight."

Carlos hid a smile. She was doing a good job of pretending to be an airhead. "You'd better not buy very much. We'll have to take it with us."

"It won't weigh anything," she assured him. "I want to buy some Mudmee silk scarves. The silk here is so shiny and soft. And I can't wait to see all the silverware." She sat up. "Speaking of silver, we're going to the Akha tribe tomorrow, right?"

"Yes," Tanit replied, frowning. "But I'm not sure how they can help you find the . . . cats you're looking for." He glanced nervously over his shoulder.

"Oh, don't worry about that." She waved a hand in dismissal. "I'm just dying to see all the stuff they make. I hear the ladies wear beautiful head-dresses made of silver coins and beads. I'd love to have one."

"Sounds heavy," Carlos muttered. He ate more food to keep from laughing. Caitlyn was one sneaky rascal. She wanted to go to the Akha tribe because she'd spent time with them before. She didn't want Tanit to know, so she was making it sound like a shopping spree.

"I should go and make sure everything is ready for our trip," Tanit said. "I'll pick you up at your hotel in the morning. Will nine o'clock be all right?"

"That's great. Thank you," Carlos replied.

"Are you sure you wouldn't like some dessert?" Caitlyn asked. "I'm going to have some ice cream."

"No, thank you. I should go." Tanit stood and pressed his hands together. "Thank you for dinner." He hurried from the restaurant.

Caitlyn watched him go. "Did he seem nervous to you?"

"Yes." Carlos glanced at Tanit's plate of Khao pad gai. "He hardly ate a bite."

Caitlyn leaned closer. "Did you notice his tattoo?"

"No. You have a thing for tattoos, don't you?"

"Only yours, because you hide it and that makes me want to rip your clothes off."

"In that case, I should tell you I have a tattoo on my rump."

Her eyes widened. "Do you really?"

His mouth twitched. "You'll never know."

She swatted his arm. "Don't be cruel."

He snorted. Cruel was sleeping on the floor, knowing that she was nearby in a bed and there wasn't a damned thing he could do about it. He knew he loved her, but he still couldn't have her.

She retrieved a small memo pad and a pen from

her silk handbag. "Tanit had a small tattoo on the inside of his right wrist just like the professor had."

"Are you sure?"

"Yes, I'm sure." She gave him a wry look. "All my years of shopping have given me a great eye for detail. I studied Tanit's tattoo when he wasn't looking." She drew the design on her memo pad.

"Looks like a Chinese symbol," Carlos said.

The waiter came to their table, and Carlos asked if they had ice cream.

"We have very nice vanilla, served with jackfruit and grilled bananas." The waiter gathered up their used dishes.

"We'll take two of those." Caitlyn showed the waiter her drawing. "Do you know what this means?"

The waiter frowned. "It looks Chinese. One of our cooks is Yao. Maybe he knows."

"Could you ask him, please?" Caitlyn tore off the page with her drawing and passed it to the waiter. "Thank you."

"You can't understand written languages?" Carlos asked.

"No." She shrugged. "I know it's strange. If I could just get someone to say the word, I would understand it."

Carlos sat back in his chair. "I have to tell you, Catalina, that hiring you was one of the best things Angus and Emma have ever done."

Her face lit up. "Why, thank you. I thought you considered me hopeless and helpless."

He smiled. "You're not the best warrior around."

"I'm not a violent person."

"I know." It was one of the many things he loved about her. She was soft and sweet. If he ever attacked her, it would be to make love. He pushed that thought aside and tried to remember the point he was making. "When it comes to investigation, you're a natural."

"Thank you." She grinned. "I'm naturally nosy." Her smile faded. "I'm still worried about this 'master' thing Pat talked about on the phone. He seemed desperate to me, and Tanit's way too nervous. There's something going on we don't know about."

Carlos nodded. "I've been thinking about that. Maybe Pat is involved with the trafficking of exotic animals. That could explain why the informant talked to him."

She placed her hand on his. "Whatever's going on, we need to be careful."

He entwined his fingers with hers. "I'm still worried about your safety, but I'm glad you came. I'm not used to having someone to watch my back. You . . . you do it really well."

She smiled at him, her eyes filled with love, and he wanted to kiss her. Hell, he wanted to take her back to the hotel room and make love to her.

The waiter returned with their ice cream. He handed the slip of paper to Caitlyn. "Our cook said it meant a worker, the kind who works for a master. No pay."

"You mean like a slave?" she asked.

The waiter nodded. "That's it." He hurried off.

Carlos exchanged a worried look with Caitlyn. Professor Pat and Tanit were intelligent, modern men who worked regular jobs. How could they be slaves? And more important, who was their master?

After an hour of riding in the backseat of Tanit's car, Caitlyn was struggling to stay awake. The mountain road swung back and forth, lulling her into a sleeplike trance. Fortunately, every time she nodded off, they'd bounce over another pothole or swerve to miss a motorcyclist.

The reason for her exhaustion was all Carlos's fault. He was stubborn as a mule. She'd lain in bed last night, listening to him toss and turn on the floor. She'd invited him to share her bed, promising not to molest him. He refused. After another hour of hearing him thrash about on the floor, she offered to switch places with him. Again he refused.

Thirty minutes later, still awake, she took matters into her own hands. She grabbed a pillow and blanket and joined him on the floor. He ordered her to leave him be. This time she refused. She was comfy and he could have the bed.

He scooped her off the floor, strode to the bed with her in his arms, and dumped her. He returned to the floor, and she lay in bed, marveling over how strong he was. And sexy.

For another thirty minutes she considered stripping and straddling him on the floor. She'd never done anything that bold before. Or pathetic. If he wanted her, he'd make a move for her. She couldn't force herself on him. And she couldn't handle being rejected again. He still wanted a were-panther mate. Her secret fantasy of him tossing that away just to have a future with her was not likely to ever happen. So she'd stayed in bed, restless and frustrated, while he remained on the floor.

The car slowed to a halt as the road dwindled into a footpath through the jungle. The Akha tribe they were visiting lived in a remote area close to the Burmese border. Since she was pretending never to have been there before, Carlos was the one insisting they visit this particular tribe. She hoped their wily old leader, Ajay, was still there.

"We have about a thirty minute hike," Tanit said as they exited the car. He glanced warily at the jungle. "There are other tribes not so remote, much closer to Chiang Mai, and they have wonderful handicrafts, too."

"We're going to this one." Carlos hefted his backpack onto his shoulders. "If the cat shifters exist, they'll be in a remote area like this."

"I suppose that's true," Tanit mumbled.

Carlos slipped some knives into his belt, then handed one to Caitlyn. He'd bought them at the bazaar last night while she'd bought three beautiful silk scarves for the were-panther girls.

She wedged her knife under her belt, then slathered insect repellent on her bare arms and neck. "Want some?" She offered the tube to Tanit.

"Thank you." He spread some on. "You know, there are worse things than mosquitoes in the jungle."

"That's why I bought this." Carlos holstered a semiautomatic pistol on his belt.

Caitlyn shuddered. She hoped he wouldn't have to use it. She fastened the ties of her khaki hat under her chin so it wouldn't fall off. Like Tanit, she was nervous about trekking through the jungle. She had visions of huge poisonous spiders dropping out of trees to land on her head. At least her hiking boots were thick enough to offer some protection from scorpion stings or snake bites.

She jammed water bottles into every pocket on her backpack, then swung it onto her back. "Ready?"

Thankfully, their trip through the jungle was fairly uneventful. Carlos spotted a pit viper in a tree, but it ignored them as they walked by. Caitlyn bit her lip to keep from squealing.

The sun was high in the sky when they entered the clearing where the Akha tribe lived. She estimated almost twenty wooden houses with thatched roofs. Each house was built on stilts, with ladders to the main floor. Several huts were at ground level, and she remembered from her previous stay that one was used to store farming equipment while the other two were village workshops for making intricate silver jewelry.

Surrounding the houses were fields where the Akha grew vegetables and rice or raised pigs and chickens. In the center of the village there was a huge fire pit. Off to the side, a wooden tower rose high above the houses.

Men stopped their work in the fields to watch them as they approached. Children ventured from the village to gawk at them. Women came, too, dressed in indigo tunics they'd decorated with silver beads, coins, and shells. The sun gleamed off their silver headdresses.

Tanit spoke to them in Thai, and Caitlyn could

tell that most of them understood him even though their own language was closer to Burmese. They smiled at Carlos and Caitlyn, eager to have tourists who might buy their embroidered handwork or silver jewelry. She smiled back, inwardly wincing at some of the women's teeth. They enjoyed chewing on betel nut leaves that had the unfortunate effect of staining their teeth reddish-black.

She listened carefully as they spoke to each other, so she could recall their language. She'd spent two weeks here several years ago and had become fluent at that time. She smiled when two women discussed how ugly her khaki fedora was. Children commented on the strange color of her hair and eyes, while a few men speculated that she'd been here before.

As the small crowd escorted them to the center of the village, Caitlyn spotted Ajay. He'd grown more frail and had lost more teeth, but his eyes were still sharp.

He approached her, smiling. "Pretty American lady," he said in their Burmese dialect. "You have returned."

She pressed her hands together and spoke in English. "How do you do? I'm Caitlyn." She bowed, and when her mouth was close to his ear, she whispered in his language, "Can I see you alone?"

His eyes widened. "Yes, of course." He motioned toward the silversmith shop.

"Carlos," she called to him, where he was standing close to Tanit. "I'm going to look at their handcrafts."

He nodded, and she hurried toward the silversmith shop with Ajay. "You remember me, then?" she said quietly in his language.

"Yes." His eyes twinkled as he opened the door for her. "You came before and sat in our tower with a radio so you could spy on the Burmese."

She winced. "'Spy' is such a strong word. I was conducting research on a possible incursion across the border."

He chuckled. "My people had to flee from Burma a hundred years ago. I was happy to help you spy on them."

She shrugged with a sheepish smile. "Okay, I was spying. How have you been, Ajay?"

"My people are happy. But very poor." He motioned toward the table filled with silver jewelry.

She could take a hint. She examined the beautiful items. "You nearly bankrupted me the last time I was here."

"Are you here to spy again?"

"No. I don't work for the government anymore. I'm helping the man who came with me. Carlos Panterra. He's searching for . . . something."

Ajay nodded with a wise look. "Aren't we all?"

"It's a little . . . unusual, and I'm not sure we can trust the guide who is with us. So I've been pretending not to understand any language other than English."

Ajay frowned. "You are deceiving him?"

"Well, yes. I'm worried he might have bad intentions toward Carlos."

"Ah." Ajay nodded. "So you are spying on him."

Again with the spying. "When we join the others, I'll be pretending not to understand anything. Our guide doesn't know that I've been here before, so I'll also be pretending not to know you."

"Hmm." Ajay crossed his arms, scowling.

"I'm just doing it to protect Carlos." She bit her bottom lip. "There's one more thing I should tell you. Carlos and I are pretending to be married."

Ajay's brows shot up. "Pretending?"

She felt her face grow warm. "It's . . . complicated."

"Of course it is. When you start deceiving people, it always gets complicated." He shook a finger at her. "It's like I always tell the children, once you start lying, it always comes back to bite you in the butt."

She grinned. "Don't worry. We'll be all right."

"We shall see."

She glanced up from the jewelry and wondered if she should be concerned about the mischievous gleam in his eyes. Ajay was a wily chieftain. No one in the village got away with anything he didn't know about.

Among the jewelry and headdresses, she spotted two engraved silver cats, each about eight inches long. They'd make good presents for the two werepanther boys. "Are these tigers or panthers?"

"Once you pay for them, they are whatever you want them to be."

She removed a handful of baht from the zippered pocket of her khaki pants and left it on the table. "Is that enough?"

"I believe they cost more when the buyer has secrets."

She narrowed her eyes at him. "Are you threatening to tell on me?"

He laughed and slapped a hand against his thigh. "No, pretty spy lady. I'm just playing with you."

She grinned at him. "You are such a rascal, Ajay."

His eyes glittered. "You have no idea."

She picked up one of the silver panthers she'd just bought. "Have you seen any panthers around here?" When he pointed to the other one on the table, she groaned. "I mean real panthers. In the jungle."

He shrugged. "Not in several years. You're not hunting them, are you?"

"We're searching for . . . this will sound strange."

He chuckled. "Everything from you is strange, pretty lady."

"Have you ever heard of people who can change into animals?"

His eyes widened. "You are looking for such a people?"

"Yes." She dropped her backpack on the earthen floor and stuffed the two silver panthers inside. "What do you think?"

"I think . . . I am glad to have you back. You make life very interesting."

"And?"

He smiled. "We must celebrate your return with a feast. You will be our guests tonight."

"Thank you." Caitlyn followed him from the shop, wondering what the clever Ajay was up to.

By that evening Carlos was growing increasingly frustrated and impatient. He'd asked Tanit to question the villagers about any panther sightings in the area, but he wasn't getting any definitive answers. Some said there were tigers a few valleys to the north. Several men talked about seeing glowing golden eyes in the jungle at night. One guy insisted a giant cat had stolen his favorite pig two years earlier. A few women tried to sell him silk cloth embroidered with golden tigers and black panthers. Even Caitlyn added to his frustration by showing him two silver panthers she'd bought for Emiliano and Tiago.

Meanwhile, the village chieftain, Ajay, insisted they stay the night and join them for a feast at sundown. They gathered around the fire in the center of the village. He and Caitlyn sat cross-legged on woven mats of bamboo close to Ajay, who lounged regally in the one chair. The fire crackled, and smoke curled up into a cloudless sky of brilliant stars. Mosquitoes buzzed about. Caitlyn coated her arms and neck with more insect repellent, then passed him the tube.

The feast was delicious but dragged on forever. Some of the dishes were so hot, he and Caitlyn drank nearly a gallon of tea. At the end of the meal, a platter of exotic fruits was passed about the circle of villagers. As everyone enjoyed their fruit, Ajay droned on and on in a monotonous voice.

About five minutes into Ajay's speech, Carlos leaned close to Caitlyn and whispered, "I need to relieve myself."

"Me, too," she muttered under her breath. "But we have to wait for him to finish."

After another five minutes Ajay finished, and the villagers applauded and shouted praise.

Caitlyn rose to her feet, pressed her hands together and murmured, "Restroom?"

Tanit translated into Thai, and Ajay pointed toward an outhouse far across the village by the rice field.

"I'll take you." Carlos jumped to his feet and escorted her across the village.

"I tried the outhouse this afternoon," she muttered. "It scares me more than the jungle."

"Then let's find some bushes." He led her toward the line of trees in the distance. "What was the speech that Ajay was giving?"

"He was reciting the list of his ancestors by memory. The Akha can go back many generations."

"Interesting," Carlos grumbled, "but we haven't learned a damned thing about any panthers in the area."

"You have to give it time. These are a proud and independent people. They're not going to tell you everything right off the bat. Besides, it's a good thing that they want us to hang around for a while. If there are any big cats nearby, they'll be drawn to me." She cast a wary eye at the jungle. "I hope they don't show up while I'm using the bathroom."

Carlos walked past a few trees, then found a large tree with a clump of bushes around it. "This looks like a good spot. You go first."

She glanced up at the tree. "What if there's something up there and it drops down on me?"

He peered up at the tree. "I don't see anything."

"There could be a snake or a spider."

"Then you'd probably pee in your pants."

"It's not funny," she hissed. "I can't do this unless I know it's safe."

He groaned. "Okay. I'll check the tree."

"How?"

"Just don't freak out and scream, okay? I don't want to draw attention." He concentrated, and a shimmer began on his hands, then ran up his arms. Claws sprang from his fingertips, then black fur sprouted from his skin. His hands turned into paws and his arms shifted into the front legs of a panther.

Caitlyn gasped.

"Shh," he warned her, then leaped onto the tree. His claws dug into the bark, and he climbed to the first set of branches. Some birds scattered, flying away.

He searched the tree while Caitlyn stood below, gawking at him. He jumped down, landing lightly on his feet while his arms returned to normal. "There's nothing there."

She didn't answer. She was looking away from him with a worried expression.

"What's wrong now?" he asked.

"I thought I heard something." She pointed to a clump of bushes next to a big boulder. "Over there."

"I'll check it out. You do your business." He ran toward the bushes, drawing a knife from his belt.

Nothing was there. He breathed deeply, but couldn't make out the scent of an animal. It smelled more like roasted chicken and bananas, which meant the person who had hidden here had also attended the feast. *Merda.* Someone other than Caitlyn might have seen him partially shift.

He went ahead and relieved himself, then returned to Caitlyn.

She was refastening her khaki trousers. "All done." She wedged her knife back into her belt.

"Me, too."

"Did you find anything behind those bushes?"

"No." He escorted her back to the campfire. He looked amongst the villagers but couldn't tell if anyone was missing.

A few of the adults grabbed him and Caitlyn by the arms and gently directed them to sit on silk pillows in front of Ajay.

"What's going on?" Carlos whispered.

"I don't know." Caitlyn tilted her head to listen as Ajay talked. Suddenly, her eyes widened and she grew pale.

Carlos glanced around but couldn't see anything dangerous. Ajay was grinning, his eyes twinkling with mirth. Meanwhile, Caitlyn was sitting stiffly with her hands clutched together. Her knuckles were white with tension, though she was carefully keeping her face blank.

Then a group of Akha women whisked her off to a house.

He stood to follow, but some men grabbed him and insisted he and Tanit drink with them. It was some kind of liquor, strong enough to peel varnish off furniture.

With his head reeling, Carlos stumbled with the men as they escorted him to a house on stilts. Tanit struggled to climb the ladder, falling off twice before he managed to make it inside. Meanwhile, the men insisted Carlos put on a baggy pair of blue pants. Since he didn't know how to argue with them, he complied. There was no matching shirt, just a pair of sandals.

"Interesting tattoo." Tanit motioned to the inked panther around his neck, then hiccuped.

"Do you know what's going on?" Carlos asked him.

"Celebration for you and—" Tanit collapsed on the floor.

"Great." Carlos grabbed his knives and revolver as the village men escorted him out. They led him to another house and urged him to climb the ladder.

He entered a small room, dimly lit with a lantern in the far corner. Fragrant flowers were strewn all over the floor. The light gleamed off the silver headdress of a woman sitting on a pallet. He stiffened. Were the villagers offering him one of their women for the night?

He retreated a step. "I'm terribly sorry, but—"

"Carlos, it's me." Caitlyn pulled the headdress off and set it on the floor next to the pallet.

"Oh, thank God." He set his weapons on the floor. "Are you all right?"

"Yes. They dunked me in a vat of cold water, then stuck me in this robe."

"They made me change, too." He glanced about the tiny house. The pallet was narrow. Too narrow. "Maybe I should bunk down with some of the village guys tonight."

"They expect you to stay here."

"It's kinda small."

"It's . . ." She hugged her knees to her chest. "I'm afraid this is their equivalent of a honeymoon suite."

He blinked. "Oh, I guess you told Ajay we were pretending to be married."

"Yes." She sighed. "That wily old buzzard. He told me that telling lies would come back to bite me in the butt."

Carlos felt a chill skitter down his bare back. "What are you saying?"

She gave him a worried look. "I don't know how to say this, but . . . Ajay married us."

Chapter Twenty

*C*aitlyn winced at the shocked look on Carlos's face. "Don't worry about—"

"He *what*?" Carlos interrupted her.

"He . . . blessed our marriage, but—"

"Didn't you tell him it was *pretend*?"

"Shh, not so loud." She scurried to the opening and pulled the draperies shut that served as a door. "We're supposed to be happily married."

"We're not supposed to be married at all. Why didn't you stop him?"

"It would have blown our cover. I'm not supposed to understand their language." She sighed. "That rascally Ajay knew I wouldn't be able to stop him. He's always been a tricky—"

"Wait." Carlos held up a hand. "Caitlyn, there are times when you let your cover drop. You know, emergencies? This was one of them. You shouldn't have let it happen."

Ouch. "Marrying me is that awful?"

"You know I can't marry you for real."

She planted her hands on her hips. "Well, I guess it's your lucky day, 'cause I don't think it's legally binding."

"That's a relief."

"Oh yeah." She glared at him. "I'm deliriously happy."

He crossed his arms on his chest and scowled back.

She tried not to notice how his biceps bulged and how wide and strong his chest was. Or how warm and sexy his bare, tanned skin looked. The villagers had dressed them in matching outfits. His blue baggy pants were the same color as her blue silk robe. The tattoo around his neck drew her attention. The black and red panther seemed to be watching her. Prowling toward her.

He motioned to the wall behind her. "There's a silver cross hanging there."

"Some of the Akha tribes have converted to Christianity." She glanced at the cross. "Beautiful workmanship, don't you think?"

"Please don't tell me Ajay is a priest."

"I . . . don't think so." She didn't want to admit that the tribe might see him as their spiritual leader.

Carlos watched her closely. "What exactly did he say?"

"You don't want to know." She pulled on some ropes that held the mosquito netting festooned above the pallet. The netting tumbled down, surrounding the white cotton pallet with a gauzy white film.

"I do," he said quietly.

She slipped under the netting and settled on the pallet. "He said we were kindred souls set on the earth to love and protect each other." She glanced at Carlos.

He was still by the entrance, his stance rigid and tense. "I will protect you. With my life."

That was nice, but he'd left out the part about loving her. She hugged her knees to her chest. "He asked God to bless our union and prayed that we would have many children."

When Carlos remained silent, she quickly added, "It doesn't matter. There was no marriage license. The marriage would not be recognized in the States."

Carlos's eyes gleamed amber in the dark. "Ajay is the leader of his people, and the words were spoken out loud, calling upon God as a witness. Where I come from, that would be enough."

Her heart lurched. Did Carlos actually consider them married? A few seconds of elation quickly morphed into wounded pride, for it was clear that he didn't want to be her husband. Her most dreaded fear crept back to crush her self-confidence. *Not good enough.*

Outside, someone started banging a drum. Then another joined in, and another. Villagers began chanting. She groaned and rested her forehead on her knees.

Carlos sat on the wood-planked floor. "What are they saying?"

"They're . . . wishing you great prowess in the sack."

He grunted.

The drums grew louder and the pace quickened. She sighed. It would have been great to make love to that urgent, pounding beat.

Carlos shifted uneasily on the floor. "How long are they going to do that?"

"I'm afraid they'll keep it up until we . . ." Oh, what the heck. At this point a little more embarrassment hardly mattered. "I know what to do."

"What?"

"Showtime." She stretched out on the pallet and took a deep breath to mentally prepare herself.

"What are you doing?" Carlos scooted a little closer.

"Nothing to see here. Return to your homes," she mimicked an officer at a crime scene.

Carlos snorted, but edged a bit closer to the netting.

She smoothed her hands down the blue silk robe she was wearing and moaned. She grazed her fingertips over the curves of her hips and up her rib cage to her breasts.

"Aah," she gasped as she palmed her own breasts. She massaged them gently and groaned even louder.

She rolled onto her stomach and then onto her back once again. "Yes, yes!" She banged her fists on the pallet. "Oh Carlos!"

She heard a hissing sound as he drew in a sharp breath. She planted her feet on the pallet and squeezed her knees together. "Oh my God!" She panted loudly and rapidly. "Yes, yes!" She let out a long scream.

In the distance she heard the villagers cheer.

She lifted her arms in the air. "A perfect ten. She scores!" With a wry grin, she turned to Carlos. "Okay, your turn."

He stiffened. "You're kidding."

"It's your honeymoon. Enjoy it."

"Fine." He let out a shout.

The villagers were quiet. Birds chirped in the distance.

Caitlyn snickered.

"They cheered for you," he mumbled.

"That was a measly little shout," she explained. "I've heard men get more excited than that over a pizza."

He gritted his teeth. "They're doubting my sexual prowess?"

She giggled. "I don't think they have any doubts."

"To hell with that." He tilted his head back and let out a long, guttural roar, followed by some victorious hoots.

The villagers cheered.

"Wow. I'm impressed." *Not.* She was starting to feel angry over being rejected once again. This was not her idea of a wedding night.

"I'm not good at faking an orgasm. I never had to before." He gave her a pointed look. "Unlike some people."

"Ooh, the cat has claws. Maybe I just never cared enough—" She stopped herself. This was getting too personal. And too damned frustrating.

"How long have you been faking it?" he asked quietly.

"Who said I was? I'll have you know that I

have an extremely high success rate, especially when I'm doing it with myself. Would you like to watch?"

He ignored her question. "Have you been with other men?"

"Of course. Legions. I set the world record three years in a row."

He scoffed. "I don't believe you."

She shrugged. "I have been known to lie."

"Have you ever been in love?"

I'm in love now, you moron. She gritted her teeth. "What do you care?"

He moved next to the netting. "Have you ever been in love?"

She groaned. "I love to experience new things. I love to travel, learn new languages and cultures, try new food and dances. But when it comes to my heart, that's where I stop being adventurous."

"Why? Are you afraid of being hurt?"

"I suppose. When I was young, I loved my sister more than anything, then I lost her. Then I loved Mr. Foofikins, and I lost him. I think that's why I kept so many treasures. I didn't have to worry about them leaving me."

Carlos nodded. "I understand. I lost everyone I loved."

You wouldn't lose me. She wanted to tell him she loved him, but how could she? He would just reject her again.

"Who is Mr. Foofikins?" he asked.

"My cat. He was beautiful. Solid black with gold eyes. He had feline leukemia, so it was doomed from the start." Tears crowded her eyes. "Sorta like our relationship."

"I am sorry."

There was a pause. Caitlyn blinked her eyes, determined not to cry.

"Have you had any lovers?" he asked quietly.

She sighed. "I don't know if you could call him a lover. He claimed to love me, but . . . I never really . . . I didn't love him. I think I was just lonely."

"Is that when you learned to fake orgasms?"

She snorted. "You seem to be obsessed with that."

"Your performance was . . . extraordinary."

"Gee, thanks. I'll have it put on my tombstone."

"I can't help but wonder how it compares to the real thing."

She glanced at him. His features were blurred on the other side of the white gauze netting, but she could see his gleaming amber eyes focused on her. A wave of longing swept over her. She would never have to fake it with Carlos. Her heart would be fully engaged up to the moment he broke it.

"In fact," he murmured, "I'm extremely curious to see how you react to the real thing."

"Curiosity killed the cat," she whispered.

"I'll risk it." He lifted the edge of the netting and slipped underneath to join her on the pallet.

Her skin tingled with anticipation, but her heart pounded with fear. "Carlos—"

"Shh." He placed a hand on her cheek. "I've never wanted a woman as much as I want you." He kissed her brow, then her nose.

Tears filled her eyes as she placed her hands on his face. She'd pursued him from the beginning, but she was not going to play the part of a pathetic, needy wimp. If she'd learned anything from all this, it was that she needed to be strong. "Carlos, if you're not going to stay with me, then don't do this."

His eyes searched hers.

It was strange, but she'd never felt closer to him than now, when she was rejecting him.

He brushed her hair back from her brow. "I want to give you pleasure."

"Why? Because I've had to fake it in the past? I won't do this because you pity me."

He sat back. "Catalina, I have many feelings for you, but never pity."

She waited to see if he'd elaborate on all those feelings, but he remained quiet. A tear rolled down her cheek.

He bowed his head. "I have pity, but for myself, that I have found the most beautiful woman in the world, and I cannot have her."

"Oh, Carlos." She reached for him.

He lay down beside her as he gathered her into his arms. She nestled her face on his shoulder, and he smoothed away the tears on her cheek.

He was warm and sweet, and she knew she loved him with all her heart. With a sigh, she closed her eyes and let herself drift into sleep.

Carlos jerked awake when sunlight suddenly burst into their room. A village woman had pulled apart the draperies to let the morning sunshine in. She saw him and Caitlyn still on the pallet and quickly averted her eyes. Another woman placed a tray of food on the floor, then the two women hurried away.

He walked to the opening to look outside. A

heavy mist hung low over the nearby mountains. He spotted his and Caitlyn's backpacks at the base of the ladder, so he climbed down to fetch them.

Ajay approached him with another villager, both grinning at him.

"I am Arnush," the villager introduced himself. "I know little English. Ajay like to wish you much happiness in your marriage."

Carlos gave Ajay a wry look. He considered questioning the man's audacity at marrying him and Caitlyn, but he couldn't. She'd felt so right in his arms all night. "You can tell your leader that I'm most grateful."

Arnush passed on the message, then said, "Ajay like to see you in workshop after you eat."

"Very well." Carlos climbed back into the house. He changed into his own clothes, then awakened Caitlyn. His wife. His beautiful wife.

Once he'd recovered from the initial shock, he no longer felt angry with her. He was angry at himself because he didn't know what to do. Part of him—an overwhelming part—wanted the marriage. He was in love with her. He ached for her. But there was still a small guilt-ridden part of him that reminded him he had to do what was right. He had to protect his species.

While she was dressing, he went to relieve himself. The village women had brought them a breakfast of guava, bananas, rice, and hot tea. After eating, they proceeded to the workshop.

Ajay and Arnush were there, drinking tea. Ajay smiled and said something to Caitlyn.

She responded, pressing her hands together and inclining her head.

Carlos mimicked her act, although he had no idea what was being said. "Arnush, would you mind finding our guide, Tanit?"

"Yes, I find him." Arnush hurried from the shop.

Ajay motioned for them to sit on bamboo mats next to him. He spoke, then Caitlyn translated.

"He says I could be right in thinking our guide is not trustworthy." Caitlyn's brow furrowed with worry. "When we went into the jungle last night to relieve ourselves, Tanit also left the campfire. Ajay says he went in the same direction we did."

Carlos winced. "Then Tanit might have seen me shift."

Caitlyn nodded. "I'm afraid so."

He recalled the way Tanit had eyed his tattoo. Caitlyn had warned him about Pat's telephone conversation. If Tanit learned anything about a cat shifter, he was to call Pat so they could alert the Master, whoever that was.

"I find him," Arnush announced as entered the shop with Tanit.

The guide gave them a sheepish smile. "I'm very sorry. I overslept. That drink last night knocked me out."

"That's all right." Carlos motioned for Tanit to join them. "I want to ask Ajay if anyone in his tribe has seen panthers in the area."

"Of course." Tanit sat on a bamboo mat and posed the question to Ajay in Thai.

Ajay nodded, then responded in the same language.

Tanit grew pale as he listened. Carlos glanced at Caitlyn, knowing she could also understand what

Ajay said. Her face was carefully blank, but her hands were clenched together.

"Ajay has not seen a panther for several months," Tanit reported. "But he says there is a creature to the north of here, a man-eating creature."

"How does he know it eats men?" Carlos asked.

"Because the men do not return," Tanit explained with a shaky voice. "There was a man from the village who went north, hunting for wild boar, but he never returned. A week later his cousin went looking for him, but he disappeared, too. Now, no one from the village will go north."

Ajay spoke some more, then Tanit translated. "There are rumors that the man-eating creature is a giant cat. Others say he is an evil creature of the night."

"We should check it out," Carlos said.

Tanit's eyes bulged. "We can't go into the jungle, looking for man-eating cats."

Carlos frowned at him. "I thought you understood what this mission was about."

"Yes, but—" Tanit wiped beads of sweat from his brow. "What if they're not cat shifters? What if they're not human at all, but like to *eat* humans?"

"Maybe we should spend a few days here," Caitlyn suggested. "The cats might come to us."

Ajay spoke some more.

Tanit jumped to his feet. "This is too dangerous. I—I can't do this." He ran from the workshop.

Ajay snorted and said something in the Akha language.

"He says our guide is too fearful," Caitlyn translated. "That he's hiding something."

Ajay talked some more while she listened. Her eyes widened and she gulped a few times.

"What did he say?" Carlos asked.

"There's a legend in these hills," she began. "All the tribes whisper the tale in the dark, but none have dared to report it to the government. Men have been disappearing for forty years. Some say it is the tigers or the panthers, but everyone agrees it is evil. The Yao say it is a supernatural creature who steals the breath of a man and leaves him as a soulless body to roam the night. They call it by its Chinese name, *chiang-shih*."

"What is that?" Carlos asked.

She gave him a worried look. "It's the Chinese equivalent of a vampire."

He sat back. "Are you serious?"

"The tribes haven't reported it because they don't think any authorities would believe them. And they probably wouldn't. No one thinks vampires are real."

Carlos nodded. "But we know better. We should check it out."

She winced. "I was afraid you'd say that. This means a trek through the jungle, doesn't it?"

"You don't have to go. You can stay here while I go with Tanit."

She grimaced. "I don't trust him. I'm coming with you."

Carlos stood and offered a hand to help her up. "You're the bravest woman I've ever known."

She snorted. "Or the most foolish." She took a deep breath. "I'll just think of it as an adventure. I love adventure. That's my story, and I'm sticking to it."

Ajay stood and spoke again. He raised his hands in the air, then rested a hand on each of their shoulders.

"He's praying for God to protect us," she whispered.

Carlos nodded. "We're going to need it."

Chapter Twenty-one

*C*arlos glanced up at the sun. If the rumor was true and a vampire lurked about these hills, he needed to find it before sundown. He looked at his watch. Almost three in the afternoon. They'd been hiking along this path, headed north, for four hours. He'd kept the pace slow for Caitlyn's sake, but she looked exhausted.

That was actually an improvement. She'd spent the first two hours looking terrified. The first time he stopped to let a cobra slither across the path, she cowered behind him with her hands clenched in his T-shirt.

They'd left the village about eleven in the morning, getting a late start after Tanit abruptly announced he was going with them. He had no backpack or gear, so it took some time for the villagers to prepare one for him. Ajay provided them with food and rolled bamboo mats to sleep on.

Arnush had pulled Carlos aside to warn him that their guide had changed his mind about going with them after making a cell phone call. But it was clear that Tanit didn't want to be with them. Every time they saw a snake or scorpion, he begged them to return to the village.

Carlos wondered if Pat had ordered Tanit to go with them. Caitlyn had been right to suspect them both.

A snap of a twig in the distance pricked Carlos's extra sensitive hearing. Sounds in the jungle were common, what with all the animals that lived there, but these sounds kept recurring. For the past thirty minutes something had been following them. In the last ten minutes he'd heard the sound more often. Whatever was following them had grown in number. He inhaled deeply to try to catch their scent, but they were staying downwind.

The path took them downhill, and he quickened their pace. Down in the valley, they discovered a creek dissecting a green pasture. Carlos leaned over to cup some water and splash it on his face. He straightened and looked around. Long grass was dotted with clumps of green ferns. On the other side of the valley the trail cut a jagged path straight uphill.

"Oh God." Caitlyn grimaced. "I need a break before we do that." She dropped her backpack on the ground and pulled a water bottle from an outside pocket.

Carlos swiveled, scanning the tree line.

Tanit dumped his backpack on the ground. "We'd better head back to the village, or we'll be stuck out here for the night."

Caitlyn sighed. "I don't think there are any cats in the area. They would have come to me by now."

"I believe they have." Carlos pointed to the tree line, where two tigers emerged. "We have company."

"Man-eaters!" Tanit squealed, and pulled the knife from his belt.

Carlos moved in front of Caitlyn and drew his pistol.

"No!" She stepped away. "Don't shoot."

Carlos lowered his weapon. "If one of them charges, I'm shooting."

"Don't hurt them." She faced the tigers, frowning with concentration.

Carlos had never seen such huge tigers. They seemed content to keep a distance, sitting on their haunches and studying them with golden eyes. They were still downwind, so he couldn't get a good sniff.

"They're warning us of danger," Caitlyn whispered.

"Of course we're in danger," Tanit snapped. "They're going to eat us!"

"You can communicate with them?" Carlos asked her.

"Sorta." She remained focused on them. "It's hard to explain. I don't get actual words, but the ideas form in my head. They clearly believe we're in danger. And they want us to know that they're not man-eaters."

Tanit snorted. "You're crazy. You can't talk to a tiger."

"Can you ask them if they know about any panthers in the area?" Carlos asked.

Caitlyn was silent a moment, then answered. "They say this is their territory. The panthers are south of the Akha village."

Carlos felt a surge of hope. He could be close to finding more of his kind. If he could discover that his species wasn't endangered after all, he might be able to stay with Caitlyn. They could have a normal mortal marriage with mortal children. She'd be safe as long as he didn't bite her while in panther form.

But before he went hunting for were-panthers, he needed to make sure the hill tribes were free from the curse of a local vampire. "Do the tigers know anything about a vampire?"

Tanit flinched, then swatted at a mosquito to try to cover up his reaction.

Caitlyn was quiet once more as she communicated with the giant cats.

Tanit shifted nervously from one foot to another. "We need to go back. We shouldn't be out here at night."

Carlos turned to him. "What do you know that you're not telling us?"

"Nothing." He shook his head nervously. "Anyone could tell you that you don't spend the night in the jungle."

"The tigers say there is an evil cave to the north, but we should stay away from it." Caitlyn shuddered. "Humans go in, but they never come out."

"We can't do it," Tanit hissed. "We can't go!"

Carlos glanced at the sun. "We'll be fine as long as we get there before sundown."

"I refuse to go!" Tanit yelled.

Carlos scowled at him. "Then go back to the village. I'm sure the tigers would love to escort you."

Tanit turned pale.

"If there's been a vampire in these hills for forty years, terrorizing the people and killing them, then I'm getting rid of him," Carlos announced. "It'll be easy enough to do if we find him before sundown."

"If," Caitlyn whispered. She took a deep breath, then shouldered her backpack. "We'd better get going, then."

Carlos's heart expanded in his chest. She was the bravest woman he'd ever met. She cowered in fear every time they saw a snake but still pressed forward.

She raised a hand in farewell to the tigers. "They say this is as far as they will go. We'll know we're coming close to the cave when we see the prayers."

"Prayers?" Carlos asked as the two tigers slipped back into the jungle.

She shrugged. "I'm not sure what they meant."

Carlos jumped over the narrow creek, then helped Caitlyn over. "You lead the way," he told Tanit. He wasn't turning his back on their guide.

With a scowl, Tanit put on his backpack and trudged up the mountain path.

Caitlyn groaned as they headed uphill once again. Almost two hours had passed since she'd communicated with the tigers. She'd sensed a true concern and friendliness from the giant cats that didn't seem to jibe with their supposed wildness.

She wished she could discuss it with Carlos, but didn't feel comfortable talking about cat shifters in front of Tanit.

They'd figured out what the tigers meant about prayers. At the top of the mountain, they'd spotted a big boulder with a symbol painted on it. With a shudder, Tanit had explained it was a prayer for protection.

As they wound downhill, they noticed several other boulders with the same symbol. Now, as they trudged uphill again, Caitlyn winced with each step. Her legs felt like wet noodles, but with pain.

Finally, they neared the summit and ran into a vertical slab of rock fifteen feet high. The path fell off into a ravine to the left. To the right, the rock wall stretched as far as she could see.

"Looks like a dead end," she muttered.

"It is." Tanit pointed to the symbol painted on the rock. "It means death."

"It might refer to the vampire since he's dead during the day," Carlos said impatiently. "The cave should be close by. Let's hurry before the sun goes down."

Tanit moved slowly to the right on a narrow path in front of the rock wall.

"Faster," Carlos ordered.

Caitlyn glanced at the sun. It was nearing the horizon in the distance.

The path suddenly widened, and the black hole of a cave gaped in the rock wall. Symbols had been painted in red on either side of the cave opening.

"We can't go in," Tanit whispered. He lowered

his backpack to the ground. "The symbols are a warning. Whoever enters will die."

"We'll be fine as long as the sun is still up." Carlos dropped his backpack and pulled out a flashlight. "So who wants to be first to go inside the dark, scary cave?"

Caitlyn snorted, then dropped her backpack so she could remove her flashlight. Suddenly, she was grabbed from behind and jerked into an elbow lock. She gasped when Tanit pressed a knife to her throat.

In a flash Carlos dropped his flashlight and pulled his revolver.

Tanit stiffened, his arm tightening around her neck. "How did you move so fast?"

"I'm an excellent shot," Carlos growled. "I can kill you without harming a hair on Caitlyn's head. Let her go."

"No." Tanit stepped back, dragging her with him. "You can't go inside. It's forbidden."

Caitlyn's mind raced as she tried to remember her martial-arts training. Could she double over and flip Tanit onto his back? No, she couldn't lean forward without slitting her own throat. Maybe backward?

She reared back, throwing all her weight against Tanit. He stumbled back, and Carlos leaped forward, wrenching the knife from Tanit's hand. Caitlyn scrambled out of their way. By the time she regained her footing, Carlos had Tanit pinned to the ground with the knife at his throat.

"Are you all right?" Carlos glanced at her. When she nodded, he said, "Get my gun. I dropped it."

She ran to pick up his pistol.

"Please," Tanit breathed. "I don't want to die."

"Talk," Carlos growled. "Whose orders are you following?"

Tanit gulped. "If I disobey, they'll kill me."

"Disobey whom?" Caitlyn ventured closer. "The Master?"

Tanit's eyes bulged. "How do you know about him? It is forbidden to speak of him except to the Guardians."

"Is the professor a Guardian?" Carlos asked.

Tanit nodded. "The Master will be very angry if we defile the temple."

"What temple?" Carlos asked.

Tanit looked toward the cave. "It's a Temple of Death. Only the Master is allowed inside." He trembled with fear. "Master Han is a great and powerful *chiang-shih*. He has killed thousands. We will die if we go inside. Please. We must—"

"Look at me," Carlos interrupted. "Your master cannot harm us during the day. We'll stake him, and then you'll be free."

Tanit's eyes filled with tears. "It's too late. I saw you shift into a cat, and I told the professor. He ordered me to stay with you until the Guardians come for you."

Caitlyn exchanged a worried look with Carlos. Why would a vampire want a were-panther?

Carlos stood and dragged Tanit to his feet. "It doesn't matter. By the time the Guardians find me, your master will already be dead. The game will be over."

Tanit whimpered. "It is impossible to kill Master Han. He can live forever."

"We shall see." Carlos shoved him toward the

mouth of the cave. He skidded to a stop in the pebbles.

Carlos wedged Tanit's knife under his belt. Caitlyn handed him the gun, and he holstered it. He picked up the flashlight and shouldered his backpack.

She did the same while her heart raced. She didn't want to admit it, but she was as scared as Tanit.

"Ready?" Carlos asked her.

She glanced at the sun. It was low enough to paint the sky pink and gold. "We'd better hurry." *And get this over with.*

Carlos grabbed Tanit by the arm and escorted him inside the cave.

Caitlyn followed. The setting sun shone inside for a short distance. The interior was a large room, wide and deep. Far in the distance, her light picked out a narrow opening. This room might be the first of many.

"What's all this?" Carlos shone his flashlight overhead. Ropes crisscrossed the ceiling over them, and yellow strips of paper dangled from the ropes.

"Those are prayers," Tanit whispered. "Buddhist prayers to keep the evil in this cave from escaping."

Caitlyn looked around the empty cave. "Who left them?"

"Him." Carlos's flashlight beam landed on a man's skeleton. His tattered orange robes identified him as a Buddhist monk.

Caitlyn drew in a sharp breath. A spear protruded from the monk's rib cage. "Someone murdered him."

"I told you!" Tanit cried. "Any who enter this cave will die!"

"Relax. It looks like it happened years ago." Carlos shone his flashlight at the narrow opening in the distance. "We need to go through there." He walked forward.

Caitlyn followed closely. Tanit hung back, his face deathly white.

Carlos took a step and froze when a metallic click echoed through the cave. "Booby-trapped."

"What?" Caitlyn didn't have time to think or react. The ground shuddered under her feet. Carlos grabbed her and leaped forward, much farther than any human could have. They landed, falling forward.

She glanced back and saw the ground caving in, taking Tanit with it. He screamed, then disappeared. A cloud of dust rose from a ditch that now divided the cave room into two halves.

"Tanit!" She crawled to the edge of the ditch and gasped. Iron spikes shot up from the bottom of the ditch, and Tanit was impaled on one of them.

She screamed and looked away.

Carlos grabbed her and held her tight. "It's all right."

"He's dead!"

Carlos grabbed her by the upper arms. "Caitlyn, we have to stay calm. The cave is booby-trapped. I think we made it past the first one because the Buddhist monk set it off."

She drew in a shaky breath. "We wouldn't have

survived the second one if you couldn't leap like a cat."

"There could be a third one. We have to be careful."

She started to shake. They could no longer get to the cave entrance. It was cut off by the ditch with spikes. And they couldn't move forward without setting off another death trap. "How can we move?"

"Don't worry, sweetheart." He squeezed her arms. "I'll get you through this." He took off his backpack and tossed it forward a few feet, angled to the right.

Nothing happened.

"Okay, that space is safe." Carlos stepped close to the backpack and picked it up. He held out his hand to Caitlyn.

She grabbed his hand and stepped close to him. Just a few feet more and they could slip through the narrow gap. "Do you think the next room is safe?"

"Probably so. That ditch was designed to take out an entire group."

She shuddered, and the beam from her flashlight quivered. Poor Tanit. They shouldn't have forced him to come inside.

Carlos tossed his backpack again, and it landed just to the right of the entrance. When nothing happened, he lunged toward it and picked it up. He reached for Caitlyn.

It was a jump for her. She leaped, but overcompensated and bounced into him hard. When she fell backward, he dropped his backpack to grab her.

Click.

A spear flew from a hidden crack in the cave wall, zooming straight toward them.

"Get down!" He pushed her down and jumped in front of her.

She fell on her rump and looked up just in time to see him jolt. The point of a spear shot through his stomach, coming to a stop inches from her face.

She screamed. Carlos shuddered, his face pale, his eyes wide with shock. He collapsed to his knees.

She scrambled to her feet. The spear had impaled him from the back. "Oh God, no."

He crumbled onto his side.

"Carlos." She knelt beside him. She could see him before her but didn't want to believe it. He couldn't die. Not Carlos.

With shaking hands he grasped the spear that protruded from his stomach. "Not much time," he rasped. He gritted his teeth and attempted to break the shaft of the spear. He cried out in pain.

"Carlos, what are you doing?"

"Have to break off the point. Help me."

She stared at the blood rapidly coating his hands.

He fumbled for a knife at his belt. "Help me."

She pulled the knife free and sawed at the spear shaft.

"Let me try again." He gritted his teeth and snapped the shaft in two. "Pull it out of me. From the back."

"It'll make you bleed more."

"Pull it out!"

Tears ran down her cheeks as she grasped the shaft and gave it a hard yank. Carlos cried out.

"Don't die on me!" She yanked handfuls of T-shirts and underwear from her backpack and pressed them against the wounds on his back and stomach. "Don't you dare die on me."

"Don't be afraid," he whispered. "I'll be here for you."

Her tears splattered onto his T-shirt. "Carlos, don't leave me."

His eyes flickered shut. His body shuddered, then went still.

"Carlos?"

He lay there, still and pale.

Caitlyn let go of the clothes she'd pressed against him. She sat back and looked at her trembling hands covered with blood. His blood. He was gone.

"No!" She flung herself on top of him. "No, Carlos, no." This couldn't be true. She couldn't lose him. She clutched at him, willing him to come back.

The cave suddenly grew much darker and colder. She glanced at the entrance. It was dark outside. And she was all alone in the jungle, in the Temple of Death.

With a shudder, she realized the sun had gone down. She might not be alone after all.

Chapter Twenty-two

*C*aitlyn fumbled on the ground and located the flashlight she'd dropped earlier. The beam quivered in her shaking hand as she pointed it at the narrow opening.

Get a grip. But how could she when Carlos was dead? A sob racked her body. *Don't fall apart now. Think, think.* She needed to protect herself. Carlos would be angry if she hadn't learned her lessons well. He would be even more pissed if he'd died in vain protecting her. *He's not feeling anything. He's dead.*

She wiped at the tears streaming down her face, then realized her hands were still coated with Carlos's blood. She rubbed her hands on her khaki pants. She had to protect herself. She had to make him proud. She removed the gun from his holster. If anything came through that opening, she'd shoot and keep shooting.

The gun trembled in her hand, and she prayed for strength. She kept the flashlight aimed at the opening and waited. And waited.

She edged closer to Carlos 'cause somehow she felt safer when she was sitting next to him. His body was still warm. And solid. Tears slid down her face, but she didn't dare put down the flashlight or gun to wipe them.

It was going to be a long night. In the dark. How long would the batteries last in the flashlight? Carlos's was still on. She quickly set her flashlight and gun down, so she could grab his flashlight and turn it off. She might need a backup.

Still nothing from the narrow opening. Maybe the vampire was gone. Maybe she was safe. Relatively safe. There was still a ditch filled with iron spikes between her and the cave entrance.

If she couldn't go back, could she go forward? She eyed the narrow opening. Maybe there was an exit on the other side of the mountain? Or maybe there were more booby-traps. Or worse.

No, she wasn't going through that opening. It was too much like the silly girl in the movies who ventured up to the attic all alone. Or the basement. In her underwear.

She dug into her backpack and pulled out her cell phone. It was worth a shot. No signal. Not surprising when she was in a friggin' cave in the middle of the jungle.

"What do I do, Carlos?" she whispered.

She dropped her phone into the backpack and noted the silk scarves she'd bought for the three were-panther girls. She smiled, remembering how

Carlos had fussed about her shopping. More tears rolled down her face.

She smoothed her fingers along the silk. So soft and shiny. And amazingly strong. She fisted her hands in it and yanked. If she tied the three lengths together, she'd have a nice rope. She scanned the cave with her flashlight and studied the crisscrossed ropes where the monk had hung the yellow paper prayers. Maybe the prayers had worked. The vampire didn't seem to be using this cave anymore.

She tied the scarves together, then tied one end to the spear shaft. Hopefully, all her exercising with Carlos had helped her upper body strength and aim.

She propped the flashlight on top of her backpack so it would light up the prayer ropes. Then she threw the spear like a javelin, hoping to wedge it into the crisscrossed ropes. The first few tries failed, and she retrieved the spear by pulling on the scarves.

It was too lightweight, she decided. She reattached the end of the scarf with one of the silver panthers. This time when she threw the spear, it caught. She tugged hard on the scarves to make sure it was secure. She needed to swing across the ditch without falling in.

She anchored the end of the scarf on her side with Carlos's backpack. She would wait till morning before attempting to cross the ditch. No way was she venturing into the jungle in the dark.

She sat beside Carlos with the flashlight and gun within reach. A new wave of grief swept over her, and more tears fell. As the hours dragged by, it seemed like she'd fallen into a nightmare that would never end.

Carlos jolted as an electric bolt of energy jump-started his body. He opened his eyes to darkness.

Something behind him jerked, and he heard a gasp and a fumbling sound. A flashlight beam struck him in the face, and he turned his head.

Caitlyn screamed and scrambled away.

"Cait—" His throat was tight, so he cleared it. It rumbled deep in his throat like a growl.

"What— Who? What?" Her voice sounded panicked.

"Caitlyn." He sat up. His eyes adjusted quickly to the dark. "Dammit, woman, don't point that gun at me."

"You—You're dead. I saw you die."

"Put the gun down. I can explain." Or maybe not. He didn't have much time. Already he could feel the Surge building inside him.

"You were dead," she whispered.

"I know." He yanked his T-shirt over his head. "I hate it when that happens." He pulled off his hiking boots and socks.

"You're alive?" She set the gun down. "And stripping?"

He unbuckled his belt, yanked down the zipper, and pulled down his cargo pants, taking his underwear with it. "I don't have much time. The Surge is coming. It always comes right after—" He jolted as the first wave of new power shot through his system.

"Carlos?" She stepped toward him.

"Stay back." He gritted his teeth and clenched his fists. So much raw power. He wasn't sure he could control it. "I'll try not to hurt you."

"What?"

He cried out as the Surge took him over. Wave after wave struck his body with increasing force, pummeling him so that he writhed and twisted as the power grew and grew. He flipped over onto his hands and knees and arched his back. His body shimmered, then transformed. But that wasn't enough. No, now he would be a level four were-panther, larger than he was before. His bones crackled, lengthening and thickening. He thought his head would burst. He roared with the pain, and the sound echoed around the cave.

He rolled his massive shoulders back and looked at the huge paws supporting his black powerful body. His claws sprung out, more sharp and lethal than ever. His vision was sharper. Even in the dark he could make out the tiniest of spiders on the cave wall.

With a low rumbling growl, he turned his head toward Caitlyn. His woman. His wife.

She stepped back, her face pale. The flashlight trembled in her hand. "Ca-Carlos? Are you there?"

He lifted a paw, then advanced a step in her direction.

She stepped back. "N-Nice kitty?"

A red haze filled the cave. Something strange was happening to his eyes. His woman seemed to shimmer in a red glow. It made his blood boil, his heart pound. He had to take her. He stalked slowly toward her.

Her eyes widened and she looked about nervously. Suddenly, she ran to a length of silk and pulled it loose from where it was anchored by his backpack. She jammed her flashlight into her belt and took a running leap across the ditch.

He roared for fear she would fall to her death, but the silken rope carried her safely across. She scrambled to her feet and faced him. He growled deep in his throat. Did she think she could escape him?

He leapt across. She screamed, and he knocked her flat on her back. He straddled her trembling body. All it would take was one bite, and she would be his forever.

"Carlos, please," she whimpered.

He bared his teeth and snarled.

Tears filled her eyes. "Don't kill me."

Kill her? He didn't want to kill her. He wanted to possess her, mate with her, keep her forever. All he had to do was bite her.

And that might kill her.

He shook, trying to regain control. He couldn't bite her. He could never bite her. He loved her too much.

He fought the beast, panting over her as she trembled beneath him. His body shimmered, and with a gasp, he returned to human form.

He collapsed beside her, breathing hard.

She scooted back on her rump. Tears ran down her cheeks. "Carlos? Are you okay now?"

No, he wasn't. The Surge wasn't over yet, not until he found release. A flood of lust gripped him, and he rose onto all fours. Blood rushed to his groin, and he grew instantly hard. His eyes narrowed on his prey and he growled deep in his throat. She was still shimmering with a red glow.

He seized her by the ankle and dragged her toward him.

"Carlos, what are you doing?"

He moved over her and pinned her down by the shoulders. "I need sex."

"Your eyes are glowing." Her gaze drifted down his body and her eyes widened. "Oh my God." She struggled to get away from him, but he pushed her back down.

"Carlos, please. I—I'm too freaked out. I thought you were dead. Then I thought you were going to kill me."

He noticed for the first time how red and puffy her eyes were. She'd been crying. A lot.

He gritted his teeth, once again fighting for control. The beast inside him howled, wanting to possess her and take her by force if necessary, but the human part of him loved her. The red haze faded away.

He backed off her. He would still need release for the Surge to end. He slowly stood and turned his back to her. He glanced ruefully at his erection, then leaped across the ditch.

Behind him, Caitlyn gasped. There was no need to fear. With his newly added power and strength, he could easily jump a dozen feet. He strode toward the narrow opening.

"Carlos? Where are you going?" Her flashlight beam caught him standing naked at the narrow gap in the cave wall.

"Don't go anywhere. I'll be right back." He

glanced over his shoulder and gave her a wry look. "It won't take long."

Caitlyn sat in the dirt, breathing heavily, wondering what the hell had just happened. Was she dreaming this? Was she so desperate for Carlos to be alive that she'd dreamed all this? She pinched herself. *Ouch.*

She should have known. Her dreams were rarely this strange.

Carlos was alive. Her heart expanded, finally able to accept the truth. She didn't know how it could be true, but it was. Carlos was alive. And apparently, masturbating in the next room.

She jumped when he roared. It wasn't quite as loud as his panther roar, but it was still impressive. He was correct. It hadn't taken long.

She beamed her flashlight at the narrow opening and rose to her feet. "Carlos?"

He emerged from the opening, frowning.

She gulped. He was still naked. No longer hard, but still magnificent.

He glanced at her. "I want to show you something."

She snorted. "I've already seen it."

He gave her a wry smile, then grabbed his underwear and pants off the ground and put them on. "There's something really strange farther back in the cave."

"There's something strange right here. You just woke up from the dead."

"Yes." He buttoned the waistband of his khaki cargo pants. "I hope you're not disappointed."

"That's not funny, Carlos. I thought you were dead. It nearly killed me. It was awful."

"I didn't enjoy it much either." He rubbed a hand over his stomach.

"The wound is gone," she whispered. "How did you do that?"

He sat down to pull on his socks and hiking boots. "That rumor about cats is true. Were-panthers have nine lives."

Her mouth fell open. "You have nine lives?"

"Actually, only five now." He tied the laces.

"What? You've died before?"

"Yes. Unfortunately, I'm getting really good at kicking the bucket." He picked up his T-shirt and grimaced at the blood. "Still hurts like hell."

She tightened her grip on the flashlight. "You should have told me. You scared the hell out of me."

"I'm sorry. I wasn't expecting to die." He walked over to his backpack and pulled out a fresh T-shirt. "It's not something I ever plan on doing. And I don't like to talk about it. It feels like a giant failure."

Her anger wilted away. "You didn't fail. You saved my life."

He glanced at her and smiled. "That's true. But I always thought a real hero should manage to save the princess without getting himself killed."

She smiled at him. "You're still here. That's what counts."

He pulled on the T-shirt, then motioned to her rope made of scarves. "You made that?"

"Yes. I was planning to swing across in the

morning, then hike back to the village. I thought the tigers might help protect me."

Carlos regarded her with a look of amazement. "You didn't need me. You would have survived without me."

"That's all it was. Survival." Tears blurred her vision. "I thought my heart had died with you."

"Catalina." He jumped across the ditch and pulled her into his arms.

She wrapped her arms around him and held on tight. Her flashlight lit up the ceiling.

"Don't cry." He kissed her brow and wiped her cheeks. "We're alive, and we have each other."

She rested her head on his chest and listened to the steady beat of his heart. Carlos was alive.

"Come now. I want to look at the rest of the cave."

He swung her up into his arms.

"What are you—" She gasped when he leaped across the ditch and landed neatly on the other side. She squirmed out of his arms. "Would you stop scaring the hell out of me?"

He grinned. "I have super strength and agility. I'm at level four now."

"Great. I'm so glad dying came with a bonus."

He chuckled, then grabbed his flashlight off the ground and turned it on. "Let's go."

She followed close behind him as he went through the narrow opening. It was a long, narrow passage filled with rock formations.

"Watch your step here." He maneuvered her to the left.

She shone her flashlight down to see what he was avoiding. It was a whitish puddle. "What is that? Rainwater with chalk or lime deposits?" She beamed her light at the ceiling to look for drips.

He snorted. "That was from me."

Her face grew warm. "Oh."

He led her forward. "There's another one here. Watch your step."

Her flashlight picked up a second puddle in the middle of the path. Her face blazed hotter. "Okay." She stepped over it.

"And there's a third one here." He aimed his flashlight at an even bigger puddle.

She gasped. "My God, you're an animal."

He laughed. "That may be true, *menina*, but this one actually is rainwater."

"Oh. Never mind." She edged around the puddle and followed him to another narrow opening.

"I peeked in here earlier. It looked . . . strange. I wanted to get a closer look." He led her through the opening.

Their flashlight beams wandered about. It was a huge cavern, almost as big as a soccer field.

"What I saw was down here." He shone his light on the floor, which was about four feet lower from the ledge where they stood.

Caitlyn gasped. There were dozens of man-sized clay figures, all lying down.

"I estimate about ten in each row." Carlos scanned the rows with his flashlight. "About twenty rows deep."

"Two hundred?" Caitlyn whispered. "It reminds me of the Terra-Cotta Warriors they found in China."

"Except these aren't warriors. They're all lying down with their hands crossed over their chest."

"Like a giant funeral." She shuddered. "Maybe that's why this is called the Temple of Death."

Carlos glanced at the nearby wall. "That looks like a torch." He unzipped a pocket on his pants, pulled out a cigarette lighter, and lit the torch.

"Here's another one." She shone her flashlight at it.

Soon Carlos had six torches lit, and she was better able to see. The ledge they stood on circled the large chamber, with torches every six feet or so. They lit more torches, then proceeded down some steps into the pit where the clay figures rested.

"They don't seem to have as much detail as the ones in China," Caitlyn observed. "They're very basic, and all alike."

"I wonder how long they've been here." Carlos knelt beside one and tapped on the clay. "That's odd."

"What?"

"It doesn't sound very hollow." He hit the clay figure on the chest with the end of his flashlight.

"You broke it!" Caitlyn's indignation quickly turned to horror as he pulled off pieces of clay.

Inside the clay figure was a human skeleton.

"Oh my God." She spun around, looking at all the clay figures. Two hundred dead people?

Carlos continued to pull chunks of clay off the skeleton. "It's hard to tell what the cause of death was, but if this is a vampire cave, then all these people were probably murdered."

She gulped. "The tigers said people go in and never come out."

"I doubt all these people wandered into the cave. I think they were already dead and encased in clay when they were brought here."

She nodded. "And the entrance was booby-trapped to keep anyone from finding them."

Carlos straightened and looked around the large chamber. "There's something very ritualistic about the way the bodies are arranged so neatly into rows."

"Like an army." She shuddered. "A dead army." She spotted another opening in the far wall. "Look."

Carlos took her hand, and they walked past row after row of dead people encased in clay. They ascended some stone steps, then entered another room. It was small, dark, and cold.

Caitlyn shivered as she scanned the room with her flashlight. Three stone slabs were raised like altars, and on top of each one lay a clay figure.

Carlos approached the first one. The clay had been shattered, as if someone had struck the figure's chest in a fit of rage. A skeleton's rib cage lay broken inside.

"Someone was angry," she murmured.

Carlos pulled off some clay shards. "Why would a dead corpse make a vampire angry?"

She leaned closer, aiming her flashlight. "There's material in there." She gasped. It was green, camouflaged material like they wore in the army. "He's a soldier."

Carlos broke off more clay around the figure's neck. He pulled out dog tags and held them under his flashlight. "United States Marine Corps."

She gulped. "There were some soldiers from the Vietnam War who were never found, but this is a ways from Vietnam."

"Not very far if a vampire teleports you here." Carlos strode to the second altar. "This one is destroyed, too."

"I don't understand." She followed him. "Once the vampire has fed off these people till they die, then what use are they to him? Why go to so much trouble with the dead bodies?"

"Maybe he was trying to preserve them."

"Preserve them for what? Some kind of reawakening?" Caitlyn eyed the shattered clay. "He certainly got angry when the preservation didn't work."

Carlos nodded. "I have a feeling all these bodies were part of an experiment. One that failed."

She walked to the third altar. "The clay on this one is intact."

"Not for long." He tapped his flashlight on the clay till it cracked, then peeled back a piece.

She gasped. There was a body inside. A full flesh and blood body. "Is he alive?"

"I don't see how he can be." Carlos ripped off larger chunks of clay.

She helped him, and soon they had the man's entire body free. He was dressed in army fatigues from the tip of his hat to the soles of his black army boots. He was a tall man with a strong, athletic build.

"He's a major." Carlos unbuttoned his shirt to locate his dog tags. "Russell Ryan Hankelburg."

She touched his shoulder. It was still firm. "How can he be dead for so many years, but not decay?"

Carlos studied the soldier. "I've seen this before. When a vampire transforms another into a vampire, he drains all the blood from his victim and puts him into a coma."

"This is a coma?"

Carlos nodded. "But the vampire usually turns the victim shortly afterward. This guy's been waiting since the Vietnam War."

Goose bumps prickled Caitlyn's arms. "Forty years? Why would a vampire put a man into a coma, then abandon him?"

"I don't know," Carlos said. "We need to call Angus. We'll have to hike back to the village so we can use our cell phones."

She nodded. A soldier in limbo for forty years. If he woke up, the world he knew would be completely changed. "Do you think we can save him?"

"The only way to save him is to turn him into a vampire."

Chapter Twenty-three

Carlos halted when he heard the snap of a twig in the distance. "We're not alone."

Caitlyn pivoted, looking about. "I don't see anything. Are the tigers back?"

"I believe so. We're in their territory now."

They'd started back to the Akha village shortly after sunrise. Carlos had left an electronic tracking device just inside the cave. He hoped the Vamps would be able to teleport straight to it. It would save a lot of time, and he didn't relish the thought of hiking across the jungle with them in the dark.

He and Caitlyn had crossed the stream into tiger territory ten minutes ago, and he'd been expecting the cats to show up. They were in a small clearing now on the hillside, about ten yards wide. The morning sun shone down on them, but in the distance, under the thick trees and underbrush, it looked dark. An easy place for a tiger to hide.

"They seemed to be truly concerned about us." She unscrewed a bottle of water and took a sip. "I thought they might be shifters."

"I wondered the same thing." He borrowed her bottle and drank. "Usually I can tell a shifter by their scent, but the tigers always stayed down-wind."

A bush in the distance shook. He passed the water back and rested a hand on his automatic.

"I don't think they mean us any harm," she whispered.

The jungle parted and a large golden-striped tiger emerged. He made a huffing sound and swished his tail.

"Well, excuse me," Caitlyn muttered. "He says we smell like death, and we're stinking up their territory."

"Great." Carlos glanced over his shoulder as a second large tiger emerged from the jungle behind them. "At least we don't smell good enough to eat."

Caitlyn paused, her head tilted. "They understand a little English. They say they're not maneaters, and you would do well to stop insulting them."

"Never make a tiger angry," Carlos agreed as he turned his head back and forth to keep an eye on both cats.

"The one in front of us is Raghu, which means swift," Caitlyn explained.

Carlos watched him with narrowed eyes. "I'm sure he is swift."

"Rajiv is behind us. His name means striped. They would like for you to take your hand off the gun."

Carlos dropped his hand. "I would like not to be surrounded and outnumbered."

"It's two against two," she murmured.

"You're not a cat, Catalina."

She snorted. "Yeah, but I'm the one who's able to communicate with them. Raghu wants us to follow him."

"Not happening."

Behind them, Rajiv growled.

She glanced back. "I believe they can be very persuasive."

"Ask them why," Carlos whispered. "What do they want from us?"

She hesitated, then answered. "They believe you're a shifter. They want to talk to you."

"Then they're shifters, too?"

Raghu made another huffing noise, then turned to walk into the jungle. Rajiv advanced on them from the rear.

"I guess we'll find out later," Caitlyn muttered.

Carlos took her by the elbow and followed Raghu. Once they broke through a barrier of bushes, there was a narrow path. It sloped gently downhill for about fifteen minutes.

Carlos walked behind Caitlyn so his back would be to Rajiv. He kept his ears tuned to Rajiv behind them and his eyes glued to Raghu. If the two tigers decided to attack, he'd be better off using his automatic than shifting. "I think we're headed back to the valley where the stream is."

After another five minutes they emerged into a clearing in the valley.

Caitlyn gasped. "It's beautiful."

It was impressive, Carlos thought. A green field stretched before them, dotted with wildflowers. On the other side of the valley a stream cascaded over a cliff, making a small waterfall that fell into a clear blue pond. Another stream broke off from the pond and meandered down the valley to the point where they had crossed it earlier.

The tigers led them toward the pond.

Caitlyn smiled at them. "It's beautiful. Thank you for showing it to us." Her smile faded and she stiffened.

"What?" Carlos asked, his nerves tensing.

"They want us to strip."

"Strip?"

She nodded. "Strip and get in the water."

"Why? Do they like their food clean?"

She winced. "Don't say that." Raghu growled, and she gave Carlos an exasperated look. "How many times do I have to tell you? They don't like being called man-eaters."

"I can see that." He dropped his backpack onto the ground. "From their scent, I'm guessing they spend part of their time as men."

Rajiv snarled.

Caitlyn lifted her hands. "Okay. We're stripping."

"We are?" Carlos turned to watch her. "In that case, ladies first."

She snorted, then looked at the tigers. They inclined their heads and turned their backs.

Carlos chuckled. "You asked them to turn around?"

"Of course. They're men, aren't they?"

"And what am I?" He ejected the clip from his automatic and secured them both in his backpack.

"According to Raghu, you're an old man who bickers too much with his woman."

He straightened with a jerk. "Excuse me?"

"He thinks you're . . . what's the word . . . henpecked?"

"What?" Carlos glared at the giant cat who sat calmly with his back to them, twitching his tail back and forth. He was tempted to give that tail a big yank. "Why would he say that?"

Caitlyn smiled as she lowered her backpack to the ground. "They think you waste time arguing with me when you only need to give orders."

He arched a brow. "They have a valid point, but do they have any idea how stubborn you are?"

Her eyes twinkled with humor as she sat on the ground to remove her hiking boots. "You discuss things with me as an equal. I think it's very sweet."

Sweet? He was a were-panther, dammit. He yanked his T-shirt over his head and threw it down. "Was I sweet when I turned into a snarling animal and pinned you down?" He ripped off his boots and socks, leaving them scattered over the meadow.

She slipped off her socks, then neatly rolled them and stashed them in her boots. "It's just a different culture here. In the western world, men have learned to be more sensitive to a woman's needs." She perched her hat on top of her boots.

Sensitive? Carlos growled as he unbuckled his belt and jerked down the zipper. He'd show her where a man was most sensitive to a woman's needs. His trousers and underwear fell to the ground and he kicked them aside.

Her eyes widened.

The longer he stared at her, the harder he became. "I believe the appropriate term is semi-aroused."

Her eyes grew even wider. "Semi?" Her voice came out in a squeak.

"Hurry up and get naked." He marched toward the pond, then called over his shoulder, "And that's an order."

Caitlyn bit her bottom lip as she watched Carlos. Could any man be more gorgeous? His bare back was strong and tanned. His skin was smooth, with no sign of the fatal wound he'd suffered the night before. His determined stride made the muscles in his buttocks flex and pull.

He was simply mesmerizing. And huge. Semi-aroused? More like semi-superhuman.

She sighed with dismay when he walked far enough into the pond that the water level covered his rump. She hadn't spotted any tattoos. He had only been teasing. He dipped low in the water, arching his back to wet his hair. Then he straightened, smoothing his shoulder-length hair back with his hands as he turned toward her.

He planted his hands on his hips and watched her with his amber eyes. His chest was broad and hairless, but a narrow trail of hair started at his belly button and descended out of view into the water.

She wondered if he was still semi-aroused. Her mouth fell open as his right hand slipped from his hip to his groin. Was he fondling himself underwater?

"I'm waiting, Catalina."

Her skin tingled with anticipation. She slowly stood. The grass was cool and soft against the soles of her feet. With trembling fingers she unbuttoned her olive-colored camp shirt. Her heart rate sped up. She'd never stripped in front of a man before.

His eyes gleamed, his gaze never leaving her.

Her arms prickled with goose bumps as she slid the shirt off. She folded it and set it on the ground next to her boots. She glanced back to make sure the tigers weren't watching, then looked at Carlos.

One corner of his mouth curled up as he focused on her red lacy bra. Her nipples responded to his gaze, pebbling against the cool silk. She felt a tightening, squeezing sensation between her legs. She'd never felt so turned on, and he hadn't even touched her yet.

Slowly, she unbuckled her belt and unfastened the waistband of her khaki pants. Her heart beat even faster. Once she entered the pool, she knew he would pounce on her. And she wanted him. She wanted his hands and mouth all over her. With a little wiggle, she pushed her trousers over her hips and let them fall.

His brows lifted slightly at the sight of her high-cut red lace panties.

She stepped out of the trousers, then leaned over to pick them up. She folded them neatly.

"Get on with it," he growled.

His impatience gave her a sudden gratifying feeling of power. He was at her mercy. She was setting the pace. And she was enjoying making him wait.

"Are you feeling . . . anxious?" She turned to give him a view of her backside. She leaned over to set her folded pants on top of her shirt.

He snorted. "Go ahead and torture me, Catalina. It'll be your turn soon enough."

She straightened and faced him. "You're planning on torturing me?"

He smiled. "I'm going to make you scream."

"Promises, promises." She reached behind her back to unhook her bra. It came loose with a little pop, and her heart lurched.

She took a deep breath to steady her nerves. Then with a flourish, she whisked the bra off and dropped it on her clothes.

Carlos hissed in a breath.

Her courage wavered under a sudden attack of modesty, and she turned her back to him to remove her underwear. The red lace fell to the ground, and she nudged it with her foot onto her pile of clothes.

"Catalina," he called softly.

Her heart swelled with love and longing. She looked up at the blue sky overhead and vowed to herself that no matter what happened, she would never regret this. She would cherish this day for the rest of her life.

She turned and streaked toward the pond.

"Ack!" It was colder than she'd thought it would be. When the water reached her hips, she pushed off her feet and swam toward the waterfall.

She came to an abrupt halt when a hand seized her ankle. "Hey!" She dropped her free foot to the bottom of the pond and turned to face her attacker. The water was only chest deep.

Carlos pulled her hard against his chest. He wrapped her ankles around his back, making her straddle him around the waist. She gasped as her most sensitive flesh was pressed against him. He supported her with one arm and slid his other hand around her neck.

He was breathing heavily. She could feel the rise and fall of his stomach pushing against her groin.

"Catalina, I've wanted you for so long."

"I want you, too. More than anything." She blinked back tears. "When I thought you were dead—"

"Shh. We're together now." He dragged her farther up his body, rubbing her tender skin against him.

She whimpered. Her head fell back as he nibbled on her neck. She dug her heels into his back, pressing herself against him. He grabbed her buttocks and squeezed.

A gong sounded in the distance.

He lifted his head from her neck. "What is that?"

She glanced toward the field. The tigers were gone. "I hope they're not in the forest watching us."

Carlos dunked down, bringing her with him, so the water was up to their chins.

Another gong sounded.

"Maybe it's the dinner bell," he muttered.

She smoothed a hand over his wet hair. "Or a fire drill?"

He snorted. "I've got a drill for you."

She giggled and slapped his shoulder. "Oh, there are people coming." She spotted two women and a handful of children coming from the forest.

"Definitely a tribe of were-tigers," he murmured. "The children won't shift until puberty. And the women probably only shift on the night of a full moon."

She gasped when the children gathered up all of her and Carlos's clothes. "Wait!" she called out to them. "We need those."

The children giggled and ran back into the forest. One of the women took their backpacks.

"She's got my weapons." Carlos let go of Caitlyn and walked toward the shore. "Hey, bring that back!" He gave her an exasperated look. "Can you tell them to stop?"

"I don't know their language yet."

The other woman smiled and showed them a bamboo tray with two clay dishes on top. She set the tray on the water and pushed it toward Carlos. Then she ran back into the forest.

"What is it?" Caitlyn asked as Carlos brought the floating tray to her.

He shrugged. "I don't know." The two clay dishes held clear, thick liquid.

She dipped a finger in and rubbed it with her

thumb. It made suds and smelled of jasmine. "It's soap."

He motioned with his head toward the waterfall. "Want to take a shower?"

With a laugh, she bounced toward the waterfall. They both lathered up their faces and hair, then stuck their heads under the spray.

"Oh, that feels wonderful." She smoothed her hair back, then noticed that he was gone. "Carlos?"

His arm shot through the waterfall and dragged her through.

"Ack!" She wiped the water off her eyes, then gasped. "Oh my gosh. It's a grotto." She pivoted, taking it in. The water fell like a shimmering, misty curtain in front of them. Behind them there was a small opening in the rock wall. There was a ledge just above water level. Surrounding the opening, green moss gave the rock wall a rich, tropical look. "It's incredible."

She looked around. "Carlos?" He'd disappeared again.

He swam around the edge of the waterfall, pushing the bamboo tray in front of him. "I brought the soap."

"That's very kind of you."

"At your service." He dipped his fingers into a bowl and tossed a glob of soap on her chest.

With a laugh, she moved closer to the ledge, where the water was only up to her waist. He followed her and smoothed the soap over her shoulders and down her arms.

She grabbed a blob of soap and rubbed it over his

broad shoulders and chest. "You're so beautiful."

He snorted. "This is beauty." He covered her breasts with his soapy palms and massaged gently.

With a groan, she arched toward him.

He pulled her against him, and their slick, soapy chests rubbed together. His erection pressed against her stomach, and a desperate need made her ache for him.

"Carlos." She ran her hands up and down his back.

He kissed her brow, then trailed kisses down to her lips. When she opened her mouth for him, he kissed her with a ferocious hunger that made her fall limp against him.

He nibbled a path down her neck, then pulled back with a grimace. "Soap." He splashed into the deeper water with her and ran his hands over her body to rinse off the soap.

She wrapped her legs around his waist and her arms around his neck. They kissed again, with the spray of the waterfall misting their faces.

He lifted her higher and with a growl, he nuzzled his face in her breasts. She giggled. His whiskers were ticklish.

She gasped when he sucked a nipple into his mouth. He suckled hard as he moved them back toward shallower water. He released her breast and reached for more soap. He slapped it on her rump, then massaged it onto her cheeks.

She dug her heels into his back and pressed herself against him.

"Ah." He looked down. "My favorite part." He

dipped a hand into more soap and slipped it between them. He rubbed her pubic hair, then delved deeper.

She gasped at the feel of his fingers exploring her folds.

"Lean back," he whispered. "Float in the water."

She fell back. He kept one arm under her hips to support her, and she locked her feet around his waist. Water lapped against her ears. The world was still and peaceful, and all she could feel were his fingers moving gently between her legs. It was sweet and delicious. She could do this for hours.

She jolted when he suddenly tweaked her clitoris.

"Something wrong?"

"I—" She gasped when he rubbed the nubbin between his thumb and forefinger. "Carlos?"

He launched into a full assault on her senses, and she floundered in the water. With a chuckle, he lifted her back into his arms, then resumed the exquisite torture.

She clutched at his shoulders, panting as tension coiled inside her.

"I want to taste you." He set her on the ledge and dove between her legs.

She cried out at the feel of his tongue, licking and tickling her. His lips clamped onto her clitoris and suckled. She screamed as all the tension in her body shattered.

He grinned and pressed a hand against her. "I can feel you throbbing. You're wet and swollen."

"I—I . . ." She gave up on speech. There were no words for it. Her body was still shuddering with spasms. She reached for him and was glad when he took her into his arms. She was far too limp and ragged to support herself.

She rested her head on his shoulder and gave a sigh of contentment. "That was perfect."

"That was just the beginning."

She jolted when something hard nudged her where she was still sensitive and swollen. "Oh."

"Wrap your legs around me." He took hold of her hips and positioned her against his erection.

She glanced down. He was magnificent. Large and swollen. Moisture seeped from her, and her skin tingled where it pressed against the round tip.

He moved his hips from side to side, wedging himself between her folds. She shuddered. This was it. She'd wanted this from the first night she'd met him.

"Will you be mine?" he whispered.

"Yes." She lifted her gaze to meet his. There was so much love in his eyes, she thought her heart would burst. She lay her hand on his cheek. "I love you, Carlos. I will always love you."

"Catalina." He kissed her lips, then rested his forehead against hers. With a sharp, sudden thrust and a pull on her hips, he buried himself deep inside her.

She gasped, stiffening a second, then slowly adjusting to his large size. "If you tell me you're only semi-aroused, I'm going to scream."

He chuckled and kissed her brow. "My God, I love you."

"Really?"

"Mmm." He kissed her mouth. "I've known it for some time."

"Really?"

"Mmm." He kissed her again.

"For how long?"

"Sweetheart, do you think we could talk after I finish screwing you?"

She feigned a huff of indignation. "Men. So incapable of multitasking."

He swatted her rump, and she gasped. "That's it. Keep your mouth just like that." He planted his lips on hers and invaded her open mouth with his tongue.

He moved her hips, rocking her against him, gently at first, then harder and harder. They stopped kissing when their breathing became more labored. Soon they were panting, and he was thrusting into her with a desperation that brought tears to her eyes.

She whimpered as her climax lifted her higher and higher, then screamed when it broke free. He let out a long groan as he pumped himself into her.

They held each other tight as their breathing slowly returned to normal.

"I can still feel you inside me, throbbing," she whispered.

"Mmm."

She smiled and rested her head on his shoulder.

A gong sounded in the distance.

He grunted. "I forgot we weren't alone in the world."

"I wonder what they want now?"

He moved through the water, still holding her, and they rounded the waterfall.

A woman emerged from the forest with something folded in her hands.

"I think they're bringing us clothes," Caitlyn murmured.

The woman set the folded material on the grass, then spoke in a dialect Caitlyn had never heard before. "Please dress yourselves, and join us for dinner." She turned and hurried back into the forest.

Caitlyn repeated the request to Carlos, then they swam to the shore. He ran to fetch the clothes, then brought them back to her.

She quickly donned a blue tunic that hung past her knees, while Carlos put on the baggy blue pants.

She glanced back at the waterfall. "I'll always remember this."

"We'll have lots of memories." Carlos took her hand and led her to the forest.

Just inside the tree line, the woman waited with her eyes averted. "This way." She scurried down a narrow path.

"Can you understand her?" Carlos asked.

"Yes, but it will be a while before I can talk to her."

They came to a village that was similar to that of the Akha tribe. Wooden houses stood on stilts, and the villagers were gathered around a central fire. They grinned at her and Carlos and nodded their heads.

"Please, sit." The woman motioned to a bamboo mat big enough for two.

Caitlyn took a seat and pressed a hand to her chest. "Cait." She gestured toward the woman.

"I am Malai." The woman smiled, then passed them a wooden plate filled with rice and some kind of grilled meat.

"I'm starving." Carlos popped a piece of meat in his mouth. "It's good. Tastes like chicken."

"Which means it could be a frog." Caitlyn pointed across the village. "There are our clothes. They must have washed them." They were hanging on a line to dry.

"Welcome." A large man dressed in baggy green pants sat on the mat beside them. He had long black hair and golden eyes. He introduced himself.

"Oh." Caitlyn was surprised. "This is Raghu," she told Carlos. "He was much furrier the last time we saw him." She smiled and bowed to him.

Carlos bowed. He pressed a hand to his chest. "Carlos." He motioned to Caitlyn. "Cait."

Raghu inclined his head. "He is a were-panther, yes?"

Caitlyn nodded and replied in English, "Yes."

"You do not speak our language?"

She shook her head no. "Not yet."

"But you understand me?"

She nodded. "Yes."

"You can communicate with us when we are shifted."

"Yes."

"That is most unusual. I have never met a human with that ability." Raghu accepted a plate of food from Malai. "She is beautiful, yes? She is my mate."

"Ah." Caitlyn nodded, then said "Yes" in his language.

Carlos leaned close to her. "What is he talking about?"

"He's married to Malai." Caitlyn smiled at the woman. "I agreed that she's beautiful."

"Oh." Carlos went back to stuffing food down his mouth.

Raghu chewed on a piece of meat. "My mate came from the Lisu. They are known for their beauty."

Caitlyn tilted her head. The Lisu were a hill tribe, completely mortal as far as she knew.

Raghu regarded her curiously. "I do not understand why you are still human."

She gave him a perplexed look.

"Your mate is a were-panther, but you are still human. Is he reluctant to bite you?"

She sat back, confused. She wasn't fluent yet in the were-tiger's language, but she managed a few words. "Why . . . bite me?"

Raghu's golden eyes shifted from her to Carlos. "He must bite you in order to make you a were-panther."

"What?" Caitlyn scrambled to her feet.

Carlos jumped up. "What? What's wrong?"

Her shock quickly sizzled into anger. "You— You jerk!"

"What?" He glanced at the empty plate in his hands. "Okay, I ate all the food, but it's not the end of the world. I'll get you some more."

"You can bite me and make me a were-panther?" she cried.

His face paled and the plate tumbled from his hands.

Chapter Twenty-four

*T*ears blurred Caitlyn's vision and she trembled with anger. How could he not tell her something so vitally important? "Why didn't you tell me?"

He leaned over to set the wooden plate on the bamboo mat. "I can explain."

"You should have explained weeks ago! What the hell are we even doing here?"

"We can discuss it later in private."

"I'm upset *now*!" She glanced around the circle of villagers who were watching her curiously. Damn, she was providing them with a soap opera. She lowered her voice, but it still shook with emotion. "At least tell me if it's true. Can you turn me into a were-panther by simply biting me?"

A pained expression crossed his face. "In theory, yes."

"Then in theory, you never had to come here

to look for a were-panther mate. You could have taken me!"

"Catalina—"

"What was wrong with me?" Her old fear came reeling back at full force. "You didn't think I was good enough?"

He scoffed. "You're all I've ever wanted. I'm not giving you up, even if I find a jillion were-panther women."

She blinked. "You—You're staying with me?"

"Yes." He scowled at her. "I thought I made that clear in the grotto."

She scowled back. "I thought that was . . . sex talk."

"That was love. I told you I love you." He pulled her into his arms and fastened one hand to her jaw to force her to meet his hungry gaze.

The village women sighed in unison.

Caitlyn thought she might melt at his feet. "So you don't want to marry a were-panther now?"

"No. I want you."

"When did you decide that?" She didn't know whether to kiss him or slap him. He had her so confused.

"I've been considering it for a while."

"And you didn't tell me?" She pushed away from him. "I'm still angry at you."

He gave her a bewildered look, then picked up the plate and handed it to Malai. "Can you get her some food?" He pointed at the plate, then at Caitlyn.

Malai nodded and scurried away.

Caitlyn snorted. "It's not about food, Carlos. It's about honesty."

He stiffened. "I haven't lied to you."

"You kept the truth from me. You didn't tell me you were planning to stay with me."

"I didn't realize I needed to. As far as I'm concerned, we're already married."

"Well, it would have been nice if you had told me. And what about your little habit of dying every now and then? You should have told me about that. I suffered needlessly."

He arched a brow. "I suffered a bit myself."

She winced. He had a point there. "You still should have told me. I'm detecting a pattern here, and I need you to be upfront with me so I can trust you."

He scoffed. "Caitlyn, I died last night to protect you. You can trust me."

She folded her arms over her chest, frowning.

Malai returned with another plate filled with food and set it on the bamboo mat. "You were right, husband," she whispered to Raghu. "They bicker too much."

He nodded. "She's a fiery one. He should wear her out with a long bout of sex."

The village men nodded in agreement while the women giggled.

Caitlyn's face grew warm.

"What did they say?" Carlos asked.

"Nothing," she grumbled.

He arched a brow. "Something about me being hen-pecked?"

She groaned inwardly. "I . . . was wrong to doubt your trustworthiness. You were willing to sacrifice yourself in order to protect me, and I'm more grateful than I can say."

When he reached for her, she stepped back and lifted her hands to stop him. "But I'm still upset that you didn't tell me I could be turned into a were-panther. You knew all along that I could be your mate and a mother for your children."

"And I knew the transformation would most likely kill you."

She paused, stunned.

"It's true, Catalina. I've seen mortals die in agony, unable to survive the transformation."

She swallowed hard. "Are you serious?"

"My cousin married a mortal, and when she attempted to go through the transformation, she died a miserable, painful death. Her father was so enraged, he massacred my people."

Caitlyn swayed from the impact of his words. All those people had died because a woman hadn't survived the transformation?

He grabbed her arm. "Are you all right?"

"I . . ." She shook her head. She could actually die? This couldn't be right. It was too cruel a twist of fate. She and Carlos were perfect for each other. It had nearly killed her when she'd thought he was dead. And now, if she tried to become his mate, she could die?

"Come, sit down." Carlos tugged on her arm. He waited for her to sit beside him, then placed the plate of food in her lap. "You look pale. You should eat."

She glanced down at the food without seeing it.

Then she looked around the circle of villagers who were all watching her like she was on prime-time television.

She attempted speaking the were-tiger language

to Raghu. "Your mate is from the Lisu tribe? She's human?"

"Malai is were-tiger now," Raghu answered proudly and smiled at his wife.

"Was it hard for her to change?" Caitlyn asked.

Raghu's smile faded. "Very hard, but my Malai is strong. Only those with the heart of a tiger survive it."

Caitlyn gulped.

"Akkarat," Raghu said to one of the men. "You tell our guest your story."

A young slim man inclined his head. "I am Akkarat from the Akha village. I ventured into tiger territory a year ago, searching for my cousin. I found him here. He'd fallen in love and didn't want to leave. When I met his mate's sister, I didn't want to leave either."

The young woman seated next to Akkarat gazed up at him with adoring eyes.

"My cousin and I decided to become were-tigers so we could be fitting husbands and worthy of our chosen mates." Akkarat glanced sadly at a young woman who sat alone with tears in her eyes. "My cousin did not survive the transformation."

"I'm so sorry." Caitlyn's heart sank. What Carlos had said was true. She could die. "I was at the Akha village, and Ajay mentioned you and your cousin. They believe you were both killed by a man-eating creature."

Akkarat snorted. "We fell in love."

Raghu growled deep in his throat. "Everyone accuses us of being man-eaters." He pointed at the plate in her lap. "We eat chicken. Try it."

She bit into a piece of grilled chicken and nodded.

"It's very good. We're actually on our way back to the Akha village. I could tell Ajay that Akkarat is alive and well."

"No, you must not," Raghu said. "It is good that they fear coming into our territory. We must keep our existence secret."

She nodded. "I understand." If Carlos's tribe had kept their secret better, they might still be alive. She glanced at him. He was watching her with a worried look.

"What have they been saying?" he whispered.

"They confirmed what you told me. Not everyone survives the transformation." She set the plate of food aside, too tired and depressed to eat.

"You look worn-out. You didn't sleep at all last night."

She gave him a wry look. "You slept like the dead."

He smiled and brushed her damp hair back from her brow. "Maybe you should rest for a while before we continue our trip."

"I would love that." She was suddenly feeling very weary. The night in the cave had been emotionally wrenching. Booby-traps, Tanit's death, Carlos's death and resurrection, the finding of an American soldier trapped in a forty-year-long coma. It was a lot to take in. And now she had another emotional quandary to deal with. Should she risk death to become a were-panther?

She turned to Raghu. "Is there a place where we can rest for a while?"

"Of course. Your clothes will not be dry until tomorrow, so you will be spending the night."

"Thank you. You are very kind."

Raghu inclined his head. "We are honored to have a were-panther and his mate as our guests. He fears losing you, doesn't he? That is why he hasn't bitten you."

"Yes."

"A man must conquer his fear so he can be with his chosen mate." Raghu glanced at Malai with love in his eyes. "Now we are expecting our first child."

"That's wonderful."

He turned toward Caitlyn. "You cannot give him were-panther children if you do not transform. If you remain human, your children will be human."

She closed her eyes briefly. Everything had seemed so perfect in the grotto, and now it all seemed wrong. "He needs to have were-panther children. His people are in danger of extinction."

"He is searching for other were-panthers?" Raghu asked. When Caitlyn nodded, he continued, "There are a few panthers south of here, but they are not shifters."

"Oh." Her heart plummeted further.

"There are a larger number of panthers east of Chiang Mai, close to Laos," Raghu said. "He may have better luck there."

"I'll tell him. Thank you." She rose to her feet, and Carlos stood beside her. "I'd like to rest now, if you don't mind."

Carlos woke when Caitlyn stirred in his arms. They'd been shown to a small house on stilts on the edge of the tiger village. Their backpacks were inside, and he'd quickly checked on their weapons. Then he'd stretched out on the pallet beside Caitlyn and they'd slept.

She stretched and opened her eyes.

He smiled. He always loved looking at the beautiful turquoise color. "Sleep well?"

"I dreamed the Terra-Cotta Warriors were chasing me through the jungle." She sighed. "What time is it?"

"The sun's still up. I estimate late afternoon, but I'm not sure. I suspect one of the tiger children is sporting a new watch."

"You took yours off when we stripped?"

He nodded. "How are you?"

"I'm wondering what I'm doing in Thailand when you never really needed to search for a mate."

"I still need to find more of my species."

She frowned. "Raghu said the panthers south of here aren't shifters."

Carlos rolled onto his back and stared at the thatched roof. Had he come all this way for nothing?

"He said there are more panthers east of Chiang Mai close to the Laos border," she continued.

There was still hope. "We'll go there after we take care of the soldier in the cave."

She sat up and hugged her knees. "I need to decide if I should become a were-panther."

"No." He sat up beside her. "We can't risk it. We'll just live like normal people."

"With normal children? What about your endangered species?"

He shrugged. "It can't be helped. I suppose the were-panther children will have more children when they grow older."

"We can't unload that burden on them. And I want my children to be like you, Carlos. I love you. I want little were-kittens like you."

"It's not going to happen. I'm not risking your life."

"It's my life, so it's my decision to make."

He winced. This was what he had feared would happen. It was the main reason he had avoided telling her the truth. "I'm not allowing you to sacrifice yourself."

"Then you would sacrifice your species? How could you live with me as a mortal without hating me someday for forcing you to give up who you are?"

"How could I live with myself if you died? It would kill me, Caitlyn."

She rested a hand on his cheek. "We can't be sure I would die. I'm terribly stubborn you know."

He snorted. "Sheer willpower might not be enough."

"How about love?" She smoothed her hand through his hair. "I love you so much."

"I love you, too." He kissed her brow. "I couldn't bear to lose you."

She tilted her head to meet his mouth, and he kissed her slowly and thoroughly. Her mouth parted for him and he stroked her tongue with his.

Already his groin was tightening, but he refused to take her quickly. He wanted to explore every inch of her. He was curious to see how she looked and tasted, curious to watch her body react to his lovemaking. Something about being a cat, he supposed.

He nibbled on her neck as he slid a hand down her thigh to the hem of her tunic. When he pulled it up, she lifted her hips to help him. He tugged it over her head, then pushed her gently down on the pallet.

Her nipples fascinated him. With just a look he could make them pebble. With some suckling he could turn them a darker color of red. With a flick of his tongue he could make the tips harden into tight buds.

Caitlyn's moans were like music, and each time she gasped his name, he wanted to roar with victory. His woman. His wife. The muscles in her stomach trembled as he kissed and nibbled his way to the feast between her legs.

With a moan she opened for him. He rested his head on her thigh so he could watch her reactions to his fingers. She shuddered, and moisture seeped from her core. Her scent made him grow harder. Her folds grew swollen and wet. Her clitoris darkened to a delicious looking red. Her passage was tight and slick around his fingers.

He stroked the inside of her as he leaned closer to flick his tongue on her clitoris. She jolted and let out a keening cry. So close. He sucked her clitoris into his mouth, and she screamed. Her passage clamped down on his fingers.

It was more than he could bear. He withdrew his fingers and plunged inside her. He didn't last long. She was still throbbing, and it sent him over the edge. With a hoarse cry, he pumped into her, then collapsed beside her.

He gathered her into his arms and held her tight. He would never risk losing her. Even if she decided she wanted to risk the transformation, he had the power to stop her. All he had to do was refuse to bite her.

The next day, Caitlyn said their farewells to the were-tigers, then she and Carlos headed toward the Akha village. It was a misty morning with the clouds settled low in the mountains. Her freshly washed clothes soon felt sticky against her body, but she reminded herself that extra humidity was good for her skin.

And extra sex was good for her spirits. For a man who had once avoided her like the plague, Carlos was making up for lost time. They'd spent the night making love, with short snatches of sleep in between.

After three hours of hiking, they arrived in the Akha village. Ajay invited them to his house for lunch, and she told him about the cave and how Tanit had died.

"We need to call our friends so they can help us revive the soldier," she explained.

Ajay nodded. "If you go to the top of the tower, you can get a signal from Chiang Mai. We call our tribesmen there who sell our silver crafts in the bazaar."

After lunch they climbed to the top of the watch-tower, and Carlos called the number for MacKay S & I.

Caitlyn leaned close so she could listen.

"Yo, Catman," Phineas answered the phone. "What's up?"

It felt strange to hear the Vamp's voice during the day, but it was nighttime in New York.

"Hey, Phineas. We saw something strange here in the mountains."

"Oh yeah? What have you been smoking?"

Carlos snorted. "There's a vampire around here somewhere, and he left a lot of dead bodies in a cave."

"No shit?"

"We found a body that looks like it's been in a vampire coma for about forty years."

Phineas scoffed. "That's whack, man. That dude is dead."

"He hasn't decayed. And he's an American soldier, a major in the Marine Corps."

"Shit. I guess we should wake him up."

"I think we should try," Carlos agreed. "It's daytime here. I'll call again when the sun goes down and it's safe to teleport here."

"I'll probably be in my death-sleep then," Phineas muttered. "I think the closest Vamp we've got to you is Kyo in Japan. I'll leave him a message. And Angus will want to know about this, too. He's in Moscow, so you'll have to wait till the sun sets there before he can teleport out."

"We'll be here. Thanks." Carlos hung up. "We have to wait till tonight." His eyes gleamed as he looked her over. "How will we ever pass the time?"

She smiled. "I believe the honeymoon suite is still available."

Chapter Twenty-five

It was after midnight when Carlos was finally able to contact Angus in Moscow. The head of MacKay Security & Investigation had been awake for ten minutes, and he'd read the report that Phineas had forwarded to him. He teleported straight to Carlos in the tower, bringing his Moscow operative, Mikhail, with him.

As Carlos shook hands with Mikhail, he wondered how old the Russian vampire was. Mikhail looked like a medieval Viking warrior, with his white-blond hair braided down his back and his piercing blue eyes constantly searching for danger. He appeared to be the strong silent type, for he barely said a word as Angus introduced him to Carlos and Caitlyn. He wore his sword on his back like Angus, but where Angus preferred his blue and green plaid kilt, Mikhail opted for black leather pants.

Kyo from Japan had arrived an hour earlier, and he'd already tested the homing device Carlos had left in the cave. He'd safely teleported to the cave and back. Then he entertained himself by showing off his samurai sword to the men in the village and flirting with the young women.

In the tower, Angus set the ice chest he was carrying on the wood-planked floor. "Emma packed us a supply of synthetic blood in case we manage to revive the soldier in the cave." He nodded at Caitlyn. "How are ye faring, lass?"

She smiled. "I'm fine, thank you."

"She's doing a fantastic job," Carlos said. "I don't know how I would have managed without her."

Angus nodded with a hint of a smile. "Then it's going well? You havena run into any danger?"

Carlos shifted his weight. "Our guide, Tanit, is in the cave, dead. Impaled on a spike."

"Bugger," Angus muttered.

Mikhail merely lifted an eyebrow.

"The cave was booby-trapped," Caitlyn explained.

"Och." Angus winced. "I'm glad ye both survived."

Carlos shifted his weight again. "Actually, I died."

"Again?" Angus gave him an incredulous look. "Lad, ye have to stop doing that."

"He did it to protect me," Caitlyn rushed to his defense. "He saved my life."

"Well, that's good." Angus retrieved his cell phone from the sporran that hung in front of his kilt. "I'm calling Robby in Budapest, so he can join us. Just in case we run into a few angry vampires."

After a few minutes, Robby arrived with Zoltan Czakvar, the coven master of Eastern Europe.

Zoltan frowned at Angus. "I heard something exciting was going on, and you didn't invite me."

"Yes, the excitement is hard to bear," Mikhail murmured with a deadpan expression.

Angus chuckled and slapped Zoltan on the back. "Ye're always welcome, old friend."

Zoltan greeted Mikhail and Carlos, then smiled at Caitlyn. "Good evening. I don't believe we've met."

"This is Caitlyn." Carlos wrapped an arm around her shoulders. "My wife."

Zoltan shook his head ruefully. "I'm always too late."

"Did ye say *wife*?" Angus asked. "When did that happen?"

Caitlyn smiled. "The tribal leader said a few words over us. It's not official."

"Yes, it is," Carlos grumbled.

She gave him an impatient look. "It's not legal."

"We'll make it that way as soon as we get home."

"Are you proposing to me?"

"I thought I already did."

"Enough!" Angus held up his hands. "We have a job to do."

Robby smirked. "They sound like they're already married."

Carlos shot him an annoyed look. "You're one to talk, Big Red. I bet you asked Olivia for permission to come here."

Robby frowned, remaining silent.

Carlos snorted, then handed the homing device monitor to Angus. "Kyo already tried it. It works."

"Where is Kyo?" Angus asked.

"There." Mikhail pointed across the village. "I'll bring him." The Russian vanished, then reappeared seconds later with a hand firmly grasping Kyo's arm.

"What?" Kyo looked around, then jumped back from Mikhail. "Holy cow! You big as a truck."

"We're ready to go," Angus announced. "Kyo, since you've been there before, take Carlos with you. I'll take Caitlyn. Mikhail, bring the ice chest."

A few seconds later Carlos materialized just outside the cave. He checked to make sure Caitlyn was all right. Then he pulled the flashlight from his belt, turned it on, and headed into the cave. "Our guide called this a Temple of Death."

"It smells like death," Angus muttered.

Carlos wrinkled his nose. Caitlyn covered her mouth and coughed. Tanit was definitely still there.

Inside the cave, Carlos pointed his beam of light at the skeletal remains of the Buddhist monk. "This poor guy activated the first booby-trap."

"We think he left the prayers." Caitlyn aimed her flashlight at the yellow strips of paper above them. "He was trying to keep the evil power in the cave from escaping."

"And ye believe the evil power is a Chinese vampire?" Angus asked.

"Yes," Caitlyn answered. "They call it a *chiang-shih*. Tanit called him Master Han. He said he was great and powerful and he's killed thousands."

"The professor in Bangkok is one of the Master's Guardians," Carlos added.

"What is this?" Zoltan tugged on the scarves that hung down from the crisscrossed ropes along the ceiling.

"Caitlyn made it to swing across the ditch," Carlos explained.

"I'd love to have the scarves back." She stared wistfully at them. "And the silver panther. I was going to give them as presents."

"Not a problem." Zoltan levitated up to the ropes to untie the scarves.

Carlos showed the rest of the Vamps the ditch with iron stakes. "This was the second booby-trap."

Angus frowned at Tanit's dead body. "We should give him a proper burial."

"We dinna bring a shovel," Robby murmured.

"We could leave him in the large burial room with the other bodies," Caitlyn suggested as she folded the scarves Zoltan had liberated. "He was a slave to Master Han, so it's fitting for him to remain in the master's Temple of Death."

Angus nodded. "Works for me. Who wants to get him out of the ditch?" He gave Robby a pointed look.

"Och, leave me the dirty job. Thank you so much." Robby peered into the ditch. "The spikes are about three feet apart. I should be able to levitate down between them."

"You'll notice if you miss," Mikhail muttered.

Carlos wondered if the Russian was joking. It was hard to tell with that stoic, rock-hard face.

"I'll help you," Zoltan offered.

As Robby and Zoltan lowered themselves slowly into the ditch, the rest of the Vamps teleported across, taking Carlos and Caitlyn with them.

Carlos glanced ruefully at the bloodstained stone floor where he'd died. "This way." He led Caitlyn and the Vamps through the narrow passage into the large burial room. He lit the torches, and all two hundred clay figures came into view.

"Holy cow!" Kyo exclaimed.

"The devil take it," Angus whispered.

Mikhail lifted a brow.

"I think we're alone, but just in case . . ." Angus drew his sword.

Mikhail and Kyo unsheathed their swords, too.

Caitlyn led them down the steps into the lower portion of the room. "At first I thought they were symbolic of a dead army, but Carlos broke a few open, and we discovered skeletons inside."

"We couldn't understand why a vampire would go to this much trouble to preserve a bunch of dead bodies," Carlos added as they walked across the room. "But when we found the soldier in a vampire coma, we figured Master Han may have been trying to put them all into vampire comas."

Angus looked about, frowning. "If that's true, then there could be others who survived."

"We'll have to check them all," Mikhail concluded. He handed the ice chest to Angus, then started down a row, cracking each clay shell with the blunt end of his sword to make sure only a skeleton lay beneath.

"I'll help." Kyo started down another row.

Going at vampire speed, the two Vamps moved quickly down the rows.

Caitlyn shuddered. "I keep imagining them all suddenly standing up and moving toward me."

Carlos wrapped an arm around her shoulder. "They can't hurt you."

Angus shook his head. "If Master Han had succeeded, he could have transformed all these men at the same time. He would have had an instant vampire army at his disposal."

Robby and Zoltan entered the large room, carrying Tanit's body. They placed him in a row of clay figures.

"This place is amazing." Robby strode toward them, his kilt swishing about his knees.

"Aye, but I can only be glad that Master Han failed," Angus added.

"How can you be sure?" Mikhail called from across the chamber as he finished cracking open the clay figures. "There could be other caves just like this."

That gave them all pause.

"Tanit said that Master Han has killed thousands," Caitlyn whispered. "There are only two hundred here."

"Kyo, I want you and your team in Tokyo to investigate this Master Han," Angus ordered.

"*Hai*." Kyo smashed the last clay figure with the end of his samurai sword. "These guys are all dead."

"Good." Angus turned to Carlos. "Show us the soldier."

"This way." Carlos led them up some steps and into the next room.

With no vampires in sight, the Vamps sheathed their weapons. Angus set the ice chest on the floor.

Carlos passed the first two altars where the clay figures housed skeletal remains. The third altar was just as they left it. Major Russell Ryan Hankelburg rested there in his green fatigues.

Kyo frowned at him. "He looks dead to me."

"He's not dead," Mikhail said. "He hasn't decayed."

"His muscles haven't withered," Caitlyn added. "It's like he's frozen in time."

Angus rested one hand on the major's chest, then lifted the eyelids to examine his eyes. "Aye, he's in a vampire coma."

"How long has he been like that?" Robby asked.

"We estimate about forty years," Carlos said.

Zoltan shook his head. "I've never heard of a person lasting so long."

"Aye." Angus drew his Highland dirk from his knee sock. "But he willna survive the night if his body rejects the transformation."

"He is strong," Mikhail said. "He will fight."

"We shall see." Angus sliced his forearm. As blood oozed from the wound, he placed it over the major's mouth.

Nothing happened.

Angus pulled the major's cap off and tapped his fingers against his temple. "Come on, lad."

Mikhail shook his booted feet.

"He's so far down in a black hole," Zoltan said. "He's probably forgotten which way is up."

Angus smeared blood on the major's mouth

and nose. "Wake up, lad." He glanced at Caitlyn. "Maybe he'll respond to a female voice."

"Okay." She leaned close and placed a hand on his brow. "Russell, do you hear me? Russell, come back. Come back home."

The major's body jerked. His mouth opened with a gasp.

"That's it." Angus dripped some of his blood into Russell's mouth.

The major coughed.

"Ye have to drink it, lad." Angus drizzled more blood into Russell's mouth.

The major swallowed, then his body trembled. He grabbed Angus's arm and drank from the wound.

"Is that what causes the transformation?" Caitlyn asked. "He has to drink blood from a vampire?"

"Aye," Angus answered. "First he must be drained dry by a vampire. All his mortal blood must be gone, and he has to fall into a vampire coma. Usually, the coma never lasts longer than one night."

The major released Angus's arm and opened his eyes. His gaze shifted from Angus to Caitlyn, and he looked confused. Then his gaze drifted up to the top of the cave. His eyes widened with alarm.

"Russell Ryan Hankelburg," he croaked. "Major, United States Marine Corps. Serial number five-seven—"

"Lad, ye're no' a prisoner," Angus told him.

"We found you in this cave." Caitlyn smiled and patted his shoulder. "You're safe now. You're among friends."

He lifted his head to look at all the people. His

gaze landed on Kyo and he gasped. "Charlie!" He struggled to sit up.

"What?" Kyo huffed with indignation.

Russell searched his uniform in vain for weapons.

"You think I look like Viet Cong?" Kyo cried. "I'm not commie bastard. I'm Japanese! Descendant from noble ninja warrior!"

"Relax, Kyo," Angus muttered.

Robby chuckled. "Yeah, tell us how ye really feel."

Russell eyed them all warily. He winced and rubbed his stomach.

"That's the hunger ye're feeling," Angus explained. He motioned toward the ice chest, and Mikhail removed a bottle of synthetic blood.

"Where am I?" Russell asked.

"A cave in Thailand," Carlos told him. "What do you remember last?"

"I was on leave in Phuket. I went into a bar and—" Russell grimaced, pressing a hand to his stomach. "I don't remember."

"Most likely, a vampire took control of yer mind," Angus said. "Then he teleported you here to feed off you."

"What?" Russell gave him an incredulous look.

"What year is it?" Zoltan asked him.

"Nineteen seventy-one." Russell's eyes narrowed with suspicion. "Why do you ask?"

"Lad, there's no easy way to tell you this," Angus said. "Ye've been in a coma for thirty-nine years."

Russell flinched. "Thirty-nine?"

"Aye." Angus nodded. "Ye'll find that the world has changed quite a bit."

Russell looked askance at him and Robby. "Men are wearing skirts now?"

The Scotsmen stiffened while the others in the room snickered.

"This is a kilt," Robby announced.

"Aye," Angus added. " 'Tis a fine, manly tradition amongst the Scots."

"Right." Russell turned to Caitlyn and smiled. "And what's your name?"

"She's my wife," Carlos growled.

Angus chuckled. "And some things havena changed at all."

"Look, whoever you guys are— Agh!" Russell doubled over, holding his stomach. "Damn."

" 'Tis the hunger." Angus accepted a bottle of synthetic blood from Mikhail, then offered it to Russell. "Here. Ye need to drink this."

Russell lifted the bottle to his nose. "Blood?" He threw the bottle aside and it smashed into a rock wall.

"Lad, ye need blood." Angus extended a hand so Mikhail could pass him another bottle.

"You're crazy!" Russell shouted. "I'm not drinking— Agh!" He slapped a hand over his mouth.

"Those are yer fangs coming in," Angus told him.

Russell's eyes widened with horror.

"I know it is hard to believe," Angus said softly. "Ye were attacked by a vampire thirty-nine years ago. He put you into a vampire coma and abandoned you here. We revived you, but yer life will be different from now on. Ye'll have extraordinary strength and speed. Yer senses will be extra sharp. Even now ye can see amazingly well in this dark cave, can ye no'?"

Russell nodded, his hand still covering his mouth.

"Ye can hear our heartbeats," Angus continued. "Ye can smell the blood running down the wall over there. And it smells good to you, does it no'?"

Russell nodded. He opened his mouth and felt his elongated fangs. "Is this for real?"

"Aye, ye're a vampire." Angus passed him another bottle of blood. "The pain in yer belly will go away if ye drink."

Russell took the bottle and gave it a dubious look. "A vampire? I didn't think they existed." He winced and rubbed his stomach. "Aren't vampires evil?"

"Do ye feel evil?" Robby asked.

Russell shook his head. "I feel the same."

"Exactly." Angus patted him on the shoulder. "Death canna change yer true nature. Now, drink."

Russell took a sip from the bottle and grimaced. "It's cold."

"Do you see a microwave around here?" Zoltan asked dryly.

"A what?" Russell took another sip.

Zoltan chuckled. "Why don't you come stay at my house for a while? Robby and I can show you how to be a proper vampire."

"You guys are vampires, too?" Russell drank more blood.

"Aye," Robby said. "We're the good Vamps."

"Cool." Russell drank more blood. "This actually tastes good." He downed the rest of the bottle.

Angus introduced everyone, then Zoltan and Robby teleported back to Budapest, taking the new Vamp with them.

"I will leave for Tokyo now." Kyo bowed. "And I will begin investigation of Master Han." He teleported away.

Angus turned to Carlos. "And what about you two? Do ye want to hitch a ride to Moscow?"

"We need to go back to the village," Carlos said. "Our stuff is there, and our guide left a car nearby. We'll leave in the morning and head east of Chiang Mai. We've heard there's a group of panthers close to Laos."

"Verra well," Angus said. "Keep in touch." He and Mikhail teleported them back to the Akha village, then went on to Moscow.

The next morning, Carlos and Caitlyn wished everyone farewell in the Akha village, then hiked back to the main road where Tanit had left the rental car. A few times, Carlos heard a twig snap in the jungle. He suspected one of the tigers had come to see them off.

They reached the main road, and he dropped his backpack on the trunk of the car so he could fish out the second set of keys.

Caitlyn leaned against the car and sighed. "I am so looking forward to a real hotel room with a real toilet and a real bathtub."

Carlos straightened suddenly and sniffed the air. Sweat and tobacco. There were mortals close by. He glanced across the road at the dense jungle and spotted the glint of a rifle barrel. He considered handing Caitlyn the car keys and urging her to drive away, but what if the car had been tampered with?

"Catalina," he whispered. "Go back to the trail, then run to the village."

Her eyes widened. "Why?"

"We've walked into a trap."

Chapter Twenty-six

Caitlyn stiffened just as gunshots were fired behind them.

Carlos pulled her down, using the car as a shield. He glanced over his shoulder. "I've been shot. Some kind of dart."

She yanked it out. "What is this?"

"Tranquilizer." He drew his pistol. "When I start shooting, run for the trail. Don't stop. Don't look back."

A chill skittered down her spine. "I'm not leaving you."

"Hurry!" a voice yelled behind them. "Get him!"

The shout had been in Thai, Caitlyn realized. And it sounded like the professor, Pat, from Chula. She eased up a few inches to peer through the car windows.

Ten men armed with rifles charged from the

jungle. One of them was the professor. An old army truck crashed through the underbrush onto the road, and three more armed men jumped out.

"Run!" Carlos yelled at Caitlyn, then aimed his weapon over the car trunk. With rapid fire he took down four armed men before the others began shooting back.

"Careful!" Pat shouted. "We have to take him alive!"

Carlos ducked down and glared at Caitlyn. "I told you to run."

She shook her head and pulled the knife from her belt. Her hand was trembling, so she gripped the handle harder.

Three armed men came around the end of the car. Carlos shot the first one, and the other two leaped back out of range.

"Look at his arm," Caitlyn whispered. The dead man had the same tattoo as Tanit and the professor.

Gunfire rang out, and she jerked at the sudden pain in her rump.

Carlos winced, then rose to his knees. "They shot darts under the car." He pulled darts from her bottom.

She yanked three darts from his rump. He suddenly pushed her head down and fired his weapon. She glanced toward the hood of the car and saw another man fall. How many were left now? Seven? She and Carlos were still badly outnumbered.

More shots were fired, and Carlos jerked. She gasped at the sight of five more darts in his back.

One of the thugs had rounded the end of the car while Carlos was busy killing the one by the front.

"Stop that!" She threw her knife.

It hit the man in his gut and he fell back.

"Bitch." He pulled a gun. "We don't need you alive."

"No!" Carlos threw himself in front of Caitlyn just as the shots were fired.

Caitlyn screamed as his body jerked with the impact of real bullets.

"Dammit!" Pat ran toward them. "I told you we needed him alive!"

The man writhed in pain, his hands gripping the knife in his gut. "I was aiming at the bitch. She deserves to die."

"You deserve to die. You failed the Master." Pat drew a weapon and shot the man in the head.

Caitlyn gasped and held onto Carlos tight. Blood oozed from two bullet holes in his chest. His breathing was shallow, but she wasn't sure if it was because he was dying or just tranquilized.

Pat and the remaining five men fanned out, their rifles aimed at her.

"Hurry, load them into the truck," Pat ordered. "Maybe we can still save him."

The men advanced toward her.

"No!" She pulled a knife from Carlos's belt.

Gunshots rang out as they sprayed her with a dozen tranquilizer darts.

With a huge roar, a tiger sprang from the jungle and leaped on the nearest man. Lethal claws ripped the screaming man apart.

Caitlyn pulled darts out of her arms, but she

couldn't reach those that had hit her on the back. Her sight blurred as she watched the tiger attack another man. Her ears rang with the din of multiple gunshots, all aimed at the tiger.

"No," she moaned as the tiger slumped onto the ground, drugged by too many darts.

The tiger shimmered, then shifted into human form.

"Rajiv," she whispered.

The men gasped, then shouted with victory.

"Another cat shifter!" Pat exclaimed. "The Master will be pleased."

Dots swirled before her eyes and their voices sounded very far away.

"Load them up," Pat ordered.

She collapsed on top of Carlos as everything went black.

Caitlyn slowly came to, her mind in a fuzzy haze. Memories of the ambush flitted through her head, and she sat up with a gasp. Where was she? A single lightbulb on the ceiling dimly illuminated the small room. The one window had been boarded up from the outside. There was a table against a wall. She was sitting on a hard pallet covered with a white sheet.

Her heart lurched. Where was Carlos?

A noise across the room made her jump. She peered into the dark corner.

"Miss Cait?" Rajiv pulled some of the white sheet covering his pallet into his lap to cover his nudity. "I apologize for my appearance."

"It's not your fault," she answered in his language. "I'm sorry you were dragged into this."

He shrugged his broad shoulders. "I was considering leaving my tribe, so I could experience the world and have interesting adventures. I thought I might find that with you and Carlos. I suppose I have."

She winced, hoping his search for adventure didn't get him killed. "Do you know what happened to Carlos?"

"No. I just woke up a few minutes ago, and he was gone. Who are those people?"

"They're working for a *chiang-shih* called Master Han."

"A *chiang-shih*?" Rajiv repeated. "I didn't know they were real."

"Apparently, they didn't know until recently that cat shifters are real." She stiffened when she heard the metallic scrape of a bolt sliding and a lock being turned.

The door cracked open and the muzzle of a rifle appeared. Rajiv growled and started to shimmer.

"Don't even think about shifting." A man swung the door farther open and shot tranquilizer darts into Rajiv. When Rajiv started pulling them out, the man drew a handgun from a holster. "Stop it. This one has real bullets."

Rajiv glared at him, then slowly slumped to the side. Two men hauled him from the room.

Meanwhile, the man pointed his gun at Caitlyn. "Don't move."

Her heart raced. "What have you done with Carlos?"

The man looked surprised. "You speak Thai?" He glanced out the door. "They're bringing your husband now."

Two men entered the room, carrying Carlos. She winced at the sight of his blood-soaked chest. They shuffled over to where she sat and dumped him on the pallet.

"Careful," she muttered.

"Why bother?" The man with the gun smirked. "The bastard is dead."

She flinched.

"That's enough, Sawat." The professor, Pat, entered the room. "Carlos's death is a tragedy."

The man with the gun scoffed. "He deserved to die. He killed a lot of our men."

"They died in the service of our Master," Pat argued. He turned to Caitlyn with an annoyed look. "You neglected to tell us you spoke Thai. We removed the bullets and tried to save your husband. We were too late."

Tears filled her eyes. She knew Carlos should revive in a few hours, but it still grieved her to think how much he had suffered. She brushed the hair back from his pale face, and a tear ran down her cheek. "Why are you doing this? Carlos considered you a friend."

"Master Han is in need of a powerful cat," Pat explained. "Once I realized cat shifters might truly exist, I knew they would be the most powerful cats in the world. I thought Carlos could lead us to a cat shifter. It didn't occur to me that he was one until Tanit told me."

Caitlyn sniffed as more tears streamed down her face. "Tanit is dead. We left him in the Temple of Death."

Pat inclined his head. "It is an honor to die in service to the Master."

She snorted. Then that was an honor she wished on the professor and the rest of his crew. "What are you doing to Rajiv?"

"We need him alive, so he will not be harmed. We are fitting a silver collar around his neck. I believe that will keep him from shifting. If not, we will have to keep him tranquilized until we can bring him to the Master."

"What will the Master do to him?"

"The real question is what will the cat shifter do to the Master?" Pat headed out the door, then paused. "We must keep you locked up until this evening. I may be able to release you at that time, but I do not know. The decision will not be mine."

She swallowed hard. "Who makes the decision?"

"Guardians of higher rank than I. I am merely a mortal, but they are *chiang-shih*. They will awaken in a few hours."

Pat and Sawat left the room, and she heard the scrape of a bolt sliding into place.

With a sigh, she touched Carlos's face. "I hope you wake up before the vampires do."

She wandered about the room, looking for a way to escape or something that could be used as a weapon. The window was covered with bars and boarded up. She found a clay pot under the table and figured it was the toilet. On top of the table was a bowl and pitcher full of water. She might be able to whack someone with the pitcher, but first she would put the water to good use.

She took the sheet off Rajiv's pallet and tore it into strips. Then she poured a little water into the bowl and set it next to Carlos. She washed the blood off his bare chest. He was still wearing his khaki pants and hiking boots.

She stretched him out on the pallet. Even though he couldn't feel anything, she wanted him to look comfortable. She emptied the blood-ied water into the chamber pot, then washed her own face and hands. With nothing else to do, she lay down beside Carlos and waited for him to come back.

She must have dozed, for she awakened when she felt Carlos's body jerk. Yes! He was going to revive again. She sat up, her heart expanding in her chest.

His body jerked again and his eyes opened.

She grinned. "Carlos. Thank God." She smoothed a hand over his chest and abdomen. The wounds were gone.

"I died again," he whispered.

"You're all right now." She caressed his face.

He glanced around the room. "We're prisoners?"

"Yes."

He sat up, his eyes wide with alarm. "Is there another room where you can go?"

"No. We're locked up together."

"Merda." He pulled off his hiking boots and socks. "The Surge is coming. I can feel it."

"It's okay."

"No, it's not!" He unbuckled his belt. "Each time it happens, the panther is more powerful. I don't know if I can control it. Caitlyn, you can't let me bite you."

She drew a quick breath. If he bit her, she might become a were-panther. Or she might die.

He pulled down his pants and underwear. "Caitlyn, promise me you won't let me bite you."

She hesitated.

He grabbed her by the upper arms. "Don't even consider it. I will not be responsible for your death."

Tears filled her eyes. "You've died twice for me. Why shouldn't I risk it once for you?"

"Because you don't come back like I do!" He jumped up and paced across the room. His gaze landed on the window. He punched a fist through the bars and shattered the glass.

"What are you doing?" She grimaced at the blood on his hand.

He pulled a jagged shard of glass from the window and dropped it on the pallet beside her. "If I try to bite you, stab me. It won't kill me, but it'll help me come to my senses."

She shook her head. "I don't want to hurt you."

"You have to." He stepped back as his body started to shimmer. "Sometimes it hurts to do the right thing."

With a roar, his body shifted. He came down on all fours and arched his back. She winced at the sound of his bones crackling and elongating. He was by far the largest cat she'd ever seen. Larger than a male lion. She suspected he was larger than a saber-tooth tiger.

He turned his head toward her and growled low in his throat. She picked up the shard of glass.

He lifted a massive paw and set it down in her direction. His golden eyes gleamed, focused intently on her. His body lowered to a few inches off the floor.

She held her breath. She'd seen this move before with her kitten, Mr. Foofikins. It was the classic crouch stance before the pounce.

"Carlos?" Her heart stuttered when his eyes turned red and began to glow. How much of him was a beast? How much control would Carlos have? If he pounced on her, would he maul her to death? Or was he simply driven to bite her and make her his mate?

A growl rumbled low in his throat. His tail twitched. Then he pounced.

His paws hit her shoulders and knocked her back. He stood over her, his legs straddling her. He lowered his head with a grumbling sound in his throat.

She gazed into his red glowing eyes, searching for Carlos. His body trembled, and she realized he was there. He was fighting the beast.

She flung the shard of glass away. "Go ahead," she whispered. "Bite me."

He threw back his head and roared. She winced at the sight of his fangs. When he lowered his head, she turned her face away and squeezed her eyes shut. A wet, raspy tongue licked her neck, and she shivered.

Pop. She gasped. His fangs had broken her skin. He licked her once again, then backed away.

She touched her neck, then drew away her hand. There was blood on her fingers.

His body shimmered and shifted back. He wiped the back of his hand against his mouth and stared at the bloodstain. He looked at her, his eyes amber once again. They widened at the sight of her neck. "No, no."

"It's okay."

He jumped to his feet. "No!" He clenched his fists and pressed them against his temples. "The beast was too strong. I tried to fight it."

"Carlos, it's all right."

He fell onto his knees. "Oh God, what have I done?"

"It wasn't your fault! It was my decision. I threw away the shard of glass. I told you to bite me."

He gave her an incredulous look. "Why?"

Tears filled her eyes. "Because I love you. And like you said, sometimes it hurts to do the right thing."

He took a deep breath and closed his eyes. "The next part of the Surge is coming. I can feel it."

"What part is that?"

His eyes opened, and they were red once again. "I need sex."

Her breath caught. Now she remembered the Surge he'd gone through in the cave. After shifting into a panther and back, he'd wanted sex. And she had refused.

He stood slowly, and her gaze went instantly to his erection. No way was she going to refuse him this time.

She pulled off her hiking boots as he walked toward her. The intensity of his red glowing eyes made her tremble with anticipation. She undid her belt and unzipped her pants.

He leaned over, grasped the hem of her khaki pants, and yanked them off so roughly she fell onto her back. He ripped off her panties, then shoved her legs apart and knelt between them.

He inserted a finger inside her and growled. "You're already wet."

"Yes." She wrapped her legs around his back and lifted her hips.

He grasped her butt cheeks and pulled her toward him. She gasped when his erection slammed into her. He ground her against him so her clitoris was tickled by his crisp pubic hair.

He thrust into her, hard and deep. Tension rose inside her higher and higher. He leaned his head back and roared. He pumped into her wildly, and she screamed her release.

Then he fell onto the pallet beside her and gathered her into his arms. Her body throbbed with aftershocks.

He stiffened suddenly and sat up, looking at the door. She heard it a few seconds later. Footsteps running toward the door.

"Get dressed," he whispered.

She pulled her underwear back on and reached for her pants. Carlos jumped up and pulled on his pants.

"I heard strange noises," someone shouted in the hallway. "It sounded like the roar of a cat."

"Impossible," another voice said. "The panther is dead."

"Open the door," the professor ordered.

Caitlyn fastened her pants. Carlos ran barefoot to the side of the door and pressed himself against the wall.

The bolt scraped, then the door cracked open. The muzzle of a rifle slid through the opening. Carlos waited, then grasped the muzzle and yanked the man into the room. As the man fell forward, Carlos karate-chopped him on the back of the neck and wrenched the rifle from his hand.

As the next armed man ran into the room, Carlos spun around and swung the rifle like a bat. The man fell on the floor.

Another armed man ran into the room, but Carlos flipped his rifle over and shot three darts into the man's chest.

Gunshots rang out and several tranquilizer darts hit Carlos in the chest. He ripped them out as more armed men ran into the room. They tried to shoot at him, but he ignored the darts and charged after them.

"Magnificent." Pat slipped inside the room. "So incredibly strong, he can defy death."

Carlos leaped at another armed man, knocking the rifle out of his hand, then punching him in the face. More darts were shot at him but he kept fighting. Caitlyn realized he was a level five werepanther now. He possessed superhuman strength and speed. He'd taken down several men in just a few seconds.

The click of pistol hammer drew her attention, and she gasped. Pat had a revolver aimed at her head.

"I suggest you stop," Pat told Carlos. "Or I will be forced to shoot your wife."

Carlos stopped, and was instantly bombarded with dozens of tranquilizer darts.

"The woman, too," Pat ordered.

Caitlyn winced as several darts pierced her skin. Her vision grew fuzzy. She saw Carlos crumble to the floor.

"What an amazing specimen!" Pat exclaimed. "He must be the strongest cat in the world. The Master will be so pleased."

Caitlyn collapsed on the pallet as everything went black.

Chapter Twenty-seven

*S*ean Whelan banged on the door at Romatech Industries, then shouted at the nearby surveillance camera. "Open up, damn you!" These damned Vamps kept the place locked up tight at night. It was infuriating that he had to beg entrance in order to see his own daughter and grandchildren.

"Open up!" They had to know he was here. The guard at the front gate would have alerted them.

The door opened and he burst into the foyer to find Shanna and that damned bodyguard, Connor Buchanan.

"Dad, what's wrong?" Shanna asked. "Is Mom okay?"

He gritted his teeth. "Do you know where Caitlyn is?" He spotted Phineas McKinney rushing into the foyer. "Where the hell is my daughter?"

Phineas gave him an exasperated look. "Relax, dude, she's okay."

"Then you know where she is?" Sean demanded.

"Yer daughter is on assignment," Connor replied. "Angus saw her last night, and she was fine."

"The hell she is! I just got a call from the State Department. A hill tribe contacted the American consulate in Chiang Mai, Thailand, and reported she was missing. They heard gunfire—"

"*What?*" Shanna interrupted.

"You heard me," Sean snapped. "The tribe said there was a gunfight, and Caitlyn was taken. The consulate asked the local police to investigate, and they found a bunch of dead bodies in the road."

Shanna gasped. Connor pulled a cell phone from his sporran.

"They also found an abandoned car and two backpacks," Sean continued. "One had Caitlyn's passport inside, and the other had a Brazilian passport for Carlos Panterra."

Phineas nodded. "They're on assignment together."

"You sent my daughter into the jungle with a damned shape shifter?" Sean shouted.

"We'll contact Angus as soon as possible," Phineas began. "He won't be awake just now."

"I have his voice mail." Connor talked into his cell phone. "Angus, it looks like Caitlyn and Carlos have been abducted. We'll e-mail you the details."

"You'd better find her!" Sean yelled. "You can tell Angus that if something happens to her, I'll hold you all responsible. I'll hunt you down—"

"Dad, please!" Shanna hissed. "We're just as upset about this as you are."

Sean fisted his hands, attempting to regain control. "Can you track her whereabouts? Don't the MacKay employees have some kind of homing beacon implanted in their arms?"

"We did that after Robby was kidnapped," Phineas said. "But only for the Vamps. We didn't think the shifters or mortals would ever be targeted."

"Well, you were wrong, weren't you?" Sean growled.

Phineas motioned for Sean to follow him. "Come to the office so we can get all the information you have. I'll broadcast it to all MacKay employees. It'll be our top priority."

Sean scoffed. "A lot of good that'll do. It's daytime in Thailand, so your Vamps won't be any help at all." He glanced over his shoulder. Shanna and Connor were following them down the hall. "This is your fault, Shanna. You just had to drag her into this foul world of yours."

Her face turned pale.

"Enough, Whelan." Connor glared at him. "Ye were going to do the same, offering her a job on yer bloody Stake-Out team."

Phineas opened the door to the MacKay security office, and Sean strode inside. He paced about as Shanna took a seat and Connor stood by the door, glaring at him.

Phineas sat behind the desk. "I was just reading the report Angus filed. He left Caitlyn and Carlos with the Akha tribe."

"I want to read that report," Sean demanded.

Phineas glanced at Connor, who frowned.

"Verra well," Connor said. "Let him see it. The information is most likely related to her abduction."

"What information?" Shanna asked.

"Evidence of a powerful Chinese vampire who appears to have mortals assisting him," Connor explained.

"They call him Master Han," Phineas added.

Sean snorted. "I should have known a vampire was involved in this. He could teleport Cait anywhere on the planet. We'll never find her."

"We have employees all over the world," Connor said quietly. "We will find her."

"Why should I believe you?" Sean sneered at him. "You've been looking for Casimir for years, and you keep failing."

Connor's eyes narrowed.

"We've been kicking ass," Phineas insisted. "We've killed off a bunch of his minions."

Sean shrugged. "They'll keep coming as long as their leader's alive, and you can't even find him."

Connor's jaw clenched. "We've located Casimir twice."

"And he always escapes." Sean enjoyed seeing the red flush of rage on Connor's face. "If anything happens to my daughter, I'll raze this place to the ground. I'll destroy you all."

Connor zoomed over to him in a blur of vampire speed and seized him by the shirt collar. His eyes blazed with anger. "Mind yer manners, Whelan. Ye need us."

Sean wrenched himself free. That damned

Connor. Once he started killing the Vamps, he'd make sure Connor was second on the list, right after Shanna's damned husband.

Carlos blinked his eyes open. The place was dark, but his eyes adjusted quickly. The floor beneath him vibrated slightly, and he could hear the hum of engines.

"There you are," Caitlyn whispered. "Welcome back."

He planted a hand on the floor to push himself into a sitting position, and felt something tug at his wrist. He was in handcuffs with a foot of chain between his hands.

He sat up and felt another tug at his neck. "What the hell?" There was a collar around his neck, and a heavy chain extended from it to a metal bar. "We're in a cage?"

"Yes." Caitlyn sat beside him, leaning back against the bars. There were no handcuffs or chains on her, and she had a blanket draped around her shoulders. "They kept you drugged for hours. They're scared to death of you." The corner of her mouth tilted up. "I can hardly blame them. You can really kick ass."

He grasped the thick chain in his fist and tugged. With his added strength, he might be able to break it. "Where are we?"

"On a plane. In a cargo hold." She wrapped the blanket tighter around her. "We've been waiting for you to wake up."

"We?" He glanced around and spotted Rajiv, the were-tiger.

The young man was dressed in baggy pants. His

long black hair hung over one shoulder in a braid, and there was a silver collar around his neck. His hands were also cuffed. He said something in his language.

"He's glad you're all right," Caitlyn translated.

"I didn't know he'd been captured," Carlos said.

"Well, you have a good excuse." She gave him a wry look. "You were knocked out and *dying* at the time."

"Better me than you." He thought back to their hike through the jungle. "I thought I heard a tiger."

She nodded. "He followed us, then tried to help us. Pat was delighted to capture a second cat shifter since you were *dying* at the time."

He arched a brow. "Do I detect a little anger?"

"I'm a bit peeved because you keep *dying* all the time. You don't have an unlimited amount of lives, you know."

Neither did she. Carlos's gaze drifted to the bite mark on her neck. It was true. He'd bitten her. His mind was so fuzzy with the aftereffects of tranquilizers that he'd hoped he had only imagined biting her.

"It'll be all right," she whispered.

He hung his head, closing his eyes.

"I was talking to Rajiv while you were sleeping," she changed the subject. "He's Raghu's younger brother. Only twenty years old. He hasn't fallen in love with any of the girls in his tribe, and his brother will be head of the tribe for life, so Rajiv decided to leave in search of adventure."

Carlos glanced at the young man who was

watching them with his golden eyes. "How can he take tiger form during the day?"

"Oh, good question." Caitlyn asked Rajiv in his language, then translated the response. "He says he's on his second life. He was bitten by a cobra when he was eighteen. When he revived, he was able to shift whenever he wanted."

Carlos nodded. "If he wants adventure, he certainly found it."

Caitlyn smiled. "He says he was somehow drawn to me, that he knew I would help him."

"Like Coco and Raquel." Carlos's gaze drifted once again to the bite on her neck. She was the most amazing woman in the world, and she was going to die because of him.

"Do you want to know what happened while you were sleeping?" she asked.

"Yes." He glanced around the cargo hold. "How did we get here?"

"I woke up when Pat and his buddies were dragging us into a large room. Rajiv was already there. And three vampires, so it must have been after dark. The vampires spoke Thai to Pat but Chinese to each other. They didn't realize I can understand Chinese."

"So what were they saying?" Carlos asked.

"They were worried about the silver collars on you and Rajiv, worried that they wouldn't be able to teleport you. Pat gave you and Rajiv a sedative, then he removed the silver collars. And then the teleporting began. It took a while since the three vampires had to make multiple trips to take us and Pat and his buddies."

"Where did they take us?" Carlos asked.

"To a small airport. I think it was on an island 'cause I could see palm trees and sand, and I could hear waves breaking. The vampires talked about being afraid to teleport any farther east."

"Right." Carlos nodded. "They don't want to accidentally teleport into sunlight and get fried."

"So I figure the island was east of Thailand, somewhere in the Pacific. And I assume we're still traveling east. They offered us blankets, but Rajiv refused his and growled at them."

"Good man." Carlos gave Rajiv a thumbs-up.

She pointed to another caged area in the cargo hold, barely visible with the dim running lights. "See those coffins over there? A while back the vampires came down here and climbed inside them."

"We must be headed into sunlight." Carlos tugged on his chain. "If I can get into their cage, I could kill them."

"With what?" Caitlyn asked. "We have no weapons. They took our shoes and belts. My feet are frozen." She rubbed her bare feet together. "And these bars are really strong. Rajiv already tested them."

Carlos curled a fist around a bar and shook it. It didn't budge.

"We might as well wait it out," she said. "I don't think any of us know how to fly a plane."

"Good point. How long have we been in the air?"

"We're not sure. We don't have watches, but it seems like a long time."

"Flying east for hours," he murmured. "It's actually a good thing if this trip takes a long time.

It'll give MacKay more time to figure out we're missing and track us down."

Caitlyn nodded. "My sister has a strong psychic link to me. I'm trying to send her images of us in a cage on an airplane."

"You're amazing." His gaze lingered on the soft golden color of her hair, the sweet line of her jaw, and the pink perfection of her lips. So beautiful.

"Don't look at me like that," she whispered. "Like you're trying to memorize every detail before I'm gone."

He swallowed hard. "I'll never forgive myself if—"

"Don't say it." She pressed two cold fingers to his mouth. "I'm going to make it."

He took her cold hand in his. "Your chances are not good."

"I'm going to fight," she insisted. "I'm not going to leave you. You know how stubborn I can be."

He smiled sadly. "So you'll survive just to prove me wrong?"

"If I have to, yes. Just because I'm a lousy warrior doesn't mean I'm not strong."

"You're the strongest woman I know."

"Thank you." Her eyes glimmered with emotion. "So what will happen exactly? Will I sprout whiskers in a few days? Or have an insatiable desire for tuna?"

His chest tightened. He knew she had to be scared, but she was putting on a brave front. "The change will remain dormant inside you until it's triggered by the full moon. That's why the first time is so dramatic and painful. The abruptness of the transformation is more than some people can bear."

"So I have until the next full moon?"

"Yes. About two weeks from now."

She nodded, then leaned back against the bars. "Two weeks."

He rubbed her hand to warm up her fingers. Whenever, if ever, they got out of this mess alive, he wanted to make their marriage legal. Tears came to his eyes when he realized how short their marriage would likely last. "Catalina, will you marry me?"

She squeezed his hand. "I thought you'd never ask."

Chapter Twenty-eight

Caitlyn was hoping she'd recognize their location when they disembarked, but unfortunately they never left the plane. At one point during the flight, Pat and his armed thugs came down to the cargo hold to check on them. She begged to go to the restroom, so Pat allowed them to go one at a time with an armed escort. Carlos and Rajiv each required three armed escorts.

She hoped Pat would talk to his cohorts so she could glean more information, but they were silent now that they knew she understood Thai. She continued to send airplane images to her sister but had no idea if she was succeeding. After many hours, she finally felt the plane descend and heard the landing gear lower.

When they jostled and bounced a little with the landing, Rajiv stiffened. "What is that?"

"We just landed," she told him in his language.

He was trying to be brave, but she could tell he was nervous. It was his first time to travel by air and his first time away from home.

"Do you know who's piloting the plane?" Carlos asked.

"No." She shook her head. "I never saw anyone in a uniform. I think one of their thugs must know how to fly."

The plane taxied for what seemed a long time.

"I counted about six mortals during our bath-room break," Carlos whispered.

She nodded. "The guy who escorted me is called Sawat."

"The huge lummox with the broken nose?" Carlos glanced at the coffins. "It would be better to defeat the mortals before the vampires wake up."

"You and Rajiv can't shift with those collars on. And we have no weapons. I think we should wait till we disembark, then try to find a way to escape."

Carlos's eyes narrowed as he considered.

"Whatever you do, please don't get yourself killed again," she muttered.

He frowned. "It's not like I enjoy it."

The plane stopped moving. Caitlyn tensed, afraid that Carlos and Rajiv would try something suicidal when Pat and his cohorts arrived.

They waited. And waited.

Rajiv curled up on the floor and fell asleep.

"*Merda*," Carlos muttered. "They're waiting for nightfall . . ."

"So the vampires can wake up," she finished his thought.

The time dragged by. She wrapped the blanket around herself and Carlos and lightly dozed.

A sudden creak woke her up. Carlos motioned with his head toward the coffins. She shivered at the sight of the lids slowly opening.

The vampires floated out of the coffins and landed on their feet. There were all Chinese, as far as she could tell, and dressed in red embroidered silk robes. Their long black hair was braided down their backs, and their fingernails were yellow and about six inches long.

They turned their heads toward her and hissed, showing sharp yellow fangs.

She shuddered and huddled closer to Carlos. She hoped she and her friends weren't breakfast.

"If one of them tries to bite you," Carlos whispered, "I'll snap his neck."

Pat and six men came down to the cargo hold. Sawat opened the vampire cage and bowed as they exited. Pat and the others bowed low. The vampires seized three men and sank their fangs into their necks.

Caitlyn flinched. The men didn't fight. They quietly submitted, then bowed low after the vampires released them.

"We have arrived in San Francisco?" the tallest vampire asked in Chinese.

"Yes, Master," Pat responded in the same language. "All is ready at the temple."

San Francisco? She immediately shot an image of the Golden Gate Bridge to her sister.

"Then it is time for us to go." The tallest vampire moved toward Caitlyn and her friends.

Pat and his six thugs ran up to the cage. Several pointed handguns at them, while the others grasped the chain connected to Carlos's silver collar. They yanked on it to pull Carlos toward them. He resisted, but the collar pressed into his throat, cutting off his air. He relented then and let them draw him back. Caitlyn winced when the back of his head hit the metal bars.

With Carlos pinned to the bars, Sawat tugged his T-shirt up in the back. Caitlyn gasped as Pat plunged a syringe into Carlos's back.

Pat glanced at her. "It's just a sedative. We need you all alive."

Sawat smirked. "For a little while."

Carlos's eyes flickered shut and he crumpled to the floor. Pat and his thugs did the same procedure to Rajiv, then opened the cage and removed the silver collars from both the cat shifters. The vampires sauntered inside the cage, and two of them grabbed Rajiv and Carlos and teleported away. Soon they were back and teleporting away the thugs and Pat.

The third vampire advanced toward Caitlyn. She stepped back, her heart thundering in her ears.

"When we celebrate the resurrection of Master Han, I will take this one," he said in Chinese. "I will drain her dry and burn her flesh for my incense."

She swallowed hard, and sent another frantic image of the Golden Gate Bridge to her sister. The vampire lurched toward her with incredible speed. She jumped back but his long fingernails had curled around her arm. He teleported, taking her with him, and everything went black.

She stumbled when they arrived and fell onto her knees as the vampire tossed her aside. She saw Carlos and Rajiv nearby, lying unconscious on the floor.

She remained huddled on the floor as she scanned the surroundings. They appeared to be on a raised wooden dais at the end of a rectangular room. Beams painted a lacquer red crossed the vaulted ceiling. Bare white walls were trimmed with more red lacquered woodwork. At the end of the room a large brass gong sat between two black doors gilded with gold. Pat stood by the gong, and he now wore a black silk robe with a hood. The six thugs stood along the back wall, armed with large ceremonial swords.

This had to be the temple the vampires had referred to. She spotted the three vampires on the other side of the dais. In the center of the dais there was an altar made of wood, inlaid with gold dragons. On top reclined the body of a tall man dressed in red silk with gold braid.

A chill crept down her spine. The man on the altar must be Master Han.

The gong sounded, and she glanced toward the entrance as Pat struck it again. The entrance doors opened and men filed in, two by two, dressed in black silk robes with the hoods drawn up to cover their heads and hide their faces. Twenty in all, she counted.

The last ones to enter closed the doors, then joined their fellow black-robed monks as they formed five rows with a center aisle between them. Each row had four men.

Pat hit the gong again.

"Master Han!" the monks shouted in unison, then dropped to their knees and bowed forward.

One monk seemed to be slightly slower than the others, Caitlyn noted, as if he didn't quite know the routine. The armed thugs along the back wall also dropped to their knees. Beside her Carlos and Rajiv stirred.

Pat marched down the center aisle swinging a brass censor that emitted a trail of smoke. Incense filled the air, and the monks began to chant.

Carlos and Rajiv sat up and glanced warily about. Caitlyn figured Carlos was counting their opponents and assessing their chances of defeating them in battle. She didn't know how well the twenty monks could fight, and there were still six armed thugs, Pat, and three vampires. That made it thirty to three. Really bad odds.

Carlos was one hell of a fighter, and could probably take down seven or eight guys before he was captured or killed. Again. She looked at him and shook her head, pleading with her eyes that he not attempt anything rash.

Pat stepped onto the dais and set his incense burner onto a brass stand. "Guardians, behold your Master!" He lifted his arms as he approached the altar.

The monks sat up and shouted, "Master Han!"

"It was forty-five years ago when Master Han brought peace to the warring factions of the three vampire lords," Pat announced. "It was Master Han who unified the vampires and their minions to one common goal. It was through Master

Han that we grew in power and territory. It was through Master Han that we realized we could take over all of Asia!"

The vampires and monks cheered.

"And then"—Pat's voice grew sad—"then the unthinkable happened. Master Han and his forces claimed victory over a village in Tibet and requested the most beautiful virgin be delivered to him as a gift. The village sent the girl, filled with poison, and when Master Han drank from her, he fell into a deep sleep."

The monks murmured their disapproval.

"We rose up to avenge our master," Pat continued. "We burned the village to the ground and slaughtered all that lived there!"

The monks cheered.

"We brought the Master here to San Francisco, where Dr. Chou is known to have the greatest knowledge of ancient folklore and herbal remedies. For five years we have tried to revive our master." Pat motioned to one of the monks. "Dr. Chou has long been convinced there is only one way to resurrect our master."

The monk stood and pushed back his hood to reveal thin, graying hair. "Ancient texts tell us that a corpse can be brought back to life if a cat jumps over it. Not any cat will do. It must be a magical cat of great power."

"And now we have the most powerful cats in the world!" Pat exclaimed as he gestured toward Carlos and Rajiv.

Caitlyn snorted. That was why they'd been kidnapped? So Carlos could shift and jump over an unconscious vampire? She looked at him and rolled her eyes.

He frowned and shook his head slightly.

And then she realized why he didn't see the humor in the situation. If he jumped over Master Han, and it didn't magically cure the vampire, they could be blamed for the scheme's failure to work. They would probably be executed. And if they fought, they were terribly outnumbered.

Pat pointed at Carlos. "It is time! You will shift and jump over our master!"

Carlos stood slowly, looked around the room, then shook his head. "No, thanks."

The monks gasped.

Pat flinched. "You do not deny the Master." He motioned for the six thugs armed with swords to approach the dais.

One of the monks, the one who had moved slower than the others, suddenly jumped to his feet and zoomed toward them at vampire speed. His hood slipped back as he jumped onto the dais, and Caitlyn thought she detected a glint of recognition in Carlos's eyes.

The vampire monk seized her from behind and pressed a knife to her neck. Her blood chilled with fear.

"You will jump over our master," Pat ordered Carlos. "Or you will see your wife die."

Caitlyn's breath hitched when Carlos hesitated.

He exchanged a look with her captor, then with a shrug, he turned toward Pat. "Go ahead. I'm tired of her."

She gasped.

Pat's eyes bulged. "What?"

Carlos waved a dismissive hand. "She's lousy in bed. She just lays there and makes me do all the work."

Caitlyn gasped again. Was he serious? Her heart plummeted when she saw all the monks murmuring and nodding their heads in commiseration with Carlos.

"Do not harm her!" Rajiv cried in his language. He ran toward the altar and shifted into a tiger as he leaped over Master Han.

"No!" Carlos shouted.

Monks jumped to their feet.

Rajiv landed on the other side of the altar and shifted back to a human. His pants had remained on, and were now ripped to shreds.

A collective gasp spread over the room as Master Han's body began to twitch. The monks jumped up and down, shouting in celebration. Master Han floated up in the air, then stood on the altar. His face was covered with a golden mask.

"Oh, shit," the monk who held Caitlyn muttered in English. He pressed a button on his wristwatch. "Angus, get over here now!"

"What?" Caitlyn turned her head to look at her captor.

He winked. "J.L. Wang at your service." He handed her the knife, then drew two swords from underneath his robe. He tossed one to Carlos.

Carlos and J.L. leaped from the dais, running toward the thugs. Caitlyn winced at the sound of clashing swords. Some of the monks fled toward the doors, but before they could escape, Angus materialized by the entrance with a group of Vamps.

Caitlyn recognized Emma, Phineas, Connor, Ian, Roman, and, to her amazement, her father.

Screams reverberated around the temple as those who challenged the Vamps were quickly killed. Rajiv ran back to Caitlyn, and on the way, he grabbed the brass stand, letting the incense burner fall onto the floor. He stood next to her, holding the brass stand like a weapon.

Sawat jumped onto the dais, his face twisted with rage as he stalked toward her and Rajiv. "I'll kill you both." He lifted his sword and charged.

She threw the knife J.L. had given her.

Sawat screamed as the knife plunged into his groin.

She winced. Rajiv gave her a wary look and stepped back.

"I was aiming for his chest," she assured him. "Really."

"Master Han!" Pat shouted. "You must flee to safety."

"No!" Carlos ran toward the dais to stop Master Han. J.L. was close behind.

Pat jumped in front of the altar, pulling a knife from his robe so he could protect his master. Carlos swiped Pat with his blade, and he fell to the side, wounded. Carlos stabbed at Master Han, but he vanished.

"No!" Carlos charged toward the three vampires. One zoomed over to the wounded Pat, grabbed him, then teleported away.

"Take me!" Sawat screamed, his hands covering his bloody crotch. He glared at Caitlyn. "I will not forget you, bitch." He disappeared as one of the vampires teleported away with him.

The third vampire teleported away with Dr. Chou. The battle came to an end with all the remaining monks and thugs either dead or surrendering.

Carlos rushed toward Caitlyn. "Are you all right?"

She folded her arms and glared at him. "You're tired of me? I just lay there, and you have to do all the work?"

He snorted. "I was just buying time, sweetheart. I knew the instant I saw J.L. that help was on the way."

"You know him?"

"Sure." Carlos slapped J.L. on the back. "He works for MacKay. I knew he wasn't going to hurt you."

J.L. nodded. "Sorry about scaring you. I knew I'd better put a knife to your throat before any of the other guys could."

"How did you find us?" Caitlyn asked.

"When your sister claimed you were in San Francisco, I went undercover in Chinatown," J.L. explained. "Angus and the guys teleported to the coven house nearby and waited for me to call."

"And since J.L.'s a Vamp, he has a homing beacon inserted underneath his skin," Carlos continued. "I knew Angus and the others would come."

Caitlyn let out a deep breath. Shanna had received the images. "Thank God." She hugged J.L. "Thank you. I was so afraid Carlos would try to fight everyone by himself and get killed again."

Carlos frowned. "I had a plan. I was going to grab that brass stand and leap onto the altar and threaten to ram it through Master Han's heart if they didn't put down their weapons and let you and Rajiv go."

J.L. nodded. "Not a bad plan."

"And what would have happened then?" Caitlyn asked. "How were *you* going to escape?"

Carlos shifted his weight. "I didn't have that part figured out yet."

She didn't know whether to scream or cry. He always put her safety before his own. "I love you so much."

He grinned and pulled her into his arms.

"It is over then?" Rajiv asked Caitlyn in his language.

"Yes." She turned toward him. "We can take you home if you like. Or if you'd rather, you could probably work for the same company as these other guys. They work for MacKay Security and Investigation, and they go around catching bad guys."

"Like Master Han?" Rajiv asked. "I would like to work with them." He hung his head. "It is my fault that Master Han rose again. I only did it because I thought they were going to kill you."

She hugged the young were-tiger. "No one blames you, Rajiv. You have proven yourself the bravest of warriors."

"What's going on?" Carlos asked.

"I think Rajiv would like to work for Angus," she replied.

"I'll introduce him." J.L. motioned for Rajiv to follow him. He turned and nearly skidded in the pool of blood left by Sawat. "Damn. He left his balls in San Francisco."

Carlos laughed and gathered her back into his arms. "Are you really okay?"

"Yes." She leaned her head against his chest. "But I'm ready for a nice long break."

His arms tightened around her but he remained silent. She could guess what he was thinking. Her break would not last long. In two weeks she would shift for the first time. And she might not survive it.

As soon as they teleported back to Romatech, Carlos asked Sean Whelan for his daughter's hand in marriage. Afterward, when Carlos's nose stopped bleeding, he called Father Andrew to make the arrangements.

They were married the next night at the chapel at Romatech. Roman offered to walk Caitlyn down the aisle since her father refused to come. Shanna was her matron of honor and Coco and Raquel served as flower girls. Carlos asked Fernando to be his best man. Constantine was his ring bearer.

It made his heart ache when Caitlyn spent their wedding night running a fever and throwing up. After returning to Romatech, he confided to Shanna and Roman that he'd bitten Caitlyn and feared they would lose her in two weeks.

Shanna, Roman, and his head chemist, Laszlo, worked all night long, developing a formula that would hopefully ease Caitlyn into the transformation. The formula consisted of synthetic blood that matched Caitlyn's blood type, plus a small amount of were-panther DNA they had isolated from his blood. They figured her chances of survival would be greater if her body was allowed to adapt slowly to the were-panther DNA rather than letting her undergo an abrupt and total change when the moon was full.

Shanna was so terrified of losing her sister that she insisted Caitlyn receive the first dose the next night, the night of her wedding. Within a few hours Caitlyn was miserably sick.

The next night she was given another dose, this one with a tiny bit more were-panther DNA. Again she was sick.

This went on for a week, and Carlos feared the worse. Were-panther DNA made her ill. How could she ever survive the transformation?

Caitlyn refused to stop the treatments, since Roman believed their plan would work. She insisted on remaining positive and hopeful. Her bright attitude was one of the things Carlos loved most about her, so he tried not to show how frightened he was.

When the night of the full moon arrived, Romatech employees were given the night off. Only Shanna, Roman, and Connor remained. Phineas and Howard stayed at the Draganesti home with Tino and Sofia. Carlos knew Shanna didn't want the children around in case the worst happened.

Shanna had attempted to make the gazebo in the Romatech garden comfortable for them. She'd placed a mattress inside with blankets. Roman had given Carlos a syringe with a painkiller in case Caitlyn needed it. As the moon began to rise, Caitlyn and Shanna hugged each other tightly with tears in their eyes.

Then with a heavy, fearful heart, Carlos led Caitlyn outside to the gazebo. He glanced back at the Romatech cafeteria and could see Shanna inside, pacing nervously while her husband and Connor stood nearby.

As the moon rose higher in the night sky, Caitlyn's breathing became more labored. The first pain hit right after they entered the gazebo.

She curled up on the mattress, her eyes squeezed shut. When the pain subsided, Carlos encouraged her to undress. She was shaking, so he wrapped her in blankets and held her tight.

Another pain hit, and she cried out. Soon she was rocking back and forth, whimpering.

"Do you want the painkiller?" he asked.

She shook her head. "I'm going to get through this, Carlos. I'm not giving up."

Tears blurred his vision. "You're the bravest woman I've ever met."

She cried out and collapsed on the mattress. She rolled onto all fours and trembled. She screamed when claws burst out of her fingertips. Her arms started to shimmer, then turned black. Her hands shifted into paws.

"You're doing it, Caitlyn."

She screamed when her back legs crackled to reform into panther legs. Then her back arched, more bones crunching and shifting. Her whimpers turned into a growl.

"My head," she whispered. "It's going to explode."

He held her tight. Her body was now sleek and black.

She screamed again. Her head shifted, and her scream turned into a roar. She collapsed onto the mattress, panting.

"You did it." He held her head in his hands and

gazed at her lovely turquoise cat eyes. "Catalina, my beautiful cat, you did it."

She licked his hand, and her tongue was raspy.

Carlos stripped and shifted. She was still lying on the mattress, but her breathing had eased. He nudged her with his head. *Come on, let's go play.*

She lifted her head. *You can talk to me telepathically?*

Yes. It was a power I gained when I reached level three. Level one were-panthers can't do it, usually, but you came into this with psychic power. He nudged her with his head again. *Come on, run with me.*

She rolled onto all fours and followed him outside the gazebo. She glanced toward the cafeteria. Shanna was inside, and when she spotted two were-panthers, she jumped up and down, hollering and punching the air. She and Roman hugged each other, laughing.

Carlos chuckled, then trotted toward the woods. *Your senses will be sharper. You'll be able to see in the dark.*

I feel strong, she told him. *Like a hunter.*

They ran all over the grounds at Romatech. She learned to leap and sharpen her claws. She even tried pouncing on Carlos a few times. When the moon began its descent, they returned to the gazebo.

The shift back to human form was less painful for her. Still, she lay back on the mattress, breathing heavily. "My God, I'm exhausted. I could sleep for a week."

Carlos shifted back, then covered her with a blanket. "You did it, Catalina. I'm so proud of you."

She heaved a sigh. "I'm glad it's over. Now you can stop looking at me with all that guilt in your eyes. It was hurting me to see you hurting so much."

Tears threatened to fall. "I don't know how I could have lived with myself if I'd lost you. I love you more than I can say."

She touched his face. "It's all right. We made it through." She smiled. "I guess Shanna was right from the beginning. I get to have kittens."

Smiling, he brushed her hair back from her brow. "Our children will be completely normal until they reach puberty and shift for the first time." He tilted his head. "I take that back. No child from you would be completely normal."

"Hey." She swatted his shoulder.

He chuckled. "I mean your children will probably be beautiful, intelligent, and psychically gifted."

"Oh. Well, that's true." Her eyes twinkled with humor. "And your children will probably know how to sweet talk their way out of trouble."

"I like them already." He kissed her freckled nose.

"Me, too." She wrapped her arms around his neck. "Maybe we should get started on them right away, you being an endangered species and all. It would be the environmentally responsible thing to do."

"I love it when you talk sexy."

She laughed. "I love it when you purr in my ear."

He nuzzled her ear and growled low.

She shivered.

He kissed a path down her neck. "Catalina, are you sure you're not too tired?"

"I'm exhausted. But then I thought I'd just lay here and let you do all the work."

He lifted his head to give her a wry look. "You're never forgiving me for that, are you?"

Her mouth twitched. "You'll never know."

"Naughty kitty."

With a laugh, she flipped him over and straddled him. Holding his shoulders down, she leaned over and nipped at his ear. "No more dying, you hear me? I won't have you dying for me."

He chuckled. "For you, sweetheart, I want to live forever."